SPOOK HOUSE

MICHAEL WEST

Copyright © 2012, 2022 by Michael West
All rights reserved. No portion of this book may be copied or transmitted in any form, electronic or otherwise, without express written consent of the publisher or author.

Cover art and illustrations: Matthew Perry Cover art and illustrations in this book Copyright © 2012 Matthew Perry & Hydra Publications.

Editor: Amanda DeBord

ISBN Number:978-1-948374-76-7

Hydra Publications
www.hydrapublications.com Second edition

*For all those who dwell in West Manor
– Stephanie, Kyle, and Ryan – where every day is Halloween.*

And in loving memory of Donald Pleasence and Sara J. Larson, who are sorely missed in Spring, Summer, Winter, and especially Fall.

"There are vibrations of different universes right here, right now. We're just not in tune with them. There are probably other parallel universes in our living room – this is modern physics. This is the modern interpretation of quantum theory, that many worlds represents reality."

~Dr. Michio Kaku, Theoretical Physicist, Professor, and Best-Selling Author

"To the scientist there is the joy in pursuing truth which nearly counteracts the depressing revelations of truth."

~H.P. Lovecraft

"You're not supposed to go up there. That's a spook house."

~Tommy Doyle, *John Carpenter's Halloween*

It is estimated that, nationwide, over 1,000 haunted attractions are produced by local fire departments and charity groups, open for just a few weekends in October or for a single day on Halloween.

While the size of these attractions and their markets may vary, a typical "spook house" can average around 7,500 paying guests, and due to fire codes and other measures, they are all extremely safe.

But then again, there is nothing typical about Harmony, Indiana...

august

CHAPTER ONE

Sheri Foster shuddered, but not because of the air conditioning. Sure, a cold breeze blew from the Pontiac's vents, laboring to combat late August heat, but that wasn't why she felt a chill. Not tonight.

Her foot tapped the floorboard, looking for a brake pedal that didn't exist. Jeff was the one driving, and there was no stopping him when his knowledge had been called into question.

Why couldn't she just agree for once? Now he had to come out here and prove her wrong. It was all so childish and stupid.

The woods were dark, even with brights on. Weeds and tall grass choked the dirt road ahead, low-hanging branches clawing at the Pontiac's metal top as it passed beneath them. Something ran across their path, caught by the headlights, a creature with huge, bright eyes; there and then gone. Sheri clamped her hands over her mouth and screamed through her fingers, not much of a scream – more of a quick yelp, really – but loud enough for Jeff to hear.

"Just a possum, hon," he said with a laugh. "Or maybe a big rat."

She lowered her hands to her lap and glared at him. "You're not helping."

He laughed again, keeping his eyes on the narrow road that wasn't really a road at all, just a very long driveway.

The trees on either side slid off into shadow, giving way to a clearing of tall, unkempt grass and dwarf bushes. Sheri could see the night sky clearly now, a velvet blanket littered with a million stars, a beautiful sight marred only by the dark, gabled roof of a farmhouse. *There it is*, she thought, *the old Fuller place.*

"See?" Jeff smiled victorious in the dim dashboard light. "Told you it was still out here. You didn't believe me."

Sheri didn't believe much when it came to this house. Oh sure, she'd heard the stories since childhood. Everyone had. Heard how the man who owned the place, Sam Fuller, had been a Grand Dragon in the Ku Klux Klan, head of the whole "Realm of Indiana."How, in 1946, he'd lynched an entire family just north of Harmony, hung every man, woman, and child, and watched them flail and kick until they'd died. And how, about a month later, according to local legend, Fuller had fallen into his own threshing machine.

Supposedly, the man's death was ruled an "accident," but no one in town seemed to buy it, then or now. And over the years, the stories of ghosts and karmic retribution had been repeated so often, and with such conviction, that they were widely accepted as canon.

Sheri's eyes shifted to the left, to the distant shadow of a barn. It leaned to one side as if tired of standing. *Is the machine still in there? Still covered in Fuller's blood?* She shuddered.

When the car finally came to a stop, the house stood squarely in its headlamps, huge and sprawling and showing both extreme age and total neglect. Windows had been boarded at random, leaving unprotected glass to shatter; the jagged shards hung from the panes like crystalline teeth. Indiana weather had not been kind to it, stripping its paint and leaving naked wood to crack and gray. Winds stole its shingles, and seasons of heavy snow had weighed down its roof until it sagged and buckled beneath the memory of past strains. Even the front door had abandoned it, leaving a vacant hole just as dark and sinister as the house itself.

Sheri stared up at it, almost hypnotized, and when Jeff spoke, she nearly leapt from her seat.

"Creepy place, huh?"

"Yeah." She looked away, glanced down at her arms, and found that her skin had turned to goose flesh. "OK, you were right, they didn't tear it down. Can we go now?"

"What?" He gaped at her, puzzled. "We didn't drive all the way out here to just turn around and leave. There's a flashlight in the glove compartment."

"We can't go *in there*."

"Why not?"

"That's trespassing." She tried to say it with authority, as if she were afraid of being caught. She was afraid all right, but not of that. They were miles away from anywhere, with no reason to believe this place was on any cop's radar. No reason to think anyone would come out here to catch them in the act. No reason to think anyone would find them at all. And *that's* what she found truly frightening.

"I don't see any signs." Jeff reached across the dash and opened the glove box, removing a neon yellow flashlight. "Besides, the house has been empty for what, fifty years? Who's gonna care? It's not like there's anything in there worth stealing."

"Probably not, but it could be dangerous."

He laughed, held the light under his chin and switched it on, casting odd shadows across his face. "It's got a death curse!"

She slapped his arm. "I'm serious! What if the floor's rotten, or the ceiling collapses, or there's a nest of poisonous snakes or spiders or–"

"Look, if you're too scared, you can stay out here with the doors locked and your cell phone ready." He aimed his flashlight at the windshield. "I'm just going to go have a quick look around. If I don't come back, call somebody."

"Come on, Jeff, you've already proved your point. Let's go back to my –"

"I just want to see it," he told her. "Just give me fifteen minutes."

Sheri sighed. She knew she couldn't talk him out of it, not when he had his mind set, but she also knew there was no way she was getting out of this car. "Fifteen minutes?"

"Fifteen. Tops."

She hauled her purse off the floor and dug through it until she found her cell phone. It would be just her luck to find no service out here. When she flipped it open, however, she found two signal bars and the faint ghost of a third. She held it up and shook it at him. "One second more and I swear I'm calling the cops."

Jeff smiled, his hand already on the door handle. "Fair enough."

He opened the door, let in the humid summer air, and climbed out into the night.

Sheri leaned across the seat after him. "You know, this is the part of the horror movie where everyone yells at the screen and calls the character a complete idiot."

"Yeah, but I'm *your* idiot." He stuck his head back inside, kissed her lightly on the lips, then withdrew and closed the door behind him.

Sheri watched him step around to the front of the car. He stood there a moment in the headlights, casting a huge shadow across the house's crumbling façade, then he moved through the tall grass and carefully mounted the steps. He paused a moment, studying something at his feet, then he crossed the threshold, the shadows swallowing him whole, and Sheri glanced back down at her phone, at the time displayed there in the corner of her lighted screen. Fifteen minutes suddenly seemed like a very long time.

"Okay, mister," she said aloud, "clock starts now."

That's odd.

The wooden steps should've been warped, cracked and pitted with rot, instead they were smooth and sturdy and bore Jeff's weight with ease. They didn't even creak. He shone his flashlight down at his feet and saw light-colored planks marbled with woodgrain, the screw heads so new they glowed like tiny mirrors in his beam.

New steps? Why would somebody put new steps up to an old house?

He lifted his eyes and his light to the vacant doorway and stepped through into darkness, his confusion deepening. The scent of fresh-cut pine hung thick in the humid air. Plywood? Yes. Someone had cut up sheets of plywood and fastened them to the hallway floor.

Jeff peered into the empty room to his left, shined his flashlight on neon yellow saw horses and scattered boxes of decking screws.

They're fixing the place up? This place?

And the way they were going about it...

Fresh wood on the hallway floor, but the rooms on either side still had their original flooring, frosted with years of dust. There were footprints, like tracks in new-fallen snow, various sizes and treads. A flurry of recent activity. The walls, however, showed no sign of being touched. The original floral wallpaper was still there; yellowed, dingy, torn in spots – hanging strips exposing a landscape of scarred and cratered plasterwork, wooden ribs showing through scattered holes – but there was no rhyme or reason to it. And attached to all this corrosion was a bright white smoke detector, fresh out of the box, its sensor light blinking red like a warning beacon in the dark.

What the hell?

Jeff continued down the hall, illuminating one mysterious anachronism after another. More new smoke detectors on more crumbling, barely touched walls. Shiny fire extinguishers in otherwise neglected rooms. Electrical outlets mounted on the outsides of walls, sometimes just above the old-fashioned, existing outlets; external wiring sealed in metal pipes that ran along the rotting baseboards to points unknown. It was as if the remodeling crew wanted to preserve all this decay.

He turned a corner into the kitchen. It didn't appear that the workmen had come this far. He found a floor that was a fresco of small tiles, some cracked, some missing; cabinets without doors, some of which had fallen from their roosts, leaving more pits and holes in the plasterwork; and a sink basin full of debris. The window above was boarded, allowing fingers of moonlight to reach in along the far wall.

Jeff turned his light and found a closed wooden door, the only one he'd seen in the house so far. The hinges were original, rusted and tarnished, the knob covered in a Celtic pattern both intricate and ornate. He paused, then reached out and opened it, wincing at the scream of metal against metal. The tiny spotlight found wooden steps descending into absolute darkness.

The cellar.

Probably a dirt floor. That's the way they did it back then, wasn't it? Dirt floors and wooden shelves full of canning jars. Would there still be fruit after so many years – rotten and mummified, mutated into all variety of science experiments? Part of him was dying to find out.

And if those stairs give way and you fall? What then? Maybe it's not dirt. Maybe it's concrete. Maybe you'll bust your head wide open and that'll be it.

Jeff nodded. He was just about to walk away and head back out to the car, when he saw something.

A light.

He froze, thinking he'd only imagined it, but no, there it was again.

A soft, yellow-green glow, fading in and then fading out.

What the – ?

He paused, thinking it over, then his curiosity got the better of him. He held his watch up to the light, knowing Sheri would follow through with her threat to call the police if he wasn't out there on schedule. He still had seven minutes, however.

Plenty of time for a quick look.

Jeff started down the stairs with caution, testing each step before applying his full weight. Cobwebs dangled in his path. He brushed them aside, then wiped his hand on his jeans in disgust. It looked as if no one had been down here in forever, and yet that light...

It came again, illuminating red brick walls and a latticework of old copper pipes that hung from the rafters.

But what the hell is it? A television screen left on? Maybe it's part of a new security system to go along with the new smoke detectors and fire extinguishers? None of this makes any sense.

Jeff reached the basement floor (dirt, just as he'd imagined) and flashed his light around. Bricks and support posts had turned the cellar into a maze of storerooms. Water-damaged boxes and wooden pallets sat stacked in corners, filling the confined space with the stench of their gradual corruption. And at the end of a very long, very narrow hall, an archway glowed with that mysterious yellow-green aura.

He stepped through the arch and a sharp odor assaulted his nostrils almost immediately, overpowering everything else. Chlorine. He coughed against it, and covered his mouth and nose with his hand to block it out.

Still the smell persisted.

Jeff looked around for the source and his eyes filled with tears. He could still see, however. He just couldn't believe what he saw.

The brick on the opposite side of the room was cracked, a single fracture that snaked its way up the entire length of the wall; nearly three feet wide at the floor, tapering down to a paper-thin line near the rafters. It glowed. The crack actually glowed, filling the room with wavy, spectral light...and something else. A thick, yellow-green fog, heavier than the surrounding air; it poured from the break, hiding dirt beneath a churning blanket of mist.

Jeff took a step toward the crack and was immediately seized by a coughing fit, that chlorine stench burning the lining of his nose. *A chemical spill? Did the workmen breach some underground tank? Oh God...what have I just exposed myself to?*

He heard an animal snarl behind him and spun around, aiming his light in the direction of the sound, seeing nothing but brick and molder in all directions. Then, in the darkness beyond the arch, something moved; he heard the whisk and patter of feet, the crash of falling debris. Whatever it was, it was between him and the stairs.

Oh shit! Jeff coughed, his nose and throat blazing, his eyes fogging with fresh tears. *What the hell is that? What have I –*

A scream made him jump, then he heard a guitar riff start in. His ring tone: Ozzy Osbourne's "Crazy Train." He shoved his hand into his pocket and yanked out his cell phone, silencing the Prince of Darkness, seeing a familiar smiling face on the touch screen. "Sheri?"

"Time's up. Get your ass out here and let's go."

He glanced into the dark hallway. Had the thing out there heard the music? Was it coming for him now? He hunkered down, trying to keep his voice low. "Sheri, listen to me...There's something down here, and it – "

"Yeah, right."

"*I'm serious!*" Jeff was rocked by another coughing fit, and tasted blood in his mouth. He wiped his lips with the back of his hand and saw red streaks across his knuckles in the flashlight.

That animal snarled again, but it was not coming toward him. It sounded distant, trailing off. He heard the loud drumming of hurried feet on wood.

It was climbing up the stairs.

Before he could warn Sheri, however, something lashed out at him from behind and wrapped itself around his wrist, something pink and laced with purple veins, something covered in a thick coat of slime. It was a tentacle. Rows of suckers on the underside flexed and puckered like countless wanton mouths. Jeff's teary eyes bulged from their sockets as the tentacle tightened its grip, its pressure crushing in on the bones of his wrist. He lost his grasp on the flashlight and it fell into the yellow- green fog that pooled around his feet.

Holy shit!

Another tentacle whipped at Jeff, wrapped itself around his waist. It was larger than the first, thicker and more muscular; it flexed and constricted and yanked him back across the floor, the heels of his sneakers digging deep furrows in the dirt, gouges that quickly filled in with mist. Jeff's cell phone slipped through his fingers and joined the flashlight in the chlorine haze. He could still hear Sheri's voice, however; she sounded more angry than frightened.

"Stop it! I mean it! This isn't funny!"

No, Jeff thought, *this isn't funny at all!*

The back of his head slapped against the brick and birthed a fire-works display in his watery eyes. More tentacles came from behind him; they curled around his chest, around his legs. They were actually extending from the crack in the wall, trying to pull him through.

Jeff opened his mouth to scream, but the tentacles bulged and tight-ened and squeezed all the air from his lungs with a glut of blood. He heard his ribs crack and break. The splintered bone stabbed through his organs, flooding him with wave after wave of searing pain. Warmth washed over his body – his blood defying gravity, flowing back into the light. The insistent tentacles yanked and tugged, and his spine snapped in two, the jagged lips of the crack in the wall raking Jeff's flesh like teeth as he was pulled through it.

Before he was wrenched completely into the break, however, before his skull finally imploded, before his brain was flattened to the thickness of a flapjack and scraped back into the yellow-green light beyond, Jeff's final thought was of Sheri.

The sudden silence on the other end of the line chilled her to the bone.

Sheri clutched the phone to her ear, her hand shaking. She sat there in the passenger's seat, staring through the windshield into the darkened doorway, and the Fuller house stared back at her with cold indifference. She cried out again, "I'm going to call the cops, Jeff."

No reply.

"I'm serious!"

Still nothing.

She lowered the phone and looked at the screen. The call hadn't dropped. Jeff just wasn't talking.

Shit.

Sheri glanced up just in time to glimpse a dark shape as it bolted from the mouth of the door and dove off the porch into the tall grass. The blades rocked violently back and forth as whatever it was neared the Pontiac's bumper. She locked her door, then reached across Jeff's seat and did the same. She ran her fingers over the steering column, trying to see if Jeff had left her the keys; when her fingernail slipped into the empty ignition, she had her answer.

Shit!

Her foot brushed against her purse on the floorboard. Inside was a Monarch Stun Pen. 1. 3 million volts. She put the phone back against her ear and shrunk down in the seat, trying to reach it, trying not to be seen, her seatbelt digging into her chin. "Jeff?" she whispered. "Jeff, something's coming for the car."

Coming for *her*.

The dark shape leapt up onto the hood, denting the metal, a jolting impact that rocked the car on its axles. Sheri's breath caught in her throat. The thing was the size of a German shepherd, but this was no dog. No. This was unlike any animal she'd ever seen, a nightmare silhouette. Its back was the serrated outline of a naked spine, and it stood on more than a dozen boney, spider-like legs that flexed and bent in odd, crazy angles, each step accompanied by the shrill scrape of claws on metal. It's long, narrow head dipped down, peering in at her.

Does it know I'm in here? Can it see me? Smell me?

The shadowy creature snarled at her. Its snout split open and the flesh peeled away from its jaws in flaps. The obscene mouth lunged at the windshield, streaking the glass with slime and spittle, its fangs scraping and scratching like diamonds.

Sheri recoiled, pressed herself flat against her seat. Her heart thumped so loud she could hear it; the beat mixed with the beast's snarl and the scratch of metal and glass to form a hellish symphony.

"*Jeff!*" Sheri shrieked into her phone, knowing now why he didn't answer, why he would never answer again, and the image sprang up behind her eyes with such suddenness that she literally jumped in her seat; Jeff lying on a rotting floor like the Raggedy Andy doll she'd had as a child, his head nearly ripped off and his stuffing spilling out, except it wasn't stuffing at all.

It was blood.

Tears ran down her cheeks. She hung up, her harried fingers dialed 922, then she hung up again and dialed the correct number. As she listened to it ring, she undid her seatbelt, reached down and retrieved her purse, all the while keeping her eyes on the windshield, on the creature outside.

Those flaps around its jaws opened and closed again. The creature hissed and snarled and bellowed its frustration. It knew she was in the car, but it could not get at her.

"Go away!" she screamed, searching blindly through her purse with her free hand. She felt her Kindle, her checkbook, a compact, her birth control pills, a small bottle of Excedrin, and folded pieces of paper that seemed so important but now meant nothing. *Where the hell is my stun pen?*

Ringing gave way to a distant female voice, "Harmony 911, where's your emergency?"

"Oh God...Help! Please help me! The old Fuller place!"

The creature snarled, then scratched the glass once more with its teeth.

"What's your emergency?"

"Send the police! Hurry!"

"What's your problem there?"

"It's trying to get in ! I think it killed my boyfriend!"

"What happened to your boyfriend?"

The thing lunged at the windshield again, and this time the glass cracked in a spiderweb.

Spider-dog, he thought incoherently. The word just popped into her mind and then exploded from her lips. *"Spider-dog!"*

"What happened to your boyfriend, ma'am? I need to know."

"It's breaking in! It's gonna get me!"

The spider-dog screeched and growled, saliva tethering the folds of its mouth to the glass in long, back-lit strands.

"Someone's breaking in right now?"

"Just send cops with guns! Guns! Hurry!"

"Who has the guns?"

"No! Listen, you stupid bitch!" Sheri held the phone up to the windshield so the woman could hear the spider-dog's hungry, frustrated snarls. *"You hear that? It's gonna kill me! Send some fucking cops out here to shoot it or I'm gonna die!"*

The voice came again, but this time Sheri didn't think the woman was talking to her. "Route Six, the old Fuller Place. Possible break-in. They say someone has a gun and is trying to kill somebody else."

Another lunge and she felt the sting of glass on her arms and her cheeks. *"Hurry,"* she screamed into the phone. *"It's getting in!"*

"They're on their way," the dispatcher assured her. "I need you to calm down. I need you to talk to me. You say someone's breaking into the Fuller place?"

The spider-dog thrust its snout through the opening in the windshield, coming within inches of her nose. It opened its mouth again. Its hot breath stank of low tide.

Sheri continued to fish through her purse, and *finally*, her fingers closed around the Monarch's rubber grip. She yanked the pen free and thumbed off the cap. She hit the wrong button, however, and turned on the high-powered LEDs instead of the stunner.

In the bright light, she saw the spider-dog clearly for the first time. The insides of those folds were wrinkled and pink and lined with rings of teeth like a lamprey. The rest of its skin was the blackish-gray color of rotting flesh. It screeched and shook its head back and forth. Its eyes were bulbous and black; there were dozens of them, various sizes and on both sides of its narrow head, but they didn't seem to have any lids.

I've blinded it!

It screeched again, and outside, those countless legs clawed and scratched and tried to pull itself free of the windshield.

Sheri glanced down at the Monarch, and this time, she armed it. She thrust it up like a sword. There was a bright flash of electricity, and the spider-dog let out a shrill cry of pain. Its head jerked backward, withdrew from the car; it slid off the hood into the grass and was gone.

For a moment, she thought she heard more creatures coming up behind her, their screeching growing louder, *closer*. When she saw the red and blue strobes in the Pontiac's rearview mirror, however, she knew it was just the police. Sheri fell back against her seat in tears, her cell phone in one hand and her stun pen in the other. And when a police officer finally knocked on her window, his gun drawn, she was slow to open it.

CHAPTER TWO

Officer Hicks drew his gun and started for the old, dark house.

So much for another quiet Saturday night.

Harmony was usually boring, even on the weekends, just the way his wife, Angie, liked it. He'd been a beat cop up in Chicago for years before Uncle Sam and the reserves called him away for back-to-back tours in Afghanistan and Iraq. And now that Angie finally had him home, after all those sleepless nights of worry, he knew she didn't want to get *that* call.

"We regret to inform you that your husband survived well-armed, well trained terrorists and roadside bombs half way around the world, but was taken down by some high school drop-out in a bathroom meth lab a few miles from your doorstep."

So they pulled up stakes and moved to this quiet little town. No gangstas. No whores. No crack houses. Just law-abiding, God-fearing people who watched out for their neighbors; a place where the only victims of gunfire were deer. This made Angie happy, which made Officer Hicks happy, but sometimes, just sometimes, he found that he still longed for the excitement of a city beat.

Now, his adrenaline was pumping again.

The Pontiac on the front lawn had been a wreck. Hood dented in. Windshield shattered. Hicks ran the plate and it came back registered to one Jeff Stone.

"He's still in the house," the woman inside the car informed him, and Hicks had seen the fear in her eyes; white hot, despite all his assurances of safety. "I think that thing got him."

The thing in question was some kind of large animal.

Spider's dog? Is that what she called it?

Whatever it was, she said she'd tasered it.

Hicks keyed his radio and said to the dispatcher, "22-06, be advised, we have a 10-91V in progress."

A 10-91 denoted anything involving an animal, and the letters signified the seriousness of the situation. There were codes for everything from stray (10-91A) to dead (10-91D). V stood for "Vicious," and judging by the damage done to the Pontiac, and the woman's terrified state, Hicks thought it was the right call.

"Ten-four," the dispatcher replied, her voice just as calm as ever. "10-91V. Will contact Miami County Animal Control and direct to your location."

"Ten-four." He frowned. It would take animal control a good forty-five minutes to get there, and if Jeff Stone really was injured, he might not have forty-five minutes to wait.

The fact that the woman could stun it told Officer Hicks that he could kill it, which meant he was going inside. He crossed the threshold, sweeping every room from left to right with his light and his Glock, making quick steps down the corridor and paying close attention to every corner. He didn't want any surprises, and Angie still didn't want that call.

"We regret to inform you that your husband tried to be a hero and was eaten alive by Cujo."

"Stone!" he shouted. "I'm here to help. Can you hear me, Stone?"

The only sound was the thud of his own footfalls on fresh plywood.

"Stone!" Hicks turned the corner and found an open door. He tipped his flashlight down a flight of stairs. There were footprints on the dusty steps; one set of shoes heading down into the darkened cellar, one set of animal tracks coming back up. *Big* animal tracks. "Jesus," he muttered, then yelled, "You down there, Stone? Are you injured?"

Silence from the darkness below.

Hicks glanced over his shoulder, then squinted into the dark ahead; he tightened his grip on his gun and started down the stairs. Bits of dust drifted through his beam like falling snow, and the smell of fresh-cut wood gave way to the dank musk of mildew. When he got to the bottom, his light played over brick walls; it was a tight corridor with several arched doorways.

Then he saw a glow. It filled the archway at the end of the hall.

"Police!" Hicks yelled. He took a few steps down the passage, checked a storage room to his right, then advanced a few more steps before sweeping another room on his left. "Stone? You in there, Stone?"

He strained to hear any response from the darkness, no matter how faint or non-verbal, but he heard nothing.

Hicks moved forward again, cautiously stepping beneath the brick arch and into the room at the end of the hall. He'd expected to see Stone, bleeding out into the dust, perhaps mauled to death. He was even prepared to confront the animal responsible – a large, feral dog, or, judging by the size of those prints on the stairs, a tiger escaped from someone's pen. Instead he found...nothing.

No animal. No Jeff Stone.

But something had happened in here all right. The dirt was disturbed in a way that suggested a struggle. Drag marks ran from the far wall to the center of the floor where a flashlight laid abandoned; its plastic lens had cracked, but the bulb within still burned brightly; the beam bounced off the brick walls, creating that glow Hicks had seen from the hall. A few feet away from the light, a discarded cell phone lay face down in the dirt; a wad of mucous stuck to its back, just below the tiny camera lens, like someone had sneezed on it.

Hicks crinkled his nose.

Let CSI touch that.

The faint smell of bleach hung in the air, and for a moment, Hicks wondered if someone might have cleaned evidence from the walls. His light revealed a different story. The brick was filthy, dark moss filling in mortar lines. The far wall was badly cracked – a long, dark, deep fissure that split the brick in two like a fault line – but it appeared to have been there for some time. No one had cleaned this place in years, if ever.

But Hicks couldn't find any blood. *No blood. No body parts. No body. Not even torn bits of clothing or a stray shoe. Where the hell is Stone?*

Hicks turned away and headed back for the stairs, studying the floor, looking for more drag marks, anything that would indicate what had happened to the man. His mind kept going back to the prints on the stairs; shoes going down, claws coming up. If someone had placed the flashlight and cell phone down here, they'd still need to get back out. And if the animal only went up the stairs, how did it get down here in the first place?

Maybe it was down here for a long time, starving, and Stone set it free from its cage?

But, as he shined his light around the other storerooms, he found no cages. No other doors, either. No clues at all.

Hicks hurried back up the stairs, hearing the old wood creak. When he reached the kitchen, he turned his light back on the steps, saw his own shoe prints amid the others, but his pointed both ways. It was a mystery.

Or a big practical joke. The paw prints could've been faked. Stone could've walked down there, dropped his stuff, then slipped on some kind of costume before he ran back up here to –

What? Wreck his own car? Scare his girlfriend out of her mind, to the point that she tasered his ass when the joke went too far?

It made no fucking sense.

Hicks lifted his flashlight to the ceiling, still needing to check out the second floor. He moved quickly down the hall, searching for a staircase. Along the way, his light washed over sawhorses and other bits of construction equipment, and when he finally found the landing, his beam caught something else.

Building permits.

They were hung on the wall with strips of duct tape, protected in plastic sleeves that glowed in his light. The licenses had been issued to the Harmony Indiana Fire Department, and they detailed electrical and structural work that was planned for the next month and a half. Hicks gave them a quick read, and he found something at the bottom of one of the forms that gave him pause.

Description of work: Temporary use for haunted house from 10/13/2012-10/31/2012 and occupy per plans.

This place was going to be a Halloween attraction? *Really?* Hicks had heard all the horror stories about this place, and he didn't buy into supernatural bullshit, but still...turning the sight of real-life tragedy into some cheap spook house? It seemed wrong to him, disrespectful, like dancing on somebody's grave.

A *thump*.

It came from upstairs.

Hicks whirled, lifted his light and gun toward the sound. The stairs bent around a corner. He proceeded with caution, one step at a time.

And then he was in the upstairs hallway, his gun like an extension of his own hand, a metal finger pointing the way. Half a dozen doorways lined the walls, presumably leading to a like number of rooms. Some rooms lacked doors, while in others, the doors stood wide open. The only closed door belonged to the room at the end of the hall.

Of course. Perfect.

He crept down the hallway, pausing to check each of the side rooms as he went. They were all empty; bare floors, bare walls. Within those walls, however, he could hear movement – a sound he knew well from his city beat. Rats. Scampering around in there, hidden behind the dingy floral wallpaper.

This isn't the city. It's probably just a family of cute little field mice.

Probably, but it still gave him the creeps.

Through the boarded slats of the front windows, he saw the red and blue strobes of his cruiser. So close, yet so far away. Part of him wanted to run for it, but that part was being drowned in adrenaline.

You wanted excitement.

He nodded to himself and marched on. The door at the end of the hall grew larger, closer, until he could reach out and touch the tarnished knob. He gave it a push and it opened easily. He waited a moment before advancing.

Rusted bed frames leaned against the walls like metal skeletons, and the floor sat buried beneath mounds of black trash bags. Hicks opened one of the bags to look inside. Old habits died hard. He'd made some pretty good busts in his day by looking through meth house trash.

The bag stank of ammonia.

Hicks holstered his Glock and reached into the bag. He grabbed a wad of fabric, then brought it out into his light. He drew out the corner of an old tablecloth with a delicate, lacy trim. Baby mice clung to it. Tiny. Naked and pink. Their eyes still tightly shut. They were anything but cute.

"Jesus!"

He dropped the fabric and stepped back, watching as the little animals hit the floor and moved away from his light like mutant slugs; their tiny arms and legs pushing and pulling them to safety beneath the mound of Hefty bags.

"Jesus," he muttered again.

His radio sounded, startling him. "22-06?"

"We regret to inform you that your husband died of a heart attack. But don't worry, ma'am, we'll be sure to honor his memory by using the story in ads for our new haunted house. That'll really pack 'em in!"

Hicks snickered to himself, then took a breath and keyed his radio. "Go ahead, 22-06."

"22-06, what's the situation on your 10-91V?"

"Ten-four. Just completed my sweep. Request 11-41 for female, approximately thirty years of age, suffering from post-traumatic shock. Unable to locate second victim."

"Ten-four, 22-06. Sending EMS unit your way."

"Ten-four."

Officer Hicks backed out of the room, calming down, his heartbeat slowing as he descended the stairs. He headed back outside to wait for the ambulance and Miami County Animal Control. As he walked away, he glanced back over his shoulder at the darkened doorway.

What would the fire department charge for admission, he wondered, and why would anyone pay to go in there?

CHAPTER THREE

The woman sat motionless in the back of the police cruiser. Robby Miller noticed the Monarch still clutched in her hand. It looked as if she'd used the little taser on herself. Her eyes were the palest blue; vacant, distant, glancing neither right, nor left, nor even acknowledging him as he knelt beside her and slipped a blood pressure cuff around her arm.

He flashed her a smile anyway. "Hey there."

She said nothing, continued to stare off into space.

"I'm just gonna make sure you're okay." Robby adjusted the earbuds of his stethoscope; he reached out with the diaphragm, paused, and said, "This might be a little cold."

He placed the metal disc against her chest and she winced.

"Sorry." He listened to the tune of her heart, strong and steady, then inflated the blood pressure cuff. "I'm Robby. What's your name?"

At first, he didn't think she would answer, but then her lips parted and he heard her say, "Sheri."

"Nice to meet you, Sheri." He watched the cuff slowly deflate. *86 over 55. Low, but she's obviously in shock.* "Can you tell me what happened?"

Sheri's face twisted into an expression of revulsion. "It tried to get me."

It? Robby frowned. Another EMT might not have thought twice about the word, but Robby's mind seized it and wouldn't let go. He blinked and looked her over, tried to redirect his mind to assessing her injuries. Tiny cuts marred the pale skin of her forearms and face; they weren't deep, no more than nicks really, and they'd already begun to scab. "Did it hurt you?"

She shook her head and held up the stun pen. "I zapped it and it disappeared."

Robby looked over his shoulder to make sure no one would hear. "You mean...like a ghost?"

She shook her head, the shock in her eyes giving way to confusion. "It ran off."

Robby let go of a breath he didn't realize he'd been holding. "So it was an animal?"

She nodded.

"But it didn't bite you or scratch you?"

She shook her head again.

"What kind of animal was it?"

Her mouth opened and she wrinkled her nose in disgust. Behind her eyes, he could see her searching for words to adequately describe what she'd seen. Finally, she gave up and just shrugged.

"It's okay, Sheri." Robby unfastened the cuff; the loud rip of the Velcro made her jump. He opened a plastic bag and removed a thick blanket; he unfolded it, then draped it around her. "This will help keep you warm."

"Did they find Jeff?"

"Jeff?"

"My – my boyfriend." She blinked out a tear and used the corner of the blanket to mop her cheek, then her eyes drifted up to the Fuller place. "He went in there."

Robby followed her line of sight. Sure, it was an ugly house, a rambling eyesore, a monument to rot, to decay, but at least it was honest. *Real.* Other homes hid Harmony's true ugliness beneath manicured lawns and polished veneers. Not this place. No. This old farmhouse told the whole sordid story with every crumbling plank and moldering brick.

"I think it got him," Sheri muttered, and with the words came fresh tears, "but I – I don't know. I need to know."

Robby nodded, then turned his attention to a small knot of officers forming in the tall grass at the foot of the steps. One of them aimed his flashlight at the ground. Robby recognized him from previous runs. His name was Hicks, and judging by the enthusiasm in his young face, he'd found something good.

"Let me see what I can find out for you," Robby said over his shoulder, but when he started to stand, Sheri reached out and gripped his forearm like a vice. He turned to look back at her and saw a sense of urgency in her eyes.

"Please," she said, "be careful."

Robby placed his hand over hers and gave it a gentle squeeze. "I'm just going to walk over and talk to the officers." He pointed them out to her. "You'll be able to see me the whole time, and I'll come right back here and tell you what I find out."

She nodded and released her grip.

He stood and stepped away from the cruiser, but his eyes were drawn back to Sheri again and again as he waded through the tall grass. When he reached the officers, Robby looked down and saw what was caught in Hicks' light. Animal tracks, but not like any he'd ever seen before. They were *huge*.

"Looks like we got another cougar on the loose," one of the cops – Kirsch – said.

"I thought cougars were extinct," Robby told him, his eyes still on the tracks. They did look vaguely cat-like; four rounded toes with long, slender claws that dug deep furrows in the dirt, but there was something odd about them. For one thing, there seemed to be tracks on top of tracks, as if the animal had walked this same path half-a-dozen times. And there were deep holes behind some of the prints, always centered, like the stiletto heel of a woman's shoe.

"Well, maybe one of these days somebody'll let the cougars know that." Kirsch snickered. "Then we won't have to chase 'em anymore."

One of the other cops spoke up: "Remember last year, that guy in Ohio? Has his own fuckin' zoo and decides one night to open all the cages before he offs himself. Those guys had to spend the whole next day trackin' down a damn menagerie. Lions and tigers and bears, oh my." He flicked his light around. "You think somebody 'round here?"

"Nobody in Harmony's that stupid," Kirsch asserted. "Most dangerous pet around here is that mangy mutt down at Robinson's Salvage."

Robby nodded at the vacant doorway. "Anybody know what happened to the boyfriend? Dispatch only mentioned the woman."

"He's not in the house," Hicks told him. "We've checked the barn too." The officer paused a moment, putting the scene together in his mind, obviously still trying to make sense of it; he lifted his flashlight to the distant tree line. "We think he might have run off into the woods to try and lure the animal away from his girlfriend."

"Okay." Robby looked up at the moon. "So you're standing out here in the yard because the light's better?"

Kirsch got defensive. "There's acres of woods and cornfields out there, Miller."

"I know that." A chill crawled up Robby's back to his scalp. "But if that thing's out there – "

"We'll deal with it." Kirsch adjusted his belt and put his hand on his holster and the Glock within. "When animal control gets here, we'll track it down."

For all his macho talk, Robby knew Kirsch wasn't going after it because he didn't want to go into those woods at night. More than anyplace else on Earth, he didn't want to go in there. None of them did. Oh sure, they would go into the barn, the place where they pulled Grand Dragon Fuller out of a threshing machine in bits and pieces, but they didn't want to set foot out there. And Robby couldn't say he blamed them.

People had a habit of disappearing in those woods.

Too many people.

"There are old cops," Sheriff Carter used to say, "and there are bold cops, but there are very few old, bold cops."

Robby used to think that he was so much smarter than Sheriff Carter. Now he wondered. Carter had long since retired and left Harmony for the Arizona desert. Not a cornfield in sight.

Why are you still stuck in this town, Miller? What are you trying to prove?

He made a fist and pointed back at the cruiser with his thumb. "So who gets to tell the girl that her boyfriend's missing?"

"I'll do it," Hicks said, and there was clear frustration in his voice. Robby could tell the young cop wanted to go out there, though the others had talked him out of it, and the decision obviously wasn't sitting well with him. Hicks was still new to Harmony, and while he'd undoubtedly heard all the stories – you can't avoid it around here – he'd not yet seen enough to really believe them.

Stick around, buddy boy. Stick around.

This is Route 6 after all, his brain offered, as if he was in need of the prompt. *Remember what happened with Paul Rice's car? How it flipped over just up the road from here? How you pulled him from the burning wreck and he laid screaming in his delirium, going on and on about demons, about how they were clawing at the glass, coming to get him, coming to take away his soul? And then there was that business at the Woodfield Movie Palace last year. Who could forget that, right? But that demon...that one you were able to stop, weren't you? You were able to send that fucker straight back to Hell, big guy. Good work! You* the man! *But it doesn't make up for all your friends that died out there in the corn, now does it? You couldn't do anything to stop that, could you? No. They died, and you couldn't do Jack Shit! That's something you'll never forget, Robby, because I won't let you. No way, buddy boy. I'll keep reminding you...every...single. . . day!*

———

At twenty minutes past midnight, Robby, the EMT, returned. Sheri knew this because she'd been staring at her watch. A present from Jeff.

He'd given it to her for her birthday in July, and the thought that it would now be the last gift he would ever give her sank into her brain like a slow-motion bullet.

A police officer accompanied Robby, a young man with a crew cut who looked more like a Marine than a cop. He knelt down in front of her, his eyes very serious. "Ma'am, I'm Officer Hicks. I pulled you out of the car a little bit ago."

Sheri nodded. "Thank you."

"I'm afraid I have some upsetting information – "

"He's dead, isn't he?"

"I made a complete search of the farmhouse, and I found a flashlight and cell phone in the cellar that may belong to him. Other officers were then dispatched here to the scene, and together we – "

"Is he dead or not?" *Goddammit, stop handling me with kid gloves and just say it!* Sheri wiped the scalding tears from her cheek with Robby's blanket. "Can you – can you just tell me?"

"Ma'am, we don't know where he is right now."

"What are you talking about?" Sheri pointed up at the old farmhouse as if they couldn't see it. "He's in there!"

"Ma'am, as I said, he's not." The officer's eyes never left hers; his voice was calm, quiet but firm. "I made a careful search of the entire house, every room, and Mr. Stone is not inside."

"Then where is he?"

"We don't know," Hicks said. "We think he may have been trying to protect you from the animal that attacked your car; that he may have run off into the woods to try and lure it away from you. We found tracks that suggest it went off in that direction."

"Jeff's alive?" The knots in Sheri's stomach loosened up a bit. She glanced up at Robby for confirmation, but he stood by, silent and noncommittal.

Of course. He didn't go in the house. He doesn't know.

"We don't know that for certain," Officer Hicks cautioned. "We did find drag marks in the cellar near his personal items, but there was no blood or other evidence of violence."

Sheri frowned. Drag marks sounded pretty violent to her. They didn't see the creature she'd seen. They didn't understand. Hell, *she* was still trying to understand.

"Jeff was – he's a big guy," she told them. "It would take something really strong to drag him anywhere he didn't want to go, unless he was unconscious."

Hicks looked at her, neither agreeing nor disagreeing, then he said, "The most important thing to focus on is that, if this animal had mauled him, we would expect to find a large amount of blood at the scene. We didn't find any."

"But you don't *know* anything, right? You don't *know* he's alive?"

"I don't want to give you false hope, ma'am, but I've been on the job a long time, and not finding blood or other evidence...it's a good sign."

Sheri nodded, feeling numb, cold. She pulled the blanket tighter, crossed her arms over her chest. She wished it was her own blanket, wished she was at home in bed, having the worst nightmare of her life. And more than anything, she wished she'd wake up.

Hicks went on, "Miami County Animal Control is on the way. When they arrive, we plan to follow the tracks into the woods. There, we'll catch or kill the animal that attacked you, and we *will* find Mr. Stone. I promise you that."

Sheri nodded, then she noticed Robby's face. The EMT didn't look at all convinced. Neither was she. She glanced off into the woods, into the darkness between the trees, and her mind did not like what it saw there.

CHAPTER FOUR

It was just after one in the morning when Austin Todd heard his cows screaming. He'd lived his whole life on a farm, nearly sixty years, and never, *ever* had he heard such a terrible, mind-splitting sound. He'd even accompanied his father to the slaughterhouse as a child, seen heifers hung up by their hind legs in the processing line, waiting to have their throats slit, and not even *then* had he heard animals make a noise like that.

"Christ almighty." Austin climbed out of bed. Wearing only plaid pajama pants and worn out slippers, he went downstairs for his shotgun.

His wife, Helen, followed him, clutching her pink bathrobe in worried fingers. "Don't go out there," she pleaded. "Call the police."

"You call 'em," he told her as he broke open his double and popped in shells. He snapped the shotgun shut, grabbed a flashlight, and was out the screen door, off on an angry march across the lawn to his barn.

The metal door stood wide open. Nothing odd about that. He often left it that way on hot summer nights. The cows were secure in their pens, and even if they managed to get out, the whole yard was surrounded by gates and fences.

Sometimes, kids came out here to try their hands at cow tipping, but they usually left disappointed. Contrary to popular belief, cows didn't sleep standing up. They might take short naps that way, but they couldn't lock their knees. So when they shut their eyes for the night, they did it lying down in their straw beds.

The screaming was deafening.

Austin stood in the doorway, aimed his flashlight up and down the rows. His girls were standing up in their pens, their heads dipping up and down, their tagged ears pinned back tightly in distress, dark eyes wide with panic. All but one.

He didn't see Betty White.

That's what Helen had named her. An all-white Holstein. If not for those dark eyes, the cow could've been mistaken for an albino.

Her pen looked empty.

Austin cocked his shotgun, hoping the sound would frighten off whoever or whatever was lurking around, but the cows were so loud, it was barely audible. He moved cautiously down the row. And, when he reached Betty's pen, when he shined his light inside, he couldn't believe what he saw.

The cow was in there all right; she lay on her side, her pure white coat stained scarlet. Her eyes were glassy, lifeless, and her tongue hung out across the straw. Something straddled her carcass, a monstrous silhouette from the B-Grade Horror movies of Austin's youth. At first, he thought it was a giant spider, but it had too many legs. It had its head buried in Betty's side, and Austin could hear it slurping up her innards.

Holy shit. It's one of those Chupacabra thingies the Mexicans always talk about. Right here in my fucking barn. Holy shit.

For a moment, he stood by in frozen disbelief, his hands trembling, then he leveled his shotgun and tried to steady his aim. Normally, he was a dead shot, but he couldn't remember a time when he'd been this rattled. This wasn't a fox or a coyote. No. This was a fucking monster!

He fired. Lightning flashed from both barrels, the resulting thunder ricocheting off the walls and ceiling. The shells missed the thing entirely, however, connecting instead with a wooden column at the back of the pen, splintering it.

Shit!

The creature pulled its blood-soaked snout from Austin's cow. It screeched, then leapt up onto the wall of his barn and began to climb. It moved like a blur, legs reaching up over the top of other legs, sharp talons digging into the wood. And when it reached the rafters, it hung down like some demon bat, hissing at him, rosy drool dripping from its fangs. Austin backed away, his hand in his pajama pocket, digging for more shells. He found some, cracked open his shotgun to reload, and –

The thing dropped to the floor and lunged for him, elongated rear legs held up like arms with clawed hands.

Austin's hands lost their grip and the empty shotgun and shells fell to his feet. He turned away, ran for the door. Behind him, the creature snarled. Austin felt it closing the gap, but he didn't dare look back; he reached the door and slid it shut just as the creature's bulk slammed into it. The thing shrieked as he fastened the lock and backed away.

The back door!

It was still open. He hoped the creature wouldn't figure that out until he was safe in his house. He spun around and sprinted back across the lawn, the screams of his cows following him the whole way.

"What is it?" Helen asked him as he rushed in and chained the front door. "Lord, Austin...you're white as a sheet! What's happening?"

Austin couldn't answer. His heart was in his mouth, and even if he had the breath for words, he wouldn't have known what to tell her. *There's a monster in the barn?* She'd think he'd lost his mind.

He grabbed Helen by the arm and pulled her down the hall and into the bathroom, the place where they took refuge when the tornado sirens blared. They sat there, on the lip of the bathtub, waiting for the police to arrive, listening to that horrible, shrill screaming.

Helen was in tears. Austin stroked her hair and held her close, feeling her warmth. His chest ached and his pulse thudded madly in his ears.

"We got insurance," he said at last, and he repeated it again and again in the hushed tone of a prayer.

Outside, the chorus of screams weakened as, one by one, the voices died off. Finally, it stopped altogether.

CHAPTER FIVE

No...Don't stop! Don't go away! I need to know where you are...to find you...to serve you...

Cayden Donnelly's eyes sprang open. He sat straight up in bed, his arms outstretched, reaching for something in the darkness, something just beyond his grasp. The animal pelt that covered him slid down his muscular chest and piled on his lap.

He leapt naked from the rented mattress, ran blindly through the blackness. When he reached the wall, his hands found drapes and fumbled with the thick fabric until it parted. Outside, Vegas burned bright as a thousand torches, blinding him, thrusting his mind into a higher state of consciousness.

He saw the doorway again, a ragged fissure of light in a dark, crumbling brick façade. And beyond, he saw the Old Ones; pressing in against it, trying to push their way through to this world, trying to be free. They called to him, their voices deafening yet muffled and faint at the same time.

"I hear you," he screamed aloud, trying to be heard above the din, "but I need more! Give me more!"

Instead, the vision spiraled away from his eyes like a flashlight tossed down a deep well, and the distant thunder of those ancient voices died in his ears.

"No!" The window shook beneath Cayden's fists as he pounded the pane. "Not yet! I'm so close!"

He pushed himself off the glass, ran his fingers through the sweaty red locks of his hair and squeezed the back of his neck.

All his life, he'd been chasing those echoes. From his home in Connemara, Ireland, to Salisbury, Wiltshire and Cardiff, Wales. Across the sea, to the shores of Easter Island and the caverns of Cenote, Mexico. And then, on to America; Maine, New Hampshire, Rhode Island, Arizona, New Mexico...He'd journeyed to all the thin places, spots where the veil between worlds had worn and frayed to form a connection; tapestries woven together in some mystic loom. And he'd always been too late. Inevitably, someone beat him to the punch and cut those threads, collapsing bridges before they could be crossed, keeping his gods at bay.

But not this time.

No. This time would be different. This time, he would find the doorway and see it unlocked. This time, he would be there to greet his lords with open arms.

Cayden staggered across the motel room and fell to his knees on the dingy carpet. He reached out for the animal skin that sat crumpled on the bed, ran his fingers through the coarse hair of its fleece. To find this new thin place, this doorway, he needed stronger magic.

He needed blood.

Under the bed, he'd hidden a satchel made from quilted leather and the finest lambskin. He dragged it out, untied its straps, unfolded its flap, and brought his dagger out into the light. The blade was as old as it was polished, jagged on both sides; the handle, carved from bone, ended with a five-pointed star in a hoop.

He stood, studying the reflection of his own dark eyes in the metal. On the desk was a flier, one of hundreds that littered the Vegas streets. Pictures of women in seductive poses stared up at him. Prostitutes; each one vying for his attention, begging for him to call the number at the bottom of the page.

Cayden picked up the phone and dialed.

CHAPTER SIX

At first light, Harmony Police and Miami County Animal Control began their search of the woods and fields around Route Six, looking for the animal that attacked Sheri Foster and later paid a visit to the Todd farm. They were also searching for Jeff Stone, but after the carnage they'd found in Austin Todd's barn –

All his heifers were dead, partially eaten, their blood painted across stalls and puddled in the dirt and straw.

- the authorities held out little hope of finding him alive.

Sheri Foster knew none of this, however. After the police towed Jeff's Pontiac to impound –

"He'll get it back," Officer Hicks assured her.

- and drove her home, she tore off her clothes and stood in the shower, trying to get rid of the stench. The reek of the spider-dog would not leave her nostrils. She used her floral-scented soap, her shampoo that smelled of cucumber, but she could not rid herself of it.

Why hadn't the police noticed it?

Maybe they did and were too polite to tell you that you stank to high heaven. Or maybe...maybe it's all in your mind.

That was what frightened her, what kept her head beneath the hot stream jetting from her shower head, her tears lost in the water that poured down her face and gave her hair weight: the fear that this smell, like the memory, was now stuck in her mind, repeating over and over like a skipping CD, and she would never be rid of it.

She threw her clothes in the laundry and went to bed naked. The sheets smelled of spring rain, but it was nearly dawn before she finally got to sleep. Even then, the spider-dog haunted the darkness behind her eyes. She sat straight up in bed, trembling like a puppy, her sheets soaked with sweat and tears. In her dream, she'd still been trapped in that car, only this time, she never found her taser; she turned her purse inside out, and it just wasn't there. So the monster climbed right in, and she saw her screaming face reflected over and over again in the black voids of its countless eyes.

She reached for her nightstand, wanting – no, *needing* – a cigarette. Instead, she found a curved container of Nicorette Lozenges. She snatched it up in her fumbling fingers; finally, the lid flipped open. She popped the breath mint-sized lozenge onto her tongue and let it dissolve.

Sheri started smoking in college. It had nothing to do with peer pressure. She was her own person, and perfectly capable of making up her own mind. But she'd been bored, and homesick, and looking for kicks. One night at a party, she thought to herself, *Hey...I'm eighteen now. I can smoke if I want to and it's perfectly legal.*

I was so damn rebellious. She snickered despite her tears and hugged her knees beneath the sheets.

Sheri had bummed a cigarette off one of the girls standing outside her dorm, just to see what it was like, and the rest, as they say, was history. She'd never been a heavy smoker, never went through two packs a day or anything. Hell, a single pack of Virginia Slims might last her a whole week. But it was that first cigarette in the morning she really craved, maybe even more than the one after sex. It was how she got going.

"Yes, Virginia," she'd whisper, after taking that first deep drag and slowly exhaling. "Now, I can start my day."

And yet, almost as soon as Sheri started, she wanted to quit. She hated the way those three or four cigarettes made her clothes smell each day, hated the dark magic they had no doubt worked within her lungs, but it was hard to grind those butts out in the ashtray and just walk away. Something always drew her back. In college, it was the stress of exams. And now, teaching English and literature to a bunch of high schoolers who couldn't give a shit about anything that didn't come from their iPods or PS3s...life was full of aggravations.

Sheri turned her face toward the nightstand. Jeff's face sat next to the lamp, smiling up at her from behind framed glass. Her lip began to tremble uncontrollably.

Jeff was the one who got her to quit smoking. He never told her to stop, never harped on health issues, or the money she spent. He never even gave her that look of disapproval so many people did when she grabbed her purse and stepped outside. No. He got her to quit because she loved him, because she saw herself spending the rest of her life with him, and she wanted that life to be long and happy.

Sheri stared at Jeff's smiling face in the picture, remembering the day it was taken, remembering how he laughed at her for snapping it and threatened to take her camera away. And then she heard his laugh, not like a memory within her head, but in the *room*. Her head snapped around and...nothing. Nothing was there.

She was alone.

Why had she let Jeff drive out to that goddamn house? Why did he have to go inside? Why didn't she go in there with him?

Because then you'd be dead, is that what you want?

No. She didn't want that.

She glanced at her alarm clock. 11:25. The alarm never sounded.

Because it's Sunday, remember?

Sheri nodded and her eyes fell to her silent phone. She grabbed the handset and checked for missed calls. Nothing from Jeff since after school on Friday. Nothing from the police at all.

Because no news is good news, right?

No, it wasn't. Not knowing sucked.

Sheri put the phone back in the charger and snatched up her TV remote, flipping through local channels. She found infomercials, sports bloopers, and cartoons for pre-schoolers, but no newscasts. She dropped the remote on the sheets with a thump and slid from the bed.

She couldn't just sit around here all day. She had to get out there and do something, *anything*. Her workout clothes were still crumpled in a duffle bag from the last time she went to the gym. They reeked of stale sweat, but that was preferable to the sour stench of the spider-dog. She put them on and went to the door.

The Harmony Herald was rolled on her WELCOME mat, baking in the mid-day sun. She clawed the rubber band off and unfurled it, flipping pages and finding nothing. Nothing about the attack. Nothing about Jeff.

She heaved an exaggerated sigh and slapped the paper down on the table. On the front page, a headline caught her eye:

PRESIDENT HAS NOT SMOKED IN MONTHS.

Good for him, she thought, still longing for her lost Virginia. She could stop at Tony's Speedway, buy a pack on her way out to the old farmhouse, calm her nerves with a good smoke before she went out beating bushes and calling out Jeff's name.

No! Jeff wouldn't want that.

Sheri didn't really want it either. She looked up from the paper and the small coffee maker on the counter drew her eyes like a magnet. She made herself a cup to go.

Virginia had been out of Sheri's life for a month now, but her scent still clung to the car interior. After Febreze, and the "new car smell" air freshener from the car wash, the tobacco stench had faded, but it still hung in the air like a distant echo.

How long? How long until I don't think about it anymore? How long until...

Sheri opened the windows and drove off.

CHAPTER SEVEN

Robby Miller drank deeply from his Thermos, trying to wake as the Fuller place slept around him. Last night, in the dark, this structure had the appearance of a tired horror cliché. The old dark house. The bad place. But now, in the harsh light of day, robbed of its shadows, it really *was*...well...

A bad place.

He strolled its crumbling corridors, his "Spidey sense" tingling. Something had happened here, something dark, something *wrong*. He could feel it all around him...dripping from the cracked ceiling...sweating from the porous woodwork...held hostage in the hanging cobwebs...

A malevolent force.

Had it been here a few weeks ago on the tour, when his captain had shown them around? Maybe. *Probably*. But Cap's excitement had been so infectious – like a kid with a shiny new toy, just eager to start playing – Robby must've overlooked it, must've chalked it up to his own idea of...

A haunted house.

After the Department had signed the temporary lease agreement, after all the fund-raising plans had been set into motion, they now had two months to make it happen. Two months to build all the sets and props, to hang the chains and skeletons, to fill every corner with rubber spiders and monsters, to plant fake headstones and crosses in an empty graveyard. But, for Robby, these time-ravaged floors...these walls marred by festering sores...these features covered over in a death shroud of dust...*these* were far more frightening than anything they themselves could create. And yet...

No blood.

Robby had answered more than his fair share of animal attack calls over the years. Dogs. Bulls. Snake bites. Hell, even an alligator. But no matter what the animal, they all had one thing in common: blood. Lots of blood. Not here. The place was filthy, sure, but there was no blood splatter on the walls, no trail of blood across the floors, no...

No body.

There should have been a carcass, or at least parts of one. Once, there was a guy who kept his own menagerie: snakes, lizards, and spiders from every corner of the globe had all found their way into the glass tanks that filled his apartment. One day, the neighbors called 911 to complain about the smell, and when the police got there, they found the man dead on his couch, covered in cobwebs. One of the poisonous spiders had bitten him and stopped his heart. Well, after a while, all those animals got hungry, and they *all* started biting. When Robby arrived, the spiders were crawling in and out of the dead man's nose, out his ears and open mouth. The lizards had torn morsels of flesh from his arms, from his torso and his face; and the snakes...well, the snakes just slithered their way inside and made themselves at home. But, here...no bits...no pieces...

No nothing!

Robby turned the corner and almost had a heart attack himself. The Thermos slipped from his hand, hit the floor and rolled forward, caramel-colored coffee bleeding from its spout. There, on the open window sill, perched a single black crow. It sat there, *staring*, its eyes glassy...black...soulless...

Go away.

But it didn't go away. It stared at him, cocking its head from side to side. Its beak hung open as if it were about to speak, as if it were about to...

Go away.

But it didn't go away. The cold black marble of its eye rolled between Robby and his spilling thermos. *Aren't you going to get that?* the look said. *Aren't you going to come closer and pick that up? Aren't you going to come over here and let me...*

Go away!

And then it did go away. The crow spread its black wings and took flight, soaring across the room and out the window on the opposite wall. But for a moment, an instant, Robby thought it was coming for him, thought it was going to...

But it didn't.

No. He stood there a moment, catching his breath, letting his pulse slow, then he snatched up his Thermos and got coffee on his fingers. He wiped his hand across the leg of his jeans as he moved off down the hall toward the cellar. A line of yellow CRIME SCENE tape had been tacked across the door. Robby pulled it aside and reached for the doorknob, knowing it would be locked...

But it wasn't.

No. The door swung open on rusty hinges. Robby glanced down the steps into darkness, gripping his Thermos tightly. He was sweating. Must be the afternoon heat...

But it isn't.

No. The crow had him spooked. This whole damn house had him spooked. Being out here alone, so close to the woods, to the fields, to...

Nothing.

He threw the thoughts off and stared down at the dusty steps. The same tracks: balled toes, long nails, a single high heel impression at the back. They came up from the darkness as if they'd been born there. As if they appeared out of...

Nothing.

And then Robby thought he heard it. Here, in the house... walking down the hallway...approaching him from behind...

Nothing!

But it wasn't nothing. It was there. And, when it reached up and grabbed Robby by the shoulder, he nearly leapt free of his skin.

CHAPTER EIGHT

Just off Route Six, a white Chevy pickup sat idle, its engine cooling in the shade, the words MIAMI COUNTY ANIMAL CONTROL stenciled in black down the side of its bed with a phone number. Wire cages could be seen through the windows of its covered bed, and a pump-action shotgun was securely locked in its cab. The driver, a tall, muscular man in a tan uniform shirt and black slacks knelt in the woods nearby; his left hand held a catch pole like a wizard's staff, the loop of its noose swaying gently in the breeze; his right hand pressed into a large animal print, one of many that now littered the soft earth between the old farmhouse and Austin Todd's bloodied barn; his eyes stared out at the trees.

It was still out here. Close by. Probably resting in the shadows, waiting out the heat of the day, waiting for the night, for the hunt.

He crouched in the ferns. His uniform shirt, now dark with sweat, clung to him; bits of leaves and pine needles were plastered to his arms and the back of his neck. His own body odor filled his nostrils, but thankfully, he was downwind.

But downwind from what *exactly?*

He glanced down at his hand, at the tracks that surrounded it. They'd told him he was looking for a cougar. He could see how an untrained eye might make that assumption. These paw prints bore similarities to those of a big cat, but they were clearly made by something different. And those starfish-shaped wounds on the dead cattle...

Chupacabra.

That's what the farmer kept calling the animal.

"It was hairless," he'd said, "with long fangs. And it made sounds like I've never heard before. Snarling and hissing...sent chills down my spine. And you saw what it did to my cows. Those heifers are sixteen hundred each!"

Chupacabra.

The name literally meant "goat sucker," but the stories had it feeding on the blood of horses and cows as well. That is, if you believed that shit, and he didn't.

What that farmer saw was more than likely a coyote with a severe case of mange. Mange was quite common in coyotes; it distorted the animals' features and often led to them being reported as bizarre, unidentified creatures.

But these tracks...they're not coyote either.

"What the hell are you?" he asked aloud.

Chupacabra!

Fuck that! He refused to believe in supernatural bullshit. Who was he, Van Helsing? No. He didn't get paid to catch zombies and werewolves. He made his living with rabid raccoons in crawl spaces, with snakes in toilets, alligators in retaining ponds, the occasional cougar or coyote in the backyard, and the dog mauling kids on their way home from school.

He'd been at it a long time, longer than most. Most people got tired of the crawling and the hiding, got tired of seeing mangled youth, tired of being snapped at by pets gone amok and owners who didn't know a damn thing about the animals they housed or let loose. But not him; he was in it for the long haul, in it for life. If God wanted him to stop hunting, He'd have to put an end to him Himself.

He took off his Animal Control ball cap and wiped his sweaty arm across his sweaty forehead, listening to the persistent silence. There was a set to his jaw, a cold, hard squint to his eyes as he studied the branches above. *No birds. No squirrels or chipmunks; hell, I don't even hear any damn bugs.*

Nature exhaled through the woods. He was grateful for the cooling breeze, but even more grateful for the sound of rustling leaves and swaying limbs, anything to break the monotony, to prove that the world was still alive.

He glanced back down at the tracks. It was something exotic all right, something that shouldn't be in these woods. But whatever it was, he would find it.

A twig snapped.

His eyes shot toward the sound. He froze, then tightened his grip on the catch pole.

Another snap, closer this time.

Something was there, just on the other side of that foliage, stalking slowly toward him. He could hear the rustle of leaves as the animal passed through them, see the tops of the branches sway. Whatever it was, it was big.

Chupacabra?

Before his mind could craft some nightmarish image, a rack of deer antlers stabbed through the foliage. The buck stepped out into the clearing, stood there with its ears pinned back against his head, its dark eyes focused and alert, wondering if it was safe. After a moment, its head dipped down to the tall grass and grazed.

It was a beautiful animal, majestic, and as he knelt there, entranced, the man's stern face lightened with a forming grin.

The teardrop-shaped radio that hung from his neck crackled; a voice that wasn't his spoke his name, "Mancuso, you out there?"

Suddenly spooked, the buck lifted its head and bolted back into the underbrush, the beat of its hooves fading into the distance.

Mancuso frowned. He reached up, tilted the receiver toward his lips, and answered the call with a curt whisper, "Yeah."

"You find anything?" the radio asked.

"Nope."

"We've got nothin' here either. A few big whitetails. Wish they were in season."

The radio laughed, and Mancuso watched the bushes sway where they had swallowed the buck whole.

"Anyway," the voice went on, "made it out as far as the old quarry. We're headed back your way now."

"Don't."

"Why not?"

"It's bedded down."

"That means it's not prowling around. That's good right?"

"Could be, if we're smart about it." Mancuso gave his scruffy beard a quick scratch; his gaze moved from the tracks to the loop of his catch pole, watching the noose sway back toward his truck. "You're upwind. You head toward me, it'll smell you comin' a mile away, and you'll blow my stalk."

"So what?"

Mancuso turned his attention back to the trees. "If you stay put, sit still enough, *high* enough, you're more likely to see it if it moves."

"You want us to just sit around on the rocks and wait?"

"I want you to stay out of my way."

CHAPTER NINE

Sheri parked in the tall grass, right next to a bright red Ford pickup. She didn't remember it being there the night before. Then again, after her encounter with the spider-dog, she didn't remember much.

What if they've got a guard in the house now? What if they won't let anyone in?

Part of her wanted it to be true, wanted an excuse not to step inside, an excuse not to go down into that cellar. That's where they told her they'd found Jeff's flashlight and phone. That's where she knew she had to look.

After a moment's hesitation, she opened the car door and stepped outside. The wind hissed at her through the trees, but she noticed that there was no birdsong, no symphony of cicadas, no chirping of crickets. No sign of life at all.

Sheri felt a chill despite the heat.

This is the last place I saw Jeff...maybe the last place I will ever see him.

She felt tears of grief welling up again, gave her eyes a quick swipe, then marched on toward the old farmhouse. Her gaze rose to the boarded windows, to the missing shingles and the fallen gutters. How many empty decades had it sat here, falling apart? She tried to imagine what the house must have been like when it was all shiny and new.

This used to be someone's home, a place where they felt safe...

She made her way up the new front steps...

...safe from the summer storms...

...stepped cautiously across the porch...

...safe from the winter cold...

...slipped through the open doorway...

...safe to live in and love in and raise their family in...

...and, as she moved down the hall...

...safe...

...Sheri wondered if she would ever know the true meaning of the word again.

Something was happening here. The skeletal frame was being clothed in fresh wood. She eyed the tools, the tiny improvements, the new flooring. Was someone trying to make this place a home again?

When she turned the corner, her confusion turned to surprise. A man stood at the cellar door, staring down into darkness. His back was to her. He hadn't seen her yet. Sheri's entire body tensed; her eyes shot back and forth between his wide shoulders and the front door, her mind holding a silent debate on whether or not to make her presence known.

Take this as a sign, she told herself. *It's not meant for you to go down there. Get out while you can. You don't know who this guy is, what he might say or do to you.*

As Sheri stood there watching the man, angry with herself for being so frightened, she saw his hesitation and came to realize that he was just as unnerved by this place as she was.

He really doesn't want to go down there alone, does he? I can tell. But maybe together...After all, there's safety in numbers, right?

Finally, Sheri reached up and tapped him on the shoulder. She thought he would have a heart attack; he dropped his Thermos down the stairs and spun around to look at her, his eyes wide. It was her EMT from the night before.

Robby.

He caught his breath and asked, "What the hell are you doing here?"

"What are *you* doing here?"

"I asked you first."

"Looking for answers," she told him. "Same as you."

Robby's skeptical eyes slid from her face to her sneakered feet, then down the stairs into darkness. "You made me drop my Thermos," he said at last.

"Sorry."

"I really like that Thermos."

"Again, sorry."

He nodded. "After what happened last night, why would you want to come within a mile of this place?"

"Believe me; I don't want to be here at all, but this is where Jeff disappeared, and I need to know what happened to him. I need to *find* him, dead or alive, I just need to know."

Robby gave an exaggerated sigh. "Well, guess I'll have to go down there and find my Thermos."

He reached into his pocket, produced a small flashlight, then lifted his eyes to meet hers. "Come on. You can help me look."

She swallowed. "Sure. It's the least I can do."

They started down. The wood bowed and creaked with each cautious step, but, thankfully, showed no sign of giving way. There were no windows down here, she noted, and without Robby's light, the darkness would've been absolute.

A sealed tomb.

The thought sent a chill racing up her back to tingle her scalp. She shook it off and continued down. Old wiring, rusted plumbing, and rotting joists crisscrossed the ceiling above their heads, and somewhere she could hear water dripping.

Robby shined his light around, whistling "Heigh Ho, Heigh Ho" from *Snow White*.

Is he really that cavalier, or is he just putting on a show for my benefit?

She had a feeling it was the latter.

When they reached the bottom of the staircase, Robby found his Thermos in the dirt at the base of a wall. He scooped it up, traced the bricks with his light, and moved off down the corridor. Sheri followed, her nose crinkling from the stench of mildew and decay. She studied the items Robby caught in his spotlight, every odd shadow giving her a start.

He paused, staring at some rotting pallets. "Why would your boyfriend come down here?"

"I don't know." She shrugged; her thudding heart felt heavy in her chest. "He was curious, I guess. Probably all those ghost hunting shows he watched – *watches* on TV."

"Right." Robby turned his light on her. "But you didn't come in with him?"

She blinked and held up her hand to shield her eyes. "No. I – can you not do that?"

"Sorry." Robby aimed the beam into one of the side rooms. "You were saying?"

She frowned. "I was scared."

"No, you were smart. That's a good thing to be in this town." He turned his light on the archway at the end of the hall. "You'll live longer."

"Yeah, well..." She ran her fingers through her uncombed hair. "I came back, didn't I? I can't be all that smart."

Robby continued down the narrow corridor. "At least you waited for daylight."

"Yeah." She followed him, passing through the shadows, trying to catch up to the light.

They passed beneath the crumbling arch and found an empty room on the other side. Moss filled in the space between bricks, and the dirt floor was covered in various footprints and markings. There had been a lot of activity in here.

"CSI came down overnight," Robby told her. He tucked his Thermos under his arm and walked the perimeter, running his hand over the brick. "They took your boyfriend's flashlight and phone. Took pictures and swabs. They haven't found anything yet, but the lab doesn't get results immediately like they do on television. It can take weeks before they really know what they have or don't have."

Sheri moved to the middle of the room, her arms crossing her chest, her eyes crossing the walls. *This is where he spoke his last words to me.* She shuddered.

"What do you make of this?" Robby asked.

She turned to find him standing near the center of the wall on her left. His light had captured something; a shape etched into the brick. It was crude, like something she'd seen in pictures of cave drawings, and reminded her of a cactus with four legs.

"Graffiti?" she said with a shrug.

"It's not like any graffiti I've ever seen." He turned his light onto the opposite wall, finding another symbol; three "C"s, intertwined like Olympic rings. And when he aimed the beam behind her, she turned around to see what looked like a sperm cell in a hoop – a long, thin tail making waves behind a bulbous head. "And they don't look like gang tags."

"*Gang tags?* Does Harmony have gangs?"

"You might be surprised what you'd find in this town, if you look hard enough."

At this point, I don't think anything could surprise me.

Robby moved over to the far wall. There was a symbol there too, split neatly in two by a large crack that traveled up the brick like a fault line; a five-pointed star with a human eye in the middle. He traced the fractured drawing and the crack with his light, then asked, "When you were little, did you believe in the boogeyman?"

"I don't know. I guess so." She remembered fearing the darkness beneath her bed, remembered brushing her teeth at night and taking a running leap onto the sheets for fear that something would reach out and grab her by the ankles and pull her down into the dark and...She pinched herself, yanked herself back to the present. "Didn't everybody?"

"I suppose." He reached out with his fingers, ran them over the etching and along the jagged lip of the rift. "But most people grow out of it."

"Didn't you?"

"I thought I did, once. Then I learned a hard lesson. There are things in this world. Bad things." He turned back to look at her. His face, in the glow of the flashlight, in the shadows of the gloom, was that of a man who had been through Hell and had never completely left it behind him. "I think you saw one of them last night."

Sheri nodded, knowing that her own face must look like an odd mirror image of his.

"The whole police force is beating bushes out there, looking for a cougar," he told her. "But what you saw...it wasn't a cougar, was it?"

"No." The words scalded her throat as she spoke them. "It was a monster."

They looked at each other a moment, neither saying a word. Just when Sheri was wondering if he would bust out laughing, or worse, call someone and have her committed, Robby simply said, "Tell me about it."

Sheri shook her head, the spider-dog pacing across her brain like a caged tiger, the brick walls closing in. She wanted a cigarette, but instead she said, "I need some fresh air."

CHAPTER TEN

The fog darkened with vague shapes; they stood for a moment undecided, ready to step forward into dawn or retreat back into darkness at a moment's notice. Finally, the haze burned away, leaving only a few wispy tendrils to snake their way between the shadows, formations slowly gaining definition. Trees. Cayden Donnelly moved, bodiless, through a forest.

But what forest? Where?

Sunlight stung his mind's eye, turning this dark world into a brilliant flare. This too faded, however, and he was soon floating down a winding river of gravel. A road, surrounded by woods and cornfields, by cows and barns.

Farmland.

Yes.

The Midwest?

He had the feeling it was.

Iowa? Perhaps Kansas?

No. It felt more distant than that.

He slowed his breathing, concentrated, reached further from the confines of his flesh and dove deeper into this pastoral void. The gods were here in these woodlands. Cayden was certain of it now. He felt them here; their vast, eternal minds called out to him, wanting him to see, needing him to find their gateway, to throw the doors open once and for all and allow them re-entry.

Yes, this was a thin place all right. He could feel how slight the barriers were here, could hear the clamor of nightmares great and small. It was nearly overpowering.

Somewhere in these woods, a bespectacled man in torn, burned clothes cried out, begging forgiveness, only to be silenced by his new dark master. Elsewhere, in a collapsing barn, the body of a blind killer sat forgotten in a dark corner; her red dress hung tattered and torn, red tears flowing from her empty eye sockets, her shade refusing to move on, still roaring about the injustices of her former life. Cayden trembled at the vision and refocused, reached deeper. Avoiding the cornfields where dark things held their congress, he homed in on the source of the Old Ones' call.

*Yes. A landmark...please...*a fucking address!

Something came into focus. A house: old, long-abandoned, in disrepair. There were cars parked in front of it. He moved toward them, the sensation akin to flying, and found their license plates.

Indiana!

The doorway had opened in Indiana. But where in Indiana? He drifted up to the house, climbed the front steps, phantom feet never touching the wood.

New steps?

Cayden crossed the porch and moved inside. It was as if someone had tied a rope around his waist, he felt an insistent tug, reeling him in. He was drawn to an open door, pulled down darkened stairs. The walls trembled down here – the contractions of a ripe womb ready to give birth, to fill the blackness with light, with *life*.

Yes!

He reached out, anxious to touch the faces of his lords.

Show me! Show me!

Instead, the light faded, grew distant. And then the line snapped altogether. Cayden was flung back; up the stairs, out the door, and out of the house. The pastoral scenery fogged, eclipsed.

No! Not yet! I'm not finished! I need more!

But his mind's eye had gone blind, his consciousness drifting once more in that nameless dark...surfacing from unknown depths... returning -

–returning to the reality of his darkened motel room, to the bed Cayden now shared with Destiny.

At least that's what the hooker claimed her name to have been.

Destiny.

Cayden had smiled at that. Strips of her flayed skin still clung to him, her blood already cold and sticky against his heaving chest. The magic was potent, but short lived. Still, he was closer now than he'd ever been. At least he knew where to start.

Indiana.

Cayden smiled into the dimness, then rolled onto his side and gazed into Destiny's vacant eyes. He ran a finger down her cold cheek, leaving a rosy streak on her pale skin, then he leaned in and planted a kiss on her still-soft lips. "Thank you, lass," he whispered. "I couldn't have done it without you."

CHAPTER ELEVEN

As he tromped through the woods, Robby wondered again what he was doing out here. He'd followed Sheri up those creaking basement steps – steps that had received more of a workout these last twenty-four hours than they'd had in over half a century – and right out the front door, and then...well, then she just kept right on walking. At first, he was grateful to put some distance between them and the Fuller place, but now, after climbing down a steep hill into a dry creek bed and then up the slope on the opposite side, his calves burned, his heart sounded in his ears, and his lungs could barely spare the air for words.

"Sheri," he called after her. He kicked a thick root that snaked across the path, stumbled, but thankfully didn't fall. "Look, slow...slow it down! After...after last night, you should...You should be taking it easy!"

She stopped and looked back at him, perspiration glistening on her forehead; when she spoke, she didn't even sound winded, "Is that your expert medical opinion?"

"No, that...that's my Murtaugh opinion." He bent over, hands on his knees, watching sweat rain from his nose to darken the dusty ground as he fought to catch his breath. "I'm...I'm having a severe Murtaugh moment here."

"Murtaugh moment?"

"You know," he glanced up at her, "Danny Glover."

Sheri gave him a blank stare.

"Oh, come on!" Robby managed to stand, placing his hand on the rough bark of a tree for support. "*Lethal Weapon?*' I'm too old for this shit!'"

She wiped her brow with her forearm. "Never saw it."

"You're kidding?" He offered her a look of genuine surprise. "You've never seen *Lethal Weapon?*"

Sheri shook her head.

"Great flick! Saw it opening night, back in '87."

That's right, you did, didn't you? In fact, you saw it at the Woodfield Movie Palace with Sean Roche and Danny Fields. You remember don't you? Back when you didn't know the theater was possessed and your friends were still alive?

Robby quickly changed the subject, anxious to talk about anyone's demons but his own. "You were going to tell me about the monster that attacked you last night?"

Sheri chuckled humorlessly. "It sounds so matter-of-fact when you say it, like you fight off monsters every day."

"Well, not *every* day."

She glanced at him with a faint grin that evaporated as soon as they broke eye contact. For a moment, she said nothing, just stood there sweeping the bushes with her gaze, and Robby knew she was afraid something might leap out at them. Finally, she told him what it was: "I've never seen anything like it before. I don't think anyone has. If they had, there'd be pictures of it, right? I mean, with all the cell phone cameras out there, you'd think somebody somewhere..." She trailed off, still looking into the brush, then she snickered and locked eyes with Robby once more. "Then again, I have a camera in *my* cell phone, I was just too busy calling 911 to mess with snapping any photos."

"You did just fine," Robby assured her.

If she'd taken time to work her camera instead of her stun gun, she might not be standing here at all.

"Yeah, well, knowing me, if I did get a picture, it probably would've been a big gray blur or a nice big snapshot of my thumbnail." The word "gray" drew Robby's attention, but Sheri didn't seem to notice; she looked down at her hands for a moment, then went on, "I called it a spider-dog. The name just popped into my head in the heat of the moment, and now it's all I can think to call it. It's as good a description as any, I guess."

"It certainly paints a picture," Robby agreed, his mind already showing him the results of successful pitbull-tarantula crossbreeding.

"Not an accurate one, I'm sure. It didn't look anything like a dog, or a spider either – other than the fact that it had a bunch of legs. It was..." She hesitated, clearly frightened, frightened of what she'd seen, perhaps even more frightened of what Robby might think of it, then she spoke her mind. "It wasn't like any Earthly creature at all. And I know how that sounds, believe me. There have been more than a few moments since last night when I've been sure I had to be crazy. But this thing – "

"You ever hear the story of the Wampus Cat?"

Sheri looked at him, startled. "The *what?*"

"Wampus Cat," Robby repeated.

"Is that anything like a Cheshire Cat?"

"No." He chuckled, then held out his spread arms. "It was big, like a cougar, and it had six legs with claws: four to run with, and two to attack you with. According to Native American legend, they were supposed to be harbingers of death. If you heard one call out, it meant that someone you knew would be buried within three days."

"So, what...you think *that's* what I saw?"

He shrugged. "Maybe you saw the same creature those Native Americans did: a big animal with a bunch of legs, leaves tracks like a cougar. They called it a Wampus Cat, you dubbed it a spider-dog, but believe me when I tell you I've seen enough weird shit in my life to know you're not crazy."

"Thank you," Sheri told him, but she looked far from relieved. She continued her silent watch of those bushes. Every muscle in her legs tensed, as if ready to sprint at a moment's notice. Robby knew the feeling all too well; he had it every time he stood near a cornfield. "I'm glad you were there in that house. I...I don't think I could have gone down there alone."

"Well," Robby confessed, "truth be told, I wasn't real hot about going down there by myself either."

She glanced around and crossed her arms over her chest as if giving herself a much-needed hug. "I feel so damn helpless! I can't just sit around. I need to be out here, turning over every leaf, searching, but I'm petrified of what I might find. Pretty pathetic, huh?"

Robby stood sweating, his gaze fixed on Sheri's face – her pale, resolute eyes, the tiny vein in her temple that showed itself like an exclamation point when she spoke, the way the breeze moved leisurely through her hair.

She's never going to find her boyfriend, his mind told him, and in that moment, he wondered if it were wishful thinking; he licked his lips, and forced himself to turn away, focusing instead on the gently swaying trees.

The sun shone down through the canopy, painting the dusty trail with shadowy leaves, creating odd shapes and patterns across the tree trunks that surrounded them. A fly buzzed into his peripheral vision, giving him a start; he swatted it away.

No, he thought. *When people go missing out here, they're gone for good. She should go home and try to get on with her life. By the way, why* are *you still here, still stuck in this shitty little town? What the hell are you trying to prove?*

He'd seen people literally settle in Harmony, staying here out of pure lethargy. They'd been born in this town, lived here all their lives under some misguided notion that it was far safer to stay put than to face an unknown life in the unfamiliar surrounds of some further metropolis. Robby noticed it in their languid strides down the sidewalks, saw it in their weary eyes as they shopped aisles at Tony's Speedway Market; they were rooted to this sour earth just as deeply as these trees. Even if the buildings where they lived and worked were swept away by tornado or flood, the thought of greener pastures wouldn't even cross their lackluster minds; they would simply rebuild and go on with their hum- drum routines until they were put in the very ground they held so sacred. It was different for Robby. He held no love for Harmony, no nostalgia. No. He stayed out of some misguided sense of duty, some need to help the helpless who were unaware of the supernatural dangers that surrounded them – either by luck or by choice. And when the scales finally fell from their eyes, he was there to provide comfort, to let them know that they were not in this battle alone.

After a long, awkward silence, he reached out and touched Sheri's shoulder, not knowing what he would say until the words were in his mouth. "I'll help you look for your boyfriend, but I've got a shift that starts in a few hours, and right now, I think you need to get some rest."

Her face darkened. "You think he's dead, don't you? You think that *thing* got him?"

"Truth?"

"Yes."

Robby shrugged. "Yeah, I think that's probably what happened. There was no evidence to prove he ever came back out of that house, no tracks heading into the woods except your spider-dog."

Sheri nodded. She looked calm, almost serene. But Robby had delivered enough death sentences over the years to know the storm of grief that would tear through her when she stopped to truly contemplate all the ramifications of her loss.

"Listen," Robby said, his hand still on her shoulder, "these woods and fields go on for miles. It's a *huge* area, but there are a lot of people out here looking. If there's anything to find, somebody's gonna find it."

"That's what scares me," she told him.

CHAPTER TWELVE

It was just after sunset when Peter Thornton heard the scratching at his kitchen door.

"Kelly," he called out, "Jacob wants in."

Kelly was his fourteen-year-old daughter. Jacob was supposed to be her dog; a Siberian Husky she'd named after the werewolf boy from her beloved *Twilight* books. Oh, she was quick to claim the furball when it wanted to be petted, to play with it when the mood struck her, but when it came to feeding it, to giving it water, to letting it out back to do its business and picking up said business when it was done...well, she was slow to claim the dog then.

But Peter wasn't going to lift a finger to do it for her. He'd made that abundantly clear. He'd never been a dog person, never been a cat person either. Growing up, he'd suffered from severe allergies. He remembered being dragged to the doctor, being held down on a table as a nurse pricked his back, exposing him to every known allergen to gauge his reaction. Then came the shots. Years of shots. It seemed so Draconian now, when Zyrtec and Claritin were available on any drug or grocery store shelf, and hard, if not impossible, to make his daughter believe it had actually been his experience, especially when she stood there, in tears, with her pouty face on because "everyone" she knew had a dog and she didn't.

Why couldn't she just be happy with the fish?

He leaned down and peered through the glass wall of his tank. A powder blue tang named Papa Smurf swam leisurely to and fro. Nemo, the clown fish, darted around stalks of bright coral, paying him no mind. A butterfly fish and an angel fish passed like cars on a divided highway. Peter had been losing a fish a week for the last month due to some kind of protozoa in the water, but after slowly increasing the salt levels, everything appeared to be fine now.

Scratching at the door again, louder, more insistent, followed by a loud yelp.

"Kelly," he yelled, "let the damn dog in!"

His daughter had asked him to install one of those plastic doggie doors so Jacob could come and go as he pleased. Peter had actually given it some thought, but then he realized that it wasn't for Jacob's benefit but for her own – just one more pet-related chore she wanted out of. No. The least she could do for *her* dog was to open and close a door a few times a day.

"Kelly!"

―――

"Okay, okay. Jeez." She slid off her frilly bedspread, wiping cracker crumbs from her white "I'm Too Pretty to Do Homework" T-shirt. Her bejeweled cell phone was still pressed to her cheek – her friend, Gwen, still in her ear.

"What's goin' on?"

"Oh, it's just my stupid Dad," Kelly replied, rolling her eyes as she marched toward the stairs. "He wants me to go all the way downstairs and let Jacob in when he's sitting right there."

"Talk about lazy."

"I know, right?" Barefooted, she moved down carpeted steps to the cool hardwood below. It was always a few degrees colder down here than in her bedroom, and the change in temperature turned her bare arms to gooseflesh. "So whatcha wearin' Friday night?"

"I have a new pink and white-striped top with spaghetti straps. What about you?"

"I haven't decided yet."

"Kelly?" her father called from the other room.

She took her mouth away from the phone and yelled back at him, "I'm doing it!"

The kitchen was dark. She flipped a light on and saw the door on the opposite wall. Kelly started toward it, then stopped.

The glass in the center of the door was pitch black, filled with night, nothing more.

"That's weird," she said.

"What?" Gwen wanted to know.

"Jacob's not in the window."

"So?"

"So, he's usually standing on his hind legs looking in – barking, wagging his tail and stuff."

Gwen giggled in her ear. "Maybe he got tired of waiting on you."

"Ha-ha." She took another step toward the door, listening for Jacob's scratching, for his whimper, and hearing nothing. "I don't like this."

"You could call for your Dad."

"And have him get more mad than he already is? No, thank you."

Kelly took another cautious step toward the door, knowing what would happen when she got there. She would walk up, every muscle tensed, then Jacob would leap up and bang his snout against the glass, scaring her half to death. Then, she would scream, she would drop her cell, and then her Dad would run in and – no, he wouldn't run in; he'd just yell at her to stop screwing around.

She steeled herself and took that final step; her hand went to the door handle, her face pressed against the glass, her eyes searching. Jacob was there. He laid on his left side on the top step, his snout pointed out into the back yard and the woods beyond.

Kelly exhaled, her whole body relaxing. "You were right. He got tired and laid down."

"Told you," Gwen said, and Kelly could hear the smile in her voice. "You are such a 'fraidy cat."

"Am not." She pulled down on the handle.

"Are too."

Kelly opened the door and the humid air rushed in. Jacob, however, stayed put. "Come on, boy. Get in here."

The dog just laid there.

She knelt down beside him, reached out to nudge him. "Come on, Jacob."

His tail normally fanned her, but now it remained a furry lump on the step.

"Jacob?" Her fingers combed through his fur, soft bristle giving way to something warm and sticky. She yanked her hand away and saw blood in the porch light. "Jacob!"

"What's wrong?" Gwen asked.

"Jacob's bleeding," Kelly told her. "I think somebody shot him!"

"Oh my God!"

Kelly turned her head toward the hall, and the family room beyond. "Dad! Somebody shot Jacob!"

I need to press my hand against his side, stop the bleeding. That's what Miss Nicholson taught us in health, isn't it?

Kelly put her hand back on Jacob's bloodied side, her fingers crawling through his matted coat, searching for the wound. *Found it!* But it wasn't round like she'd suspect a bullet hole to be; she traced the edges, finding tapered points, like a star.

"Is he breathing?" Gwen wanted to know.

"I don't know..." She looked at the husky's still side. "I don't think so."

Her head shot up and she looked around. The porch light illuminated the steps, a dome-shaped area of grass, the edge of her trampoline, and some leaves from neighboring trees. Beyond that, only darkness.

"Dad!" she called again, and with the word came tears, blurring her vision, scalding her cheeks.

At the edge of the woods, something stirred in the shadows.

Another dog? Had Jacob been in a fight?

"Daddy!"

Without warning, it dove at her, a blur of legs and teeth. Kelly didn't have time to stand, didn't have time to run; she didn't even have time to scream. The shape struck her square in the chest, knocking her down, knocking the pink, bejeweled phone from her hand. Its fangs tore through her white "I'm Too Pretty to Do Homework" T-shirt and stained it red.

Peter hurried down the hall in the direction of his daughter's frantic calls. The back door was open, swaying gently on its hinges. He ran across the kitchen floor, hearing his daughter's name.

"Kelly? Kelly what's going on?"

He looked down and saw her cell phone. She always had it turned up too loud, same as her iPod. He was always telling her to turn it down, telling her that she would lose her hearing if she wasn't careful.

He reached down, picked it up, and pressed it to his ear. "Who is this?"

"Mr. Thornton? It's Gwen, Mr. Thornton. Is Kelly okay?"

Peter stood in the doorway; his eyes fell to the back steps, to Jacob's motionless body, then shot up and scanned the darkness of the yard. He called out Kelly's name, then spoke to Gwen, "What happened?"

"I dunno, she said somebody shot Jacob. Should I call the cops?"

Peter saw something out of the corner of his eye, something streaked across the kitchen floor, something red.

Blood.

His heart paused in his chest, icicles forming in his ventricles like stalactites in a cave. He slowly turned his head, following the wide, scarlet hash mark, finding another, then a red exclamation point, and then another streak shaped like a comma, leading behind the center island. There was something back there. He could see movement reflected in the onyx face of the stove.

"Yes, Gwen," he whispered. "Call them. Call them, now."

He lowered the phone and crept into the kitchen, following the trail of blood.

Kelly's?

Peter shook his head. He couldn't bring himself to think it, couldn't bring himself to even speak her name until he saw what it was over there in the corner. He heard the sound of claws raking the tile, the way Jacob's did when he was excited, and his eyes darted up to the funhouse reflection in the stove, trying to make some kind of sense of what he saw there.

He reached out for the counter, used the marbled lip to steady himself, to pull himself along. And when he took another hesitant step, he saw his daughter's bare feet sticking out around the edge of the island. Peter had the sudden urge to rush forward, and his mouth opened to call out Kelly's name, but the sight of a nightmarish creature hovering over her killed both desires in an instant.

Gray, hairless skin creased and furrowed with wrinkles and patches of scale. Oddly-jointed legs formed weird angles, and there were too many for Peter to count in a single, shocked glance. The thing shifted from one clawed foot to another, and its tapered head ended in a fan of grotesque, triangular flaps – like the petals of some alien flower. Its mandibles dug into his only daughter's chest, holding her up off the floor as if she were the prize in the claw game at Chuck-E-Cheese; her head and arms hung limp, doll-like, rolling and flapping from side to side as the creature moved across the tile, her feet dragging behind, her blood sprinkling the ceramic.

But worst of all were the sounds the thing was making– grotesque, wet slurping sounds, like a child trying to get the very last drop of a milkshake through a straw.

Do something! Peter's mind cried, trying to be heard over the thunder of his own blood. *That's your little girl over there!*

He fought through his paralysis, forced his arm to move, forced his hand to reach out blindly for the sink, for the knife block beside the sink. His fingers found the handle of a butcher's blade and slowly pulled it free. He clutched the knife to his chest, his knuckles white as Kelly's teeth. She'd wanted him to buy a box of those Crest White Strips before school started, wanted to look presentable for her first day of classes. He bought it for her, of course. She was his daughter, the light of his life, the apple of his eye. He'd do anything for her. Anything.

Peter lunged at the monster, and he managed to find a voice: a long, shrill shriek, filled with panic and fear, which was a far cry from his own. He grabbed hold of its slick, leathery skin and brought the butcher's knife down; the metal skidded harmlessly across hard, raised vertebrae on the thing's hunched back. He tried again, stabbed with all his might, this time finding soft flesh and burying the blade up to its hilt.

The creature released Kelly and it threw its triangular head back; those horrible slurping sounds stopped, replaced by a screech of agony. Its mouth petals writhed and convulsed as it squealed, and for the first time, Peter saw its teeth – row upon row of glistening fangs, each dotted and streaked in his daughter's young blood. The air was tinged with the acidic odor of drain cleaner, and it took Peter a moment to realize it was actually the creature's foul breath he smelled.

He rolled off the squirming beast, scrambling for Kelly and lifting her off the floor. She felt so heavy, so limp and lifeless in his arms. A star-shaped wound covered her chest, blood bubbling up and pouring across her torn shirt like tomato soup from an overheated pot, looking far too thin to be real, and only adding to Peter's feeling that this was all just a very bad dream.

When he got to his feet, Peter adjusted his daughter's weight in his arms, hugged her to his chest, and hurried for the open door. At the back of his mind, a million questions fought for answers. *Did Gwen call the police? Are they on their way? Is Kelly going to be all right? Thank God her mother's not here to see this, right? Oh God, how's she going to react when she finds out?* And over and over again: *What the hell is that thing anyway?*

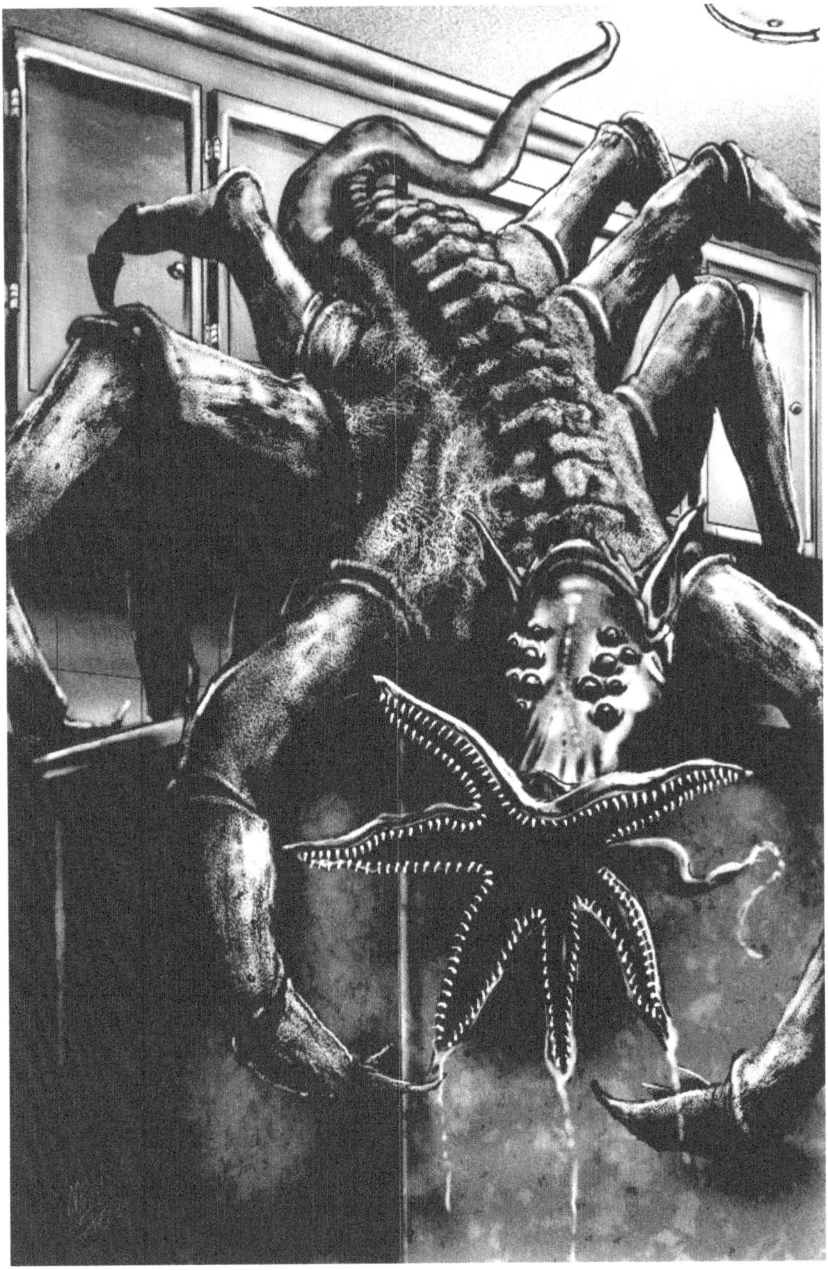

The monster climbed up onto the center island behind him and growled, giving him a start. He spun to face it, seeing the knife handle still protruding from its back like a stunted limb. It snarled menacingly and nipped at the air with terrible eagerness, strings of rosy drool tethering the petals of its mouth to the counter.

Peter felt warmth run down the legs of his pants. At first, he thought he'd lost control of his bladder, but he soon realized it was Kelly's blood soaking through his slacks.

He turned to run again, and the thing leapt down in front of him, blocking the door. It reared up on four or more of its hind legs until it was almost as tall as Peter. Its countless eyes glinted; they were black and unreadable, but Peter could sense the beast's fury.

It was not going to be robbed of its meal.

Front door!

Peter backed away slowly. He'd heard that you should never turn your back on an animal, that you should never show it fear. He adjusted Kelly's weight in his arms and the creature glanced down at her, the petals of its mouth flaring.

"Hey!" he yelled, his voice now more recognizable as his own. "Don't you look at her!"

The animal's gaze shifted, locked with his for a moment, then quickly returned to Kelly. He could feel its stare land firmly upon the opening it had torn in her chest, on the blood that now flowed over Peter's arms and down his legs like warm water from a tap.

"No," he told the thing as if it were some disobedient pet in need of a good scolding. "You can't have her!"

Peter continued backing away, one careful step at a time, sweat beading on his furrowed brow, his laden arms trembling.

If I can make it around the corner, I can turn and run. I can make it out to –

The ruthless creature lowered itself back onto the floor; it stretched out its neck and made one deliberate step forward, threatening.

Peter froze in panic. *Shit...it's going to –*

It scuttled across the tile after them, its many-jointed legs a flurry of momentum.

Peter whirled away from it. He rushed down the hall, the muscles in his arms burning from Kelly's dead weight. The walls flew by him in a mad blur, covered in happy, smiling faces under glass: his face, Kelly's face, and Gale, his wife.

Thank God she's not here. God, she doesn't know.

Whatever the animal was, it kept up with him – crawling from floor to wall, then back again with swift ease, always snapping at his heels. He led it into the family room as he bolted for the front door and his Toyota Tundra in the driveway beyond. It caught up to him in front of the couch and leapt up onto his back with lightning speed, digging in with its claws, knocking him off balance.

Peter ground his teeth against the pain; he staggered forward toward his fish tank. With all his remaining strength, he turned his feet and tucked his shoulder as if he were still on the high school football team. He managed to spin around, falling backward into the tank, insuring that the creature bore the brunt of the impact to come.

The glass wall smashed in and fifty-five gallons poured out, washing over them, pushing them forward, and sending Peter's face down onto the newly-soaked carpeting.

An ear-splitting scream filled the room, the shriek of the damned burning in the pits of Hell itself. Peter winced, and when he craned his neck, he saw that the thing on his back was actually melting. Its gray skin smoldered, emitting a yellow-green smoke as it bubbled and liquefied, sliding down the thing's side like ice cream down a cone on a hot summer day. The unmistakable stench of bleach filled his nostrils, and the molten flesh dripped down onto his back, making him nauseous.

The animal pitched forward and climbed off Peter's back. Peter scrambled to crawl as far away from it as he could. He grabbed Kelly by the arm, dragging and pulling her with him across the soaked carpet toward the door. His fish flopped and spasmed around them; Papa Smurf and Nemo, sick and oh so recently cured, their gills now flapping and pulsing useless air as they suffocated.

Yowling in pain, the thing swung its narrow head back and forth, flinging heavy gray droplets of dissolving flesh. It bucked and spasmed, but if these were death throes, the creature wasn't dying very fast. It staggered across the floor, smoking and dripping, its hind legs becoming entangled with its other scrambling limbs. It stumbled and fell into his couch, streaking it with grime. Then it stood again, making clumsy, leap-frogging jumps toward the hall, becoming partially hidden in the yellow-green fog that poured from its wounded back and side.

The chlorine stench was almost unbearable, causing Peter to cough and retch.

"Go away!" he screamed at the thing when he was able. He was crying now, and the tears burned hot lines down his cheeks as he struggled to get to his knees, as he fought to lift his daughter's dead weight off the wet floor, to get her out of the room, to get her to safety.

A siren droned from somewhere far away, nearly lost beneath the wailing creature's fit of agony.

The police!

A geyser of hope erupted in Peter's chest. He hugged Kelly tighter, her limp arms flopping as he broke into a kind of lurching run.

Gwen called them! She called!

Behind him, the creature continued its retreat. Its yowls sank down the hallway into the kitchen, becoming fainter until they all but disappeared, replaced by the building scream of sirens. They sounded as if they were right outside his front door, just out of reach.

"Help us!" Peter cried, and when he threw the door open, he saw a patrol car skid to a halt. "Help me, please! Help my little girl!"

He tripped over his threshold and stumbled onto the front lawn like a drunkard, Kelly's blood sprinkling the grass as he wept.

CHAPTER THIRTEEN

Robby's partner Julian was overweight. In fact, the Wii Fit back at the station house said he was "obese."Sure, the guy could stand to lose a few pounds, but it wasn't like he was a candidate for the next season of *The Biggest Loser* or anything. And while Julian would be the first one to admit that he wasn't the quickest on his feet, when the man got behind the wheel, he drove like he was qualifying for the Indy 500.

Tires struck deep craters in crumbling pavement.

Robby's head nearly hit the roof of the cab; only his seatbelt saved him from seeing stars. "Jesus!"

"Sorry," Julian said absently, his eyes never leaving the pitted road.

Years ago, these old gravel roads had been paved over and made smooth. But it didn't last. Indiana winters and asphalt were age-old enemies; the constant freezing and thawing conspired to find every imperfection in the pavement's armor, slowly chipping away, creating crumbling war zones of pits and canyons. Now, the grassy shoulders were littered with rusted, dented hubcaps – trophies nature displayed with pride, daring the next vehicle to venture on at its own risk.

Their "bus" careened around a sharp bend, tires squealing, flashing lights illuminating overhanging branches and trees on either side of the road. Trees and more trees, blurring by Robby's window, making him tense. He waited for the strobes to reveal something horrible in these darkened woods – something so alien that, upon seeing it for the first time, Sheri had found the name "spider-dog" so apt. If anything had been lurking out there, however, the endless *whoop-whoop* of their siren had probably scared it away.

Just as well. Robby was in no mood to deal with monsters or any other supernatural bullshit this evening.

It was a full moon, and he didn't need his "Spidey-sense" to know people went crazy when the moon was full. Crime rates rose, there were more suicides, more accidents...people just tended to snap. They said it had something to do with the fact that the human brain was mostly water, that the moon influenced this fluid in the same way it held sway over the tides. No matter what the cause, Robby had witnessed the effects far too many times over the last twenty-plus years. Add when you added the late August heat and humidity to the mix, it was a recipe for impending disaster.

Robby sighed. After the excitement of the last twenty-four hours, was a quiet night too much to ask for? A nice, uneventful shift, followed by a few well-deserved days off, would be just what the doctor ordered.

The dispatcher clearly had other plans.

Gunshot victim, the radio told them. A teenage girl.

God, how Robby hated these full moon nights.

Shootings were always a physics lesson. What was the velocity of the bullet when it entered the body? Velocity would determine the depth of the wound. What type of bullet was used? Some bullets flattened on impact, crushing tissue and creating permanent cavities. Other bullets kept a sharp point and sliced cleanly through. And still other shells fragmented on impact, creating tiny shrapnel that could do huge damage throughout the body. What tissue did the bullet strike? Did it puncture the heart, slice through a lung or a kidney? Or did it lodge itself in the victim's spinal column – making even the slightest movement of the body potentially lethal?

All of these possibilities were playing out in Robby's head as they sped down this winding road, an endless parade of actions and reactions, points and counterpoints. He wanted to be prepared for any contingency, wanted not to be surprised by what he found so that his hands could move quickly, and with the appropriate level of skill and authority needed to save a life.

Up ahead, the red and blue glow of police strobes formed a beacon in the darkness, marking their destination. Julian had barely brought the bus to a halt before Robby was out and grabbing up their equipment. EKG monitor, ambu-bag, and heavy black drug box. They made their way across the lawn to their patient.

Kirsch met them halfway there, walking backwards at first, then turning to match their stride. "Girl got bit."

"Bit?" Robby shot Julian a confused glance, the glut of in-route preparation that had flooded his brain suddenly draining away. "Dispatch said gunfire?"

"Yeah, same here," Kirsch pointed back at a distraught-looking man drenched in crimson gore, "but Mr. Thornton here says they were attacked by some weird animal, probably the same thing from last night."

Hicks, who'd been kneeling next to the girl when they pulled up, now stood. He looked like a doctor fresh out of surgery; his gloved hands were covered in blood. So much blood. It seemed too bright, too thin, to be real. "Still no pulse," he told Robby, "and she's not breathing. I've been doing CPR for the last four or five minutes, but I don't know how much good it's done. I think she's got a sucking chest wound."

Robby gave him a quizzical look. "Sucking chest wound" wasn't the type of thing he'd normally expect to hear from Harmony's finest.

Hicks elaborated, "I saw more than my fair share in Afghanistan and Iraq."

"You've got to help her," Thornton pleaded, tears clearing lines down his grimy, ashen face.

"We'll do everything we can," Robby assured him, trying not to let the fluster show in his voice. "What's her name?"

"Kelly."

Robby nodded. "How long has Kelly been like this?"

Thornton shrugged, his eyes lost.

"Call came in ten minutes ago," Hicks told them.

Robby frowned. Any resuscitative effort was essentially bringing the dead back to life. What kind of life the patient returned to depended greatly on how long their brain had been deprived of oxygen. The magic window was four minutes, and that window had long since slammed shut.

He gloved up and got down on his knees, tilting Kelly's head back, placing the ambu-bag over her mouth and nose to simulate respiration.

Sure enough, he heard it: a wet hissing sound. Something had punctured the girl's chest cavity, allowing air to rush in during inhalation, collapsing her lung. They needed to treat it immediately.

Julian was on it; he reached in and ripped open Kelly's bloodied shirt. "Christ."

As crazy as it sounds, the only thing Robby could think of was a Dr. Seuss story from his youth: "The Sneetches." It was the tale of bird-like creatures; some were born with stars on their bellies, and some were not. Kelly now sported a huge red one across her young chest.

Robby gave the wound a closer examination. The skin appeared burned...almost melted, as if someone had used a caustic chemical to brand this poor girl for life. At the center of the star, he found the deep puncture; his index finger sank in up to the first knuckle, but he could tell the wound went much deeper than that.

Julian prepped electrode patches, hooked up wires, and Kelly's heart rhythm went live on their small EKG monitor: a flat, uninterrupted line of green light.

Robby's frown deepened; he set the ambu-bag aside for a moment and ripped the plastic off a sealed syringe. Epinephrine. He pinched the syringe between his lips, held the empty wrapper over the hole in Kelly's chest, and taped it down on three sides, leaving the forth end open to form an occlusive patch. Now, when she exhaled, air would be expelled from her chest cavity, escaping through the open edge of the patch. But when Robby pushed air in with the ambu-bag, the patch would stick to her skin, closing off her chest and re-inflating her lung.

Robby quickly found a vein and injected the epi.

No response on the monitor.

He tore the wrapping off another syringe, this one filled with atrophine. He pushed it into the same vein.

Still no change.

Come on, Kelly.

He followed up with a second injection of epinephrine, shaking his head at that stubborn flat green line.

"You need to shock her," Thornton cried.

Robby sighed. *Thank you, TV.*

Everyone expected first responders to immediately charge paddles and yell, "Clear!" Hell, some people even thought you could tap someone's chest with a live power line and make them jump up and dance. But Robby wasn't Frankenstein, defibrillators weren't magic, and flatlines weren't shockable – you can't stop a rhythm that doesn't exist. And that's exactly what defibrillators did; they didn't start hearts, they *stopped* dysfunctional rhythms in the hope that the heart's own intrinsic mechanisms would restore normality, like pressing a reset button.

The EKG monitor, however, told them it was "game over," continuing to draw its thin, green line, completely uninterested in their frenzied efforts.

Robby gave her a few puffs of air from the ambu-bag, then laid his hands on her chest and started compressions. "Get the stretcher."

Julian stood and hurried back to the ambulance, leaving Robby to continue CPR.

"What's going on?" Thornton asked, fresh tears streaming down his cheeks as he glanced at the monitor, at that unyielding line. "Why aren't you shocking her? They shocked that boy on the basketball court at the high school and he was fine. You need to – "

"Mr. Thornton," Robby's voice was loud and firm between compressions, but he didn't yell; yelling wouldn't do either of them any good. "Right now...your daughter's got...no heart rhythm.

Shocking her won't do any good. We're gonna get her...to the hospital...get her the help she needs."

He paused to squeeze more air into Kelly's lungs, and his eyes were drawn back to the star-shaped wound in her chest, back to the blood. *So much blood. So bright. So thin.*

It didn't seem real.

Julian climbed in through the back door, breathing heavy, dragging the head of the stretcher with him. Robby pushed Kelly's feet inside and joined them; he hung IV bags and reattached an EKG lead that had come loose. The green line on the monitor still wasn't budging.

Robby resumed CPR as Julian climbed up into the driver's seat.

Gentlemen, start your engines!

Hicks helped Mr. Thornton up into the back of the bus.

"Sir –" Robby's arms pumped like pistons, sweat beading on his brow. "– you should call your wife...meet us there. Nothing you can do back here."

"I can hold her hand," Thornton told him.

Hicks looked up at Robby; "Your call," his eyes said.

Robby nodded, shaking loose the drop of perspiration that clung to the tip of his nose.

Hicks closed the doors and gave them a loud pat.

Julian hit the siren – its *whoop-whoop* making Thornton jump in his seat, then he flattened the gas pedal and the bus lurched forward. As he drove, he got on the radio, giving dispatch their situation and their ETA to Stanley University's Med Center. Ten minutes, but knowing the way Julian drove, they'd be there in six.

Six more minutes of CPR.

Robby wiped his forehead with his light blue uniform sleeve. His glove gleamed in the overhead lamps, now completely red up to his cuff. How could so much blood come from such a small body?

Kelly's father sat to the right of her stretcher. He reached out for her pale hand and held it tightly in his own, his lower lip quivering, his shoulders bobbing. "She's dead, isn't she."

As an EMT, Robby couldn't pronounce anyone dead even if he wanted to. That power was kept exclusively for the doctors and the coroners. Unless the patient was missing a head, cut in half, or blown to bits, they had to attempt resuscitation and rush them to the ER. From there, it was out of their hands.

"Her heart's not beating," Robby told him, not wanting to sound encouraging, but not wanting to crush all the man's hopes. He'd seen doctors work miracles before. And he knew first-hand that anything was possible. "What was it?"

Thornton blinked. "What?"

"The thing that attacked you...what was it?"

"Monster," the man muttered.

Robby continued his compressions for a moment before asking, "Was it...like a big spider?"

Thornton's eyes shot up to him. "You've seen it?"

"A friend did."

"I hope it kept melting," the man said. "Hope it melted away to nothing."

"It was...melting?"

Thornton nodded, wiping tears from his face with the back of his free hand. "When the fish tank broke, it...it got wet, and then it melted...like...like the witch in *The Wizard of Oz*."

Robby said nothing. He stared for a moment into the man's pale, grieving eyes, then turned away, focusing instead on Kelly, on his own bloody hands on her chest, on what this thing, Sheri's spider-dog, had done to such an innocent girl, and wanting desperately to believe that he could stop it from happening to someone else.

When they wheeled the stretcher through the automatic doors and into the emergency room, the staff rushed over from the Nursing Core to meet them. Robby felt a hand on his shoulder and looked up from his compressions to see a familiar face: Dr. Tyler Bachman.

"Talk to me."

"Kelly Thornton," Robby told him. "Age fourteen. Penetrating chest wound caused by some type of animal. Massive blood loss. Flatlined and unresponsive."

Tyler pried the girl's eyelids open and turned on his pen light. "Fixed and dilated. How long has she been down?"

"At least fifteen minutes."

Tyler looked up and pointed to the right. "Get her in trauma two."

They wheeled the stretcher into the trauma room, then transferred Kelly onto the vacant triage table within.

"We'll take it from here," Tyler told them.

Robby stepped back, grateful for the relief. He was out of breath, every muscle in his arms and shoulders aching. *I'm getting too old for this shit.*

Mr. Thornton stood in the doorway, staring and swaying like a zombie. One of the nurses went over to him, saw his bloodied clothes, and asked, "Sir, are you injured?"

Robby stepped in, massaging his left elbow and pointing to Kelly as he spoke, "It's her blood. She's his daughter."

The nurse nodded and rejoined the knot of staff that had formed around the triage table, a chaotic mass of moving hands and equipment.

Robby stood next to Thornton. "We really should step outside and let them work," he told him.

"No. If she...if anything happens, I need to be here with her."

"Mr. Thornton," Robby laid his hand on the man's shoulder. "She's had no heartbeat in over fifteen minutes. If it happened, it happened already, and you *were* with her. All they'll do now is call out a time for the certificate."

The man sniffled and let out a long, shuddering breath.

Robby tugged at his shoulder. "Come on, let's give them some space so they can do what they can."

"I should...I really need to call my wife."

"I'll stay here with Kelly, just in case," Robby told him, then looked over at his partner who was pushing the empty stretcher back out into the hall. "Jules, can you show Mr. Thornton where there's a phone?"

Julian nodded. "Sure thing."

They moved slowly, Mr. Thornton holding onto the stretcher's metal railing as if he needed it to remain upright. Robby tried to imagine what the man would say when his wife answered that call; would he come right out and tell her what had happened? Robby hoped not. This was the kind of news that needed to be delivered face-to-face.

And it wasn't long before Robby heard the inevitable.

"Time of death: 11:23 PM." Tyler stepped away from the table; he walked over, pulled off his bloody gloves with a loud *snap*, threw them in the waste bin and said, "We really have to stop meeting like this."

"Tell me about it."

"It's always terrible to lose a patient, but now that I have a little girl of my own..." Tyler ran his fingers through his hair, then lowered his voice to say what was on both of their minds, "Tell me this isn't another demon."

"Why? What'd you find?"

Tyler looked both ways down the hall, then turned Robby around to face the room. "See for yourself."

They moved back over to the triage table, to Kelly's lifeless body. All the EKG wires had been disconnected and the monitors were now blank. No beeps. No pings. No alarms. The nurses had pulled a gray sheet up to her chin. Her eyes were shut, her pale skin glowing in the bright surgical light. If not for the plastic airway jutting from between her lips and the single, rosy drop staining her chin, a passer-by might have mistaken her for sleeping.

Tyler peeled back the sheet.

They'd opened Kelly up, using a metal rib spreader to gain access to her chest, and Robby saw now why they'd been unable to get her heart started again. It wasn't there. Her heart, liver, pancreas, spleen, even her stomach...all *gone*. In their place: a bright, frothy pool of crimson soup. And what little remained of her lungs was pitted and corroded, with the lower portions of the bronchi eaten away entirely.

"Jesus," Robby muttered, not wanting to look at it, but unable to turn away. "What the fuck could do something like this?"

"You can't smell it?"

He leaned closer to the body, and the acrid stench struck him like a punch, burning his nostrils; he coughed and pulled back suddenly. "Oh, God...Doc. What the...Is that Drano?"

Tyler nodded. "Hydrochloric acid. Something's pumped her full of the stuff."

Robby continued to stare in disbelief. "Digesting her from the inside."

"Right. And since I don't know of any creature in *this* world that can do that, I was thinking you might try and talk me into another exorcism."

"An exorcism won't work this time, Doc, but if her father's right...I think I know what will."

The two of them stood there a moment, side by side, neither saying a word.

CHAPTER FOURTEEN

Sheri didn't sleep at all. She'd popped Nicorette lozenges all day long like they were Tic Tacs, emptying the container. So, when she finally crawled into bed, she just laid there, crying, and when she finally managed to stop crying, she moved restlessly beneath her tear-stained sheets. Her irritated eyes drifted back to Jeff's smiling face on the nightstand again and again, wondering why this had happened to him, to *them*, then watching the illuminated numbers change on her alarm clock. Finally, she forced herself to turn over and stare at the wall instead. Of course, the few times she managed to shut her eyes, the spider-dog was there, waiting to pounce on her groggy brain and sink its claws and fangs deeper into her psyche.

God, I need a real fucking cigarette!

She'd actually been looking forward to going in to work, to throwing herself into her lesson plans, hoping that, if she stayed busy, she could keep thoughts of Jeff and the nightmares at bay. But the creature took even *that* away from her. Just after six in the morning, she got the call. School was cancelled for the day due to safety concerns; the superintendent didn't want kids out waiting for the bus with a "dangerous animal" – Principal Polk's exact words – on the loose.

Dangerous animal. Sheri chuckled humorlessly. *He doesn't know the half of it!*

She finished getting dressed anyway, and when she opened her front door, the Monday edition of the *Harmony Herald* was waiting on the front step. This time, she didn't have to hunt for any mention of the attack. The article was right there on the front page. Hell, the article *was* the front page: a banner headline that capped all six columns of newsprint.

HUNT CONTINUES FOR DEADLY "PREDATOR"

HARMONY, Indiana – Authorities are now warning residents to stay indoors at night, to keep their doors and windows locked at all times, and to keep a close eye on small children, livestock, and pets until a mystery creature believed to still be roaming the woods and fields just north of town can be captured or killed.

A 42-year-old father, his fourteen-year-old daughter, and another, unrelated 32-year-old man were the victims of separate, violent attacks that occurred within twenty-four hours of one another off Route Six.

"Fourteen years old," Sheri said aloud. Her stomach sank. She took a big gulp of her coffee, tried to drown her urge for a cigarette, and read on.

According to police, the animal entered a north side home when the family opened a door for their dog. They were attacked by a deadly predator that savaged the fourteen-year-old girl and her father. Both were rushed to Stanley University Medical Center, where the young girl later died from her injuries.

. . .

Although the search continues for Jeff Stone of Pleasant View, missing since the report of a similar incident on Saturday evening, officials now believe it is unlikely that he will be found alive.

Animal Control officer Victor Mancuso has been tracking the animal and displayed plaster casts of paw prints found at the scene of both attacks. The fierce-looking prints are the size of a large dog or small bear.

"It's a big predator alright," Mancuso said as he held the plaster claws. "People need to take it seriously."

Police believe the creature they are searching for is a big cat, possibly a cougar.

Although eastern cougars are believed by many experts to be extinct, sightings continue to crop up in Miami County from time to time.

Authorities say the animal is aggressive, appears to have no fear of humans, and is therefore considered to be highly dangerous. A herd of dairy cows in an open barn were also believed to have fallen prey to the cougar over the weekend, and the large cat is thought to still be prowling the woods and fields off Route Six.

Police and animal control officers are in the process of trying to capture the feline and are asking onlookers to stay out of the area for their own safety. Anyone with information relevant to the case is urged to call...

Sheri let the paper drop to her kitchen table and then pushed it aside, unable to read any more. A cougar? Were they serious? A little girl was dead –

And a bunch of cows. Mustn't forget the cows!

- and Jeff was still missing, and now the police were just giving up on him. And they had no idea what they were even dealing with.

It was all so damned frustrating!

A vivid image slid into her mind like a thief, unbidden and unwanted; she imagined that poor, frightened girl, a girl even younger than her own students, caught in the spider-dog's grasp, screaming for help as her flesh was shredded to a bloody pulp by the death blossom of its mouth.

That could've been me.

With the realization came a sudden, unexpected wave of nausea. Sheri stood, covered her mouth as she hurried to the sink, and then vomited into the basin. Afterward, she stood there coughing, spitting and crying, then she ran the water and flipped the switch on her disposal.

What the fuck was that? I've never thrown up before without being sick.

What's wrong with me?

The phone rang, startling her. She reached out and answered it, trying to compose herself. "Hell – " She cleared her throat. "Hello?"

"Is this Sheri Foster?"

The voice was male, but she didn't recognize it, and she was in no mood for telemarketers, reporters, or any other strangers. "Who's asking?"

"It's Robby Miller."

The EMT? "How did you get my number?"

"You had to write it down on the waiver."

"Waiver?" She reached out for her blinds and pried them apart, half expecting to see him standing in her yard.

"You signed a waiver of treatment form the other night. They have you put down your number so they can call you back and make sure you're still okay."

"Right." She let the blinds fall back into place and rubbed her temple. "I'm fine, thank you for checking. I took your advice, came home yesterday and got all kinds of rest, so I really don't need –"

"That's not why I'm calling," he told her. "Did you see the paper this morning?"

Sheri's eyes shot back to her table, the frustration rising in her voice as she spoke, "Yes, I saw it. I read about that fourteen-year-old that got killed last night. I *also* saw that they're basically writing my boyfriend off."

"Yeah. Sorry about that."

"*Sorry?*" The word came out more harshly than she'd intended, but so be it. She hated this helpless feeling, and at least getting angry was doing *something*. "You're *sorry* about that?"

"If you'd seen what I saw last night, you'd..." He trailed off a moment, then came back on the line. "Look, I don't think you want to hear about this stuff over the phone."

"Then why the hell did you call?"

"I found out something important, something I think we could use to stop this thing before it kills anybody else."

She leaned back against the kitchen counter, waiting to see if he would say more, but he remained silent, perhaps waiting for her. "Go on," she prodded.

"Like I said, not over the phone. Can you meet me in town? We can talk over lunch or coffee or something?"

Sheri considered her response carefully. Why was this stranger so accepting of her story? What was his stake in all this anyway? Finally, she told him, "Give me twenty minutes."

When she walked into Emma's, the local greasy spoon, Robby was already there waiting. The diner might have been something back in the '50s, but now it resembled a rundown Steak 'n' Shake, with its black and white-tiled walls and metal bar stools around the counter. The younger crowd avoided it like the plague, choosing to hang out at the shiny new Starbucks instead. And the very young crowd would rather congregate at the McDonalds just down the street. No. This place had become the private realm of the older sect who remembered its glory days – a time when it was the only game in town.

An old guy in suspenders sat at the counter, reading the same *Herald* Sheri had cast aside. A couple of silver-haired old ladies shared breakfast and pictures of their grandchildren in a booth by the window. Despite all the other empty seats, Robby had picked the farthest booth from the door, in the far corner near the restrooms, as if he didn't want to be seen here.

That makes two of us.

She took a deep breath and marched over, sliding quickly across the smooth, red pleather bench. The glittery coating had cracked and been repaired with a Band-Aid of red duct tape; that too had since torn, re-opening the wound, revealing white stuffing within.

"Twenty minutes on the dot, teach," Robby commented. "You must run a tight ship."

She said nothing, but her eyes drifted to the old-fashioned cigarette machine that sat between the red men's and ladies' room doors, just below a huge NO SMOKING sign. The machine had probably been there for sixty years, but the sign was far more recent. There weren't even any of those glass ashtrays on the tables anymore.

Why sell the stuff if you're not gonna let anybody enjoy it?

They probably sell condoms in the men's room too, her mind countered. *It doesn't mean they want you to have sex right here in the booth.*

She frowned.

"You smoke?" Robby asked, following her gaze. She shook her head emphatically.

"I used to."

He chuckled at that. "That's like a drunk who says he *used to* drink, or a girl who says she *used to* snort cocaine. Addiction is addiction, it's all chemical reactions and biology, and once you're hooked, you're always hooked."

"I guess so."

"Being an addict is easy, it's just giving up. But making that conscious decision, sticking to it, wrestling with it day-in and day-out and showing it who's boss, that takes a helluva lot of strength."

"I didn't come here for some Dr. Drew lecture," she told him, irritated.

A waitress pounced on her like a lioness in wait, giving her a start. "Can I get you something to drink, sweetie?"

"Coffee," Sheri replied.

"Cream and sugar?"

"Black."

The woman nodded, then turned her attention to the two glasses in front of Robby; one was half full of water, the other held only crushed ice. "Another Vanilla Coke, hon?"

"You have to ask?" he said and smiled at her like they were old friends.

The waitress scooped up his glass and moved back behind the counter, leaving them alone. Sheri felt suddenly uncomfortable, wondering how much more small talk she would have to endure, but instead Robby got right to the point.

"I know how to kill your spider-dog."

"How?"

He held up his water glass. "With this."

Her brow furrowed. "What? We offer it a drink?"

"Not exactly." He took a sip and set it back on the table. "Back in high school, I had this friend, Paul Rice. He was what you might call a horror movie freak. I mean this guy watched just about every slasher, monster, or supernatural film ever made. And of course, since we were friends, I watched more than a few of them with him over the years."

She shrugged. "What's this got to do with – "

He held up his hand, begging her indulgence. "I'm getting to it."

She nodded, her glance shifting back to that shiny metal cigarette machine and the huge sign above it that begged her to look away.

"A party favorite of ours used to be this low budget gem called *Neon Maniacs*. Bad acting. Cheap special effects. But it was one of those fun little popcorn movies that we would slide into the VCR from time to time whenever the gang got together. It made the girls scream and the boys laugh. Only after what I saw last night, I'm not laughing."

"What did you see?"

The waitress returned with an empty cup and a steaming coffee pot. She set the cup down in front of Sheri, then filled it to the brim.

"Thanks," Sheri told her. She reached for the cup, feeling warmth seep through the china and into her bones, keeping the forming chill at bay.

"You're welcome," the woman said with a smile, then she glanced over at Robby. "I'll be right back with that Vanilla Coke."

"Take your time," he told her, and he waited until the woman was back behind the counter before continuing. "I saw a fourteen-year-old girl with her whole life in front of her, dead on a table. The thing had latched onto her and pumped her full of so much of its stomach acid, that her insides turned into soup."

Sheri gripped the coffee cup even tighter than before. "God."

"I think it's like a big leech, only it doesn't just suck out your blood; it sucks out *everything*. It wants to turn you into its own personal milkshake."

"And you think that's what it did to Jeff?" She winced at the thought, her voice hoarse, thick with anger and grief.

Robby looked down into his water, turning the glass in his hands, probably trying to think of a delicate way to answer her. In the end, he was as blunt as ever, "Yeah, I do. Your boyfriend's footprints go down into that cellar, but they don't come back up, and there was no trace of him anywhere in that house."

She nodded, shuddering as if from a sudden chill. Fresh tears welled in her eyes and she fumbled with the napkin wrapped around her silverware. When it finally unfurled, her fork, spoon, and knife tumbled out onto the table. She felt her face warm. "Sorry."

"No, you're fine," Robby assured her. "If you didn't cry, I'd start to wonder about you."

Sheri gave her closed eyes and cheeks a rough swipe with the corner of the napkin. Then she took a deep breath and chased it with a gulp from her coffee, liking the sudden burst of heat that filled her belly, banishing the chill, at least for the moment.

"Here's your Vanilla Coke," their waitress said as she set the glass in front of Robby. "Can I get either of you anything to eat?" When the woman looked at Sheri, her pleasant grin wilted and concern flared in her eyes; she reached out and put her hand on Sheri's shoulder. "You okay, sweetie?"

She nodded and forced herself to smile. "I'm fine."

The waitress withdrew her hand, but her face held onto that look of sympathy.

"Really, I'm okay," Sheri assured her. "I'm just not...just not really hungry right now."

Robby, however, ordered steak and eggs. "Over hard," he told the woman as she wrote in her note pad. "I hate runny yolks." And when the waitress finally left them alone again, he went back to that movie. "Anyway, *Neon Maniacs*. Dumb fun. I hadn't thought of it in years, just one of those lost bits of trivia that gets filed away, then last night, after talking to the girl's father, I couldn't stop thinking about it.

"It was a movie about creatures from another dimension, monsters that could be dissolved with water."

"Water?"

"Plain old water. Rain. Swimming pool. Straight from the tap. Didn't matter."

"Sounds like a pretty stupid fucking movie."

"Like I said," Robby took another sip of his Coke, turning dark ice white, "dumb fun."

"And what about this dead little girl made you suddenly think of 'dumb fun?'"

Robby glared at her. "I'm not some cold, callused asshole, if that's what you're thinking."

"I didn't say – "

"I've seen a lot of death in this town, and I'll admit that doing this job, day in and day out, it does numb you to some things, but not this. I felt *sick* about what happened to that girl. Sick and *angry* as Hell."

Yes, sick and angry as Hell. That about sums it up doesn't it?

"Why else do you think I called you here?" he asked. "I want the damn thing dead, same as you."

"I'm sorry," she told him, hoping he knew that she meant it. "It's just that, personally, I wouldn't be thinking about some stupid movie at a time like this, that's all. But I understand...I *know* that everyone handles things differently."

"Yes they do." Robby nodded, his expression softening again. "Anyway, it wasn't what happened to the girl, it was what the father said happened to the spider-dog." He glanced over at the counter, then back at Sheri. "The thing was right on top of him, and it would have done the same to him that it did to his daughter except for the fish tank."

"The fish tank?"

He nodded. "They fell into it, shattered it all to hell, and when the spider-dog got wet, the dad saw the thing actually start to melt."

"Melt?"

"Uh-huh."

"Like the monsters in the movie."

"Just like the monsters in the movie."

"You're joking?" Sheri looked him in the eye and quickly reconsidered. "Okay, you're serious. But water...*really*?"

"Water to you and me," he corrected, "but to this thing, it acts like battery acid."

She tried to picture it: such a loathsome thing melting, like candle wax, like a Popsicle on a hot summer day. She shook her head. "No."

Robby looked puzzled. "No?"

"You're talking about something out of a bad science fiction movie like it's real. It's not real. It can't be. Think about it...how could this thing survive without ever taking a drink? Without ever getting rained on?"

"It couldn't," he agreed, "if it's from this world."

"You think it's from outer space?"

"More like inner space."

"*What?*"

"There were stories, when I was growing up, about the Fuller place, about what Sam Fuller did behind closed doors. Some people say he was even into devil worship."

She stared. "You think he opened up a gateway to Hell?"

"A gateway to somewhere. Another dimension, maybe. Although, I doubt you'd find much water in Hell."

The waitress slid a plate in front of Robby, this time giving *him* a start; a T-bone steak and two eggs. "Can I get you anything else?" she asked.

"I'm good," he told her.

She glanced over at Sheri, her face flashing that look of compassion once more. "What about you, sweetie?"

"Fine," she told her, trying not to sound irritated. The woman meant well, but last thing Sheri wanted right now was someone feeling sorry for her.

The waitress smiled, but kept that pity in her eyes as she returned to the counter, leaving them to their surreal conversation.

Robby sliced into his eggs, and they bled yellow. "God damn it."

He stabbed them with his fork and ate just the same.

"Jeff would've sent them back," Sheri told him.

"Yeah, well, Jeff probably ate the cook's spit more times than not. No thanks."

She chuckled dryly, then sighed, feeling the emptiness once more where her lover used to live. *I'm not going to accept that he's really gone until I see some proof. I have to hold onto some glimmer of hope, no matter how faint it might be. I have to.* After a moment, she pressed Robby to continue. "Another dimension? Why would you even believe something like that?"

"Those symbols carved into the cellar walls. They were like something ancient, something you might see in some kind of occult ritual." He took another sip of his drink, then went on, "And the foot prints on the stairs. The spider-dog's tracks only went one way: up. So, either it was trapped down there for a very, very long time, or it just appeared down there and climbed its way out."

"So, just to be clear, you think somebody was holding a séance down there, or maybe tried their hand at playing Harry Potter, and just... conjured it up?"

"It sounds silly when you say it like that."

"That's because it *is* silly," she assured him. "It's ludicrous."

"You teach literature, right?"

"Right."

"Didn't Conan Doyle write something like, 'Eliminate all other factors, and whatever remains, however improbable, must be the truth.'"

"That's *fiction*, Robby. This is reality. Join me in it, would you?"

"Have you ever seen anything like the spider-dog before in *reality*?" he asked her. "In any zoo you've ever been to? In any textbook you've ever read?"

Sheri opened her mouth to offer some rational argument, but nothing came to mind; she shrugged her tired shoulders. "No. I've never seen anything like it before."

"Exactly," Robby said through a mouthful of steak.

"And you can kill it with a glass of water," she said doubtfully.

"Look, if you'd seen this guy, if you'd heard him – "

"He was in shock. You're an EMT for Christ's sake. You should know better."

"And a 'spider-dog' sounds so much more plausible?"

She frowned. "You didn't see it."

"No, but I believe you did, even if you were in shock."

Sheri blushed. "Fine. So...what? We sit around, pray for rain, and hope for the best?"

Robby shook his head. "It could be days or weeks before it rains again, and I really don't want to see anybody else wind up like Jeff or that little girl, do you?"

"Of course not."

"Well then, I was hoping you might help me take a more proactive approach."

"Like what?"

He smiled. "There's an End of Summer Clearance sale at the drug store."

CHAPTER FIFTEEN

Mancuso had tracked the animal since sunup without much difficulty. Whatever the little girl's father did, he'd hurt it, and as a result, the beast left dark clots of itself behind in the dirt – a trail of gory breadcrumbs to follow in addition to its numerous paw prints. Still, the animal control officer moved cautiously, knowing all too well that, wounded, the beast would be even more dangerous than before. An injured animal couldn't think clearly; all it knew was pain and rage, and in that fog of agony, it would lash out at anything that moved.

Not for much longer, my friend. I'll soon put you out of your misery. He tightened his grip on the rifle. The time for catch poles and cages had passed; this was a search and destroy mission now, and while he hated to see any animal put down, after the carnage he'd seen this past weekend, he knew it had to be done. *I'll make it quick. I promise.*

People were calling this thing a monster.

La Chupacabra.

Mancuso knew better. There were no monsters in this world, not really. Even if there was a "goat sucker" out there, it was not something supernatural. Just another animal we knew very little about.

There were only predators and prey; you were either one, or you were the other. And yet, as he read the morning paper, as he heard the chatter on the radio and local television stations, he had to shake his head. They wanted to ascribe some diabolical intent to this animal, as if the thing knew what it was doing when it attacked, like the Devil himself had a hand in natural selection and took a personal interest in breeding a killing machine. But Man was the only animal with the capacity to do good or evil, for all other beasts on this planet, it was simply a matter of instinct. Animals did what they did to survive. No more. No less.

Bad luck more than anything else, he thought with a nod. *But maybe I can turn it around.*

To catch a beast, you just had to be smarter than the beast. And Mancuso had yet to find the animal that he couldn't outthink. There was a first time for everything, he supposed, but it wouldn't be today.

He paused to look and listen. The forest played dead, quiet and still as the day before. Only leaf-laden branches moved overhead, rising and falling on the swells of the wind, sounding like a waterfall.

As he stood there, Mancuso felt suddenly serene – the enveloping sense of awe and calm that he always had when he hiked this deep into the woods. He breathed deeply and was slow to exhale, smelling the sweet aroma of flowers and the musty tang of moss and mold. He was alone in the green, speckled with bright shafts of light through the canopy above, at one with nature.

Mancuso took another step forward, peeling back thick ferns with his rifle barrel. The ground fell away in a steep slope, ending in a stream bed, no more than a trickle of runoff, perhaps fifty feet below. He squatted down to examine the tracks in the soft earth.

The beast had changed direction, circled back.

He tensed and turned slowly around, trying to find the slightest hint of movement from the underbrush behind him, his finger on the trigger, every muscle a rubber band ready to snap.

I'm upwind from it now. Has it picked up my scent?

Mancuso shook his head, trying to focus. He scanned the underbrush again, but saw nothing. Certainly nothing that could be caused by his quarry.

Where did you go?

He leaned his head down and wiped the sweat from his brow with his equally sweaty bicep, then stepped forward, hunched over as if to shield the rifle from view. His eyes swept the ground, once more picking up the trail. The claw marks took him west for about fifteen minutes before he realized where they were going.

Backtracking, heading toward that old farmhouse where the first attack occurred.

The Fuller place.

Of course, he realized. *It's hurt. It wants to go home. Perhaps it has cubs back there, maybe that's what caused it to attack in the first place. It felt threatened.*

Mancuso scouted over a few low hills. His gaze swung from left to right and then back again. Every step led him closer and closer.

The clots and droplets of goo grew smaller, more sporadic, and he found himself wondering if the animal would keel over from its injuries before he caught up to it. Part of him hoped that would be the case. He hated the thought of gunning down any animal, but the idea of shooting something majestic and powerful, something truly rare...well, that wasn't sitting well with him at all.

A loud, shrill screech filled the woods; it echoed off the trees, sent hidden birds airborne in a panic, and froze Mancuso in his tracks.

Jesus!

He stood there a moment, holding his rifle in a death grip, trying to figure out what on Earth could have made such a terrible sound, and then he heard a very human scream.

CHAPTER SIXTEEN

"I feel so ridiculous."

Robby turned to look at Sheri. He didn't see what she had to complain about. She wore a pair of blue jeans shorts that showed off her long, muscular legs; and a gray T-shirt with "Property of Harmony High Athletics Department" stenciled across the chest in red, block lettering. She'd pulled her hair up into a ponytail, her eyes hidden behind dark, fashionable sunglasses. And in her hands, she held a red, white, and blue plastic Super Soaker "Tornado Strike" water gun like an expert sniper.

Robby carried a matching weapon. He also had a pack filled with water balloons strapped to his back. "Better ridiculous than dead."

"This is a stupid idea," she told him, wiping her glistening forehead with the back of her arm. "You feel this humidity, right? It's like we're hiking through a sponge right now. If there really were such a thing as a creature allergic to water, it would melt away to nothing just standing still."

Robby shrugged. "Maybe it's something in the tap water that does it."

"You said it was a fish tank, right?"

"That's what the man said."

"Well, don't they have to add all kinds of chemicals to fish tanks to keep the water clean? Was the tank fresh water or salt water?"

"You know, these are all questions you should have asked *before* we got out here in the middle of the monster-infested forest."

She frowned. "That was before I picked up more Nicorette at the drug store. You seemed so much more convincing when I was going through withdrawal and wasn't thinking clearly."

Robby nodded at the Monarch stun pen she kept in her hip pocket. "At least you were thinking clearly enough to bring that along, just in case I'm wrong."

He could feel her glaring at him from beneath her sunglasses. "I don't intend to get that close to the thing again."

"Maybe you won't have to," he said hopefully. "Maybe it was hurt so bad that it crawled off and died."

"I'd still want to see the body. It might make the nightmares go away if I know it's gone."

"Yeah." Robby knew all about bad dreams. He'd had them since that night in the corn. After years of studying exorcism, hoping to one day return to those fields, hoping that he could rid himself of the nightmares if he could rid the town of that evil, he'd thought that the Woodfield Movie Palace would prove a successful test, would help him work up the nerve to actually perform the rite on a grand scale, but coming face to face with that demonic force had only served to show him that he wasn't ready. Not yet. And part of him doubted that he would ever be up to the task.

He pressed his finger firmly against the Super Soaker's trigger, ready to fire at a moment's notice. *Guess I'll just have to build up my confidence by killing one monster at a time.*

They walked on for a bit in silence, the humid air growing thick with the smell of pine. Soon they were stepping on a blanket of dry needles, green branches overhead nearly blotting out the sun. Robby kicked a large pinecone out of his path, watching it bounce and skid across the exposed roots.

When they emerged from the pine grove, the sunlight streamed through deciduous leaves, refracting off the moisture in the air to create rainbow patterns.

"This place is beautiful," Sheri proclaimed.

"So's a coral snake, until it sinks its fangs into you."

She snickered humorously. "Not much of an optimist, are you? I don't understand how –"

A loud caw made both of them jump. Robby looked up. A large crow sat perched on a low-hanging branch, a black stain on the green; it stared down at him with those soulless, onyx eyes, its mouth hanging open, its head twitching.

Fuck!

"Jesus," Sheri said softly, shading her eyes to get a better look at it. "That's a big crow."

The bird paid her no mind; it focused squarely on Robby's sweaty face.

"Looks like it knows you."

"Not funny," Robby told her once he managed to catch his breath.

"I'm serious. I read this study by...oh, who was it? Some university in Seattle, I think. Anyway, they found that these birds can recognize human faces, can even pick individuals out of a crowd."

Robby felt suddenly dizzy, as if someone were moving the ground beneath his feet. *You're dehydrated*, he thought. *Take a drink and you'll feel better.* But he couldn't move; he couldn't even blink.

The crow didn't blink either, as if it were locked with Robby in a staring contest.

"Not just crows," Sheri went on. "Ravens and seagulls too. And once they learn a face, they can somehow pass that information on to the rest of a flock, even pass it down to other generations. It helps them to avoid dangers."

Or to keep tabs on the one that got away.

"Pretty creepy stuff, huh?"

"Yeah." Robby squeezed the trigger on his Super Soaker and sent streams of water spiraling up into the branches. The powerful jets struck the crow, dousing its black body, causing it to cry out and flap its wings in a panic – water, loose leaves and feathers raining down onto the ferns below. Finally, the streams lost pressure and the drenched bird managed to get free of them and take flight; it swooped down, streaked over their heads, then disappeared from view, the echo of its infuriated caw dying on the breeze.

"That was mean," Sheri told him.

Robby lowered his water gun and glanced over at her unapologetically. "Maybe now it will go and tell the rest of its flock to stay the hell away from me."

"Well, even if it doesn't kill the damn thing, I hope the spider- dog likes water about as much as that crow."

A loud, shrill screech filled the air; an inhuman sound that made Robby's blood run cold.

"What the hell was that?" he asked aloud, but he knew the answer even before he saw the frightened expression on Sheri's face.

It struck from his right.

Robby heard the *snap* of breaking branches and turned his head in time to see the spider-dog pounce. Sheri had been right; the picture he'd painted in his head had not done the thing justice. Bony legs radiated from the long, sinuous body of a cheetah. It knocked him to the ground, snarling as it swung the arrowhead of its snout; the skin peeled back, blossoming into the star shape he'd seen burned into the Thornton girl's chest. And then Robby smelled it: drain cleaner; the same acidic drool the thing had pumped into that poor girl so that it could melt her down and suck her dry.

Now, it meant to do the same to him.

Sheri opened fire with her Super Soaker. Cyclonic streams struck the side of the creature's snout. It reared back, growling and screeching, snapping at the fountain as it backed off Robby, allowing him a chance to get to his feet and scramble away.

Thornton had been right. He'd wounded it. The creature's entire left side was an open sore. Yellow-green puss bubbled up from between layers of flayed musculature, only to be washed away by Sheri's spray.

Her gun suddenly lost pressure, the stream dwindling to a trickle from the end of her barrel as her eyes widened with terror.

The spider-dog wheeled around on its numerous legs. It snarled and lowered itself to the ground, preparing to leap, but Robby reached into his backpack and lobbed a red water grenade. The balloon exploded with a splash against the creature's open maw; a jagged piece of rubber snagged one of its fangs and dangled from it like a piece of gristle. But its face didn't melt. It didn't even smolder. It just shook the water off and roared.

"I think we're just pissin' it off!" Sheri yelled as she slid another water clip into her gun.

Robby didn't understand it. *Look at that wound,* his brain cried. *If the water didn't do that to it, what did?*

He lobbed another balloon, this time striking one of its spiny legs as it moved toward them. Once again, it appeared to do the thing no harm.

What the hell was in that fish tank?

The thing advanced rapidly on its countless legs; it was nearly on top of them now. Without thinking, Robby dropped his useless water gun and lunged; throwing himself against the creature. Sheri shrieked in terror as he knocked it onto its back and fell on top of its bony body, pinning it down to the ground.

Robby balled his hand into a fist and punched the creature repeatedly in its wounded side, his knuckles colliding with soft, slimy tissue and hard bone in equal measure. The alien beast screeched in agony and nipped at the air; Robby ducked, dodging the toothy petals of its jaws as it squirmed and bucked beneath him, its numerous legs kicking out and folding in to beat his back.

"Run!" he called to Sheri, who stood by frozen with the Super Soaker still in her hands. "Move!"

Her paralysis broke, but instead of running away, she strutted up to the struggling forms and squeezed her trigger, dousing the spider-dog with more water.

"What the hell are you doing?" Robby yelled over the animal's high-pitched squeals.

Sheri reached into her hip pocket and brought out the the Monarch. She thumbed the cap and armed it, making it hum. The spider-dog seemed to screech louder, if that were possible. "Yeah," she said, "you remember that, don't you, bitch?"

Holy shit!

Robby rolled off the soaked creature just as she thrust the small taser into its dripping face. He saw a bright flash, heard the crackle of electricity as it traveled through the water to various parts of the spider-dog's strange anatomy, causing it to convulse wildly.

And then it grew still, silent.

For a moment, Robby wondered if he'd gone deaf, but then the sounds of the forest began to return: the chirping of distant birds and the buzz of cicadas. He managed to get up on his hands and knees, sucking wind, then he was up on his feet – parts of him numb, others feeling the sting and burn of scratches and bruises.

Sheri stood over the motionless creature, still clutching the Monarch by its rubber grip.

He went to her and croaked, "You didn't run."

"No, but I did move." She blinked. "I can't believe you tackled that thing."

Robby smiled in spite of his pain. "Well, it was either that or run away while it ate you. I think I made the right choice."

"I guess I owe you then."

"I'd say we were pretty even." His eyes fell to the stun pen. "Just warn a guy next time, okay?"

"Trust me, there won't *be* a next time."

Robby kicked the spider-dog in the side to see if it would move, but it remained lifeless. *What the hell are you?* he wondered, and then he said aloud to Sheri, "Come on, I'll take you home."

She looked at his injuries. "Uh, wrong. I'm taking you to the Immediate Care. You should see yourself!"

"I'm fine. Trust me."

"Last time I trusted you, we almost got eaten."

He touched his side, winced and hissed at the pain, then brought his fingers up to his eyes. They were red with blood. "Yeah, okay. Maybe you're right."

"Jesus," she said, "Are you going to be able to make it back to the truck?"

"I'll make it," he told her. *I'm not staying out here in these woods alone.* "I'll be fine."

"You look like shit from where I'm standing."

"I'll make it."

They started back down the path toward the pine trees. Sheri bent down to pick up Robby's Super Soaker, then she hurried over to his side and shook her head.

"Water," she huffed.

"Hey, it worked in the movie."

"I'll say it again: stupid fucking movie."

"Yeah."

Having watched as many stupid horror films as he had over the years, with and without Paul Rice, Robby should have known that the spider-dog wasn't dead. But when he heard the growl, when he turned and saw the thing crouching there on its oddly-jointed legs, ready to pounce, it still caught him by surprise.

It seemed to jump in slow motion: snarling, drooling from the open blossom of its mouth, and then –

A gun shot.

The blast caught the spider-dog in mid leap, turning its narrow head into a flower of blood and shrapnel. It fell to the ground at their feet, flopped a moment, and then grew still once more.

Robby continued to back away from it, not wanting to take any more chances. He looked up and saw a uniformed animal control officer standing at the edge of the foliage. The man lowered his rifle and stared down at the carcass in disbelief.

Sheri started to cry in an odd, hiccupping sort way, her whole body shaking. She turned away and buried her head in Robby's scratched and bleeding chest. He reached up and rubbed her back.

"It's okay," he assured her. "It's really gone now. It's over."

The animal control officer walked over to them, and Robby saw the name MANCUSO stitched just above his breast pocket. "You folks all right?"

"Perfect," Robby told him. "Just perfect."

CHAPTER SEVENTEEN

The sun had yet to fully rise, but large lamps on stands made it bright and warm as day. A red light ignited atop the high definition camera and Sheri's stomach felt strange. She shifted a bit in her chair.

How many people on the other side of that lens? Millions? Millions of strange eyes on me now. Watching. Judging.

She looked away from the ogling camera, tried to focus on something else. The woman in the television monitor looked like a stranger. Sure, she recognized the clothes as her own – a pink, short-sleeved shirt with beaded embroidery around the neckline, and a black skirt that stopped just shy of her knees – but the face was alien to her; too pale in some places, too dark in others, worn out and worn down.

I look like a meth addict or something. Just what America wants to see first thing in the morning. Oh so sexy!

The image on the monitor made it appear as if she were sitting in the middle of the woods – perhaps the same forest where she'd confronted the spider-dog, but it was all a lie. In reality, her chair sat safely in the Harmony Police Department parking lot, with a row of ornamental trees and bushes behind her, miles from where the creature had died. Miles from where her lover had vanished from her sight and from her life.

This all seems so wrong. So very wrong.

Sheri drew in a deep breath, then let it out slowly in a broken stutter.

I'm not going to cry on live television. I'm not.

Matt Lauer was in her ear, asking the same questions all the reporters seemed to care about. Questions she still wrestled with herself. "Up next, what was it like to come face to face with a vicious predator and live to tell about it? And was this strange creature really the legendary goat sucker, *La Chupacabra*? We're going to find out. But first, this is *Today* on NBC."

Crazy, Matt. All of this is crazy. It wasn't supposed to be like this. No. Everything was supposed to be quite different.

The red light went dark.

"And...we're clear," one of the technicians said. "Back in five, everyone."

Sheri stared at the monitor until a car insurance commercial filled the screen, then she relaxed a bit and reached for her coffee cup. Coffee had become her new vice. She was on her third cup and it wasn't even eight yet. She'd recently read a study that people who drank four or five cups of coffee a day lived longer. If that were true, at this rate, she might become damn near immortal.

Robby sat next to her, handsomely dressed in his EMT uniform. The same uniform he'd worn the night Jeff was kill–the night Jeff disappeared. He looked at her, his eyes gentle and full of concern. "Did you get any sleep last night?"

"A bit." She thought that seeing the spider-dog dead at her feet would slay the nightmare monster that now stalked her dreams, but when she closed her eyes, it was still there –waiting in subconscious shadows, ready to pounce.

The tigers come at night.

That line kept popping into her head. Was that from some story she'd read and forgotten? Maybe a pop song on the radio? She couldn't think of the source, but it was very apropos. The tigers *did* come at night, and they were far too hungry.

She blinked and turned back to Robby. "You?"

"Not much."He took a sip from his own coffee, then asked, "You sure you can make it through this?"

"I know I look like shit, but – "

"No, you look fine."

"– I'll be fine."

They said "fine" in unison.

Jinx, buy me a Coke.

Sheri snorted and shook her head. She didn't even really know Robby, and yet he'd just risked his life for her own. True, she'd had to turn around and save his ass, but Robby hadn't expected her to do anything but run. He'd been ready to die, so that she could go on living.

She lowered her eyes and found Jeff's smiling face in her lap. She'd brought the framed picture from her bedside table. It felt like the right thing to do – to hold it up and ask people to help look for him, to help find him, even if...

Shit.

Sheri didn't know how to feel anymore. She loved Jeff, or...at least she thought she had. Lord knows she'd told him so enough times. It should still mean something, shouldn't it?And yet, as she sat here, mugging for a morning show, all she felt was numb. "I don't even know why we're here."

She heard a loud, quick burst of laughter; a piercing bark. Mancuso. The animal control officer sat on Robby's left, forming an odd mirror of Sheri – clearly out of his element, apparently far more comfortable wrestling animals in the wild than smiling for cameras. And like Robby, he'd taken the time to dress in his work uniform, clean and ironed, making her feel severely underdressed.

"We're here," Mancuso told her, "because the news has branded us heroes."

"I didn't do anything heroic," she said grimly. "I just wanted the thing dead."

If anyone should be crowned a hero here, she thought, *it should be Robby.*

The man nodded as if he agreed. "The only reason I'm here is 'cause I shot it. Nothing heroic in killin' one of God's creatures."

"I don't know where that thing came from," Robby said with a frown, "but I'm pretty sure God's not claiming it."

Mancuso shrugged. "It's not up to us to judge. Nature is eat and be eaten."

Robby rolled his eyes. "Please don't start singing 'The Circle of Life.'"

"This is news, simple as that. Just like an earthquake is news, or a fire, or a kidnapping, or a school shooting. People want to watch all the evil shit that happens in this world from the safety of their own homes. They want to know what happened. They want to know *why* it happened. And they want to hear about it from people who were there in the middle of it all. If we weren't here to give our side of the story, they'd just talk about us anyway."

Robby cocked his eyebrow. "Which is why I'm here. I'd rather hear about me from me than listen to some suit in New York who's never met me spout all kinds of crazy half-truths and rumors." He turned to Sheri once more. "You sure you're okay? You look like you're about to be sick."

"Don't worry about me," she told him.

"We're about to go live," the technician told them; he held up his fingers, dropping each in turn as he counted down, "in five...four... three..."

The light on the camera flashed red again. On the monitor, another shot of them sitting there, and then Sheri watched as they played a pre-recorded package, listening as the narrator described the horrors of the past week in the dry, detached, almost clinical manner of someone who had never met Jeff or the young girl who was killed, someone who had never seen the demonic face of the spider-dog when it was alive.

When this intro concluded, the voice in Sheri's ear was Savannah Guthrie, "And Sheri Foster, Robby Miller, and Victor Mancuso are joining us now exclusively from Harmony, Indiana. Good morning to you all."

"Good morning," they said, nearly in unison.

Jinx...

"First of all," Savannah said, "Robby and Sheri, you went into those woods despite the fact that there were warnings about this viscous animal being out there. What were you thinking?"

Sheri opened her mouth, not really knowing how to answer and yet knowing that she was obligated to say *something*. "Well...um...as you mentioned in your intro there, Jeff, my – my boyfriend, is still missing. I guess that was really my only thought, you know, finding him."

And slaying the dragon. Don't forget to tell her how good it felt to shove that taser into its side and watch it fry, the rush you experienced as it twitched and spasmed in front of you...

Robby said, "I was basically thinking of the situation we were in, which wasn't very good. You had people dead, people missing...You know, there are a lot of farms and houses in that remote area, many with small children, and as an EMT, I know how long it takes for help to get out there – "

Savannah cut him off, "Yes, I understand that you felt like you had to do something, but – "

Robby returned the favor, "Right, I was pretty concerned with what might happen next if we didn't go out there and do something."

Savannah nodded on the monitor and moved on, "And it was lucky for both of you that Victor Mancuso happened upon you when he did. Mr. Mancuso, you're the one who actually shot and killed this creature. In your time as an animal control officer, you've had to deal with some pretty dangerous situations. Anything compare to this one?"

Mancuso straightened up a bit in his chair. "No, not really. At first, they told me we were dealing with a big cat, maybe a cougar, but I could tell from its tracks that it was something else entirely –"As he spoke, Sheri noticed the monitor; they had cut away to a cell phone video someone had taken of the spider-dog lying dead in the dirt, a pixelated blur where its vulgar head had been. "– I just didn't expect it to be so alien looking. I wish I could have captured it alive, I know the folks at Stanley would rather be studying a living specimen right now instead of a dead one, but given the circumstances, it just wasn't possible."

The monitor now displayed a split image: the spider-dog's corpse stuck in a loop on one side of the screen, Savannah's inquisitive face on the other. "You mentioned 'alien' just now, which brings up an interesting point. The internet is buzzing about this creature. This cell phone video we're currently airing was uploaded to YouTube, and as of this morning, it has had over one million hits. I know the farmer who lost his cows has said this was Mexico's legendary *La Chupacabra*, others are saying it was some kind of alien. What do all of you think it was?"

Sheri spoke up, "I don't think it really matters what it was. I'm just glad that it's gone, and that no one else has to go through what we've been through."

"Well – "

"*And*," Sheri went on, needing to get this out; it was important. She held Jeff's picture high as she spoke, her knuckles turning white around the frame, "I want to thank everyone who's helped look for Jeff. Even though this monster's no longer out there, I hope people will continue to volunteer, continue to search, and that we can find him very soon."

"With everything that's happened," Savannah said, "do you still have any hope of finding him alive?"

Sheri felt her eyes narrow. When she answered, she could hear the quiver in her own voice, "Of course I hope he's alive. But, even if...even if he's not, I want some closure, for me and for his family."

"Well, our thoughts and prayers are with you," Savannah said. "You're all very brave for facing this creature and to come on TV and talk about it. Thank you so much, we really appreciate it."

Robby nodded. "Sure."

And then the red light was extinguished for good and the monitor went dark.

"Well, that went well," he proclaimed, and by his tone, Sheri couldn't tell if he were serious or joking.

And then a wave of emotion caught her by surprise. Her grip on the picture frame loosened slowly as her jaw and throat tightened. She was dimly aware of a technician's hands on her collar, removing her microphone. Was there more she should have said while she had the nation's ear? Would it have made any difference if she had?

No.

Would this be the end of it, then? After this, if there was no more news, no body, no grave marker, no proof of any kind, could she just simply go on with her life? Could she spend day after day, smiling behind her desk and talking calmly at her chalk board, expecting so much from the students who came and went from her ten by ten cell, year after empty year? Was that her future now? Growing old and dying alone?

She leaned forward, her stomach still aflutter, afraid she would be sick, but she covered her eyes with her hand and pressed down hard with her fingers until the urge subsided.

"Sheri?" She felt Robby's gentle hand on her shoulder, heard the concern in his voice.

"I'm fine," she croaked. "Just...give me a minute."

And then she heard Mancuso say, "You know, Guthrie didn't ask the one question that's been bothering me."

Robby snickered. "Only one thing about this has been bothering you?"

"Yeah. What the hell were you two doing out there with *squirt guns*?"

"Playing tag."

"Bullshit."

"The girl that was killed," Robby began.

Sheri pulled the hand away from her face and sat up in her chair. "Please, don't," she urged, but Robby evidently didn't hear her. Maybe she'd only thought it.

"Her father said that water from the broken fish tank splashed on the creature. He said...he said it started to melt. So, we thought, maybe–"

Mancuso threw his head back and laughed again, so like a dog barking.

"I know how it sounds, alright," Robby told him defensively, trying to use the same logic – or lack thereof – that had convinced Sheri to go along with him, "but if you'd heard that girl's father, you wouldn't just laugh it off."

"Oh, I'm not doubting the man," Mancuso told them with a crooked grin. "It probably did happen, just like he said. It explains the trail of goop the thing left behind in the dust, the way its skin was scorched and melted, but I don't think the water did that."

"Then what?"

"It was probably the salt."

There was a gaping pause. Finally, Robby said simply, "Salt."

"Yeah. That was a salt water tank. I don't mean to tell you your business, but anybody with any knowledge of animals at all could've looked at those dead fish on the floor and figured out the were salt water varieties. Plus, have you ever been to the ocean or a big aquarium somewhere? Salt water has a much different smell than fresh."

"I never went in the house," Robby admitted, his shoulders slumping.

Salt water. I knew it. Sheri wanted a smoke, wanted to elbow Robby and scream, "I told you so," but she drowned both urges as quickly as they surfaced with another sip of her coffee. The warmth felt good, and the ache in her head slowly began to subside.

"The thing must've had the same reaction to salt as a snail or a slug," Mancuso told them, genuinely intrigued. He paused, thinking it over, then he started laughing again.

Robby's jaw tightened. "I'm glad you find this so fucking funny."

Mancuso held up his hand. "Sorry, it's just that...the two of you thinking that plain old tap water could act like some kind of battery acid. Oh my!" He shook his head, clapped his hands on his knees, then got up out of the chair. "At least it's over now."

"It'll never be over," Sheri said, or at least she thought she did. It was like a dream, a nightmare. Later, she was unsure if she'd actually spoken that morning at all.

september

CHAPTER EIGHTEEN

There's an old saying in the state of Indiana: "If you don't like the weather, stick around fifteen minutes. It'll change."

And change it always did, as quickly as if someone had flipped the switch on a thermostat, but this was seldom an easy, peaceful transition. No. Every March, winter was forced from the territory, kicking and screaming; blown away by hurricane-force gales, snow showers replaced overnight by torrential rains, homes and farmlands pummeled by hail or erased from the map completely by a tag-team of tornados and floods.

When the flood waters subsided, a blazing sun reigned, baking the land for months. Calendar spring, calendar summer; Indiana weather didn't know and it didn't care. Green grass browned beneath scorching heat. By late July or early August, the parched earth belched dust with every step.

And in September, just when it seemed as if the heat and humidity would never end, fall made the most theatrical of entrances; announced by the ominous music of thunder, and accompanied by a brilliant fireworks display of lightning. Winds performed last rites on autumn leaves, leaving behind skeletal branches; a dead world, awaiting the first icy shroud of frost.

That year, calendar fall didn't officially begin until Saturday, September 22; when darkness and light held equal sway, and the corn turned brown before the harvest. But Nature paid no mind to civilization's times and dates, especially in Indiana. So, with Labor Day still looming large in the rearview mirror, the air turned suddenly cold, and bitter rains came down in sheets.

About 78 miles south of Harmony, in the center of the state capitol, Indianapolis, Britney Clark ran down Meridian Street. She ran away from her warm, dry cubicle in a high-rise bank tower. And as she ran, she pulled her jacket up over her ears, trying to shield herself from the deluge, failing miserably.

Why did I go off and leave my stupid umbrella back at the loft?

Good question. After all, the weather girl's forecast mentioned a chance of showers tonight, didn't it?

True. But it was so sunny this morning, so nice, *that I thought I could make it home before it started raining. I didn't think I'd have to worry about getting caught out in this shitty downpour!*

So now, she found herself drenched, and her open-toed sandals made certain that every step on this uneven brick gave her feet a frigid bath. She reached the intersection of Meridian and Maryland and glanced around, searching for quick shelter. A few high-priced restaurants lined the opposite side of the street, eateries that would most likely frown upon her sitting around and waiting out the rain.

When she turned to her left, however, a sign glowed like a lighthouse beacon in the storm: a smiling, bug-eyed, buck-toothed cartoon animal in a trucker hat; and below the image hung the words "Wild Beaver Saloon."

Not "Bar," she noted, but "Saloon." Not the type of place Britney normally frequented. But a white hot fork of lightning, and the sonic boom of thunder that came almost simultaneously, convinced her to run inside.

She scanned the room. Christmas lights hung in the corners and along the ceiling. In the distance, Britney saw a wooden door to the restrooms labeled "CRAPPER." Patrons crowded around small round tables, drinking and cheering. She turned toward the bar and saw what all the fuss was about.

Three girls were up on the counter. They danced in a line, shaking it to Christina Aguilera's "Dirrty." One wore skin-tight jeans, another wore red short-shorts, and the third wore fishnet stockings with a skirt so tiny that her black panties were clearly visible.

Britney stood by the door, wide-eyed and shivering.

What kind of place is this?

Not *her* kind of place, she quickly decided. She was about to turn around and make another run down Meridian, hoping she might have better luck – *feel a bit more comfortable* – in one of those high-end restaurants. Then she heard a voice; it wasn't shouting, but it was still loud enough to be heard over the crowd – male, pleasant, friendly, and with just a hint of an accent.

"Looking for a place to sit down, lass?" At first, she didn't think it was addressing her, but when she turned around, she saw the most incredible looking man staring right at her. His eyes –

Oh, my God, those gorgeous eyes...

-were brown, spellbinding, giving her that "come hither" look she'd only read about in romance novels. He wore a striped dress shirt, unbuttoned, over a plain white tee and ripped blue jeans. His finger-combed tussle of red hair made it look as if his head were on fire. And his face –

Perfect, like the statue of David...

-combined with that foreign accent –

Is that British? No...it's Irish. Definitely Irish.

-chased away the chill.

He leaned closer to her, pulled a vacant barstool out from his table. "I say, are ya lookin' for a place to sit?"

"Oh..." Britney blinked, water dripping from the wet spirals of her hair. Instead of backing out the door, she stepped over and took the seat. "Sure, thank you."

"The pleasure's all mine," he told her with a bit of a boyish, mischievous grin. "I know most people out there wouldn't piss on ya if you were on fire, but I like to help out a poor, unfortunate soul when I can."

Poor, unfortunate soul. That describes me to a tee.

She saw a napkin dispenser on the table and grabbed a few, dabbing the water from her face. "I must look a mess."

"Not at all." He took a drink of his beer, then said, "I know this is gonna sound like a fuckin' cliché, but what's a beor like you doin' in a place like this anyway?"

"A *bee-yo*?" she repeated, confused.

"That's Irish for a very attractive woman."

"Oh." She smiled and laughed, feeling warmth flood into her frozen cheeks. "I thought you were calling me a bitch or something."

His smile widened, charming and disarming. "Not at all."

"I – I got caught out in the rain and I just wanted to come in and get warmed up."

"Aye. It'd freeze the balls off a brass monkey out there for sure."

She giggled at that. "I just love your accent."

"Okay, lass, go ahead an' ask me."

"What?"

"Ask me to say it."

She shrugged. "Say what?"

He cleared his throat, squinted, and made a fist. "They're always after me Lucky Charms!"

Britney burst out laughing, then covered her mouth with her hands. "I'm sorry," she told him. "I wasn't going to have you do that."

"Uh-huh." He gave her a skeptical look, still grinning. "Sure."

She lifted her hand to her chest. "Honest."

He nodded, then finished his beer in one gulp. A black stone hung from a cord around his neck. There was an image carved into it: a five-pointed star with an eye in the middle; it was crude, almost like a child's drawing.

"That's an interesting necklace," Britney told him, pointing it out. "Does it mean something?"

He reached up and touched the stone, tracing the shape with his index finger. "What? This ol' thing? It belonged to my dear ol' Da, God rest his soul. An old Celtic rune stone. Been in the family for generations."

She nodded, staring at him. "So..." she finally ventured. "Do you live here in town?"

"Just arrived."

"From Ireland?"

"Vegas, actually."

"Oh really? Have any luck?"

"Not at first, but it took a turn for the better."

So has mine.

She smiled, then wiped her hand with the napkins and held it out to him. "I'm Britney, by the way."

He wrapped her fingers in his strong, warm grip. "Cayden Donnelly."

"Cayden," she repeated, liking the sound of it. *So foreign. So fascinating.* "Pleased to meet you."

"Very pleased to meet you too, Britney."

He gazed at her with those incredible eyes, and she actually felt her stomach flutter.

How old is he? Thirty? Thirty-five?

When he finally let go of her hand, for a moment, she didn't know what to do with it, and it hung there in the air between them as if suspended by marionette string. Britney withdrew it quickly, self-consciously, putting it in her lap and out of sight, where it could not embarrass her further.

A waitress seemed to materialize from nowhere and stood by their table. Britney realized it was one of the girls who had been dancing on the bar, the one with the skin-tight jeans. She wore a T-shirt that read: *Save a tree...Eat a beaver*; her eyes were squarely on Cayden. "Another Guinness?"

"Yeah, an' the lady'll have..." He turned to Britney. "What will the lady have?"

Britney blinked. "Oh...A rum and Diet Coke."

The girl nodded, snatched Cayden's empty glass off the table, and disappeared back into the crowd.

"So, Cayden Donnelly," Britney began, anxious to know more about him, "if you don't mind me asking, what brings you here to Indy?"

He shrugged. "I've been here and there, you know, knockin' people up."

"Excuse me?" She had no way to know what he would say, but *that* had been nowhere on her list of possibilities. "You go around knocking people up?"

Cayden nodded as if it were no big deal.

Britney cocked her eyebrow and gave a shocked little giggle. "Are you a fertility doctor, or a gigolo?"

"What?"

"You go around getting girls pregnant?"

He threw back his head and laughed. "No, lass...no, no, no. Knockin' somebody up in America means gettin'em pregnant?"

"Yeah, it does."

"Ahhhh Bee'Jaaysus, are yih serious?"

Britney nodded.

"In Ireland, it means callin' on folks for business."

She felt her face warm again. "Oh...Okay."

Cayden shook his head. "Well, so far, I've done this all arseways, haven't I?"

"Sorry?"

"I say, I've made a complete mess of this."

"Not at all. I'm having a lot of fun, actually."

He smiled at that. "I'm glad."

The waitress returned with their drinks. Cayden lifted his glass and said, "Sláinte!"

"And what's that mean?" Britney asked.

"That's Irish for 'To your health!'"

"Oh, well then...To your health." She touched her glass to his with a *clink*, took a sip, and frowned. Why could she never get a good rum and Coke at a bar? They always put in too much Coke and far too little rum. She looked back at Cayden and asked, "So what kind of business are you in?"

"I'm a bit of a missionary."

"Really?"

"As sure as God made apples." He took a drink of his beer, and added, "I travel the world, hoping to bring people closer to their creator."

She nodded, caught off guard, her smile wilting a bit; hopefully he wouldn't start spouting scripture and trying to somehow convert her. "I bet that's rewarding."

"Frustrating, actually." He held the rim of his glass between his thumb and forefinger and rocked it, staring down into the foam as if trying to divine some hidden fortune. "Nobody gives a flyin' fuck."

Britney's eyes widened at that.

He sure doesn't talk like a missionary.

And how would you know? her brain countered. *Have you ever met one before tonight?*

She blinked and said, "Well...I just don't think people like to be called sinners and told they're going to Hell all the time."

"Goin'?" Cayden glanced up at her and chuckled humorlessly. "Lass, we're already here! Look at the news, for fuck's sake? All the shitty atrocities men do to other men, to women and fuckin' children. It's bloody chaos out there!"

She nodded, focused on nothing but the intensity in his beautiful, wonderful eyes, feeling an unbelievable eagerness tug at her viscera.

It's been over a year. More than twelve months since I've had a man...

"But my Da," Cayden went on to say. "See, he wanted to change all o' that...wanted to help bring order to this godless fuckin' world. He was...he was a missionary too, a very wise and passionate man."

Britney nodded and took another sip of her mostly-Coke. *Wise and passionate, just like your eyes.*

Cayden looked back down into his beer, and his fingers found the black rune stone around his neck once more. "He spent all his life trying to bring about change, but he died a heart-broken man, never able to really see the face of his true father."

"You mean God?"

He blinked at her, then shrugged and said, "God...yeah."

"Well, nobody can *see* the face of God," she snorted. "I mean, you hear about people who find Jesus in a taco shell, or the Virgin Mary in a stain on the wall, but those people are –"

"Crazy?"

Britney's mouth hung open a moment, then she found her voice again. "I didn't mean to say that *your father* –"

Cayden let go of his necklace and held up his hand. "No, you're right. There are a lot of nuts out there. And, to most people, my Da was one mad yoke – they thought he was a bit off, but they admired him. *I* admired him."

He slowly lowered his hand and placed it on Britney's arm; she liked the feel of it – warm, and strong, and comforting. She found herself wondering how it would feel to have that hand touch other parts of her anatomy, and the thought ignited an excited little spark that shot through her whole body.

"And, when that great man was on his deathbed," Cayden went on to say with that pleasant Irish lilt, giving her arm a gentle squeeze, his tone one of great respect and reverence, "I *swore* to him that I would carry on with his great work, that I would bring about the change he'd fought his whole life for, but was never able to see, bring order to all this chaos."

He smiled at Britney, and she couldn't help but smile back at him.

"And now you think I'm a pure balubas drunk, don'tcha!"

Britney giggled and blushed. "No."

He pointed at her. "You think I'm trippin' balls!"

"Not at all," she told him honestly, not understanding half of what he was saying, her grin once more in full bloom. Her eyes lowered to his ring finger, searching for the tell-tale white stripe of a freshly-removed wedding band and finding none. *Funny, and handsome, and single*, and *works to promote social change...he's just too good to be true.*

And I want him.

And with that thought came sudden warmth between her thighs. She found herself trying to remember which pair of underwear she'd slipped on that morning in her hurry to get out the door. It wasn't the sexy silk panties, she knew that much, but she hoped it wasn't an old pair with holes worn in it. She hadn't planned on winding up in bed with a stranger. Given her recent track record with men, it seemed a very unlikely prospect indeed. She wasn't seeing anyone, wasn't the type of girl who had one night stands, and yet, there was something different about this man.

Hey, I didn't plan on getting caught out in the rain either, and so far, that's worked out pretty well.

"At least you're smiling," Cayden told her.

"I am."

"And you're still here."

"You sound surprised?"

He shrugged. "I mean, I know I don't look like the back end of the bus or anythin' – "

Major understatement...

"– but when I start talkin' religion, most girls can't walk away fast enough."

"Well, it's not like you're a priest." She eyed him cautiously. "Right?"

Cayden gave a loud snort and chuckled, holding up his glass as if making a toast. "Ah well, truer words were never spoken."

He killed the rest of his beer in one gulp, but his glass didn't stay empty for long. The waitress brought more drinks for both of them. And when those were gone, she brought a couple more. And a couple more after that.

Finally, Britney held up her hand and asked for water instead.

Sitting there with Cayden, she felt herself growing more and more–

Horny

-tipsy, and she didn't want to get drunk. No. If she was going to climb into bed with this man, she wanted to enjoy it. And if she drank too many more, she knew she'd only wind up hugging the toilet all night instead.

Cayden rolled the rim of his glass between his thumb and forefinger and asked, "Wanna bobble?"

"What?"

"You wanna get outta here? Go someplace else?"

Don't sound too eager, you don't want him to know how desperate you are.

"Um...sure, okay."

She stood. Her legs felt a bit trembly beneath her. Cayden grabbed up his black leather jacket, and they made their way toward the exit. A Red Bull chalk board hung by the door, and someone had scrawled "thanks 4 coming in our beaver" across its slate face.

Outside, the rain had stopped. Wet streets shimmered, reflecting the glow of arc lamps and overhead traffic lights. Wind whipped between the buildings; trash danced with dead leaves in the shadows.

They strolled leisurely down Maryland. Well, Cayden strolled leisurely. Britney put one foot in front of the other with great focus and effort.

Don't fall, Britney thought with every deliberate step. *Don't fall. Don't fall. Don't fall.*

Thankfully, she didn't have far to walk.

Gotta love Indy. You can stagger home from just about anywhere.

"So where's the craic tonight?" Cayden asked.

"What?" Britney's eyes widened. "You want to go find some crack?"

"No, lass. The craic! You know...good times, fun!"

"Oh...Well...I know we just met and all, but..." Britney brushed the hair from her face. "I-I've got this loft not far from here."

"A loft? Like in a barn?"

"No, no. An apartment."

He smiled at that. "In Ireland, we call that a flat."

She giggled. "My flat. Yes. Would you like to come back with me to my flat, Cayden Donnelly?"

His grin widened a bit. "Abso-tively! I thought you'd never ask."

They walked down Meridian arm-in-arm, and Britney felt much steadier. "Where are you from in Ireland?"

Cayden glanced down at her for a moment, then back into space, his fingers on the rune that hung from his neck, slowly stroking the dark, polished stone. "Here and there, towns you've probably never heard of. I was born in Dungarvan, but I was pretty well raised in a place called Connemara."

"I bet it's beautiful there."

"Aye. Wonderful scenery. Grasslands, lakes, rivers, mountains, castles –"

"Castles?"

This is like some kind of fairy tale...

"Aye. Castles, churches, earthen forts. See, there's a power there. It's faint now, just an echo really, but a few hundred years ago, the place was rife with it."

"What...like magic?"

"Magick, yes. The oldest and strongest of magicks."

"And now you're gonna tell me that you're some kind of magician too."

He glanced back down at her and smiled. "I am."

"Really?"

"Shwear down."

Britney shook her head, not comprehending him, his Irish slang still mysterious and her mind still fuzzy.

He chuckled. "You think I'm full of shit like a Christmas turkey?"

"No, no...I'd just like to maybe see a trick sometime, that's all."

His smile faltered a bit. "They're not *tricks*, lass. They're a channeling of great power, and not to be attempted lightly."

Now it was her turn to chuckle. "So you're a traveling magician priest?"

Cayden nodded. "All that and so much more."

Let's hope you're also an amazing lover...

They turned onto Georgia Street. The wet cobblestone was deserted. Cayden helped her up the steps of her building and into the elevator. And when the doors slid closed, she turned and put her arms up around his neck and pressed her lips against his. His lips were rough, chapped, and warm. His whole face radiated warmth. She felt her insides flutter, crying out like a thirsty castaway who'd been lost at sea for far too long.

The elevator dinged as the doors opened on her floor. Their lips parted, and Britney took him by the hand, leading him down the hall to her door. She could not find her keys fast enough, but soon, she pulled him inside and turned on the lights.

"My humble abode," Britney told him, sweeping the room with her arm.

His dark, incredible eyes saw none of it; they were focused only on her. He reached out and pulled her to him, his arms sliding around her waist and his strong, rough tongue sliding between her lips to play with her own.

"Now," Cayden said when their lips parted, his voice low and husky, "I'm gonna need to slip into your skin."

Britney giggled. "I know what *that's* Irish for."

"No," he told her, his face darkening. "I don't think you do."

CHAPTER NINETEEN

"The Porta-Potties have arrived," Robby Miller commented as he watched workmen offloading large blue latrines from a flatbed truck. "I guess we're really going through with this."

Lou Davies, his fire captain, chuckled and said, "Glad you could finally take time out of your busy schedule to join us, Hollywood. Come on in. I'll show you around."

Hollywood.

Robby shook his head. It had been weeks since he'd been on television, but the nickname didn't appear to be going anywhere soon.

Gotta love working in a fire station. These guys are merciless!

They strolled across the wet grass toward the Fuller place. Robby hadn't been back here since the day he toured the cellar with Sheri. Truth be told, he didn't really want to be here now either, but he wasn't going to be the only member of the fire department who hadn't given of their time.

Several volunteers sat on their butts on the front porch, cutting and sculpting two-inch-thick sheets of insulation into fake rocks and graveyard headstones with hot knives. Smoke and the smell of burning Styrofoam hung thick in the air.

"Jesus," Robby told them. "You guys'll be high as kites breathin' these fumes all day."

One of the guys, Charlie Meadows, gave him a goofy grin and said, "Why do you think we volunteered for this, Miller?"

Captain Davies smiled. "It was even worse inside. We moved them out here for better ventilation."

Robby followed him through the front door. The layout of the house had changed dramatically since the night that Sheri's boyfriend had disappeared. He used to be able to walk straight down a long hallway from the front door to the kitchen. Now, what looked like a brick wall stood in his way.

Davies gave the wall a pat. "Looks pretty good, doesn't it."

Robby nodded. "Yeah."

"The landlord tried to tell us that, per building codes, we had to use sheet rock for all of our temporary walls. I told him, 'Look, I'm with the fire department. Flame treated lumber, flame retardant paint, and a spray coating of flame retardant on everything will get us the flame spread rating we need.' Plus, you ever try moving a sheet rock wall? Heavy as fuck! These temp walls here can be carted around pretty easily, and we can store them up for next year."

"Next year? Getting a little bit ahead of yourself, aren'tcha, Cap?"

"Just hopeful is all."

"I mean, if doin' a spook house was such a goldmine, wouldn't everybody be doin' it?"

"I've done my research. In order to make the money we need, we just have to be able to get seven hundred people an hour through this place."

"Seven hundred?" Robby chuckled. "That's about half the town."

"We'll have radio spots running on the campus station at Stanley U, ads in the *Harmony Herald* and the Stanley paper...If we can get all the young couples, the high school and the college kids, the ones who drive out to other towns and cities for a professional haunted house, if we can get them to stay in Harmony, to spend their money here instead...we might really be able to do some good. Upgrade equipment.

Buy some of those defibrillators for the elementary schools and the library."

Davies moved on, leading Robby farther down the new path, moving left into what should have been a living room or study. Now it resembled the woods where the spider-dog died. Tree trunks went from floor to ceiling; thick branches choking the path.

"You believe these are just cardboard carpet tubes?" Davies asked, grabbing one of the fake trees.

"Wow."

"We got holes drilled in the bases with lights inside. On opening night, we'll have two kinds of fog in here. We've got a regular fog machine to just fill the room, and what they call a 'fog chiller' to make this real thick, heavy stuff that'll cover the floor." He made sweeping gesture with his arms. "Then those holes make all these rays of light that shine through and make this creepy glow. We get an eerie little atmosphere going *and* the path gets lit at the same time."

Robby nodded. "Impressive. You going to have Jason come out with a chainsaw or something?"

"People are going to jump out, yeah, but unless you want all the money we make in here to go to legal fees for copyright suits, we need to have original ghosties and ghoulies, not those movie slashers. No *Texas Chainsaw*, no *Scream* – "

"No *Scream*?" Robby feigned upset. "Oh, come on!"

"Not unless you've got the money to pay Miramax. And if you did have the money to pay Miramax, we wouldn't have to put on this here haunted house in the first place. The last thing we need after all this work is to have a Cease and Desist order handed to us on opening night."

"Fine," Robby huffed.

Davies moved out of the faux forest. Robby followed him, a step or two behind, as if they were tethered by rope.

All I need is to get lost in here, he thought uneasily as he pushed the last branches out of his way.

They walked through a wrought iron gate (PVC pipe and wood painted black, actually), and into a narrow corridor. Lengths of chain hung down from the ceiling; Robby raked them out of his way. Skeletons lined the walls, covered over in a thick layer of artificial cobweb, their wrists shackled above their heads like forgotten prisoners in some movie dungeon.

"There'll be a strobe light in here," Davies informed him.

"Naturally." Robby reached out and touched the webbing with the tip of his finger, expecting it to be moist and sticky; instead, he found it dry and stiff. "So is there a theme to this haunt, or is it just a bunch of random, non-copyrighted horror crap?"

"There's nothing random about it. Every one of these rooms fits into an overall design based on the Fuller legend." Davies lowered his voice, trying his best to sound like the narration from Disney World's Haunted Mansion. "There are some places in this world that go far beyond any normal definitions of 'haunted.' These places are so evil, so *diabolical*, that they become gateways to Hell itself. The Fuller Farm is one such place.

"It's said that old man Fuller conducted bloodthirsty, indescribable acts within these walls, dark rituals and human sacrifices, all in an attempt to gain the ultimate knowledge, the ultimate *power*. And then, he was killed, horribly murdered on his own lands, leaving his home to stand as a vacant monument to his wickedness. But once a door is opened, it can never really be closed."

Robby frowned, and his thoughts turned once more to the crack in the stone wall beneath their feet.

"Now," Davies continued, "the stars are right, and the gateway is ready to once more unleash the unspeakable."

Unleash the unspeakable.

If all the stories turned out to be true, if by blood and black magic Fuller had somehow managed to open a doorway –

To what? Another planet? A parallel dimension? Hell itself?

Then the spider-dog might only be a harbinger of something truly wicked yet to come, something that still waited on the other side, biding its time all these years, waiting for just the right moment to strike.

Before his mind's eye could conjure up all manner of otherworldly horrors, Robby heard Davies laugh maniacally – a mix between Vincent Price and Snidely Whiplash. He winced and said, "Holy shit, Cap. We might need to start worrying about you, sleep with one eye open at night."

Davies chuckled and went on, "Anyway, that's our storyline. I talked to a lot of guys who've done this for years, and they all told me that it really helped to have one. It let everybody understand what we were goin' for before we even started building anything. People took different rooms and kind of made them their own, you know, but everything fits into the story.

"We're even making these big signs with the legend on them to stick outside in the waiting area. That way, everyone can get psyched up and freaked out even before they step into the place."

Robby nodded and rubbed his chin. "I thought the department was strapped for cash. Where's the money coming from for all this stuff?"

"Most of it's been donated: the wood, the foam, and building materials. The rest is whatever we've been able to beg, borrow, and steal. A few of the guys are out looking at garage sales, if you can believe that." He chuckled, then pointed back into the forest room. "I personally went dumpster diving behind Floor World for those cardboard tubes we used to make the trees."

They entered the next room. Robby saw people using what appeared to be hot glue guns with propellers on the ends to cover everything in the room with fake cobwebs. There were more bodies hanging around in here too – attached to the walls and suspended from the ceiling by thick, white ropes of webbing.

A gigantic black widow spider dropped down right in front of them. Its red eyes glowed brightly, its pincers and legs flexed and kicked, and it made a terrible, unnatural screeching sound.

Robby clutched his chest with one hand and the door frame with the other. "Jesus Christ!"

Davies laughed until he coughed.

Robby glared at him. "That shit's not funny."

"Yeah, it kinda is," Davies said, then he laughed and coughed some more.

"Somebody's gonna punch that thing."

"I don't think so. It's far enough back that they can't reach it from the door. They'll probably be too busy clutching their scared girlfriends and making a run for it."

Robby frowned and spoke from personal experience, "I don't know. Fear can make people do some pretty crazy things."

"If they do try anything –" Davies pointed to the corner of the room; a tiny black camera, not much bigger than a web cam, had been mounted to the wall, barely noticeable in all the natural rot and man-made décor. " – we've got the whole place wired for video. We'll have signs up, telling them they're being watched, and that we'll prosecute the little fuckers if they don't behave themselves."

"Looks like you've thought of everything."

"Tried to, but I'm sure there's something I missed that will come back to bite me on opening night."

"Opening night," Robby repeated with a smile. "Who's gone all Hollywood now?"

"Come on, I need to finish this tour so I can put you to work."

The next hallway had plain, white-painted walls.

"What's going in here?" Robby asked.

"Bleeding walls."

"No shit? Won't that stuff get on people's hands and clothes when they walk through? My friends and I used to use that stage blood stuff in high school. That shit stains. We're gonna end up with somebody's dry cleaning bill."

"Relax, would you. I've thought of everything, remember. Wait here."

Davies disappeared around a corner, leaving Robby alone in the dimly lit corridor. After a moment, lights came on overhead, illuminating the walls on either side. A drop of blood ran down the white-painted wall, leaving a crimson streak in its wake.

Robby reached out to touch it, but found nothing there. Nothing wet. Nothing sticky. Nothing at all. Then, a second drop appeared, this time running down the wall and over the top of his outstretched arm.

He smiled.

A projection.

A third streak followed, then a fourth, and so on, until the entire wall had been covered in red.

"Pretty slick, Cap," he called out.

Davies turned off the projector and stepped back into the hall. "Thanks. There's this company out of Bloomington called FearMart. They create all kinds of different projections for haunted attractions. I can have bugs crawling down the walls too, if we want."

"Bugs might be better," Robby told him. "I mean, coming out of the spider room and all."

"Nah, when you think of a haunted house, you think of bleeding walls."

No, when I *think of a haunted house, I think of* burning *walls, demon-possessed statues, and zombies with knives doing their best impersonation of the Human Torch, but maybe that's just me.*

Davies led him next into what looked like a mash-up of a torture chamber and an Aztec temple. Manacles were screwed into stone walls on three sides, some with emaciated bodies dressed in tattered, bloody rags, others empty and ready for new prisoners. The focus, however, appeared to be some kind of stone altar in the center of the room.

"This is where the Satanic farmer performed his human sacrifices," Davies told him. "We'll have somebody chained to the table, screaming their head off, while our zombiefied farmer threatens to cut out their heart with a knife."

"Where does the scare come from?"

"What do you mean?"

"Don't get me wrong," Robby pointed at the altar, "the room looks great, but if I walk in, and all there is here is some girl screaming, to me...there's nothing scary about that."

"Well," Davies went over to one of the empty manacles and put his hands up through it, making it appear as if he were hanging from the wall. "We'll have some actors in here made up to look similar to the fake prisoners, so the people won't know what's real and what's not –" He took one arm out of the restraint and reached out menacingly for Robby. "– until the real people break free."

"I think you missed your true calling, Cap. You should be working for Disney World or Universal Studios or something."

"It's a lot of fun, I ain't gonna lie, but I'd miss eating smoke too much to stick with it more than a month out of the year."

They left the altar behind and stepped into the kitchen, which had been transformed into a veritable cannibal buffet. Blood now splattered the tile walls and crumbling cabinets. Hanging meat hooks speared severed limbs and decapitated heads whose faces were frozen in rictus screams. And, in the center of the room, a bloody meat cleaver lay amid clumps of gore on an even bloodier chopping block, awaiting the hand of some fiendish master.

"The Butcher's Room," Davies said, proudly sweeping the abattoir with his hand. "Every haunt has to have one."

"Of course."

"We're going to have the farmer's wife in here. She'll be chopping up bodies when the people come through, then she'll chase them with that meat cleaver."

Robby nodded absently, his eyes drifting to the basement door. There was a shiny new Master Lock on it now. "You're not going to do anything down in the cellar?"

"Nope," Davies said. "Only one way in or out of that place, and we didn't think it was wise or safe to have people bottlenecked on those stairs in case of a fire."

"Shame," Robby told him. He couldn't seem to take his eyes off that padlock, the way the silver shone like Excalibur in the light, as if it held some sort of mystical power. And then, his mind's eye moved beyond the door, down the stairs into the total darkness it kept at bay. "I hear that place is creepy as hell."

"Wanna see it?"

"What...the basement?"

"Yeah. You wanna go have a quick look while we're here?"

"Seriously?"

"Why not."

"Sure, I guess." Robby shrugged and tried to act unimpressed. "You only live once, right?"

Davies chuckled. "You hope. Otherwise, you might find Sam Fuller down there, and he might not be happy to see you."

Ghosts were the least of Robby's worries, but while he knew the spider-dog and whatever else might show itself weren't supernatural, they were still far from natural. He reached into his jacket pocket, found the small plastic tube he now kept there, and curled his fingers around it.

Salt.

Ordinary table salt. He carried it with him, just in case. He didn't know if he would run into anything, and he didn't know if it would have an effect if he did, but he figured it couldn't hurt.

Davies walked over with a ring of keys, found the one that fit the new lock, and opened the door. "Here you go."

Robby took a step forward. "You comin', Cap."

"No thanks," he said with a smile, "but I promise not to lock you in."

"You're all heart."

Robby stepped onto the decades-old scaffold of stairs and began his descent. He took the small flash light out of his pocket, used it to light his way, keeping his other hand firmly on the vial of salt. So far, however, his spider-sense had yet to scream out a warning.

Because there's nothing to be scared of, he told himself. *You've been down here before, remember? Nothing was down here then, and nothing will be down here now.*

Nothing.

He reached the dirt floor and turned into the narrow hall. Blackness filled the yawning archway at the end of the passage. The smell of the place had not improved since his last visit, nor had the feel.

"You okay there, Miller?" Davies called down.

"Just fine, Cap." He aimed his faint light into the side rooms as he moved. "A shame we can't bring people down here. Lots of places to hide and leap out."

"I bet."

Robby reached the chamber at the end of the hall. The symbols were still there. And the back wall remained broken.

Did you think you'd find anything different?
No. He didn't. Still, he entered with caution.
Nothing to fear. Nothing at all.

Robby let go of the salt container for a moment and dug into another pocket for his smart phone. He flicked it on and aimed the tiny camera lens at the first etching, the one that looked like a many-legged cactus. Was this someone's idea of what the spider-dog looked like?

He snapped a photo of it with his cell and moved on.

On the opposite wall, Robby took a picture of the three interconnecting "C"s. He then swung to take a picture of the snake curled up inside the ring, wondering what they symbolized. Perhaps they were meant to be in the opposite order – a creature imprisoned, lying in wait until the vessel that holds it is smashed and broken?

Robby turned back toward the final symbol: the star with the human eye at its center. When most people saw a five-pointed star like this, a pentagram, they just assumed it was Satanic. While that would fit in nicely with the Fuller legend, Robby had done enough research on Pagan religions and the occult over the years to know these stars were not always used for evil.

A true Devil's pentagram would have featured a goat's head as its centerpiece, not this crude human eye. And at the very least, Fuller, or whoever created the star, should have drawn it pointing down, toward the dirt floor and Hell below, not aiming for the rafters.

Okay, so it's a Pagan religion, but not a Satanic one. Robby frowned. *That really narrows it down.*

Whatever belief system this symbol sprang from, Robby knew that all upturned pentagrams worked roughly the same way. Four of the points were used to represent elemental forces in nature –

Earth, wind, and fire, just add water...

– while the fifth and final point, the one facing the heavens, was meant to signify "the spirit." When pointing up, as this one was, a pentagram represented the spiritual world holding dominion over the physical one, all working in communion to create new life.

But what kind of life? Robby wondered. *And from where?*

Not all the lines were straight, he noticed. In fact, the center part of the star reminded Robby of the *Star Trek* symbol; curved on the left side and arched at the bottom beneath the eye. Although whether this was intentional, made by someone in a far too big a hurry, or simply proof that Fuller had absolutely no artistic ability was still unclear.

Davies called out again, "You still alive down there, Miller?"

"Comin', Cap."

Before he left, Robby snapped a quick picture of the cyclopean pentagram, wishing he knew what it was meant to see.

CHAPTER TWENTY

Yes, I see! I see it, my lords...my gods! At last...at long last...
Cayden Donnelly felt the images slipping away again, felt the powerful sensations dulling once more, leaving him numb, but this time, he wasn't upset to see it all fade. And when he awoke, he awoke with a smile on his face for the first time in years.

He sat up and looked around. Another strange room. Another strange bed. Another stranger's skin draped over his body in heavy, wet clumps.

The girl's body lay next to him, growing cold beneath the warm blanket. She stared up at the ceiling, her eyes clouded and unseeing. But in death, she had made Cayden's vision gloriously clear.

Harmony.

No, that wasn't her name at all. Cayden couldn't actually remember *what* her name had been, and quite frankly, it was of little importance. All that mattered, all that ever really mattered, was finding the identity of his final destination – the place where his existence would finally have meaning.

And now, he'd found it.

Cayden peeled the flayed bits of stranger's flesh from his chest, from his arms and lower body, then tossed them aside. Some of the blood had clotted and hardened against his skin, but much of it remained sticky. He swung his legs over the side of the bed, resting his feet on the carpet. It felt soft and warm, like a sheep's pelt.

The blade sat on a bedside table. Cayden snatched it up and went looking for the *Fir*. He had to clean himself up, to clean the blade, but first and foremost on his needs list: he had to take a piss.

He walked down the hall, stepping on his and hers clothes along the way. The first door he came to opened on a *pantrach*; boxes of granola, Quinoa Flakes, and jar after jar containing various varieties of nuts.

Bloody hell. Was she a fuckin' squirrel?

The next door opened to a washer and drier, but the third room he came to, thankfully, had a toilet. He lifted the lid and relieved himself, his cock in one hand and the blade in the other. Cayden moaned loudly at the ceiling, then looked around.

Long stemmed flowers bloomed from glass vases on the granite countertop, matching the blossoms printed on the shower curtain. A glass bowl lay beneath the tall, curbed faucet instead of a traditional sink. Towels had been rolled and stacked neatly in a wooden cabinet. Make-up and skin care products sat on a mirrored tray. And a huge looking glass reflected Cayden's wide eyes and muscular arse.

Jeezus...More of a Mná than a Fir.

He chuckled, gave his member a final shake, then turned the shower on. The water warmed quickly. He stepped into the spray, set the blade down on the edge of the tub, then picked up the soap and sniffed it – a fresh scent, but not overpowering.

Don't want to smell like I fell in a vat of perfume, now do I?

Cayden washed himself, watching the water turn crimson as it ran off his feet and circled the drain.

Nothing more powerful in this world than the blood of a woman.

Of course, there was nothing more dangerous either. He knew that. He was no fool. Too many dead bodies pop up skinned in your wake and you might as well leave your fucking calling card for the police. But he'd never been this close before, and he couldn't risk losing again.

The rune stone dangled from his neck, water washing over its flawless black surface, the eye winking at him from its star. Cayden frowned down at it.

There had been bad images in this last vision. One of the Old Ones had been killed, slain by the hands of men. Well, two men and one woman, the same woman who had escaped its grasp that first night, when the gateway had opened just a crack.

Nothing more powerful in this world than a woman.

Cayden knew his lords feared that power, and they were right to do so. After all, it was the *first* woman, Eve, in which the seeds of their exile had been planted. So now, it was only fitting that one of her descendants would be the key to unlocking their prison.

Sherry, like a fine wine, like a celebration.

No. It wasn't spelled that way, was it? He concentrated, trying to remember.

It's Sheri, with an "I," as in "I am the key."

Cayden reached out for the blade, brought it under the stream and washed it until the metal gleamed, until he could see himself in it. His smile slowly returned; his eyes sparkling, nearly manic with joy.

"When Irish eyes are smiling," he sang, staring at his own reflection in the blade. "All the world seems bright and gay."

For once in his life, he knew exactly where he was going, what he was meant to do once he got there. For once in his life, things were going his way.

"And when Irish eyes are smiling, sure they steal your heart away."

He turned around and around beneath the water, actually dancing a little jig. There would be no stopping him this time.

CHAPTER TWENTY-ONE

When her iPod shuffled to Rhianna's "Rude Boy," Sheri normally dropped everything, got up on her feet, and made a complete fool of herself. Today, however, she didn't feel much like dancing. Instead, she sat on her couch, surrounded by stacks of paper, grading book reports.

Her students had been assigned to read Nathaniel Hawthorne's *The Scarlet Letter* and then to write five hundred words on its themes. Did Hester Prynne's punishment fit the crime? Why or why not?

In Hawthorne's day, the upper case letter "A" stitched to your frock was a symbol of mortal sin, a badge of shame for all to see and shun. But, in the age of MTV's *Jersey Shore*, *16 and Pregnant*, and *Teen Mom*, these teenagers had an entirely different notion of sin and guilt. And, so far, Sheri hadn't scrawled many scarlet letters across the results of their work.

"They knew what would happen and they *still* didn't use a condom," one student commented. "They got what they deserved."

She wondered for a moment if it were possible to get an "F" in history and literature with a single paper, then she thought about how sad it was that she actually knew the date the first condoms went on sale.

Another of her students wrote, "All the Puritanical craziness was crazy. They'd all die of heart attacks if they were still alive today watching Snooki and Jwoww."

But her absolute favorite had to be: "The people back then were stupid. Hester thought the old man she married was dead. Why wouldn't she sleep with somebody else? What, she's supposed to be a nun for the rest of her life?"

It's hard to argue with that, Sheri thought before reading on, her red pen tapping the page. *You just might earn yourself a scarlet letter! We both might.*

Hester's husband, Roger Chillingworth, had supposedly been lost at sea. No body. No bones. No bloody clothes. No proof of any kind. But everyone assumed he was dead, until he just showed up one day unannounced and found his wife had given birth to another man's child.

You know what happens when you assume, she thought, then chuckled to herself humorlessly. *Should've used a condom. Then nobody would have to know, right? No sin. No guilt. No problem. .*

Sheri set her red pen down and rubbed her tired eyes. She'd been with Jeff for such a very long time, but she had no more tears left to shed, no curses left to be uttered against God and this cruel universe of His. The well had gone dry. And that led to a deep sense of remorse, to her own feelings of guilt and shame.

Stop it, she told herself. *Shame and guilt are just some crazy Puritanical craziness, remember? What, are you just supposed to become a nun?*

When the phone rang, Sheri no longer answered it because she thought there might be news. Gone was that mix of dread and uncertainty that had plagued her early on, because now she knew that whoever spoke on the other end of the line had nothing new to say about the case. There *was* no case anymore. Oh sure, there had been a few half-hearted searches since that interview on *Today,* but the police had switched into recovery mode – they only went out there to look for a body, to cross the "T"s and dot the "I"s on their reports – and they had recovered nothing.

It took them thirty-two years to find the bloody clothes from that baby in Australia, the one the dingoes ate. Do you really want to put your life on hold for thirty-two years? And what if they never found anything at all? What then?

No. No one wanted that. No one wanted to wait. Not the police. Not the courts. Not even Jeff's family.

So, as of a week ago, Jeff had been ruled dead. Normally, in the absence of a body, it would have taken a court order to get them to issue a death certificate. But, as the cold, legally-worded letter to Jeff's parents had put it, "in this case, there is circumstantial evidence that would lead a reasonable person to conclude that this individual is deceased on the balance of probabilities," and so the state had killed him on paper.

It wasn't unheard of, the speed with which the authorities had acted. Without so much as a bone or scrap of cloth, they had declared the missing passengers and crew of the *Titanic* legally dead; they'd done it just as soon as the *Carpathia* hit New York harbor with its load of survivors. In September of 2001, death certificates had been issued for the 3,000 victims of the World Trade Center within days of the attack. When soldiers went missing after a major battle, the military usually did the same. And, when that aforementioned Australian baby first vanished into the wilderness, even when no one actually believed she'd been eaten alive, the authorities had seen fit to declare her dead in short order – if for no other reason than to get on with the business of railroading her innocent mother.

Guilt, innocence...let society be the judge.

Jeff's family held a memorial service. Sheri had never been to a funeral without a casket before, and it provided yet another chance for everyone to cry, but very little in the way of true closure. It just didn't seem real.

She reached into her pocket and popped another Nicorette onto her tongue, wondering how long it would be before the cravings stopped. And how sad would it be if it actually took longer for her to get over cigarettes than it did to get over Jeff? What would that say about her?

Everyone grieves differently. The books all say as much.

Sheri had downloaded more than one book on grief, and they all told her that what she'd been going through was perfectly normal, that feelings naturally faded in time, became less raw, but none of them gave her the answers she sought. Not one could tell her *how much* time. And she could find no hint as to when it was right for her to have feelings for another man.

You're not looking for answers. You're looking for permission, *and you're not going to find that in any book.*

She'd finished with the self-help books and moved on to lying to herself, which hadn't been much help either. She tried to convince her confused little brain that this attraction wasn't real, that she'd simply been lonely without Jeff. But the harder she tried, the more she knew different.

When her phone rang at night, Sheri certainly didn't hurry to answer it because of Jeff. No. She was quick to pick up that receiver because she hoped to hear Robby Miller's voice on the line.

He'd called frequently to check on her, to see how she'd been doing, and best of all, just to talk. It was so nice to have a conversation with someone and not feel like she had to have her guard up the whole time. Those conversations had been the lone bright spots of her otherwise dreary days.

But with each call, at the back of her mind, she kept wondering: *Is he going to ask me out this time? And, if he does, what will I say? Will I take a moment to think it through, or will I just blurt out an answer and hope it's the right one?*

"I really like him," she said aloud, her voice anemic, almost apologetic. There. It was finally out in the open. She'd uttered it with complete frankness, complete honesty. She liked another man, and it felt so...

Wrong.

Robby was a good-looking guy. Muscular. Mature. Funny. Intelligent. And he certainly wasn't afraid to say what he was thinking, to stick to his convictions, no matter how they might sound to Sheri or anyone else.

And this attraction hadn't been a one way street either. Oh, no.

Sheri had caught Robby glancing at her on more than one occasion, when he thought she wasn't looking. Not sympathetic glances, either, but the appreciative glances of someone who liked what they saw.

She'd actually had dreams of being with him, fantasies of how it would feel to touch her lips to his, her *body* to his. She'd found these thoughts a bit disturbing at first, but then, as they grew more intense, more *passionate*, the visions frightened her more than any nightmare of the spider-dog. How could she think of making love to Robby when she should still be mourning Jeff?

Her feelings of guilt deepened, as if by letting go of Jeff's memory she was slowly killing him all over again. But as that fear of being unfaithful grew within her mind, so too did her strong attraction to Robby.

You haven't done anything wrong. Jeff would want you to be happy.

Sheri shifted uncomfortably in her seat and tried to focus once more on her grading, trying not to see herself as a modern day Hester Prynne in need of a good branding. Then again, based on these papers, it appeared that she could walk around Harmony with a big, fat scarlet "A" on her breast and nobody else but her would even give a damn. She uttered a long, trembling sigh and wondered if she should make the first move, let her feelings be known to Robby the next time he called. She wanted to, she really did, but she feared his reaction, no matter what it might be.

As the books said, there's no right answer. Everyone's different. Everyone needs –

The doorbell rang, making her jump.

Sheri got up, walked barefoot across her living room to the front door, and peered through her peephole. She saw Robby Miller standing outside, waiting patiently on her stoop, looking like a bobblehead figure in the fish-eyed lens.

Speak of the devil!

She spun toward the mirror on the wall behind her, gave herself a quick once over, ran her fingers through her hair, then turned back, her heartbeat quickening in her chest as she fumbled with the chain.

"Making house calls now?" she asked, trying not to smile.

"I'm not a doctor," Robby replied; he held a bottle of wine in one hand and a bucket of chicken in the other. "I'm just an EMT."

"You're a bit more than that," she told him, leaning against the door, feeling the cool wood against her flushed face. Her hand was firmly on her hip, as if to scold one of her students for forgetting their homework. "You're a celebrity, remember? A monster slayer. All the papers said so."

"I get enough of that crap from the guys at the station." He chuckled. "*You* were more of a monster slayer than I was, Queen Taser."

She smiled in spite of herself, her cheeks still uncomfortably warm. "So...What brings you out here?"

"I know it's late, and I probably should have called first, but I needed to talk to you, get your opinion."

"And you felt the need to soften me up with chicken and booze?"

He looked down at his laden arms and shrugged. "I hadn't eaten anything yet, so I stopped off and got this. Guess my eyes are bigger than my stomach, because there's no way I'm going to eat all this chicken by myself. So see, you have to let me in. You wouldn't want it to go to waste, would you?"

Sheri nodded at the bucket, still smiling. "Original or extra-crispy?"

"Both."

"Well, what are you waiting for?"

She held the door open for him and Robby stepped inside. He wore a navy blue T-shirt with a white HFD – Harmony Fire Department – across the chest, and tight blue jeans. Sheri couldn't help but notice the way his eyes darted to and fro as she led him back into her living room, as if he were expecting to see someone else here in the house. Perhaps he detected the ghosts of cigarettes past, the odor of stale smoke that all the Febreze in the world had failed to evict. If so, he made no mention of it.

More likely it's Jeff's ghost he's looking for, she thought humorlessly, and a chill waltzed up her back. *Waiting to see if stuff starts hurling at him from around the room.*

On the mantel, her iPod dock started broadcasting Framing Hanley, a cover of Lil Wayne's "Lollipop." Sheri rushed over and quickly turned it off. "You...uh...mind eating in here around the coffee table?" she asked, her hand suddenly on her forehead, stroking her temple. "My kitchen's kind of a mess."

He smiled. "That's how I eat at home."

She pointed to the bottle in his hand. "What's that?"

"Wine."

"I can see that."

"Oh..." He chuckled. "Right. It's *Oliver* wine. Mango."

"Mango? Does mango-flavored wine go with fried chicken?"

Robby shrugged. "To be honest, I didn't know *what* kind of wine went with fried chicken."

They both giggled at that, and then they stood there a moment in awkward silence.

Sheri quickly pointed into the kitchen. "I'll just go get us some glasses and a screw – corkscrew." She made a few awkward steps toward the doorway, then added, "Make yourself at home."

She turned the corner, frowning.

Make yourself at home? Sheri shook her head. *Jesus!*

For a moment, she stood at the sink, her fingers gripping the edge of the countertop, her eyes on her own reflection in the window. She hadn't died in that car with the spider-dog scratching at the glass. She'd fought for her life. She'd wanted to live. It was time she actually got around to *living*.

She opened the silverware drawer, found her corkscrew, and called out, "Is the wine supposed to be cold, or room temperature?"

"Beats me."

She took two wine glasses from her cabinet. "Would it be totally uncouth if we had wine over ice?"

"That's fine. I've never had much couth to begin with."

Sheri smiled at the ceiling, then walked over to her fridge and let it spit ice cubes into the glasses. "You...uh...said you had something to talk to me about?"

"We'll get to it," he told her. "But first, let's eat. I'm starving!"

When she came back into the room, she found Robby kneeling at the coffee table in front of an empty paper plate. A matching plate lay on her side of the table, and tubs of coleslaw and mashed potatoes sat between them.

"You came prepared," she said.

"Didn't think it would be nice to show up at your door and expect you to do dishes."

Add thoughtful to the list.

Robby picked up his wine bottle and reached for the corkscrew. "Allow me to do the honors."

She handed it over, then knelt down and placed the glasses in front of him.

"You know," he said, "they actually make a Bill Clinton one of these."

"A Bill Clinton corkscrew?"

"You can find them on Amazon. The corkscrew is..." He stabbed the cork and twisted. "Well, where Little Bill should be."

Sheri smiled, feeling that twinge of guilt again. "They could make one of those for just about any politician anymore. I don't know what it is about men and power, but as soon as they get it, it seems they start screwin' around."

Robby popped the cork and said, "That's why they also make a Hillary nutcracker."

She stared at him a moment with her mouth open, and then she burst out laughing. It was a short, hard burst, as if a dam had just broken and released all the tension that had been building up within her. Best of all, the laughter felt good.

He laughed too, not as loud or as hard as she did, but she could see him relax a bit afterward. Robby poured the wine over ice, then handed her a glass. "Should we make some kind of toast?"

"How about...to laughter and good times?"

"Sounds good to me."

Their glasses came together with a loud *clink*, and they laughed again.

He shoveled coleslaw onto his plate and nodded at the papers that still littered her couch. "Did I interrupt something?"

"Just a fun-filled night of marking up assignments. My red pen's almost out of ink."

"Ouch! Glad I'm not one of your students."

"They're reading Hawthorne. He's pretty dense."

"As in dumb?"

She snickered. "*No.* As in hard to read and understand."

"Oh, come on. When I was in school, I found his Cliffnotes fascinating."

Sheri rolled her eyes at him. "He's an important American author, but half these kids don't read much at all, and the half that do read find him completely boring. If they really wanted me to get the kids excited about literature, they'd let me teach *Harry Potter* or *Twilight*."

"They don't let you teach *Twilight*?" Robby grinned. "The school board must have gotten a whole lot smarter since I went there."

"Stop," Sheri told him. "At least it gets them to read *something*."

"When I was a kid, I used to love Ray Bradbury. *The Martian Chronicles. Fahrenheit 451.*"

"I bet *Fahrenheit* is a big hit down at the fire station." She took a bite of chicken, chewed slowly, then said, "I'm going to have them read *Something Wicked This Way Comes* in October for Halloween. It's hard to get enough books for the class right now. Since Bradbury died, his stuff has been in high demand. I always think it's sad that an author, or any artist for that matter, is never truly appreciated until after their death."

Robby put down his spork and held up his hand in a dramatic pose. "Death, the undiscovered country, from whose bourn no traveler returns."

"*Hamlet*," she said with a smile, pleasantly surprised. "You know *Hamlet*?"

"Not all of it by heart, but yeah, I've read it a few times." He chuckled. "Maybe I've got some couth after all."

"With all you know about...you know, horror stuff, I just figured you more for a Stephen King, Dean Koontz kind of guy."

He shrugged. "I guess I get too much supernatural, paranormal, horror crap in my real life. The last thing I want to do is read about it. Not really my idea of fun."

They ate in relative silence after that, but Sheri found her gaze being drawn to him again and again, and at one point, their eyes met. There had been a spark in that instant, not the grand finale of the Fourth of July show, but it had been white hot while it lasted. She guessed Robby felt it too.

He looked away first and was slow to find his voice, "So...I – I did do some reading this afternoon."

"Do tell."

"I was out at the Fuller place again earlier today."

Sheri frowned and lowered her eyes to her plate, moving the mashed potatoes around with her spork. "Are they still going through with that haunted house thing?"

"Oh yeah. I don't think I've ever seen Cap this excited. You should have been there."

"You'd have to tie me up and drag me."

Robby was quiet for a moment. He took a bite of chicken, washed it down with some wine, then went on, "I was there doing my bit to help out, painting props and what-not, but I was able to sneak away long enough to snap a few pictures of those symbols we found."

"Are you taking up scrapbooking?"

"*No.* I went and did some research on our friend Farmer Fuller, spent a few hours down in the basement of the Harmony Public Library, digging through old copies of the *Herald* from the forties. Some very interesting reading."

"I bet." She took another sip of her wine. "World War II. Always my favorite period in American history. Did you know that the P-47 fighter-plane was manufactured right here in the great state of Indiana?"

"No shit?"

"I shit you not." Sheri giggled and lifted her glass. "In Evansville, to be exact."

"Well, did *you* know that, from 1940 to 1946, half a dozen people went missing in this town?"

Her smile withered; she lowered her glass and felt her stomach sank right along with it.

"Half a dozen people in six years," he continued. "One a year, to be exact. All of them vanishing between the months of August and October – right around the harvest. Three young, unmarried girls between the ages of twenty and thirty, and three children, the youngest only two years old.

"They just..." He lifted his hands and wiggled his fingers. "... disappeared."

"Jesus."

"Want to know how many people went missing in the next six years, after Fuller met the threshing machine?"

"Zero," she managed, her mouth now totally dry.

"No, two."

She slumped, put her elbow on the table, and rested her forehead against the heel of her hand. "Okay, you just lost me. I mean, if people were still disappearing after Fuller's death, I don't see – "

"People go missing all the time, Sheri," Robby told her, "especially in a rural area like this. People get lost in the woods and die of exposure. Kids get hot, they take a dip in the limestone quarry, and they drown.

"But the two that went missing from 1947 to 1953 got lost at different times of the year, one in July, the other in February – an eighty-year-old widow who evidently left her front door open and decided to go for a walk in the middle of a blizzard."

"And how about the first one?" Sheri asked.

"A toddler who wondered off into the woods during a family barbeque," he said as if it were unimportant, then went on with the story he apparently wanted to tell, "And, here's the key difference: their bodies were found. They came across the old woman after the first thaw, and a group of hunters eventually stumbled on the little boy's bones. Those other people, the ones who went missing while Fuller was still alive, were *never* found. No bodies. No bones. When I said 'disappeared,' I meant it. All six vanished off the face of the Earth."

"Like Jeff."

"Yes, just like Jeff."

"So, you think that he was...What? Literally spirited away by Sam Fuller's ghost?"

"Not exactly."

"Then what?"

Robby reached into the red and white bucket for another chicken leg. "How much do you know about the Druids?"

"Didn't they worship trees or something like that?"

He finished the leg off in world record time, then said, "Julius Caesar claimed that they practiced human sacrifice on a massive scale. 'Their gods delight in the slaughter of prisoners and criminals,' he said, 'and when the supply of captives runs short, they sacrifice even the innocent.'"

"And we know what a shining example of humanity Julius Caesar was," Sheri pointed out.

"Well," Robby said, dropping the naked chicken bone onto his empty plate, "the Celts didn't keep a written history, so the Romans' word used to be all there was to go on."

"Used to be?"

"There's been some recent archaeological finds in Britain and Ireland," Robby explained, working on his own glass of wine. "Some pretty gruesome stuff that suggest Caesar wasn't stretching the truth. If anything, he may have even sanitized it. We're talking about cannibalism and...the ritual sacrifice of women and children."

They exchanged a glance, but this time there was no heat to it. No. This time, Sheri felt a chill that cut her to the bone.

"Are you saying what I think you're saying?" she asked, not sure she wanted to hear the answer.

"Those symbols we found in the cellar?" Robby said, then he upended his glass and drained the last drop of mango wine before continuing. "They belonged to an ancient Druidic sect, kind of a cult within a cult."

Sheri heard herself say, "Like my Russian Nesting Dolls."

Robby flashed a grin at that, but it faded as quickly as it had appeared. "The Romans came back from Britain with all kinds of horror stories about the priests of this sect. They said that, by eating the flesh of women and children, the cultists gained both physical and spiritual strength. They also said that the magic was most potent if the sacrifices were performed during this time of the year."

"Military propaganda," Sheri began, "trying to make the enemy look like a bunch of savages. Getting back to World War II, look at all the racist posters that showed Japanese soldiers as big-toothed rapists! 'Keep the horrors from your home,' they said. 'Buy War Bonds!' they said. It was all to make the bad guys look...well...*bad*, and the home team grand by comparison."

"I'm not denying some of that went on," Robby admitted, holding up his chicken bone for emphasis, "but you've got modern scientists now finding bodies that have been *gnawed* on – human teeth marks on human bones, children's bones. And these symbols are carved into all of them."

"And you got all this from the library?"

"Well, the library and Google."

Sheri chuckled at that. "And we all know that anything you find on Google is a hundred percent accurate!"

Robby sat there for a moment, smiling at her, but the grin never touched his eyes. When at last he spoke, he sounded both weary and worried, "Even if it's only fifty percent accurate, it still scares the shit out of me."

"Let's say you're right," Sheri granted, and she could not help but shiver at the thought of it. "Let's say Fuller was some Ku Klux Klan cannibal, doing human sacrifices and barbecuing babies in his cellar so that his corn grows taller – "

At the word "corn," she noticed Robby jerk; the color drained from his face with the suddenness of mercury in a freezer thermometer.

"Are you okay?" she asked.

"I'm fine," he told her. "Go on."

She hesitated a moment, then said, "Well, what happened to all the bodies? Did he bury them there in the cellar? Did anybody bother to take a look after he died?"

"I doubt it," Robby told her. "I made the connection between Fuller and the disappearances, but the papers didn't. There were probably as many serial killers lurking around then as there are now, but I think we're just more conscious of them now, more *aware*. I don't think it even occurred to the police and reporters of the time that this kind of thing could be possible."

"And where was Mrs. Fuller during all this?" Sheri wanted to know. "Did she have any idea her hubby was pulling a Jeffrey Dahmer down in the fruit cellar?"

Robby cocked his head, his color slowly returning. "I don't know if she knew about the kidnappings and the sacrifices, but something sure spooked her. She took off one night, dragged the kids down to her sister's place in Atlanta, and never set foot in the house again. And back in the forties? Well, that shit just didn't happen.

"The cops actually thought she might have pushed Fuller into that thresher for a time. Rumor has it, when they called her to tell her that her husband was dead, she said, 'Thank God.'"

Sheri shook her head. "Sounds like he was a real winner."

"Problem was...the wife had a truckload of alibis. There was a half-hearted investigation, but ultimately, they ruled it an accident."

"An *accident*," Sheri repeated, making air quotes with her fingers. "You think somebody else found out what he was up to? Someone actually had to *kill him* to get him to stop?"

"Maybe." Robby shrugged. "Or maybe he thought that the sacrifices he'd performed had made him *so* powerful that he'd become the *ultimate* sacrifice. Maybe he thought that, with so much power, if he sacrificed himself, the door he'd opened just a crack over the years might finally open all the way. Maybe – "

"Maybe he realized that he was one sick son-of-a-bitch psycho torturer, and he committed suicide because he just couldn't live with it anymore."

Robby shrugged. "I guess we'll never know."

"Exactly. We'll never know."

The conversation seemed to skip a beat then – as if they both needed a moment to catch their breath.

Then Robby said, "But, Sheri...What if that doorway is still open, even if it's only a small crack?"

"If that's true, why haven't we seen a spider-dog before now? If there is this crack, why haven't dozens of them slipped through it over the years?"

"I've wondered about that." He pointed at her with his spork. "You remember that story I told you about the Wampus Cat?"

"Yes."

"Well, what if there *have* been spider-dogs before?"

"A Native- American legend would pre-date Fuller."

Robby nodded. "The gateway might be a lot older than we know."

"Still...I leave my door open just a crack for five minutes and my house is full of flies. If this door's been cracked for sixty years, or even a hundred and sixty years, I would think that —"

He cut her off, "We've been down there in that basement a few times since that first night, right?"

"*You* have."

"And we've never seen any mystic door."

"And what does a mystic door look like?"

"I don't know," Robby admitted, "but I would think we'd recognize one if we saw it."

Sheri grinned.

"The point is," Robby went on to say, "what if somebody's decided to pick up where Fuller left off? What if the gate only opens if there's a sacrifice? What if Jeff was it?"

"Because Jeff fits in so well with the Celts' modus operandi of women and children."

Robby frowned. "Maybe it was a crime of opportunity. Jeff was in the wrong place at just the right time."

"No argument there."

"And what if the spider-dog was only the opening act? What if the main event is still to come?"

"That's a whole lot of 'what if's," Sheri told him.

"I suppose it is."

"So where does that leave us?" she asked.

"In serious need of another drink," Robby told her. He reached for the bottle, half-filled his own glass, then held it out to her. "More wine?"

"I better not," she told him. "Too much wine and I get..."

"Silly?"

"Horny."

"Oh." He looked at her, startled, then put the bottle down. "Well, we don't want that."

"Don't we?" She set her glass aside, then turned back to him, trying to think of what to say, and shocked to hear that she'd already started speaking, "I have to know...You *are* attracted to me, right?"

Robby reached across the table and took her hand in his own. "I'm *very* attracted to you."

"Good." She exhaled and gave a slow nod. "That's good."

"And I *do* want you."

Her smile withered before it had even fully bloomed. "There's going to be a 'but,' isn't there?"

"*But –*" He gave her hand a gentle squeeze. " – I don't think you're ready yet."

"You sure about that diagnosis, Not-a-doctor Robby?"

"It doesn't take a doctor to know that you're still hurting."

"So, help me stop hurting."

Robby stroked her hand with his thumb. "If we...went through with this tonight – "

"Yes." Sheri flashed a grin that was meant to be sexy, but she felt her lips trembling; she shivered all over.

" – I'd just be taking advantage of you. And I like you too much for that. To quote another great, important American writer, Quentin Tarantino..." He cleared his throat and tried to sound dramatic again. "I might be a bastard, but I'm not a fucking bastard."

She snickered in spite of her disappointment, and they looked at each other wordlessly for a time.

"I should go," he said at last, nodding at the unfinished grading on her couch, "let you get back to crushing the dreams of our youth."

He hesitated, thoughtful, and she could not help but wonder what he was thinking. Then, he leaned across the table and gave her a kiss. It was brief, maybe five seconds, but she liked it. She liked Robby.

Add gentleman to the list.

"Rain check?" he asked when their lips parted.

"Any time."

"I can find my way out." He got to his feet, his eyes never leaving her, his face serious. "Do you have any salt in the house?"

"There's a big thing of Morton's in the pantry."

Robby nodded. "Do me a favor? Keep it close, just in case."

"I will," she promised, watching him walk across the room. "Don't stop calling to check on me."

"I won't," he assured her; he checked the locks and then he was out the door, leaving her alone once more.

Sheri sighed. She reached across the table for the wine bottle and refilled her glass.

Well, that went well, she thought.

CHAPTER TWENTY-TWO

Winding sidewalks crisscrossed Stanley University, connecting students from the various dorms and fraternity houses to their crowded lecture halls, their classrooms, and their labs. Dr. Graeme King strolled down one such walkway, headed for Orr Hall – home to the zoology department. At four stories, it was one of the tallest buildings on campus; it was also one of the oldest – fashioned of Indiana limestone, dug from a quarry just north of Harmony, and covered in a healthy growth of ivy.

Graeme looked up at the heavens. Even in a rural area like this, there was still too much light pollution to see the stars clearly. Jupiter was visible, however. He could see it low to the horizon, just above the trees; a bright yellowish ball of light.

365 million miles, 588 million kilometers, 0.0000621 light years away, or just a hop, skip, and a jump across an Einstein-Rosen bridge.

He chuckled to himself and turned his attention back to the path. On more than one occasion, he'd been walking with his head quite literally in the stars, studying the planets and constellations, calculating the time it took for their light to reach his eyes, and he'd barreled right into students and other faculty, nearly knocking them down. The walkway was clear tonight, however, and he continued on his trek, making quick work of the steps to Orr Hall.

Dr. Kathy Ward met him at the door with a smile. "Glad I could drag you out of your office and away from your work, Graeme."

He smiled back at her. "The universe will still be there when I return. Besides, it's a beautiful night for a walk."

"That it is."

"So, you said you had something exciting for me to look at?"

Kathy's smile widened. "I did, and I do."

"I have to admit, I'm a little bit curious to know why a zoologist would need to consult a theoretical physicist."

"When you see what I've been working on these last few weeks, everything will become quite clear."

Graeme followed her inside, through a few more sets of swinging doors, and down a metal staircase into the bowels of Orr Hall. It was here, in the locked rooms that lined these shady corridors, that the university kept its vast collection of specimens for study. They entered one such door, and the good doctor turned on the overhead lights.

Kathy's lab was the size of a subway station. Rows of metal examination tables filled the room. Various anatomical charts had been tacked to the walls, mapping the skeletal and muscular structures of a dozen or more species. Wooden models of dinosaur skeletons sat between two microscopes and three computer monitors and keyboards. Shelves were lined with jars, filled with fetal pigs, cow heads, brains and stomachs, hearts and bladders of some variety. And, on the opposite wall, a row of freezer doors, the kind you might find in a grocery store, except what lay inside was not meant for consumption.

She moved toward one of the exam tables and covered it in a surgical drape. "You keep up with the news, don't you, Graeme?"

"I do my best."

"Then, you've probably read or seen reports of the strange animal that was causing some trouble over in Harmony a few weeks back." Kathy reached into the pocket of her lab coat and produced a pair of blue, plastic gloves; she slid them onto her hands with a snap and a puff of powder hung in the air, the particles drifting. "It fed on the local livestock and killed two people."

Graeme nodded, excitement and curiosity making his heart thump wildly within his chest. In his mind, the same question, stuck in a Mobius loop: *What does she need* me *for?* "I saw some fuzzy video, heard them say it was the Mexican goat sucker, *La Chupacabra.*"

She chuckled at that. "You might also have heard that the body of said animal was turned over to this fine university for identification and study."

"I do recall hearing something about that, yes."

"And study it we have." Kathy gripped the freezer handle and gave it a tug.

The door opened with a hiss, releasing a white fog that billowed out into the lab. The temperature of the room plummeted, and Graeme recoiled from the chill.

"We took X-rays, blood and tissue samples, ran its DNA, and we found some very surprising results." Kathy glanced back at him, then disappeared inside the cold storage.

For a moment, Graeme was tempted to peek around the corner into the freezer, then thought better of it. "Are you familiar with Schrödinger's cat?"

"No," she called back, and Graeme heard the sounds of plastic bags crinkling. "Anything like Pavlov's dog?"

"Not exactly." Graeme crossed his arms over his chest. "It's basic quantum mechanics.

"There is a cat inside a closed box. Schrödinger proposed that, while the lid remains shut, the animal simultaneously exists in both living and dead states of being; it is only when the box is opened, and an actual observation is performed, that the cat settles into one of the two possible states."

"So," Kathy called, still tinkering around within the cooler, "are you saying that, on any given day, I've got a 50/50 chance of opening up this freezer and finding a bunch of pissed off specimens waiting to pounce?"

Graeme chuckled. "If you believe Schrödinger."

"If a tree falls in the forest, and there's nobody there to hear it, does it still make a sound?"

A squeaking sound filled the air, like a shopping cart with a bad wheel, followed by the dull thud of something large striking metal.

"Is that what you do all day long in that office of yours, Graeme?" Kathy asked. "Sit around and think up mind benders?"

"Part of the fun of theoretical physics."

"Well," Kathy countered, "*this* is part of the fun of being a zoologist." She finally reappeared from the unseen depths of the freezer, pushing a squeaky-wheeled cart on which rested what appeared to be a body bag. "Actually *finding* mind benders."

Graeme's eyes traveled the length of the bag's lumpy, irregular shape, trying to picture what it concealed. Kathy slid it onto the exam table and kicked the squeaky cart out of her way; she then unzipped the bag and motioned for Graeme.

"Come on over," she said. "Have a look. Believe me, the fuzzy video did not do it justice."

As he strode carefully over, Graeme reminded himself that, while curiosity was what had driven him to science in the first place, it was also what killed the figurative cat.

Schrödinger's cat.

There was an alternate interpretation of the puzzle's quantum mechanics: the many-worlds interpretation, which stated that, when an observer lifted the lid and looked in on the cat, reality splintered; it forked, creating a world where the cat was dead, and an alternate world, a *parallel* world where the cat went on living. Both occurred. Both really happened.

Many worlds, one reality.

It was the explanation to which Graeme had always subscribed. There were many worlds, many alternate dimensions, all existing in the same space. And so now, as he stepped up to the open specimen bag, he couldn't help but wonder: was this the reality where he looked inside and saw a frozen sample? Or was this the world where something jumped out and chewed his face off?

The creature within showed no outward signs of life. It lay inert; a block of ice, evaporating into a cold steam beneath the heat of the overhead lamps. Not a cat, he noted, and not anything he could readily classify.

"Good lord," Graeme muttered; he hesitated, then reached out to touch it.

"I wouldn't do that," Kathy cautioned, handing him a pair of plastic gloves. "Not barehanded, anyway. The creature may not still bite, but the frost does."

Graeme nodded, unable to take his eyes off the thing in the bag, off the ragged stump that appeared to be its neck. *Where's its head?* he wondered. *What had it looked like?* He put on the gloves in a hurry, then caressed the creature's chitinous exoskeleton. He took hold of its spikey, folded, crab-like legs, ran his fingers along the naked vertebrae of its spine, and a child-like grin of awe and wonder bloomed across his lips.

"It's beautiful," he said. "I've never seen anything like it."

"That's because there *isn't* anything like it. Well, not on this planet anyway."

"Extra-terrestrial?" Graeme's hand stopped as if it had been quick frozen to the specimen's glacial flesh. His heart pounded. It couldn't be, and yet here it was. He was *touching* it. "How can you be sure?"

"All life here is made up of six basic components: carbon, hydrogen – "

Graeme finished for her, "Nitrogen, oxygen, phosphorus, and sulfur."

"Very good." Kathy sounded mildly impressed. "As I said, those six elements form the basic building blocks for all life here on Earth. I mean *all* life, everything from the tiniest microbe to the...the giant squid. Everything here shares those same rudimentary six, the essentials of DNA." She laid her gloved hand on the specimen, right next to Graeme's. "Everything but this. This creature's DNA is *completely* alien to what we know today, working differently than every other organism on the planet. Instead of carbon, this thing uses silicone, and it's swapped out phosphorous for chlorine."

"Silicone?"

Kathy nodded, her face practically beaming. "This is a silicone-based life form." She looked back down at the specimen. "Of all the labs in all the world, thank God you waltzed into mine."

"The implications of this –"

"Are enormous, yes, I know. I mean, true, NASA did discover an arsenic-based microbe back in 2010, but no one has ever found an organism this complex before. Sure, we've theorized they existed, but–"

"But..." Graeme shook his head and tried to think clearly. "Where did it come from? And how did it get here?"

A booming voice filled the lab, giving both doctors a start, "That's what I'd like to know."

Kathy's head snapped up and Graeme followed her line of site to the door.

Two somber-looking men crossed the room; one – a tall, broad-shouldered African-American, sporting short-cropped, military-style hair – led the way, while the other – a shorter, smaller Caucasian, who modeled a slightly longer, spikier cut – trailed closely behind. Both wore dark suits and ties with bright white shirts that appeared to glow in the dimness. The brawny man gave them a slow, appraising glance, then his attention fell to the other-worldly specimen in the bag between them.

"Can I help you?" Kathy asked, mildly annoyed.

The burly man smiled, his teeth just as white as his shirt. "You'll have to forgive me, doctor, I'm new, and still gettin' used to all these formalities."

He raised his right hand, reached into his breast pocket, and produced a piece of official-looking identification. The card featured a picture of his smiling face and what appeared to be a government seal – an eagle with its wings spread wide; an olive branch clutched in its left talon, arrows in its right, and a shield covering its chest.

"I'm Agent Preston," he told them. "My friend here is Agent Andrews."

The other man nodded and said nothing. "FBI?" Graeme asked.

"Homeland Security."

Kathy leaned in to get a closer look at the agent's ID. "Earl L. Preston, Jr," she read, "U.S. Department of Homeland Security. I've never seen one of these before, but it looks authentic."

"Oh yes, doctor, trust me, it's very real."

Kathy's eyes rose to meet the man's face, her tone much more dismissive and impatient than her words, "How can we help you, agent?"

"We're assessing a possible threat to our national security." Preston put his ID away and pointed to the still-steaming plastic bag on the table. "May I?"

"Oh..." Graeme blinked and stepped aside. "Certainly."

"Looks like we have ourselves one gigantic monstersicle." The agent produced his own set of plastic gloves. He snapped them on and stepped up to the exam table. "Now there's somethin' you don't see every day." He tossed his stoic partner a glance. "You ever seen one of these before, Andrews?"

Though he was still six feet away and hadn't even laid eyes on it yet, Andrews said simply, "No."

"Me neither."

"Can I ask what your interest is in this?" Kathy asked.

"You can ask," Preston said with a chuckle.

Neither Kathy nor Graeme laughed; in fact, Kathy was actually scowling.

The agent shook his head. "No offense, but I think you two been down here too long in the dark with the monsterpops. Cold's got to you or somethin'. You need to go out, find yourselves a sense o' humor."

What on earth is this man here for? Graeme found himself wondering. *And, for that matter, what am I here for?*

Preston returned his attention to the creature. "I'm sure you fine doctors have heard of a little town called Colonial Bay, heard about the..." He paused a moment, as if choosing his next words carefully. "... dangerous, amphibious animals that were discovered there."

"I'd heard reports of strange carcasses being recovered," Kathy confessed. "As a zoologist, I was naturally intrigued –"

"Naturally," Preston interjected, his eyes still on the specimen.

"–but I've seen very little about it in professional scientific journals. The mainstream media is quick to show sensational pictures of the odd-looking remains that wash ashore on any beach from time to time, and then print their 'sea monster' headlines. Usually, after careful study, what was once thought to be a new and unique species winds up being just bits and pieces of a very old and familiar one."

"Fair enough," Preston told her with a respectful nod. "But, having had those particular creatures try and kill me, we'll just have to agree to disagree as to their...*uniqueness*."

Kathy grunted.

"And," the agent went on, "your good ol' Uncle Sam found them to be intimidating enough to want yours truly on the job, investigating any threat they – or any other strange, previously unknown creature – might pose to the public health and welfare."

"So...What?" Kathy asked, nodding at Preston and then to Andrews behind him. "You're Mulder and he's Scully?"

"*I'm* Scully," Preston corrected. "I don't believe shit unless I have proof or can see it with my own eyes."

"Well, you can see that it's dead," Kathy told him. "I don't think it poses much of a concern anymore."

"Another thing I learned in Colonial Bay, Doc: monsters don't usually travel alone. Where there's one, there's usually more. Maybe even hiding in plain sight."

Kathy eyed him suspiciously. "What's that supposed to mean?"

Preston offered no further explanation. Instead, he peeled back the plastic and continued to give the creature a thorough exam with his eyes. Graeme had to confess, the agent had him confused. And even more curious than he'd been before.

Curiouser and curiouser...

"I read the police reports," Preston finally told them; something on the carcass had caught his attention. "A man who lost his only daughter to this thing claimed his tropical fish tank exploded all over it in the scuffle, claimed that when the water hit its skin, it actually started to bubble up and melt." Preston indicated a mottled, pitted area on the creature's side where the flesh had been eaten away, the skin around it appeared blackened, almost scorched. He looked up and locked eyes with Wade. "There a scientific reason for that, Doc, or am I stuck in a bad M. Night Shyamalan movie?"

"Salt water," Kathy snapped.

"Salt water?"

"The man's *salt water* fish tank, for salt water fish. We don't say 'tropical.'"

Preston grinned indulgently. "Well, be that as it may, is there a reason a *salt water* tank would make this thing look all *Phantom of the Opera*?"

"In the case of Earthly snails and slugs, it would be an osmotic pressure response to extreme concentration differences."

"Wanna try that again in English, Doc?"

"Their skin is a semi-permeable membrane – it keeps vital organs in, but allows water to pass through quite easily. The water solution on both sides of the membrane wants to be isotonic – to have the same level of saltiness. If you put a highly concentrated saline solution outside that membrane and pure water on the other side, the water on the inside passes out to equalize the saltiness. Since that kind of massive water-loss isn't conducive to continued biological functioning, the animal's structural integrity fails, or in English, they melt."

"I see," Preston said, clearly pleased with either the information or the way in which Kathy had delivered it. "And, not that it has anything to do with the case, but more for my own curiosity...When I go out to a fine, fancy French restaurant, and spend half my government pay on a plate of nasty-ass snails, why can I salt the hell out of 'em without having to slurp up a bunch of goo through a straw?"

Kathy grinned thinly; she didn't raise her voice, but her impatience was plain nonetheless, "When you *cook* snails, you raise the temperature of their cells enough that their proteins become denatured."

"Denatured? Like with alcohol? Is that why they cook 'em in wine?"

At that, Kathy did finally laugh.

Preston's smile widened. "See, Doc, I knew I could help you find a sense of humor."

"So you do know what 'denatured' means?" she asked him.

"No," the agent admitted, still smiling, "but I'm glad you found my ignorance so damned funny."

"Denaturation is the application of external stress, like heat, to disrupt cellular activity," Kathy explained. "When you denature a snail's cells, you alter the structure of the cellular membranes so that they now allow diffusion of water and solute in *both* directions. This keeps the snails' insides in, where they belong."

"Well, that is some fascinating shit, I ain't gonna lie." Preston let go of the plastic bag and stood tall, removing his gloves with an audible snap. "But what I find even more fascinating is the fact that we've got an honest-to-God alien in a Ziplock bag. Now, getting back to the question that –" He pointed to Graeme. "– your name, doctor?"

"King. Dr. Graeme King."

"Dr. King," Preston repeated. "Fine name!"

"Thank you."

"As I was saying, getting back to the question that Dr. King was asking when we so rudely barged in, where did this thing come from? And how did it get here?"

All eyes went to Kathy.

"Well," she began, "that's why I asked Dr. King to come here, actually."

Their eyes swung back to Graeme.

He blinked, at a loss. "Me?"

"Yes," Kathy explained. "Given the test results, and the eyewitness accounts, I doubt this creature could have hitched a ride on, much less built, some spacecraft. While it's *possible* a meteorite might have crashed nearby, and alien microbes or viruses *might* have survived inside it, shielded from stellar radiation and the heat of entry, so that there may have been enough genetic information to spawn a new life form, I seriously doubt one would have grown to this size without being discovered long before now. That leaves only one possibility: it walked here from somewhere else."

Graeme understood now. "A traversable wormhole."

"Wormhole?" Preston gave them both a skeptical glance. "Like on *Star Trek*?"

"In a way," Graeme told him, excited once more, finally feeling like more than just a fly on the laboratory wall. "Lorentzian traversable wormholes could allow travel from one part of the universe to another very quickly, as seen in *Star Trek*. Even more exciting, however, is the fact that they would also allow travel *between universes*."

"I never did care much for *Star Trek*," Preston said. "Hundreds of years in the future, all these other planets and equality for all, and the only black woman on the show has to answer the phones." He chuckled to himself, then turned to face Graeme, his arms crossing his chest. "So, Doc, what you're tellin' me is that somebody left the gate open, and instead of a fox getting' into the henhouse, this thing gets through from some other world into ours?"

"Aptly put, Agent Preston."

"Thank you. I try to make my mama proud. But, if you're right, where would we find this door, and how do we know more flies won't get in?"

Graeme shrugged. "Many people think wormholes or singularities can only happen in the depths of space, but it's been theorized for a while now that such events could appear anywhere, even in this very room. Other dimensions, other *worlds*, are all around us all the time. We're just normally not permitted to see or interact with them. The door could be anywhere."

"You're not making our job very easy," Preston said, then looked back over at Andrews.

Graeme observed their unspoken interaction with great interest. Finally, he turned to Andrews himself and asked, "Do you ever say anything?"

"He doesn't let me," the agent replied, deadpan.

CHAPTER TWENTY-THREE

Robby shined his flashlight around, looking for a few severed fingers. Four severed fingers and the better part of a palm, to be exact. So far, he wasn't having much luck.

They'd been on a handful of runs already that morning, the most memorable being the three-hundred-pound naked lady. Her weight had made her diabetic, and after a romantic evening with her equally hefty husband, her blood sugar plummeted to the point where she'd become nearly comatose. They'd given her a shot of glucose to bring her level up, but when she failed to respond, they'd been forced to carry her down a flight of stairs and out the front door, wrapped in the bed sheets to preserve some sense of her dignity.

Robby thought the exertion was going to send Julian, who wasn't a small guy either, into cardiac arrest; he saw himself there, holding up this woman's bloated feet, while his partner fell to the landing below, clutching at his own chest. Thankfully, it never happened. And, as luck would have it, by the time they had the woman in the back of their bus; she was awake and responsive. She signed a waiver refusing further treatment, and that was that; Robby and Julian were off on their next run.

Charlie Spunkmeyer, age fifty-three.

Charlie had decided to build pipe bombs in his basement workshop. Now, Robby knew that farmers used explosives from time to time to blow tree stumps and break up large boulders that littered their fields. He'd even known them to use a few good blasts to loosen up tightly packed soil for planting, especially in seasons that lacked a lot of rain. But those farmers probably had more in the brain department than good ol' Charlie here.

When Charlie filled his last section of pipe with gunpowder and sealed it, he'd come to the realization that he'd forgotten to make a hole for his wick. Not wanting to throw out a perfectly good bomb, he decided instead to drill one through the metal cap, creating a small spark. The resulting blast blew off half of Charlie's right hand and sent metal shards into his right arm, shoulder, and eye.

What is it with these crazy farmers and their basements? Robby wondered as he sifted through blood and shrapnel, looking for those missing digits. He couldn't help but wonder what a search of other farmhouse basements would yield, not liking what his mind saw there: S&M torture chambers, pot farms; long-lost daughters, held captive in secret rooms, birthing their fathers' mutant, inbred, love children; more pagan altars opening even more doors to even more hellish dimensions.

Robby's gaze shifted to another corner of the cinderblock room even as his mind turned back to Sheri. It seemed the more he tried to steer his thoughts away from her, the harder they fought to return. He felt like a high school boy again, excited to find out that the hot girl in class, the one he'd been crushing on all semester, actually liked him in return. But he wasn't a high school boy anymore. No. The high school Robby would have had no problem sleeping with Sheri last night. The high school Robby would have had his fun, dressed, and promised Sheri he'd call her sometime as he hurried out the door. But that cavalier, selfish boy died a long time ago. He'd died there in the corn.

The corn.

It always came back to the corn.

He wanted to tell Sheri what had happened to him that night. He wanted to share everything with her. And that surprised him as much as it frightened him. He was frightened of what she might say, of what she might think. And he wondered, even if Sheri could get over her past and find the strength to move on, would *he* ever be ready to join her?

Robby made an effort to concentrate on the search once more, to busy himself. He knelt down and looked around. Underneath a metal shelving unit, a fingernail reflected the glow of his flashlight.

"Found one!" Robbie called out, then strained to reach it with his gloved hand.

"Which is it?" Julian asked, still searching on the opposite side of the room.

Robby held the severed bit up and examined it. "Since he's not a giant, I'd say it was the middle one."

"Good. Charlie uses that one a lot."

Robby chuckled, then quickly bagged the finger and put it on ice in a small cooler. They would take whatever they could salvage to the hospital, and the doctors might attempt reattachment, but he doubted they would have much success. The edges were far too jagged, and they had been separated from the body for too long after the blast.

Officers Hicks and Kirsch stood over by the blood-splattered workbench, doing a search of their own. When the cops and paramedics had first arrived, Robby had busied himself with Charlie's wounds, with stabilizing a patient for transport, but if the man recovered from this, he would be in a whole new world of hurt. In addition to the thirteen pipe bombs, Harmony's finest had found an arsenal of weaponry: handguns, shotguns, high-powered rifles, even a few flash grenades.

"Probably to blind the deer before he shoots 'em," Kirsch had joked.

Now, the cops had their work cut out for them. Everything had to be photographed, had to be bagged and tagged and then logged into the evidence locker. Serial numbers would need to be checked, as would all of Charlie's paperwork with the feds.

"I don't think we had this many guns in our whole platoon," Hicks commented. He held up two pistols, one in each hand. "A Glock 19 and a Walther P22. These were the guns that bastard used in the Virginia Tech shootings."

"And out in the barn, you've got yourself a shitload of ammonium nitrate and fuel oil." Everyone's eyes turned toward the unfamiliar, booming voice. A dark man in an even darker suit stood on the basement stairs. He stepped down onto the floor and added, "Which is what the bastards used in the Oklahoma City bombing."

They continued to stare at him a moment in silence.

"Sorry to interrupt, gentlemen," the man said at last; he reached into the jacket of his suit and produced some ID. "Agent Preston, Homeland Security."

"Jesus," Kirsch exclaimed. "We only called this in about forty-five minutes ago. You guys move pretty fuckin' fast!"

"Got to be quicker than the terrorists," Preston told them with a smile, his bright white teeth glimmering in the dimness.

Robby snickered. "Charlie Spunkmeyer's an idiot, but he's no terrorist. Just a redneck with too few brains in his head and too much time on his hands – er, hand."

Agent Preston strolled over, eyeing the name stenciled above Robby's breast pocket. "Miller. You're just the man I came here to see."

"*Me?*"

"If you could step outside with me for a minute, I'd be happy to explain."

Robby glanced over at Julian, then handed him the cooler. "You got this?"

Julian nodded. "Go on. I'll start raising your bail money."

"Ha-ha. Very funny." He turned back to Preston and motioned for the stairs. "After you, Agent."

Preston wasn't a huge man, not built like a wrestler or a football player, but he was still pretty imposing. And for some reason, he had his sights set on Robby. But *why?*

The agent led him out onto the porch and leaned against the wooden railing. "So, you don't think this Spunkmeyer guy's a terrorist or anarchist or whatever other 'ist' there is?"

"I think he's a farmer who has fertilizer and fuel oil because he's a fuckin' farmer. Pardon my French."

"Don't worry about it. I used to be in the Coast Guard, so I cuss like a fuckin' sailor myself."

"I *also* think he's got enough guns to arm the Indiana National Guard. But, since we're not exactly Facebook friends, I don't know if he's penned any wacko manifestos or not."

Preston smiled. "Gotta love Midwest folk and their guns, huh? Did you know that gun sales are up fifty-five percent in the last three years?

Robby shrugged. "I gotta admit: I've never had much use for anything other than a squirt gun. Don't know why people think they need so many. If you're gonna shoot something, one would do the trick just fine."

"One of us finally gets into that big white house and it makes all the white people nervous."

"You really think that's the reason?" Robby asked, shuffling his feet uncomfortably.

"One of the reasons, sure. Everybody's afraid he'll clamp down on gun ownership, take away their right to bear arms and all that shit. But there are other factors that got nothin' to do with politics."

"Such as?"

"Well, you got your standard 'doomsday preppers,' the ones who are always convinced that the end is nigh, and it's gonna be like the Wild West all over again. And then, there's the whole zombie apocalypse thing."

"Zombies? Really?"

"People eat that shit up," Preston told him. "No pun intended. You know, right now, as we speak, there are more than a dozen gun manufacturers out there makin' and marketin' guns specifically to kill zombies? One even changed the damn safety setting. Instead of 'safe' and 'fire,' they actually marked the positions as 'dead' and 'undead.' You ever seen a zombie, Miller?"

Preston's eyes were dark brown – inquisitive, piercing and direct, and they fixed firmly on Robby's face. Robby had heard stories of people who were "human lie detectors," individuals who could determine if you were telling the truth through facial tics and by how many times you blinked. Yes. Robby got the distinct impression that he would not want to play poker with Agent Preston.

"I've seen a few strange things in my time," Robby admitted and provided no further detail. In fact, he wondered if he should really be saying anything at all. Patriot Act or no Patriot Act, this was still America. Unless Agent Preston here came with a warrant, Robby was under no legal obligation to tell him anything other than his name and address, which Preston probably already had. No. Robby didn't need to say another word, not about zombies or ghosts or monsters from Hell, not about anything at all. The last thing he needed was to be branded a nut case by Homeland Security and shipped off to Guantanamo Bay.

Preston nodded. "I know," he said. "I've seen what you saw. Of course, I bet it looked a whole lot more threatening when it was alive."

The spider-dog, Robby realized. *This is about the spider-dog.*

"I'm gonna level with you, Miller: I didn't come to this town 'cause o' some gun happy redneck. I came here to solve a mystery."

"What? Are you like the government's answer to Scooby-Doo?" Preston chuckled.

"Scooby-Doo. I like that. I like you, Miller. You're a funny guy."

"Thanks."

"You ever seen anything like that creature, Miller?"

"No."

"Neither have I, and I've seen some shit you would not believe."

"You and me both."

"I've read your statements to the police and the media. But I don't think you just happened on this thing by accident. I think you and your girlfriend went out there looking for it. I think you know where it came from."

"And I think you're wasting your time," Robby told him. "You can quote me on that in your little report if you want."

"I don't think I am. Mama always says, 'a fool looks for dung where the cow never browsed.' Maybe you don't know where it came from *originally*, but you can sure as Hell help me narrow my search." Preston's smile widened. "And that makes you my new best friend."

CHAPTER TWENTY-FOUR

At Harmony High, a bell rang out. Seventh period, everyone's final class of the day, had just ended. Sheri's students practically leapt to their feet, scooped up their books and belongings, and rushed for the doors as if they had just been signaled that the building was ablaze.

Sheri tried to be heard over the commotion, "Don't forget to read 'A Rose for Emily' in your textbooks and answer questions one through six for tomorrow. Okay? Have a great evening. See you all tomorrow."

As the mass exodus subsided, she turned back to her chalkboard, erasing the notes she'd scribbled there. Not that anyone paid much attention to her wonderful insights. The girls were too busy texting while her back was turned, and the boys just stared at her ass.

Ahhhh, the joys of teaching.

"Miss Foster?"

"Yes?" She turned around, expecting to find a student. Instead, she found an adult standing there; a tall man with short, spiked hair. He was dressed as if he were ready to attend a funeral – a black suit and matching tie.

"Agent Andrews, ma'am," he told her, extending his hand. "Homeland Security."

She took his hand and shook it. "Homeland Security?"

"Yes, ma'am." He showed her his ID to prove it.

"Has there been some threat against the school?" she asked, trying to remember all of her A.L.I.C.E. training.

A.L.I.C.E. stood for Alert, Lockdown, Inform, Counter, and Evacuate. All Harmony school teachers had been required to take it over a year ago so that they could be prepared in the event of a school shooting. It provided teachers and students with various scenarios and role plays, up to and including how to actively engage and neutralize a shooter. She'd hoped to never need it.

"None that I'm aware of, ma'am," Andrews told her, stone-faced. "I'm here to investigate the strange creature that attacked you last month. If you don't mind, I'd like to ask you a few questions about it."

"Oh, but I do mind," Sheri wanted to tell him. *"I mind quite a bit."*

Instead, she simply shrugged and put down her eraser. The noise of students chatting and laughing in the hallway outside had faded, as had the slamming of lockers; everyone gone to their cars and their busses. She and Andrews were all alone in a room full of empty desks.

She leaned against her own desk and motioned to one of the vacant chairs in front of her. "What would you like to know?"

Andrews walked over. He laid a manila folder on the desk and had a seat. "I understood from the local police report that you went out into those woods to search for your missing boyfriend?"

She stared down at him, her arms crossing her chest. "Jeff."

"Jeff, yes."

"That's right," Sheri said, wondering why Andrews needed to talk to her about this. After all, there were plenty of interviews out there now – a public record that Andrews could watch and read and do whatever else he needed to do with. "We didn't find anything."

"I'm sorry for your loss," he told her. His hands sat on the manila folder like paperweights, his fingers interlaced. Sheri couldn't help but wonder what it held.

"Thank you," she said.

"In light of the news coverage the creature received, we've been speaking with everyone who encountered it, trying to make a clear assessment of the threat this thing might pose."

Sheri nodded. "Understandable."

"Do you like riddles?" Andrews asked casually.

She blinked. "Riddles?"

"Yes, do you like them?"

"Sometimes."

"Good." Andrews grinned; a crack in the stone. "An FBI psychologist came up with this one. They asked fifteen convicted serial killers this same question and all of them got it right. So, I'm going to ask you if you know the answer."

Sheri frowned. "To see if I'm a serial killer?"

"No, no...Although, if you do get it right, I might have a few follow-up questions for you." Andrews looked at her a moment, still grinning, then went on, "Okay, here goes: a woman attends her mother's funeral, and while she's there, she sees Mr. Right. I mean, this man is *perfect*. He's everything she's ever wanted, her soulmate, and she falls head over heels in love with him the moment she lays eyes on him. There's only one problem...she doesn't know who he is."

"She doesn't walk up and ask him?"

Andrews shook his head. "No, she doesn't."

"Well, if I met my *soulmate*, I might want to at least walk up to him and ask for his name."

"She doesn't have time," the agent told her, waving his hand. "But a few days later, she turns around and kills her sister. Why?"

Sheri shrugged. "She's crazy?"

"Certainly, but the answer's a bit more specific than that."

"She found out the sister was sleeping with him?"

"Drama," Andrews remarked. "Good guess, but no."

Sheri glanced out into the hallway and up at the ceiling as if she might find a Post-it Note with the answer written on it. Then she thought, *If giving the right answer means I'm a serial killer, do I even want to guess?* Finally, she said, "I give up. Why?"

"The woman kills her sister because she believes, even if *she* didn't know who the man was, her mother obviously did, so it stands to reason that her sister might know him too. Therefore, she kills her sister in the hopes of seeing Mr. Right again at another family funeral."

"She couldn't just go ask the sister if she knew him?"

"Again, you and I don't think like crazy people, thankfully."

"Was that your way of testing me?" Sheri wondered aloud. "Making sure that, if I tell you something that sounds pretty off the wall, I'm not really crazy?"

"It was only meant to be an ice breaker," the agent assured her. "But, now that you mention it, our recent probe into strange creatures and events has shown us that people are less likely to tell the truth if they think they'll be perceived as lunatics."

"Also understandable."

"Well, we know *you're* not a lunatic, so you can feel free to tell me anything."

Sheri eyed him narrowly. "You sound more like a shrink than a federal agent."

"I do have a degree in psychology," Andrews admitted, "but I'm not here to give you a psyche evaluation, or to ask you how you feel about your father. I won't even tell you, 'Sometimes you've just got to give yourself what you wish someone else would give you,' or any other wonderful bits of wisdom Dr. Phil might prescribe."

Sheri relaxed a bit, but she couldn't fully quell her suspicions. Andrews said they were interviewing everyone. She wondered if they'd talked to Robby yet, wondered how well he'd handled it. Did he tell them about Fuller? The symbols? Human sacrifices and gateways to other dimensions? And how did he answer Andrews' little quiz?

"Now, about that creature..."

Sheri slowly uncrossed her arms and gripped the edge of her desk. Psychologist or not, she knew she could cope with Andrews. "Yes?"

"Did it seem at all intelligent to you?"

"It seemed like it wanted to kill us."

"So, would you say that it was acting more on instinct, like say, a bear or a great white shark, and not with any conscious intent?"

She chuckled humorlessly. "I don't think it was secretly plotting an attack against the United States, if that's what you're asking. It was an animal. All animals have some level of intelligence, but Mr. Mancuso, the animal control officer who killed it, would probably know more about animal behavior than I do. You should ask him."

Andrews nodded. "Yes, we'll be interviewing him as well. Let's move on to something else." He finally opened the folder, studied the top page within, and said, "They recovered Jeff's cell phone the night of the first attack. It was covered in a slimy substance. The lab results show—"

"Let me guess, they've never seen anything like it."

"No, they have. They just can't account for it."

"I don't understand?"

"It was similar in to cephalopod slime."

"Cef-lo-what?"

"Octopus," Andrews explained, looking up at her, studying her reaction. "It had the same consistency as octopus slime."

Sheri wondered if she looked as confused as she felt. "Octopus?"

"The chemical properties were quite different, but that was the closest match the lab could come up with."

"How would octopus slime get on his phone?"

"I was hoping you could tell me. The creature that attacked you didn't possess it."

She shrugged, at a loss. "I have no idea. I was talking to him on his phone, and then the line just went..."

Dead. The word you're looking for is dead. Jeff's dead. The state of Indiana said so.

"The call just ended," she managed. "And then the spider-dog came out of the house and attacked the car."

"Spider-dog?"

"That's what I called it."

He nodded. "And that was the only creature you ever encountered?"

Then it hit her: *Oh my God, Robby's right. The spider-dog's not alone. There's more out there. It's not over yet.*

"I didn't see anything but the spider-dog," Sheri told him, feeling a sudden chill and trying not to shudder. "I'd never seen anything like it before, and I hope to never see anything like it again."

If Andrews saw her shiver, he made no mention of it. In fact, he appeared quite satisfied. He closed the folder and rose to his feet. "I think that about covers it," he told her. "I hope I haven't made you feel uncomfortable."

The agent extended his hand again, and Sheri shook it. "You're just doing your job," she told him. "I don't know that I was much help."

"You were very helpful. Thank you." He started to walk away, then turned back to her and said, "Again, I'm sorry for your loss."

Sheri nodded and watched him walk away, her heart thudding in her chest. And, when she released her grip on the wooden desk, she found she'd broken a few nails.

CHAPTER TWENTY-FIVE

Earl L. Preston Jr. had never seen a haunted house outside of the movies. He didn't even know if they truly existed. Oh sure, he'd been to the fun house variety that cropped up around Halloween, usually in an old warehouse or an abandoned store. As a kid, one of his neighbors even put a spook house together in their garage; walls of black Hefty bags and cardboard coffins, but an honest to God haunt, where actual Evil dwelled with a capital "E"...never. When they drove out of the woods and parked in the tall grass in front of the Fuller place, however, he thought: *If any place was* ever *haunted, this had to be it.*

Of course, the agent had no trouble believing in spirits. There were many days, in fact, when Earl felt his own father's presence, as if the dead man had just stopped by for a visit – keeping up on the bullet points of his son's life. And, as he approached the age his father had been when he'd passed, when an Iraqi bullet stole him away during Operation Desert Storm, Earl wondered what the man might think of him now? Would Earl Sr. – the hardcore Marine, the war hero who gave his life for his country – even want to claim a boy who made his living running around the country looking for monsters?

I'm doin' it for my Uncle Sam, Dad. God bless the U.S.A.!

Earl felt a change in the environment as soon as they left the woods. The air grew still; void of bird song, void of any sound at all, as if the old house had created some kind of vacuum. He drove across the scruffy lawn – which had remained brown and dehydrated despite the recent rains – and parked.

The grass in front of the porch had been trimmed, the lawn transformed into a large queue area – a place where people would be herded into lines and forced to stand and wait their turns to enter the haunt. These lines were shaped and organized by chains hooked to poles, and the poles had been made to look like bones topped with skulls. A large sign had been fastened just above the entrance: two skeletons, covered in a faux, greenish-gray sludge of rot, framing a black board scrawled over in a wicked-looking red script: THE FULLER FARM.

"Damn," Earl exclaimed. "You folks go all out!"

"Wait until you see the inside," Robby told him.

They got out and snaked their way through the empty rows. As Earl followed Robby, he reached out and let the chains slide through his fingers, feeling a bit like the first child through the gate at the amusement park. The sound of hammers and saws drifted out from the door, killing the eerie silence.

"When are they planning to open this thing again?" Earl asked. From the commotion within, it sounded like the place was far from ready.

"Friday night," Robby told him. "It runs September 30th through Halloween."

"Nothing like a little last minute tweaking."

"They'd wanted to be done earlier, but the spider – " Robby began, looking up at the boarded second floor windows as if he expected to see something peeking out between the slats. "The thing that attacked Sheri and her boyfriend kind of threw a monkey wrench into things."

"Monsters tend to do that kind o' shit."

Earl followed Robby through the door, finding a forest in the foyer.

"Damn," he repeated, impressed. "Where to?"

"The basement," Robby told him. "The doorway's in the kitchen, but it's locked, and Cap's got the only key I know about."

"Then let's go find your captain."

Robby led him through this maze of strange rooms and odd corridors. All around them, strangers continued to work feverishly, putting final touches on their ghastly internal decorating, unconcerned. They all seemed to know Robby, giving him a smile, a wink or a nod, so Earl evidently got a free pass by association.

A man stood in the corner, hanging speaker wire with a staple gun. He saw them out of the corner of his eye and asked, "You puttin' in some more time, Miller?"

"Maybe later," Robby told him. "I'm on the clock right now. You seen Cap?"

The man pointed down the hall with his staple gun. "He was over there in the bathroom."

"Oh."

"The fake one around the corner, splatterin' blood around or somethin'. Don't worry, he's not in there takin' a shit."

"Good to know," Robby said.

The man grunted, then went right back to stapling.

They moved on and found a bathroom straight out of some gory remake of *Psycho*. A white, plastic shower curtain had been covered over in red handprints. The sculpture of a woman's mutilated body sat in the corner, slashed and opened, her "intestines" uncoiling out into the tub, probably made of rubber or foam; Earl wasn't going to touch them to find out.

The man in the center of the room looked like a surgeon gone mad. He wore a white, one-piece coverall that had been splattered with red. A white surgical mask covered the lower half of his face, and it too was dotted red.

"Hey, Cap," Robby said, walking up to the man.

"Hey, Miller," was the muffled reply. The man reached up, pulled the mask down to his chin, and said, "What are you doing here? I thought you were out on a run?"

"I was, but then I ran into Agent Preston here."

Earl stepped forward, flashing his badge. "Homeland Security."

Robby's captain leaned forward to look at the ID, then his eyes shifted to Earl's face. "What can I do for you, Agent Preston?"

Before the events of Colonial Bay, Earl had never been good at making up stories–

Lying. Let's call it what it is.

–but he had come to understand that there were some things that people didn't need to know. And even if they did know, he doubted they would believe. Then where would they be? Everyone out there thinking their government was wasting their tax dollars chasing Bigfoot, the Loch Ness Monster, and little green men. That's where.

No. It was better if people went about their business in blissful ignorance, better for them, better for everyone. And there were times that Earl wished he could turn back the clock and do the same.

"Sorry to bother your – " He waved his badge at the blood-splattered walls. " – whatever, but I'm here to check the place out prior to you opening it up to the public. We've intercepted some chatter that leads us to believe that a terrorist cell might be planning something against haunted attractions during the month of October."

"Jesus," the captain muttered. "Fuckin' terrorists."

"Yeah. We just want to make sure that everything here looks secure."

"We're gonna have off duty officers outside every night."

Earl slid his badge and ID back into his breast pocket. "Oh, I've got no doubt that you're doin' everything you can, sir, but we just want to be sure. A bunch of young people crowded in these confined spaces...I'm sure you can see the concern."

The captain nodded. "What do you need from me?"

"We just want – " Earl caught the toilet in the corner of his eye. They'd filled it full of what appeared to be spray foam insulation and painted it brown. Chunks of the stuff also littered the seat and splatted up the porcelain face. *These people are fuckin' sick.* He shook his head and went on, "We want to make sure that there are no places for someone to hide a device."

"A device? You mean like a *bomb?*"

"I'm not gonna lie." *Liar.* "A bomb is one possibility, yes."

The captain touched his forehead with the inside of his wrist and wiped away the beading sweat. "Christ, that's all I fuckin' need."

Earl held up his hand. "I'm sure everything will check out just fine, but we need to be sure. Does this place have a basement?"

"Yeah."

"I can take you down there," Robby said, "but I don't think there's anything to worry about. It's locked up, and Cap here is the only one with a key." He frowned and glanced over at the captain. "You are the *only one* with a key, aren't you, Cap?"

"Yeah." His hand went to his pocket. "Yeah, nobody else can get down there."

Or up? Earl wondered.

"Good to hear," he said. "But, do you mind if we go down and check it out, just to be sure?"

"No, no. Of course. Whatever you need."

The captain ushered them into the kitchen in a hurry, fumbled with his keys, and unlocked the padlock. The cellar door swung open, its unoiled hinges whining in protest. Earl looked down into the darkness beyond, then glanced over at Robby.

"Okay," he said, stepping aside. "After you."

Robby chuckled. "Thanks."

Earl fished the thin black flashlight from his pocket, ignited it, and followed him down. At the base of the rickety stairs, the basement made an L-turn. Earl turned his light to illuminate their path, but Robby already knew the way.

The captain's voice filtered down, "I'll just wait up here."

"You do that," Earl called back, shadowing Robby down the claustrophobic stone corridor. As they approached the dark archway at the end of the hall, he reached up and unbuttoned his suit jacket, allowing easy access to the Glock he kept in his side holster, just in case.

Robby glanced back over his shoulder. "I think you really got to Cap with that bomb story. I don't think he'll sleep at all between now and Halloween."

"Good. He'll be more alert now, more watchful, just in case it wasn't bullshit."

"Wait...was it or wasn't it?"

"That's the trick, isn't it," Earl said, aiming his flashlight around, getting a sense of the room's shape. "And this is where they found the boyfriend's cellphone?"

A cellphone in a basement, covered in octopus slime. Sea creature gunk, in landlocked Indiana? Nope, nothing odd going on here.

Before another Colonial Bay flashback kicked into overdrive, Robby answered, "Yeah. This is where that creature came from. There are no windows, no way in or out except the door we just unlocked. And on the night of the attack, the thing's tracks went *up* the stairs, but not down – up and out the front door, like it just...*materialized* down here."

"So...This Jeff guy's footprints came down the stairs, and the thing's tracks went up the stairs?"

"That's right."

"And the thing is dead, and nobody's seen hide nor hair of the man since?"

"Right again."

"And nobody finds that weird?"

Robby chuckled humorlessly. "I find the whole thing weird, but what part are you talking about?"

"Well, I mean the man comes out here and disappears, and at the exact same moment, this creature no one's ever seen before just shows up and starts goin' on a killing spree, and now it's dead, and he's still gone, and nobody saw them both together at any point in –"

Robby chuckled. "What? Like he Hulked out or something? Actually *became* the animal?"

Earl shrugged. "Just a thought."

"A pretty off-the-wall thought."

Speaking of walls....Jesus...

Earl saw the strange makings etched into each of them, feeling déjà vu wash over him all over again. What began with missing persons and cryptic symbols did not end well. He stepped over to one that looked like a four-legged cactus and ran his hand over it; the shape held no apparent meaning, yet he knew from experience that it undoubtedly spoke volumes about their current situation.

"I don't suppose you guys made these markings for your little haunt?" he asked.

"Nope," Robby informed him. "I think they were carved about sixty years ago by the man who built this house."

"Fuller?"

"Yeah. I did some research, found that they're markings that were used by an ancient Druidic sect. Archeologists think they practiced human sacrifice."

"Oh, this shit just gets better and better." Looking around the ripe, dank cellar, it wasn't hard to believe it had been the scene of past horrors. "You know, they found 143-year-old blood up in Gettysburg."

"Really?"

Earl nodded. "They used this new latent blood reagent and sprayed the hell out of the floorboards in this attic where these Confederates got killed during the Civil War. Pretty amazing stuff. If they sprayed some of that shit around down here, I wonder what they'd find."

He ran his fingers over the carving once more, tracing the curves and angles in the stone.

Maybe I should give Carol Miyagi a ring, get my own archeologist up in here, see what she has to say about it.

Even if he could reach her, Earl doubted Carol would come. Last he'd heard, she'd gone back to Japan. Her grandmother had evidently been hurt in the big earthquake or one of the aftershocks that followed.

Earl sighed and turned his light toward the opposite side of the chamber. The brick wall looked like it had been through an earthquake of its own; a deep fissure bisected it. He stepped over, ran his fingers along the jagged edge of the crack, wondering.

No, he decided. *If this was some kind of doorway, the things that squeezed their way through would all look like fuckin' flounders by the time their asses got here.*

In Earl's mind, a wormhole should be bright, glowing, with ribbons of fluorescence and nebulous gasses all swirling around a dark well, like water circling a drain. He saw nothing like that in this dank, moldy cellar. He saw nothing like that at all.

"So," Earl began, glancing around the room, feeling the answer staring him right in the face, and yet too blind to see it. "You ever search for something, Miller, and have no idea what the fuck you're lookin' for?"

Robby gave a snort and said, "All the time."

CHAPTER TWENTY-SIX

"Mr. Mancuso?"

The animal control officer turned around and saw a man with short, spikey hair and dark clothes standing on his front lawn. "Yeah?"

"I'd like to talk to you about the creature you killed up in Harmony," the stranger said; the street light behind him glowed brightly in the fading twilight, granting him a halo.

Mancuso frowned. He worked an area that covered over five hundred square miles of rural Indiana countryside, including Harmony, Pleasant View, and all the little satellite neighborhoods and collections of farms that were too small to really be called towns. Today, he thought he'd crossed damn near all of it. He'd hoped to come home, pop open a beer, put his feet up and just relax. But no; here was somebody else who wanted to question him about the fuckin' *Chupacabra*.

"Look," Mancuso pointed to his county-issued truck with his keys, "I just got home after a really long day. Why don't you stop by the office tomorrow and – "

"I am sorry for disturbing you," The stranger held up his hand and moved closer, "but this is quite important, I can assure you."

"If it's official, and you got some kinda badge or warrant you wanna show me, fine." Mancuso paused, waiting to see if the figure would produce some identification, and when none came he went on, "But since you don't, it's not so important that it can't wait 'til morning. Now, get off my grass and come by the office during normal hours like everybody else."

The stranger just stood there, saying nothing, the glowing outline of a man. He lifted his hands and slid them into the pockets of his dark coat, lowering his head as if to study Mancuso's lawn.

"I mean it." Mancuso backed up toward his front door, his keys clutched tightly in his hand; he turned toward his front door long enough to mount the steps, then glanced back over his shoulder. "If I look out here in five minutes and see you still standin' there, I'm callin' the sheriff. I don't care who you are, or *think* you are."

Something in his head said *call now*, but he ignored it. Even in silhouette, this guy was far from imposing; he was all of five-ten, and his clothes hung loosely from his slight frame. Probably some college kid from Stanley, just trying to write a story for the school paper or something. Maybe even an exchange student. That was an Irish accent after all, wasn't it?

Mancuso turned his back on the man for only a moment, just long enough to slide a house key into the lock, but a moment was all it took. The figure rushed up behind him, clamped fingers around his head in a vice-like grip, and repeatedly slammed his face into the painted steel. Once –

Pain rang through Mancuso's skull.

-twice –

His eyes filled with bright showers of sparks.

-three times.

And everything went dark.

The reason for Cayden's existence, his sole purpose in this wretched world, which until now had only sputtered and stalled, was finally up and rolling, and not just rolling, but *racing*; it was as if his entire being had suddenly shifted into overdrive, barreling ahead toward some unknown finish line, a finish line that drew nearer with each passing mile, each passing *moment*.

And now, he had arrived.

Harmony, Indiana. Such an apt name for the town where everything would finally come together in perfect unison. The ultimate thin place, the very gateway to the gods, and above this tiny hamlet, the stars, set into motion countless eons before, were spiraling into position once more, forming a precise alignment. All pieces moving in flawless synchronization, like notes in a cosmic symphony awaiting its premiere performance.

Cayden only lacked the final instrument: the key, and time was wasting.

He stared down at Mancuso, who now sat lashed to a kitchen chair with strips of his own torn-up uniform. Blood flowed from the man's forehead, painting red, squiggly lines down his scruffy face and dripping down his bare chest and into his lap. Cayden frowned; he curled his fingers into a fist and punched him hard across the mouth.

"Wake up," Cayden told him.

Mancuso's head swung violently to the side. He coughed and moaned, then his eyelids fluttered open as he turned back, looking up at Cayden with the lost and frightened expression of someone who'd just dreamt of falling. He parted his split, bloody lips to speak, sounding just as confused as he appeared, "What – ?"

Cayden struck him hard again, then turned away, relishing the sound of Mancuso's groans in his ears as he massaged his knuckles. "Stupid fuckin' wanker. You've got no idea what you've done, do ya?"

Mancuso's house was small, but neat and organized; a place for everything, and everything in its place. Even the junk mail that had been brought in from the mailbox outside sat on the kitchen table in an orderly stack. How ironic that such a meticulous man had been the one to slay that which would have brought order to the chaos of this world.

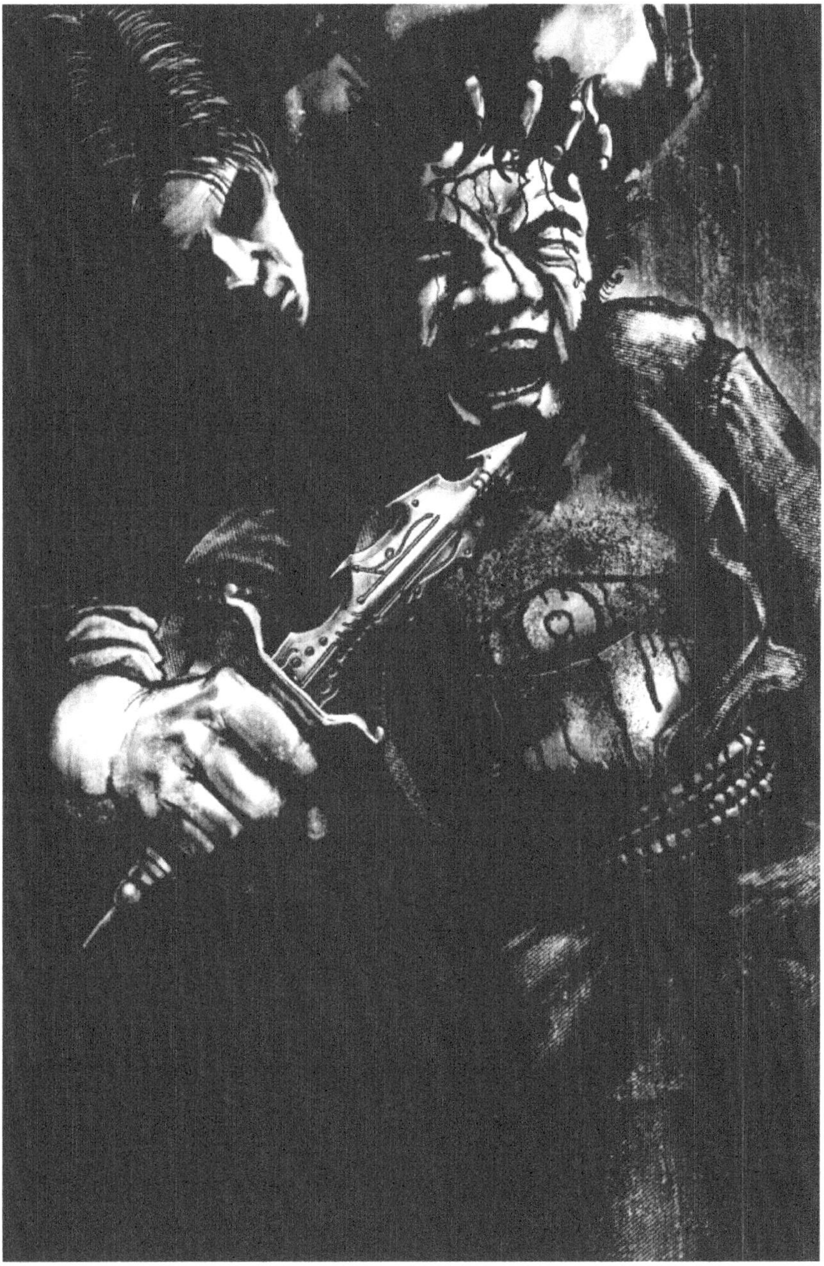

"No..." Mancuso's voice became clogged, and he coughed and spat blood several times before he could continue. "I haven't done anything to you. Please, just...just take what you want and go."

"You think this is a bloody *slad*...that I'm some common thief?"

"I don't even fucking know you!" Mancuso exclaimed, and with the words came a few tears; they ran from the corners of his eyes and mixed with the scarlet veins that had been drawn down his cheeks.

"Oh, but I know *you*, Dog Catcher." Cayden leaned over and clamped his hands around Mancuso's knees, looking him dead in the eyes. "The gods have shown me your face, whispered your name in my ear, and told me your crimes."

"What crimes?"

"Murder, Dog Catcher. *Mharaigh tú.* You murdered a fuckin' *god!*" Cayden spat in Mancuso's face and stood upright once more, watching the thick mucus slide down the side of the bloodied man's nose. "Feel its power, did ya? When you pulled the trigger and snuffed its eternal flame, did ya feel a fire ignite in your fuckin' gut?"

Mancuso shook his head, sweat glossing his naked arms and torso. "I didn't have a choice."

"You were just doin' your duty?"

"Yes."

"Savin' the world?"

"*Yes.*"

"Well..." Cayden reached into his jacket and produced the dagger. Its blade caught the overhead light and glowed as if it were ablaze. "Aren't we all?"

Mancuso screamed; he tensed and squirmed in his chair, trying to break free. Cayden pinned him down with one knee and began to sketch across his chest with the blade's sharpened point. Mancuso continued to writhe and call out for help as the drawing took shape; an open eye, spanning the space between his nipples, weeping a dozen bloody tears. Cayden paused a moment, admiring his own handiwork, then he spoke the ancient words to give his actions meaning; not Latin or Gaelic, but a far older and more lyrical tongue. Outside, neighboring dogs howled and bayed at the moon, providing music to Cayden's libretti, nearly overpowering Mancuso's shrill, tortured shrieks. And finally, when Cayden had finished his prayer, when he'd lifted the ritual dagger above his head, when he'd brought the bifacial blade down with all his might, there was silence.

"What do you suppose passes to the man who kills a god-killer, Dog Catcher?" Cayden asked, not knowing if he could still be heard, or if he was now only talking to himself.

Sharper than any scalpel, the knife sliced Mancuso's still-beating heart from his body and into Cayden's waiting hand. He brought the warm, quivering organ to his lips, opened his mouth, and took a huge bite. Hot blood gushed down his chin and dotted the linoleum flooring at his feet. The meat was tough, chewy, and when he finally swallowed, Cayden felt the heat slide down his throat, felt it fill his belly and radiate through his entire being.

"*Jaysus!*" he exclaimed, almost laughing, his teeth dark with gore, and his eyes bright with awe. "*Cumhacht!* So much fuckin' power!"

Cayden took a second bite, then a third, and he continued to feast until he'd had his fill.

"Not far to go now," he said as he stepped outside and gazed up at the stars, "but time is short."

The animal control truck sat ready in Mancuso's drive. Cayden stepped over to it, whistling and twirling the dead dog catcher's key ring on his index finger. He peeked through darkened windows, then moved to unlock the tailgate. When he opened the back doors, an overhead light came on, illuminating a treasure trove of cages, catch poles ending in limp nooses, high-powered rifles, tranquilizer pistols, and an ample supply of drugs and darts.

Cayden's smile widened. "Glory be."

He shut the doors, climbed up into the truck's cab, and drove off into the night.

CHAPTER TWENTY-SEVEN

Robby's Spidey sense had been tingling ever since they left the old Fuller place, and he didn't like it. Not at all. Something bad was about to happen; he could feel it in his bones. And, as he followed Agent Preston into the old Howard Building, Stanley University's home for Mathematics and Science, he hoped that it wouldn't happen here.

They moved through the brightly lit halls, the sounds of their footfalls echoing off tiled walls and floors, growing louder and stranger the farther they marched into the massive, aging structure. A security guard directed them to Room 422, so they found the nearest staircase and Preston bounded up the steps, leading Robby away from the labs, the vast lecture halls, and onto the fourth floor. Up here, away from the public eye, the building had taken off its make-up to show its true age. Cracks marred faded walls, dark water stains spotted formerly white ceiling tiles; stacks of boxes clogged the main arteries, adding to the claustrophobic feel of the place. Several overhead lights were either turned off or burned out, as if trying to hide all the imperfections, and an ominous quiet hung in the air.

"Are you sure these guys are still in?" Robby asked, checking every dark corner, prepared for anything.

"They'd better be."

Office doors lined the halls, and they followed the numbers to 422. Preston placed his hand on the knob and, at first, Robby thought the agent was just going to barge in, but then he knocked and announced their presence.

"Dr. King?"

"Come in," a man replied.

They opened the door and stepped inside. The office was small, cramped, filled with filing cabinets and a large wooden desk. The walls had been covered over in dry erase paint and were now filled almost from floor to ceiling with various mathematical formulas and calculations. To Robby, it was like gazing at the confines of an Egyptian tomb, or staring at those mysterious etchings down in Fuller's cellar; he knew it all meant something to somebody, but it was an alien language to him.

A thin man in a blue sweater stood with his back to them, scrawling more numbers and symbols on the opposite wall. He was not alone, either; a woman sat in one of the room's two chairs, her arms folded across her chest and a sour express on her face. Preston seemed to know both of them. "Thanks for meeting with me again," he said.

"Did we have a choice?" the woman asked, none-too-pleased.

"Dr. Ward," Preston said with a bright, gleaming grin, then he nodded at Robby. "Mr. Miller here is one of the people who bagged your alien for you, and he was kind enough to show me where it first appeared."

"Did I have a choice?" Robby asked sarcastically.

This got the woman, Dr. Ward, to smile.

Preston went on without skipping a beat, "But we have no idea what we're really looking for, or what to do when we find it. What the hell does a wormhole look like?"

The man who had been writing on the wall, Dr. King, chuckled. He capped his black dry erase marker and turned to face them. "No one really knows. Their existence, up to this point, has been purely theoretical."

"So's E.T.," Preston countered, "but Dr. Ward's got one ugly motherfucker on ice in her lab right now."

"Very true," Ward agreed.

"But," King began, "much like E.T., nobody's actually seen a wormhole outside of a science fiction film. It's simply a tunnel through space-time, connecting two different points; a bridge. The entrance could be some bright, spinning vortex, or it might be totally invisible to the naked eye. We just don't know."

"Just for my own curiosity," Robby said, "how would somebody open one of these tunnels to begin with?" Images of Farmer Fuller eating babies in his basement still clung to his brain, and no matter how hard he tried, he couldn't shake them.

"In order for someone to create and maintain a stable wormhole," King answered, "it would require an incredible amount of exotic material, a theoretical substance with negative mass – once again, something that we've never seen. Now, it's possible that these wormholes might occur naturally, but without that negative matter to hold them open, they'd be highly unstable, and they'd likely collapse just as quickly as they appeared. Think of it like a tornado. If conditions are right, a funnel will form. It could last for a minute, or it could continue whirling around and causing destruction for some time, but eventually, as conditions change, it simply falls apart."

Robby nodded, then asked, "You know how they say lightning never strikes twice?"

"Yes," King replied, "but it's not true. Lightning can, and often *does*, strike twice."

"Well, I believe the door to this tunnel has been opening in the same old, abandoned house for over sixty years. But, every time I've been down there to have a look around, like when I took Agent Preston here earlier today, we can't find shit. Is it possible for these wormhole thingies to open and close in the same place over and over again?"

"Again, it's *theoretically* possible," King told them. "Just as there are places in the country that are labeled 'tornado alleys,' because certain weather conditions mean funnels frequently form there, it might be possible to have a 'wormhole alley,' where the same circumstances needed to create a tunnel occur at random again and again." He paused a moment, considering, then added, "It could also be a case of orbital alignment."

"Orbital alignment?" Preston repeated, rolling his eyes. "Now, why didn't I think of that?"

King made a sweeping motion with his hands. "Everything in our universe is constantly moving, orbiting and expanding. And, just as we revolve around our sun, another planet out there would be circling its own star. If this wormhole is a tunnel through space-time to one world in particular, it's possible that it only forms when both planets are at the same point in their orbits, when everything is perfectly synced."

"So...it might be seasonal?" Robby asked, still thinking of his research; all those missing people, each one taken during the same time of the year.

King shrugged. "It's possible, certainly."

Preston opened his mouth to say something, but before he got the chance, Dr. Ward spoke up from her chair, clearly impatient, "Am I just here to watch you gentlemen talk, or is there something you want me to add to this conversation?"

"Dr. Ward," Preston replied, staring down at her. "If we do somehow manage to find one of King's purely theoretical wormholes, I was hoping you might be able to shed some light on what we can expect to find on the other side?"

"You're going through it?" Dr. King asked, suddenly excited.

"*Hell, no,*" Preston snapped. "But my mama always told me never to open a door in a blizzard. So, I wanna know what this thing's lettin' in to my house."

"You mean diseases and pathogens?" Ward asked.

"I mean *everything*, the air it breathes, the – "

"Well, we really have no idea what it breathes," Ward told him, "or even *if* it breathes in the way we think of respiration. It might absorb the gasses it needs through the semi-permeable membrane of its skin, the same porous membrane that allows you to melt it with salt. I find it hard to believe its atmosphere would be exactly the same as ours, and yet it obviously was able to exist here for a time without difficulty.

"Honestly, gentlemen, I'm going to agree with my friend Dr. King on this. Anything I tell you at this point would be purely theoretical. Conjecture...nothing more than an educated guess. I'd be a lot more helpful to you if I had a living sample to work with."

"Yeah," Preston told her, "that's not gonna happen if I can help it."

"What kind of atmosphere?" Robby asked.

Ward blinked. "Sorry?"

"You said you'd be surprised if its atmosphere was like ours. If it doesn't breathe oxygen, what else could it breathe?"

She shrugged. "Well, scientists have theorized for years that there might be lifeforms out there that exist in pure methane or even a chlorine atmosphere."

"Chlorine gas?" Robby asked.

"Right."

Robby frowned. The spider-dog had reeked of chlorine, and it had filled that teenage girl with hydrochloric acid. He knew from his training that exposure to chlorine gas was deadly to humans; it caused the throat to swell and the lungs to fill with water, it also changed the acid levels in the blood, eventually destroying every organ.

How could anything *breathe that shit?*

Music filled the room, someone singing the theme from the movie *Black Dynamite*, "Dy-no-mite...Dy-no-mite."

Preston's ringtone.

The agent instinctively reached for his phone and looked at the screen. "Sorry, I've got to take this." He put the phone to his ear, said, "Yeah," then turned toward the back corner of the room.

"Dr. King," Robby said.

Behind him, Preston let out a surprised, "When?" And then the agent listened to the voice at the other end of his phone.

Robby glanced over at him, then returned his attention to King. "If we do find a real wormhole, how can we close it? I mean *for good*."

The scientist thought for a moment, then took a deep breath and said, "If it's a stable wormhole, you could simply get rid of the negative mass keeping it open, and again, I can't tell you what that would look like. Or you could try over-stressing it."

"Over-stressing it?"

"Right. Man-made bridges have a weight limit to keep them from collapsing, and a wormhole would have its own mass limit as well. If too much material moves through it all at once, it might force a collapse."

"So...what? We need to drive a big Mac truck through it, one of those flatbeds with a house on the back or something?"

King chuckled. "Something like that. Again, this is all conjecture." He pointed to the markings on the walls. "It's all been numbers and theories until now."

Robby nodded, still frustrated.

Preston lowered the phone from his ear, and turned around. He massaged his eyelids with his thumb and forefinger for a moment, then opened his eyes to look at Robby, his expression deadly serious. "We need to go,"

"What's happened?" Robby asked, his Spidey sense switching into panic mode. For some reason, an image of Sheri suddenly popped into his head – beautiful and smiling – and his stomach reached for his toes.

Preston was blunt, "Your friend Mancuso's dead."

"Christ." *Another spider-dog?* Robby wondered, then he came out and asked, "How?"

"Murdered," Preston told him, and before the sting of this first punch had a chance to fade, the agent struck him with another, "Somebody ripped his fucking heart out."

CHAPTER TWENTY-EIGHT

They got to Mancuso's house just after ten, and Earl noticed two things almost immediately. First, the only cars in the driveway were police cruisers. And second, a splash of blood, now dried and rust-colored, stained the front door.

Andrews met them at the door, notebook in hand, and not all of the news was bad. The killer had been quite sloppy. Fingerprints were everywhere, and judging by the size and style of a shoe print on the kitchen floor, perfectly preserved in a pool of Mancuso's blood, they knew that they were looking for a man. And Earl's first observation had been correct: the killer took Mancuso's county-issued truck.

"Did you put out a BOLO for it?" Preston asked as he walked through the immaculate living room, looking for signs of struggle and finding none. The only hints of violence were a few stray blood drops on the carpet, hardly enough to be called a trail.

"Yes," Andrews told him. "The State Police and Harmony PD are on the look-out. So far, nothing."

Earl nodded. There weren't a lot of Miami County Animal Control vehicles, and unless the killer ditched it somewhere, it should make him pretty easy to spot. "Contact the Chicago PD and the FBI, just in case."

"Way ahead of you," Andrews told him.

He glanced back and saw Robby Miller walking behind him in silence, his eyes mirroring Earl's, making their own sweep of the room. "Have you ever been here before?" he asked, hoping the EMT might know if something were missing or out of place.

Miller shook his head. "No. I didn't really even know him. He shot the – the creature, and we did some interviews together, but that was about it."

They went into the kitchen, where Earl got his first look at the body. He felt a chill creep slowly up his spine. He'd seen his share of crime scenes over the years, including the gory interior of Jerry and Karen Hoff's yacht, the *FantaSea*, but he'd never seen anything so disturbing as this. "Holy fucking shit."

Mancuso still sat in his chair, naked from the waist up, his arms and legs bound by strips of torn beige cloth. His eyes were wide open, staring blankly at the linoleum, his face covered in scarlet threads, and, of course, there was that gaping wound where his heart should have been. But what bothered Earl the most was the bloody drawing of an eye that now stared up at him from Mancuso's chest.

Not just an eye, his mind corrected, *but an eye in a* triangle, *like the back of a dollar bill. "In God We Trust," and all that.* Earl frowned. God had nothing to do with this. At least, not the god he knew. It was the same symbol he'd seen in the spook house basement, the one with a long crack running right down the middle of it. This one had been cleaved in two as well, sliced through by the killer on his way to Mancuso's heart.

Miller saw it too, and his lily-white face turned deathly pale. "Jesus," he muttered. "Preston, they sacrificed him, just like the Druids, like Fuller."

Earl nodded. "Looks that way."

"Holy Christ...God, it's because he shot the thing, isn't it?"

"We don't know that," Earl told him.

"What other explanation is there? This wasn't fuckin' random! They didn't draw his name out of a hat!"

"You're probably right. With all the news coverage, the killer probably found out where he lived and came here for some payback."

Miller's eyes widened, and he ran his fingers through his hair. "Then, Sheri and me..."

Earl held up his hand and tried to sound as reassuring as possible. "I'll put you both into protective custody. This guy's crazy, sloppy. He won't get far and we'll have the sick fuck behind bars before breakfast."

Miller was sweating. He reached for his cell phone, then stepped back and to the left, dialing frantically.

"Who are you calling?"

"Sheri," Miller told him, lowering his eyes to the floor, and after a brief pause he said, "It's ringing."

Earl frowned, hoping the woman would answer, considering the same possibility that Miller had to be thinking about right now. *What if the killer had driven straight to her house after leaving here?* His eyes drifted back to Mancuso's desecrated form, wondering if they would find a similar scene over at her place, wondering which one of the symbols would be carved into her chest, wondering –

"Sheri?" Miller's head snapped up, and Earl watched as a great, sweeping relief washed over him. "Oh, thank God!"

Earl let go of the breath he'd been holding, glad they would not have to clean up another mess. Then, he turned back to Andrews, still trying to make sense of this one.

The phone rang.

Sheri glanced up from her papers and looked at the clock. *10:15? Who'd be calling me at this hour?* It had been a long day, and she was just about to get off her couch, take a shower, and hop into bed. When she picked up the wireless receiver, however, she saw Robby's name on the screen and instantly perked up. She'd been thinking of him all day, even before her encounter with Agent Andrews, but for some reason, whenever she thought of calling him, she never followed through. He'd given her space, been *sensitive*. It had been unexpected, and now she had no idea how their relationship should progress, or even if it should progress at all.

She put the receiver to her ear. "Hey, there."

"Sheri?" he sounded alarmed. "Oh, thank God!"

"What's wrong?"

"Something's happened. I'm on my way over there."

Sheri sat up on her couch, her stomach turning over. "What is it? Does it have something to do with the guy from Homeland Security? He came to the school today and interviewed me."

There was a long pause on Robby's end, then he said, "I'll tell you when I get there."

The doorbell rang, giving her a start.

She shook her head and chuckled in spite of her dread.

"Well, that was fast." Sheri stood up and walked across the room. "Why didn't you just wait until you got here, you goof."

"What are you talking about?"

She opened the door.

The man on her doorstep wasn't Robby. She'd never seen him before in her life. He had red, spiked hair and there was red on his chin as well. And, when he smiled at her, she even saw red on his teeth. "Sheri," he said. "We meet at last."

Before she could say anything in reply, or even slam the door in the stranger's face, Sheri heard a pop, like an air bubble bursting. She felt a sudden sting in her chest and instinctively looked down. There was something red there now, a feathery cone; it protruded from her left breast, as if someone had glued a small Badminton shuttlecock to her T-shirt. She gazed down at it, stupefied, then lifted her eyes toward the man on her front step.

He held a camouflage-painted pistol in his red right hand.

"Gun," she said aloud, her voice groggy. She felt suddenly tired; her eyes drifted closed on her, and she fought a losing battle to keep them open. *No. Can't sleep. Not now.* "Shot…"

"Sheri?" Robby called into her ear; he sounded so distant, his voice faint, echoing, as if he were speaking to her in a dream. "Sheri!"

The phone slipped through her fingers; it fell to the floor and she followed it down.

Robby had his seatbelt off even before the car had come to a complete stop. Sheri's front door stood wide open, light from her house spilling out across her lawn. He leapt from the passenger's seat and sprinted inside.

Gunshot. She'd said there'd been a gunshot.

Her phone lay on the tiled floor, but he didn't see any blood. There were no shell casings either, but the killer could have taken those with him. He scanned the walls, searching for bullet holes and finding none. The mirror opposite the door was even still intact.

He rushed into the living room, finding Sheri's papers neatly stacked on the couch. An empty glass sat on the end table, unbroken and still holding ice. Again, he found no blood, no bullets, no proof of violence of any kind, and no sign of Sheri.

His eyes strayed toward the archway on the far wall.

The kitchen.

Robby didn't want to go in there, not after Mancuso. When he had seen the man tied up like that, seen the symbols and the blood, Robby had been terror-stricken. His mind was immediately transported back in time, back to the corn. It always came back to the corn. He'd seen far too much that night; too much bloodshed, too many inexplicable horrors, and far too many good friends lost...*killed*...gone forever. It was more malevolence than anyone should have been exposed to at such a young age – a crazed frenzy that had polluted this normally quiet, boring town just as thoroughly as if a reactor had gone into meltdown; the soil, the water, the trees and the buildings...everything had been contaminated that day. *Everything*, including Robby's soul.

Scarecrow, he remembered thinking upon entering Mancuso's kitchen. *He's become another scarecrow!*

And now, the thought of finding Sheri that way...it was all too much. He didn't want to see her vacant eyes staring up at him, silently wondering why he hadn't been there to help her. If he did, Robby thought that, after all these years, his mind might finally snap.

He forced himself to go on anyway, to step into the kitchen and look around, and he was relieved to find nothing more than dishes drying on a rack beside the sink.

"Thank God," he muttered aloud.

A hand fell on Robby's shoulder and he spun around to see Agent Preston standing behind him, his eyes narrowed and his service pistol drawn and ready. "What the hell do you think you're doin'?" Preston asked, straining to keep his voice low. "You ever hear of making a sweep? What if the asshole's still in here?"

"Mancuso's truck isn't parked out front. I think he's taken her somewhere."

"He could have parked the truck a few blocks away and hoofed it."

Robby hesitated a moment, thinking it a waste of valuable time, then he pointed down the hall and said, "There's a bedroom, a spare room, and two baths I haven't checked yet."

"So, you've been *here* before."

"Yeah, I've been here before."

They searched the other rooms together, and just as Robby thought, they found nothing. The house was empty.

The Super Soaker water gun he'd given Sheri sat next to a cigarette lighter on her bedside table, as if she'd kept them there for protection. Robby reached out and grabbed them up as they left the room.

"What do we do now?" he wanted to know as he slid the lighter into the front pocket of his jeans.

"Just hold your damn horses for a minute." Earl holstered his weapon and put his cell phone to his ear. "Andrews? The house is clear. Foster's not here, our perp's taken her somewhere." He paused, then said, "They have? Where?"

"What is it?" Robby asked, still haunted by the sight of that gaping hole in Mancuso's chest.

"Harmony's finest just made Mancuso's truck," Preston told him, "heading east on Route Six."

"Toward the Fuller place," Robby said, thinking of some unknown madman dragging Sheri down to the cellar, of what he might do to her when he got her down there, and of what horrors might come if he succeeded.

CHAPTER TWENTY-NINE

Cayden Donnelly sped on toward his destiny, toward the moment he'd been planning for his entire life. And even though he'd never actually been to Harmony, he navigated every twist and turn in the road like a native. After all, he'd been down this same path a hundred times in his sleep, and it always led him to glory.

The world was about to change, to be reborn. It was written in the stars, the stars that lit the skies of this deceptively quiet Indiana night.

It was time for the true owners of this land to finally reclaim it. They'd been here before Adam. Before Eve. Before Jesus. And they were still out there, growing stronger, more powerful, biding the endless passing of centuries, awaiting any opportunity to return to their throne. And now, their patience was about to be rewarded; the hour of their release, their *resurgence* was at hand.

Cayden thought of his father. The man had been forced from this world as well. Man's toxins had filled him up with a malignancy and robbed him of his triumph.

But Man was the true cancer – spreading out across this world, poisoning it. He was a tumor that had to be removed, irradiated and eradicated until he could be made benign. Until he could be ruled. The gods would be the surgeons, and Cayden their instrument.

I wish you could be here to see it, Da. I really do.

He glanced over at the sleeping form in the passenger's seat. The woman's head hung limp from her neck, wagging back and forth as they traveled down this uneven road; her hair hid her face like a veil, her seatbelt the only thing keeping her upright. She'd been lighter than Cayden had imagined, and he'd been able to snatch her off the floor and carry her across the lawn with great ease. He was no weakling, mind you, but he'd expected to have a harder time of it. After all, getting Mancuso into that kitchen chair and tying him up had taken a considerable effort.

It's the heart, Cayden realized, and a grin of near ecstasy bloomed across his lips. *A bit of the gods' power now flows through me, giving me strength!*

"Not long to go now, lass," he told Sheri. "Not long at all, then it'll all be over, and the gods will finally be free. Long may they reign!"

Cayden turned his attention back to the road. As he drove, his headlights reflected off something white up ahead. A car; it sat parked in the grass between the woods and the road. He was nearly on top of it before he saw HARMONY POLICE stenciled across its back.

Oh, for fuck's sake.

He sped by, then looked in his rearview mirror, expecting to see its headlamps flare like eyes in the darkness, its light bar painting the night red and blue as it roared after him. Instead, the cruiser just sat there and the black void swallowed it whole.

Maybe nobody's inside of it, he thought. *Could I be that fuckin' lucky? Maybe it's just a trick. You know, tryin' to get people to slow the fuck down. I've read about small towns doin' shit like that. They don't have enough manpower, so they put some store mannequin in a police car and make it look like a fuckin' speed trap.*

Cayden glanced at the road ahead, then back in his rearview mirror, still finding nothing but darkness behind him. He smiled. *The gods are with me. I feel their power coursing through my veins.* "Nothing can stand in my way," he muttered. "Nothing."

A siren wailed in the distance.

His smile faded and his eyes shot to the wing and rearview mirrors, searching for its source. The police cruiser raced around a bend in the road behind him, its lights flashing.

"Oh, bloody hell."

Cayden's eyes shifted from his mirrors, to the road, then back again. He tightened his grip on the steering wheel and tried to focus, tried to *think*. He'd been careful to avoid any unwanted attention until now, always managing to fly just below the radar. He'd never really stopped to ponder what he might do if he were ever caught; he'd never even considered the possibility.

Bollocks! Not gonna happen, not now, not when I'm this close.

He glanced over at Sheri, still out cold. The dart gun lay on the seat between them, but these weren't Piccadilly Bobbies he was dealing with. No. Cops in America had real guns, didn't they? And they weren't afraid to use them. There were rifles and bullets in the back of the truck, of course, enough for a small army, but he would never make it to them in time, and even if he could arm himself, they would surely be wearing Kevlar. All he had was a CO2 pistol full of knock-out darts and his blade. What possible chance did he have?

The police cruiser loomed larger in his rearview, closing in.

Cayden felt his foot grow heavy on the gas pedal; he thought of making a run, then quickly reconsidered. He'd seen more than his fair share of car chases on the telly, and while there were variations to the theme of bright lights and helicopters, of bullets and barricades, of flat tires and collisions, they all had the exact same conclusion: the runaway driver never got away. Be it in handcuffs or a body bag, ultimately, their ride ended, they were carted off.

Game over.

No. It was best to just confront them now, maybe even before they had a chance to radio for reinforcements. "I believe in you, my lords," Cayden said aloud. "My gods." He flipped on his turn signal and pulled off onto the grassy shoulder. "I *believe*."

The police car followed him over, hanging back, parking about three meters off his rear bumper; its lights still flashed, but at least they had killed the damned siren. He could see movement within, two shadows, talking it over, probably calling in his license plate number, just to be sure. They obviously knew he killed Mancuso, that he was dangerous. Why else were they being so cautious?

"Do they know about you, lass?" Cayden put his hand on Sheri's limp leg and gave it a pat. "Do they know how precious you are?"

In his mirror, the police cruiser's doors swung open. The shadows were climbing out onto the grass, coming for him, coming to ruin everything.

He had to act quickly.

"For you," he muttered, and his hand wrapped around the rune stone that hung from his neck, around the all-seeing, all-knowing eye. "All for you."

And grabbed his ceremonial dagger by the hilt and poked the tip of his left index finger, drawing blood.

"22-06," the dispatcher called over the radio, "be advised, changing from a Code 10851 to Code 207."

Officer Hicks looked over to Kirsch for confirmation. "Kidnapping?"

The older cop nodded. His eyes were still on the stolen animal control truck that sat parked in front of them. Its motor was still running, and their motor was still running, ready to give chase if the perp tried to make a run for it.

"Suspect considered armed and dangerous," dispatch warned. "Proceed with caution."

"Ten-four," Kirsch said, "Proceeding with due caution."

"Ten-four. All units hold the air until I hear word from 22-06."

Kirsh had one hand on his Glock and the other on the door.

"Let's rock and roll."

They climbed out of the car, their guns drawn, and Hicks thought once more of his wife, Angie, hoping she wouldn't be getting that call tonight.

"We regret to inform you that your husband can no longer rock and/or roll."

The truck sat there, its tail lights glowing like angry red eyes. Hicks glanced up the passenger's side to the sideview mirror, but he saw no movement within. Still, something didn't feel right. He could hear the chirp of distant crickets, could smell the hot exhaust, and he felt his whole body tense. It reminded him of one night in Iraq, just before a roadside bomb went off.

That thought made him particularly nervous.

Kirsh glanced across the roof of the cruiser at him. "Whatcha think?"

"I don't like it."

"Me neither." Kirsh held his gun out and moved his free hand to the set of handcuffs that hung from his belt. "Cover me."

Hicks nodded. He watched his partner step away from the cruiser and slowly work his way up the driver's side of the truck. Kirsh peered into the windows along the bed cap, evidently saw nothing threatening, then moved on.

The driver's door opened and a man leapt into view. He was tall, dressed in a dark leather jacket and jeans. His hair was bright red, as if his head were on fire, and there were symbols drawn across his face in blood like war paint – an eye on his forehead, and something that looked like a cactus on his cheek.

Jesus...What a whack-job!

"Stop!" Kirsh ordered. "Let me see your hands!"

There was blood on the man's hands, too, and something else. "Gun!" Hicks yelled.

Kirsh saw it. "Drop your weapon," he yelled, "and get down on the ground!"

The man didn't respond at first. Then, he smiled – a wide, sinister grin, like the Joker from a Batman comic.

*God almighty...*Hicks stared at the suspect with amazement and disgust, and his grip tightened on the butt of his Glock. Fear tugged at his nerves, triggering all sorts of warning bells in his brain. *This guy's* *not gonna drop it*, he thought. *He's a fuckin' loon. He's not gonna get down, and we're gonna have to put him down.*

But the man acted as if he might actually comply with Kirsh's orders. He held up his hands in surrender, backed up a step, and started to bow down. But he still held the gun.

Spittle flew from Kirsh's lips as he yelled, "Drop the fucking weap–"

The crazy man fired at Kirsh with his head still bowed, and a dart speared the cop's left eye. Hicks knew guys in his platoon who could have made a shot like that, but not without aiming first, not without even looking at their target at all. Kirsh screamed; he reached up, grabbed the feathered end of the projectile, and when he plucked it free, blood ran down his face in a flash flood.

Hicks instinctively pulled his trigger, but the suspect somehow managed to evade him. The man was there, dead in his sights, and then, in the blink of an eye, he was somewhere else. His speed was unbelievable.

The painted man ran up to Kirsh, looking like a savage warrior, a serrated blade glittering in his bloodied hand.

A knife? Hicks' mind was still reeling. *Where'd he get a fucking knife?*

In an instant, the man slit Kirsh's throat from ear to ear. Blood erupted from the cop's opened neck, shimmering in the bright light from their headlamps; it sprayed the side of the animal control truck, tinting the windows red. And then the killer picked Kirsh up off the ground – actually lifted the cop off his feet, as if he were a dummy stuffed with newspaper or straw instead of a man who weighed more than two hundred pounds – and tossed him back.

Hicks tried to catch his friend, but Kirsh struck him in the chest like a sack of potatoes, knocking the air from his lungs and pushing him to the ground. He struggled to get to his knees, but by that time, the killer had climbed back into the stolen truck. Tires spun, kicking up a cloud of dust, and the vehicle lurched onto the road. Hicks lifted his gun, fired off another shot, and shattered the back window of the bed cap. The killer never slowed. He sped off into the blackness, leaving the policemen behind.

Hicks looked down and saw that he was now covered in sticky gore. He quickly patted himself down, searching for a wound and finding none. All the blood belonged to his partner.

He placed his hand over Kirsh's neck wound and pressed down hard, feeling warmth jet against his palm, feeling the force behind it ebb away. Hicks keyed his radio and screamed, "I need a bus! Officer down! Officer down!"

When Robby and Agent Preston arrived at the scene, Officer Kirsh was already dead. His partner, Hicks, sat in the back of an EMS bus, getting checked out by another EMT. The officer was still understandably stunned, but physically, he would be fine.

"What about Sheri?" Robby asked, grabbing the officer by the arm. He felt the tears welling up behind his eyes, heard the shaky urgency in his own voice, but he couldn't help it. He had to know.

Hicks shook his head. "I never saw her. Kirsh looked in the back of the truck, but if he caught sight of her, alive or dead, he didn't say anything to me, and now..."

Robby nodded and released his grip. "I'm sorry," he told him. "Kirsh was a good man."

"Yeah."

"Can you describe the son of a bitch who killed him?" Preston asked. "Who are we lookin' for?"

"That guy..." Hicks looked at them, confusion still swimming in his eyes. "I don't know what he was on...crank, PCP...I don't know, but he was *strong*, I mean...he was fucking Superman, and fast. He drew these designs on his face with blood and – "

"Designs?" Robby frowned. "What kind of designs? What did they look like?"

Hicks blinked and searched for words. "He had...an *eye*, on his forehead, and...I don't know, some squiggly shapes on his cheeks that looked like cactus or something."

Robby frowned. He climbed past Hicks into the back of the bus, knowing exactly what he needed and where it was kept.

Hicks turned to look at him. "That means something, doesn't it?"

"It means I know where he's headed." Robby found clear bags of saline solution, grabbed them up, and glanced back at Officer Hicks. "You want to get this guy?"

"Of course I do!"

"Well then, I need you to go back to the station and sign something out of the evidence locker. Can you do that?"

Hicks shrugged, still more than a little confused. "If you need me to, yeah, I can do that."

"What about us?" Preston asked. "Where are we goin'?"

Robby nodded at the open door, at the darkness beyond. "There's a Department of Transportation hub just up the road a bit, between here and the Fuller place."

"You think he's ditching the truck, stealing a new ride?"

"I don't know if he is or not," Robby told him, "but we are."

october

CHAPTER THIRTY

The Fuller Farm haunted attraction opened for business on Friday, September 30th, at just after seven in the evening. The "just after" was due to the fact that there had been a minor technical glitch with the credit card reader in the box office, and some of the actors were not done with their make-up and in position when they should have been. Other than that, the night had gone well, even better than Captain Lou Davies could have hoped for. And now, here it was, just after midnight on the first day of October, less than an hour until close, and they still had a line that snaked half way around the house.

While people of all ages had been through the haunt over the last five hours, a bulk of the guests were in their late teens or early twenties, many wearing Stanley University sweatshirts to keep the late-night chill at bay. *Probably because of the half-price coupons in the college paper,* Davies thought, and he wondered just how much they'd really made off the crowds. Still, considering all the potential ways this could have gone wrong tonight, he had to be pleased.

The patrons seemed to be happy as well. They were laughing and screaming their heads off. Some even left the house in tears.

Davies filled with pride. They'd been painting and putting last minute touches on the haunt until a few hours before opening, and he was simply amazed they had been able to put together something *that* frightening. Of course, the stories surrounding this place, and the fact that the tales were based, at least in part, on fact, probably hadn't hurt their cause.

I hope the rest of the month goes just as smoothly, he thought, and he reached out and knocked on one of the wooden supports for good measure.

Davies had walked through the house more times than he could count tonight, making sure his actors had water, making sure the kids didn't tear down in one night what it had taken nearly a month to put together. He glanced up at the small surveillance camera in the corner. They had them throughout the haunt to keep an eye on various props and displays, their feeds going to a black and white monitor in the box office. They had signs up at the entrance that vandals would be prosecuted. Davies didn't know if anyone actually read them, but so far, there had been no issues, and the guests had been surprisingly well behaved.

He passed through a darkened hallway and forgot about one of the steel-framed pneumatics. When he set off the motion detector, a zombie sprang up out of a hole in the wall, accompanied by an ear-splitting shriek. Davies actually jumped, nearly dropping the walkie-talkie he held in his hand.

A moment later, when the radio crackled and spoke, he jumped again. "Cap," it said, "you there?"

Davies lifted it to his mouth. "Yeah, I'm here. Where else would I be?"

"We just got a call from Harmony PD. They said we've got some trouble headed our way."

"What kind of trouble?"

"Well, they said that some –"

The rest was lost beneath the shrill sound of frightened screams. Davies rolled his eyes. Between all the screaming, the loud mood music, and the roar of the chainsaws, it was a miracle he could still hear anything it all.

After a moment, however, Davies noticed something different about these particular screams. They didn't come from within the rooms or even from the back exit where the "chainsaw killer" had been. No. They came from *outside* the house.

They came from the kids who were waiting in line.

Huge yellow trucks sat parked, waiting all in a line, backed up against the fence with their snouts facing out – *CAT*, in chrome, centered on their huge, black grills. They were used for hauling, no more than glorified dump trucks during these warmer months – their wide front blades removed and stacked off to one side – but Earl Preston knew their true purpose; they were snow removal vehicles.

Salt trucks.

The gate was padlocked and chained. Robby shook it violently, then threatened to climb up and over the chain link. Luckily, Earl had a set of bolt cutters in his trunk. "For search and seizures," he said as he snipped the lock cleanly in two.

They hurried across the tarmac. Sodium lamps turned the compound into a glowing, yellow oasis in the middle of the darkened woods off Route Six.

"I don't suppose they keep keys in the ignitions," Earl said.

"No."

"How you plan to start 'em up?" Earl asked, and when Robby turned to look at him, he frowned. "Don't you dare ask me if I know how to hot wire, Miller. I'll punch you right in the mouth."

"No, no." Robby pointed to a small building on the other side of the enclosure. "They keep all the keys locked up in the office."

Earl followed Robby over to the structure, and he noticed a camera turn to look at him as it surveyed the lot. He reached into his pocket and held up his badge for the electronic eye to see. Later, there would be some explaining to do, some paperwork to fill out, probably more than one report to file, but only if they made it through the night.

Robby tried the door and found it locked. He jiggled the knob, pounded on the wood, then held out his hand. "Let me see those bolt cutters," he said.

"You can't cut off a doorknob with bolt cutters," Earl told him, but he handed them over anyway.

Robby took the heavy tool and tossed it through a plate glass window to the left of the door. Despite the noise of shattered glass, no alarm sounded. Broken shards rained down onto the asphalt, and Earl leapt back from them.

"Jesus! How 'bout a little warning?"

"Sorry." Robby reached through the jagged opening, unlocked the door, then went inside. He picked the bolt cutters up off the floor and frantically scanned the room.

Earl shook his head and asked, "Do you even know what the fuck you're looking for?"

"Some kind of lock box."

"What, like that one?"

Earl pointed to a grey metal box mounted to the back wall, above and behind what must have been the supervisor's desk. Robby ran over, found the small padlock that kept it closed, and used the cutters to snip it open. Inside, rows of keys hung on tiny hooks; round, cardboard circles assigned numbers to each of them.

"Wasn't the truck on the end labeled 22?" Robby asked.

Earl turned and peered out the hole where the window should have been for conformation. "Yeah."

Robby snatched the truck key from its hook, then tossed the bolt cutters back to Earl as he went out the door. "You open up the shed," he told him. "I'll pull 'er around."

The salt shed looked like a giant, concrete igloo. Earl rushed over to it, once again using his bolt cutters like a skeleton key to open the padlock. Inside, stored road salt had been piled high, forming light green dunes that sparkled in the moonlight. There was an old, beat-up snow shovel to the right, and Earl found himself wondering if they would have to use that to fill the huge truck one tiny scoop at a time.

Behind him, one of the trucks roared to life. Earl turned in time to see Number 22 pull away from the other parked vehicles and speed across the lot. As it sped toward him, Earl hoped Robby understood the size and weight differential between his little Ford and that beast of a diesel he was now driving; it wasn't going to stop on a dime.

The empty salt truck did stop, however, and when Robby climbed out of the driver's seat, he sprinted in the opposite direction, away from the shed. *Where the hell is he goin'?* Earl wondered. And a moment later, he had his answer.

Loud, piercing beeps filled the air, and a big-wheeled loader backed into view with Robby at the controls. He called out, "I'd move, agent, if I were you."

Earl nodded and stepped aside, allowing him access to the piled salt. Robby dug into the dunes, filled his scoop-shovel, then shifted gears and backed out of the shed. *Beep...beep...beep...* The tractor spun around, rolled up to the side of the truck, and dumped its load into the back end. Robby repeated this process three more times, until the dump bed was filled to the brim; fifteen tons of road salt.

"You really think we need all that?" Earl yelled as Robby parked the loader.

"I hope we don't need any of it," he called back. "But I think we want to lay it down thick. We don't want any of those things to get out."

Earl nodded. It really was a brilliant plan. They would drive the truck around, encircling the old farmhouse with road salt, creating a barricade, a dry moat that the creatures could not cross – well, at least not without hurting themselves.

Then, Earl had a terrifying thought. "What if something different comes out?" he asked. "Something that can leap really far, or maybe something that can even fly?"

Robby shrugged. "Then we'll have to think of something else."

They climbed up into the cab. Robby shifted gears, drove out through the open gate, and then he stopped abruptly.

"What is it?" Earl wanted to know. "What's wrong?"

"Nothing. I just need to get some supplies from the car real quick."

Robby opened the door and climbed out. Earl watched him as he grabbed a squirt gun off the cruiser's front seat – the same toy he'd seen him take from Sheri's place. Robby shoved the water pistol into a black duffle filled with IV bags from the ambulance. He slung the pack over his shoulder, then scrambled back up into the truck, tossing it onto the seat between them.

"What's all that shit?" Earl asked.

"The something else," Robby told him. He gripped the wheel, shifted gears again, and they drove off toward the old spook house.

The house stood more than a kilometer off Route Six, but something told Cayden to stop his stolen animal control truck when it was still a ways off. *Those coppers would've radioed ahead, wouldn't they?* he realized. *And, even if they didn't know I was headin' here, they would've warned 'em that I was comin' this way.* Not Cayden, per say – he was quite confident that his actions had been so quick, so shocking, that he would be little more than a shade to haunt the surviving cop's nightmares – but Mancuso's truck was another story.

Cayden needed to ditch it, and fast.

He drove off the winding dirt road and into the woods. So far, everything had been just as he'd envisioned it, and for that he was grateful. Like most magic, visions were tricky things. They could be quite literal, showing Cayden actual places and events in real time, but more often than not, they were impressionistic, giving him the flavor of what was happening, the emotion of it, rather than any real substance, and it was left for him to make sense of it all. And, because the gods were... well...*gods*, it was often difficult, if not impossible, to decipher their true thoughts and intentions.

And yet, Cayden had done everything they had asked of him. He'd performed his duties without question, like a little tin soldier with a wind-up key sticking out of its back. And they had wound him up good over the years. They had sent him all over the globe, chasing shadows, straining to hear the faintest of whispers, but tonight...tonight it would all pay off.

Tonight, it was all so simple.

Tonight, everything was clear.

No matter what the police had radioed ahead to their brothers in blue, Cayden came this way for one reason and one reason only: because the gods knew their time had finally come, because they believed the gate could now be opened, here, in this place, and because they believed that he and he alone could open it.

Cayden would see it done, whatever the cost.

He would see it done.

When Cayden turned off his headlamps, he expected the woods around him to go completely dark, but moonlight granted the entire scene an ethereal glow. He paused in his seat for a moment, taking in the natural beauty. It truly was a magical night. Cayden smiled, then he climbed from the driver's seat and walked around to the back of the truck, to the contents within.

He grabbed what he thought he would need – a roll of duct tape, a muzzle and leash, a chain and small padlock – then he walked up the passenger's side to where Sheri sat. He smacked her lightly on the cheek and said, "Wakey, wakey."

She moaned and her head rolled toward him, her eyes opened, but remained half-lidded slits. She was quite docile now, but Cayden knew it wouldn't last. As soon as the sedation wore off, her spirit would return.

"Come on, lass," he told her, "time to fulfill your destiny." Cayden tore off a strip of duct tape and smoothed it over her lips, then he slipped the muzzle over Sheri's head and tightened it. "And mine."

The restraints were made for animals, of course, and they did not fit as well as Cayden would have liked, but he thought they would do the job. He hooked the leash around her neck, then bent her forward so that her cheek rested on the dash. She fought a bit, but there was no real strength behind it yet, more of a flailing, really, a child in the throes of a bad dream. Cayden took the length of chain, lashed her limbs together behind her back, and secured them with the padlock. Satisfied, he backed away and yanked on her leash. "Let's go."

At first, she didn't budge, and Cayden thought he might have to carry her the whole way. He smiled a bit at that, because, if he really had to, Cayden believed he could do it. Tonight, he believed he could do anything. Cayden grabbed her by the hair and pulled her out of the truck. She moaned, or perhaps it was her attempt at a scream, but the duct tape and muzzle prevented it. Once he had her on her feet, Cayden gave the leash another, more insistent tug, and this time, Sheri obeyed.

"Good dog," he muttered. "Now, let's go for a walk."

Cayden still carried the dagger, and he was covered from head to toe in blood – much of it Mancuso's, but some of it his own. Sheri moved behind him like a drunkard, her muzzled head bowed, her hands tied behind her back, her gait slow and unsteady. Occasionally, she would stop dead in her tracks and mumble, but when Cayden gave the leash a good tug, she grew quiet and staggered forward once more. When they made it out to the dirt road, they strode along the shoulder, kicking up dead leaves with their feet. A few cars passed them by, leaving the Fuller place and heading back out to Route Six; headlamps bathed them in bright light, giving drivers and passengers a good, long look. They honked, they screamed and cackled, but none lifted a finger to halt his advance. Hell, some of them even leaned out their windows and cheered Cayden on!

If the building that housed the gateway had been in a major city, or even along Main Street in Harmony, this march might have been a bit more problematic, but they were out here in the middle of nowhere, headed toward a haunted house. To these passersby, it looked as if they were arriving in costume, or perhaps they were even a part of the show.

I'll give them a show, Cayden thought, tugging once more on Sheri's leash. *I'll give them a show they'll never forget!*

They continued along the winding road until the woods opened up to form a clearing. He paused for a moment, and Sheri walked into his back; she moaned and yanked back on the nylon strap that tethered her to him, but Cayden held the blade up to quiet her. This was no dream, no vision; he was looking directly at the old house. A huge sign loomed over the front porch, lit up like Christmas: THE FULLER FARM. Cayden's face filled with joy. He was actually here, in the presence of his almighty gods; he could hear them knocking on the doorways of his mind, demanding him to come closer and set them free.

The front lawn had become a parking lot filled with cars, and the kids who belonged to those cars were all lined up like ducks in a carnival shooting gallery, talking and laughing in their ignorance, each waiting their turn to get inside and meet their fate.

Cayden lingered at the edge of the trees for a moment, taking it all in, then he tugged on Sheri's leash. "Come on, lass. Let's not disappoint them."

When he stepped away from the tree line, Cayden noticed a fire truck and several police cars parked at the perimeter of the lot, up closer to the house; security. His smile faltered for a moment, then quickly returned. He had nothing to fear from the authorities. After all, soon there would be no authority on this earth but his and his lords'. Oh sure, the police might complicate things a bit, if Cayden's plan didn't go just right, but he had faith it would all go his way. And, more importantly, he believed that, after all these empty, nomadic years, his faith was about to be rewarded.

Cayden yanked on Sheri's leash again, dragging her behind him as he snaked his way between parked cars, headed toward the front door. "Come along with me," he muttered, "the real show's about to begin."

Blackness lifted like curtains before a show, and the silence gradually filled with noise – as if someone were slowly adjusting the volume on Sheri's stereo. Screams and cheers; they enveloped her, echoing in her ears, coming from everywhere. She found herself walking, putting one foot in front of the other, with no idea how she got here or where "here" even was. Everything was fuzzy, blurry, even her memories: answering the door, something red on her breast –

Shot! I was shot!

Sheri strained to reach for her chest, to feel for a wound, and felt pain instead. Her hands were now tied behind her back. No, not tied... *chained*. She could feel the cold metal against her skin, grating on the bones of her wrist as she struggled to move.

What...?

She blinked, trying to bring her world back into focus. Her mind was still on the Sit 'N Spin, working to trace what had happened to her, what was still happening even now. Sheri felt a rough tug on her neck and saw nylon strap trailing off of her, growing taught as it demanded her to move.

Sheri's head snapped up and she saw that the man from her doorstep now held onto her reins. He was still covered in blood; in fact, it looked as if he had been drenched in even more blood than before. His entire face was now a red blur, and he held a long, serrated blade that shimmered in the dimness.

She screamed. The scream went nowhere, however, just an impotent wind whistling through her nose. Whoever the man was, he'd bound her head too; a shadow stretched from her forehead to the tip of her nose, right between her eyes, and she smelled tanned leather; she felt the smooth metal links of chain across her ears and the top of her skull, and when she tried to open her mouth, Sheri found that it had been taped shut, and the more she worked against it, the more the straps bit into her forehead and jaw.

And yet, she still heard the sound of screaming. And yelling...and *laughing...*

Sheri turned her head as much as her bondage would allow and she found a huge crowd just standing there, no more than a few feet from her face. Men and women, boys and girls, some young enough to be her students – they pointed at her; a few screamed and shied away from her, only to have their laughing friends try and push them back again. None of them came to her aid, however. They didn't even seem to know that she was in danger.

"Yeah," her bloodied captor yelled at them, his eyes wide and crazed; he was waving that knife blade right in their faces. "She is but the first," he said. "You will all feed them! The fathers will feast on your flesh tonight! They will gnaw the marrow from your very bones! You are their cattle, in line for the slaughter!"

The crowd only laughed and cheered in reply.

Why aren't they tackling him? Sheri's mind cried, feeling tears at the back of her throat. *Why aren't they helping me?*

"You're next!" the red man screamed into the crowd, and they screamed and laughed and yelled right back at him. They actually seemed to love it!

As Sheri's vision cleared, she noticed that the red smear of blood on the man's face had taken the form of symbols – the same pictograms she and Robby had found down in the cellar. He was a Druid, part of the same sect as Fuller, as those ancient peoples Robby had studied. What had he told her over dinner? *Their gods delight in the slaughter of prisoners... cannibalism...the ritual sacrifice of women...*

"Come on, lass," the blood-soaked man called over the sounds of the crowd. "There's nothing to be *afraid of.* Come on!"

Sheri now saw where he was leading her: the front door of the Fuller house, and no doubt that basement room beyond. *No, no, no...* She squeaked and moaned and stopped in her tracks, refusing to take another step forward. Her heart pounded and she shook all over.

"Come, my sweet," the man urged, and he yanked on her leash. "There are things inside that want to meet you!"

Sheri shook her head violently, still trying to scream, to call out for help, but the tape and muzzle conspired to make it impossible. She felt her eyes widen and squirmed against her bonds, her feet remaining set despite the more insistent tugs on her reins. *I can't go in there. I'm dead if I go in there. I'm gone if I go in there, like Jeff, like those kids from the forties... never to be found, never to be seen or heard from again...*

"I don't think she wants to go inside," the bloodied man said with a frown. "I think she's too scared!"

The crowd booed her. Some made chicken sounds – *bock, bock, bock, bock, bock, begowwwwk* – while others held out their down-turned thumbs, like spectators in a Roman arena.

"Can I get a picture with you?" one of the women asked.

The bloody man chuckled and smiled again. "Sure, lass. Sure."

They think this is an act, Sheri finally realized. *Just a part of the big show...*

The woman from the crowd stepped over and stood next to them, smiling while her friend snapped a photo with her cell phone. Then, when she stepped back into the line, the madman took a step toward Sheri. He grabbed a fistful of her hair, and twisted it viciously. "What do you think? Should she come inside? Should she be my next sacrifice?"

"Yeah," they cheered, nearly in unison.

"You heard them, lass," the madman said. "We all want you to come inside!"

He grabbed her by the arm with the same hand that held the long, serrated blade; the metal touched her skin, and Sheri felt something sticky on the end of it. She cringed and moaned again.

"*Now*," the man growled in her ear. Then, he tugged on her arm and her hair in unison, and she felt the ruthless, unyielding strength in his grip as he dragged her up the steps toward the front door.

He's so strong! *How can I fight him when he's so strong?*

The answer became painfully obvious: she couldn't. Before Sheri knew it, she was inside the old farmhouse, the cheers of approval from the crowd outside dying in her ears.

Robby couldn't think about Sheri dying. He couldn't allow himself to even consider the possibility. And dealing with the salt truck's unaccustomed shift configuration on the sharp curves and hills of Route Six helped to keep his mind off it.

Loaded down with fifteen tons of road salt, the hulk handled like shit, and Robby was frequently over the center line. At one point, while going down one of the road's many slopes, he thought he might lose control of it all together, but somehow, he managed to keep it upright and on course. Luckily, there was very little traffic on this road during the day; and absolutely nothing at this time of night.

Robby gripped the steering wheel just as tightly as fear gripped his spine. His eyes were focused on the road ahead, knowing exactly where it went, yet having no idea where it would ultimately lead him. His foot flattened the accelerator on the straightaways and eased up on the curves, and he glanced over at the digital clock in the dash, watching the numbers change as time ticked by. Too much time. He only hoped he wouldn't get to the Fuller place a minute too late, or wreck old Number 22 somewhere along the way.

Please, God, let me get us there in one piece, and please, please *let Sheri be okay...*

Agent Preston sat next to him, muttering a few prayers of his own; his hand wrapped around the roll handle above the door so tightly that his black knuckles had turned to pale coffee. "So what do we do when we get there?"

"We end it," Robby told him.

"Yeah, but *how?* I get how we stop the creatures from getting out of the house, but how do we stop this fucker from opening the door in the first place? And, if he does open this wormhole thing, how do we close it up again?"

Robby frowned. He knew that, in the kidnapper's mind, opening the gateway would require blood sacrifice or worse, and Sheri was his intended victim. Again, not something he wanted to think about, not something that he would ever allow. But, the door was already open, if only a sliver; and it had been since the forties. At least now, Robby thought he knew what was needed to finally slam it shut. "You remember that stuff the professor guy said?"

"Who – Dr. King?"

"Yeah, King. He said that, to keep a gateway open, to keep it *stable,* you'd have to have a lot of negative mass, some theoretical shit that they think *might* exist but can't prove and have never even seen."

"Yeah, okay, so?"

Robby shrugged. "So, what if it's not negative *mass* that keeps this thing open, but negative energy?"

"What kind of neg –?"

"*Spiritual* energy." Robby took his eyes off the road long enough to look Preston dead in the face. The agent stared back at him in disbelief. "I'm serious," he told him. "What if all those sacrifices, and murders, and God only knows what, created so much negative energy that it...I don't know...poked a hole through outer space or inner space or whatever and opened a door right into this other world?"

Preston frowned. For a moment, he was speechless, thinking it over. "So," he said at last, "you're trying to tell me that the place you guys turned into a spook house really is haunted, that we've got monsters coming out of the woodwork now because there were ghosts in the woodwork before?"

"Sort of. I'm not talking real ghosts or poltergeists and demons, not really, and believe me, I know what I'm talking about in that area."

"I have no doubt," Preston told him, and it sounded like he meant it.

Robby smirked, then went on, "I think it's just more of a residual thing, you know? I mean, these Druids believed that all the blood they shed created magic, right?"

Earl shrugged. "I guess so. I know the Aztecs did."

"Right. Well, what if it's true? What if all the horrors and fear, all the bad emotions those atrocities generated, what if everything that happened in that hell house filled it with so much negativity that it keeps the doorway open, like some kind of perpetual motion machine?"

"Okay, I'll bite," Preston ventured. "Let's say you're right...how do we stop the motion and close it up again? We say 'sorry for what happened to y'all, no more hard feelings, goodnight,' and then we just hope and pray that all the negativity just goes away?"

They both chuckled at that, but even as Robby chuckled he still felt scared out of his mind. He was scared for Sheri, for what her captor might do to her at any moment, scared of what the madman may have already done, and scared for what might happen to all of them if they failed to stop him. When they were done chuckling, Robby shook his head and said, "I had something a little different in mind."

"Like what?" Preston asked. "I want to know."

Robby smiled humorlessly. "What's the matter? Don't trust me?"

"I hijacked a salt truck with you, didn't I?"

"*Commandeered*," Robby corrected. "I know you're new to this job, Agent Preston, but you really need to learn the lingo."

The agent rolled his eyes. "Whatever! The point is, my ass is on the line for this, probably more than yours, and I'd just like to know what you're planning to do before you go and fuckin' do it."

"Fair enough," Robby agreed, and then he told him, "I plan to save Sheri, then I plan to bring the whole place down around that motherfucker's ears."

Cayden's ears filled with the sounds of discordant music, with groans and shrieks and every other sound effect the designers could conjure up to elicit fear. And, while he could feel the terror sweating from Sheri's every pore, could feel her trembling and quaking with dread in his grasp as he pushed and dragged her through the various rooms and corridors of the Fuller house, fear was the furthest thing from Cayden's mind. Strobe lights kicked on, trying to disorient him, giving his motions the odd, jerky quality of a stop-motion monster, granting the blade he held a brilliant, unearthly glow, but his path and his purpose were clear as crystal. All around them, people leapt from the shadows in rubber masks and elaborate costumes: growling, yelling, and screaming, attempting to rattle him, to produce some kind of shock and alarm, but nothing could shake the smile from Cayden's face, not tonight.

He practically danced through this house of horrors, danced and laughed like a loon. There was entertainment to be had in this place, but it was not to be from this mockery of pain and suffering, from foam and latex creatures springing up from the shadows. No. The fun was to be had from *true* pain, from *real* suffering, and from the ultimate release they would yield to his fathers, from the flesh and blood creatures who would soon rise to embrace him as their disciple, as their *child*.

Yes, once his lords were freed, freed by his hand, there would be plenty of entertainment for all.

Cayden pulled Sheri around another sharp corner, and the winding corridor opened up into a large chamber. The walls were painted grey, made to look like stone, and there were skeletons chained to them, bodies covered over in lacy drapes of cobwebs. In the center of the room, a faux stone altar had been erected, and a rubber body lay eviscerated, opened from neck to groin. Behind the altar stood a man in ratty, brown monk's robes, he held a dagger in one hand – made of plastic bones and an equally plastic blade – and a rubber heart in the other.

The man pointed at them and said, "Who dares disturb this ceremony!"

Cayden howled with laughter. He threw back his head and laughed long and hard. He laughed until tears streamed from his eyes. "Oh, my," he said, wiping his face with the back of his hand, smearing blood across his cheeks, still cackling. "Aren't you the scary one?"

And then he held up his own dagger.

"Sorry, mate." Cayden lunged forward, slashing out. "Mine's bigger."

The fake monk took a step back, his eyes questioning whether or not Cayden's blade was real, then the point of the dagger sliced through his ratty, brown robe, creating two cuts: one straight across, the other down and diagonal, like the beginnings of the mark of Zorro.

"Jesus Christ," the monk exclaimed; he dropped his plastic weapon and flattened himself against the back wall. "You're crazy!"

"No, brother," Cayden told him, still pointing at his chest with the blade, "If you stay in here, I'd say you're the one who's crazy."

The false monk moved away, still hugging the rock wall. When he was safely out of reach, he bolted for the exit, his eyes never leaving the dagger in Cayden's blood-stained hand.

Sheri moaned and squirmed, fighting against her bonds. Cayden smiled at her, wondering if she knew what was to come. He took another step toward the altar and pushed the fake body aside, watching its rubber limbs flop as it hit the floor.

This got him laughing all over again.

Cayden looked down at the mock altar and shrugged. *Well, it's not the dog's bollocks, but it'll do in a pinch.* He gave Sheri's reins a good, hard yank and said simply, "It's time."

She shook her head back and forth, denying it.

"Sorry, lass." In a single, swift motion, Cayden grabbed Sheri by the waist, picked her up off her feet, and slammed her down on the altar. "Actually, I take that back. I'm not sorry at all."

A pained moan filtered through the duct tape as she struck the table, and Sheri rocked to and fro. Both hands were still chained behind her back, and they slapped and dragged across the fake stone as she bucked and writhed and tried to pull away from him, her back arching and twisting like a worm on a hook.

"*Yes,*" Cayden said, and then he giggled. "I can't believe I've never chained a girl up before. Call me kinky, but...I do think I like it."

He released the nylon strap to her leash, wrapped his newly free hand around her throat, and pressed down on her windpipe. Then Cayden leapt up onto the altar and straddled her; he sat down on her legs, pinning her to the altar, prompting another loud groan.

Cayden stared down into her eyes, saw the kindling of rage burn bright within them, and said, "Ah, you're a strong one, lass. You'd kick my bollocks from here to Sunday if I gave you half the chance, wouldn'tcha?"

Sheri moaned, more with fury than with pain or fear. If she could, Cayden knew she would spit in his face just as he'd spit in Mancuso's.

"You know, you should be thankin' me," Cayden told her. "I'm goin' to reunite you with your boyfriend... Jeff."

Her eyes widened and she stopped squirming beneath him.

"I watched him bleed, ya know, watched him feed the fathers. His death helped to hold the gate open, just a crack mind you, but open all the same. See, the blood of a man makes for weak magic. But the blood of *woman* ..." Cayden brought the ceremonial dagger up, held it in front of her face, and watched her wide eyes fill with terror. "Now that's real power. That's *life*. And for the fathers, it's the key to freedom."

He moved the blade down the front of Sheri's blouse, slicing through the fabric, exposing her jet black bra and the pale canvas of her flesh.

"I do hope you're a screamer," Cayden told her with a smile. "I do so love a screamer." Then, he spoke the ancient words, the ritual of summoning, handed down to him by his own father, and his father's father before him.

He took the point of his blade and began to draw.

A bright light appeared in the darkness, drawing wavy patterns across mossy, stone walls.

Like the deepest natural cave, Fuller's cellar knew nothing of the sun, knew nothing of the moon and the stars that had guided explorers to these shores for countless centuries. No. The only Earthly light the cellar had ever known came carried in the hands of men. But this *other* light, this yellow-green luminance...oh, it was no stranger to that.

The light began as it always did: a dot, a glowing pupil for the carved eye. Then it snaked out, slithering up and down the wall to form a jagged line. It filled in the fissure that divided the stone in half, then spilled over the edges to flood the neighboring bricks. Soon, the light had expanded into a small, vertical pool of spectral fire, a lake with a spinning whirlpool at its core.

A chlorine mist poured out through the vortex; thicker and heavier than the surrounding air, it fell to the cellar floor in a splash and spread like a slick in every direction, covering the dirt in a churning, billowing mass of yellow-green fog. And there was something else, something that crawled rapidly through the haze like insects from a crack in the killing jar. Dark, liberated shadows, they stained the pale, glowing cloud of vapor, crawling over and under one another in an excited frenzy. Strange, unfamiliar sounds filtered down from the rafters: sounds of distress, of suffering, of *food*.

The fleet-footed creatures hissed and headed for the stairs. They made their climb out of the fog, out of the darkness of the cellar, and whatever they were, they were hungry.

Robby brought the salt truck to a stop and looked through the dusty windshield at the entrance to the Fuller house. His mind raced, descending into the darkness of the cellar beyond, and his heart pounded in his chest, going out to Sheri. He took a deep breath, then climbed down out of the cab. Whatever was going to happen next, he hoped they were ready.

Agent Andrews was already on the scene. He ran over to Preston and said, "They went into the house about five minutes ago."

Five minutes. Robby frowned. He wondered how long it took to carve someone's heart out, then felt the cold dagger of fear stab deep into his own.

Preston glared up at the security guards who stood by on the porch. "Nobody bothered to stop him?"

Andrews shook his head. "They didn't realize it was him until it was too late. He had the girl chained up, lead her around by a leash, and they thought they were some actors from the haunt, trying to energize the crowd."

Captain Davies ran over as well, eyes and mouth opened wide with confusion and alarm. "I just saw them on the video monitors. He took her into the –"

"The cellar," Robby finished for him. "We know."

"No, no," Davies corrected, annoyed at the interruption. "He's got her in the sacrificial chamber."

Robby's stomach dropped.

"You built the man a fuckin' sacrificial chamber?" Preston shook his head at Davies and looked up at the moon. "What the hell is wrong with you people?"

Cap got defensive, "We didn't build it for –"

"Yeah, yeah, I know. Just ..." Preston pointed to the off duty officers on the porch. "Have them keep the crowds back. In fact, get them out of here, send 'em home!"

Cap glanced at the distant trees, then gave an audible gasp. "You think he's got the bomb you were searching for?"

"Well, since *you* didn't stop and search him, I don't really know, but if the house explodes, I want these college kids out of harm's way."

A siren wailed in the distance, drawing near. Robby's head instinctively turned toward the sound, watching as a police car sped up the dirt drive. *Please, God, let that be Hicks.*

Robby's prayers were answered when the car stopped and the officer emerged from within with a large black duffle bag, PROPERTY OF HARMONY POLICE DEPARTMENT stenciled in white down the side. Hicks unlocked the shotgun from his dash, then ran over to where they stood.

Robby met him half way. "Did you get 'em?"

Hicks nodded. He dropped to his knees and unzipped the duffle for Robby's inspection. Inside were sealed plastic bags containing some of the evidence from Charlie Spunkmeyer's basement armory: pipe bombs and a flash grenade.

"Did you have any trouble signing them out?" Robby asked.

"No," Hicks told him. "Your friend called ahead, said it was a matter of national security, but it's my name on the dotted line, which means it's my badge they'll come after, Miller, not yours and not his. I hope to hell you know what you're doing."

"So do I." Robby zipped the duffle back up and asked, "Can you drive a stick?"

"A -" Hicks blinked. "Sure, yeah."

Robby pointed to the salt truck behind him. "Think you can handle *that*?"

"I drove transport trucks in Iraq," Hicks told him, looking up at Number 22 with a shrug. "I wouldn't think it would be too much different."

"Good," Robby told him. "Come on. Let me show you how to lay down the salt."

"Salt?" Confusion seized the cop's face and he gave a nervous little chuckle. "What the hell, Miller?"

Robby wanted to tell him everything – monsters, wormholes, ancient Druids, the whole nine yards – but too much time had already been wasted, and Robby couldn't stand the thought of Sheri spending another minute with that madman. Besides, even if Robby told the officer all that had happened, and all that might happen if they failed, there was still a chance that he might not believe, that he might refuse to go along with the plan, and Robby couldn't let that happen. There was too much riding on this.

"Listen to me, Hicks," Robby said, trying to convey the seriousness of their situation. "We need you to drive around the house and spread this salt in a big circle. Keep circling and laying it down until you run out. The bastard that killed your partner is going to release something from this house, and the salt will keep it from spreading."

"What, like some kind of chemical or biological weapon?"

"Biological, yes. Can you do it?"

Hicks looked him in the eye, and Robby could tell that he knew it wasn't entirely true, but he went along with it all the same. "Show me how to work it," he said.

They climbed up into 22's cab. Robby showed him the gears, and more importantly, the button that needed to be pressed in order to start the salt flowing. "You got it?" Robby asked.

Hicks nodded. "Got it."

"I'm counting on you."

"I got this," he assured him. "You go get that son of a bitch."

Robby nodded. He grabbed the other duffle bag, the one that held the Super Soaker and saline solution, and he climbed down onto the grass. Hicks started old 22 up, the diesel engine growling like a beast, and the truck lurched forward. A moment later, the spreader began salting the earth.

"Hold the phone," Preston said, walking over. "Why aren't you drivin' the truck?"

"Because I'm goin' in there after that bastard."

Agent Preston frowned. "You mean after your girlfriend, don'tcha?"

"What difference does it make? They're together aren't they? If I find one, I'll have to deal with the other."

"Wrong," Preston corrected. "We both will."

"I can't ask you to – "

"Right, 'cause this cluster fuck is under *my* jurisdiction, so I'm ordering *you* to accompany *me* in there while I negotiate the release of a hostage. After all, the girl might be injured and in need of a trained medic." Preston drew his Glock, checked the chamber, then asked, "How's that for knowin' the lingo?"

Robby snorted and said, "Not bad. Thanks."

"You can thank me by not blowin' my ass to Kingdom Come."

"No promises. Now, come on."

Preston watched him walk away, a duffle bag in each hand, then the agent pointed back at the entrance with his Glock. "Door's that way, Miller."

"We need something else before we go in."

"Somethin' else? You can barely carry what you got!"

Robby led Preston over to a fire truck that sat parked beside the farm house. He dropped the duffle bags to the ground and opened the metal doors below the ladders and hoses, finding oxygen tanks and glass breathing masks. He pulled a couple out, then handed one over to Preston. "Put this on."

"We goin' scuba diving?" Preston asked with a frown.

"One of those scientists said these creatures might breathe a different atmosphere than we do, methane or chlorine. If that gate opens, I want us to be prepared so we don't suffocate or drown in our own fluids."

"Shit." Preston began strapping on the tank. "This night just gets better and better."

Robby strapped on a tank of his own, then looked up. Above his head, a fire axe rested on two metal brackets, its metal blade gleaming in the moonlight. Robby slid it out of the brackets and into his grasp, knowing that, if he went into that house and found Sheri dead, he would use it to chop her killer's head off.

―――――

Sheri wanted to cry out, to scream her head off, but she could barely even breathe. The madman held her throat in a vice-grip; he forced her down against the fake altar, sending intense waves of pain crashing through her skull. His arm was like some kind of pneumatic press with a thousand pounds of pressure behind it; so much pressure that Sheri thought this hand might actually crush her windpipe at any moment, might just tear right through her neck muscles and connective tissues – decapitating her, sending her head rolling back over the edge and onto the floor below.

She wanted to bite that hand, but the tape and the muzzle wouldn't allow it. She tried to kick, tried to knee him in his scrotum, but his weight on her legs made it impossible. And her arms, bound behind her back and pinned beneath her own weight, were just as useless.

Her abdomen was an active, crawling hornets' nest. The jagged edge of the man's blade burned stinging lines and excruciatingly elegant curves across her flesh. And, though she couldn't see what he was doing to her, what twisted art he was creating with her body, her mind painted quite an unpleasant portrait.

And that smile. *The man's smiling and laughing while he does it. Oh, he's having a ball!*

That was the worst part. Worse than this feeling of powerlessness, worse than the rancid smell of his breath in her face, worse even than the pain; that sick grin, that positively giddy, demented cackle of his. The absolute pleasure he derived from her agony; it was like he didn't even see her as a human being.

Crazy, Sheri thought of him, and the word echoed through her reeling brain like a shout down a well. *Crazy, crazy, crazy...*

Murderer.

Yes. That's exactly what he was.

The bastard says he watched Jeff die. He didn't say how he did it, but he did it. I believe him. Jeff's dead. He's really dead...and I...I'm about to join him.

Sheri closed her eyes; tears of fear and rage streamed from the corners and ran down into her ears. She heard her attacker crying out, even above the din of Halloween music and all the nerve-jangling sound effects, but the man was talking gibberish. Nonsense words that were unrecognizable even as language. And with each unintelligible syllable came another cut; fresh blood.

Her blood.

Her power, the madman had called it.

Her *life*.

It flowed across her stomach, forging scalding hot streams. The heavy drops ran down her sides and fell onto the altar below. She thought she might have lost consciousness for a moment, or perhaps for an hour. She really had no idea how long it had been.

How long...

How long could she go on like this before she passed out again, feeling him carve her up, feeling each slice and cross-cut, feeling the rhythmic sobs of her heart as it wept though each yawning new wound, and helpless to put an end to any of it?

At some point, Sheri knew that her body would release a flood of endorphins to try and drown out the pain, to make her numb to the burn and the sting, and then what? Would she simply lose consciousness again? Just float away into the great beyond and leave all this suffering, leave *everything* behind?

Sheri craved a cigarette; she could almost taste the smoke. And that sudden, undeniable need filled her with disgust. They were cancer sticks, poison, a slow and painful death. How could she do that to her body, to *herself?*

Her self-loathing kindled a sudden fire in her belly. She wasn't going to kill herself, and she wasn't going to let this crazy bastard do it for her either. No. She would not go quietly into that good night. She wanted to live, not for Jeff, and not for Robby, but for herself.

She was going to live!

Sheri twisted from side to side, trying to give her arms some room to move, to maneuver. She turned her wrists, tugged at the chains that bound her hands together. If she could only free her hand, just one hand, she could hook her fingers and scratch at her captor; rake him across the face. No. She could do more than that. She could claw the bastard's eyes out. She could be free of his weight, his grasp, his blade. And, best of all, she could turn that insane cackle of his into a scream.

Yes, hearing this murderer scream would be wonderful, something to work for, something worth the stabbing pain in her wrists, worth the warm gush of blood the chains brought to the surface as it tore into the skin above her thumbs. Yes, seeing this son of a bitch get what was coming to him would be a mighty fine thing indeed.

The madman stopped. No more chanting, no more cutting. He looked up, the dagger still clutched in his hand, and when Sheri saw her blood on the blade, when she saw it shimmering there in the harsh, eerie spotlights, she felt her stomach roll.

Her attacker paused, and he listened, and then Sheri heard it too. A thud; it was so quiet and stealthy that, at first, it was barely audible above the soundscape of the haunt. It was followed by another, louder thud, however, and then another, and another. They came in rapid succession now, like someone rapping at the door.

"You hear that, lass?" the madman asked, and the tone in his voice reminded her of a child on Christmas Eve, one who stayed up late to try and catch a glimpse of Santa Claus, one who heard a scratching in the night and thought it to be reindeer on the roof.

The knocking continued, growing louder, more insistent. And wherever that door was, Sheri heard it begin to crack and splinter beneath the weight of the thing, or *things*, on the other side. A moment later, she heard a loud crash as the wood finally gave way all together.

The smell came first, heralding their approach. It flowed in from the hallway, the reek of bleach, of drain cleaner, that chemical tang of chlorine. It drifted through the shadows of the haunt like a ghost, conjuring up memories of the spider-dog, but this stench was stronger.

So much stronger.

The madman looked up and smiled into the darkness.

"It's working," he told her, his voice full of pride, of religious glee. *"They're coming!"*

They came through the fake forest, Robby clutching the handle of the fire axe and Preston gripping the butt of his gun. They had consolidated the pipe bombs, flash grenade, and IV bags into one duffel, and Preston now had it slung over his shoulders like a backpack. "Feels like I'm back in basic," the agent huffed.

The neon-yellow Super Soaker hung from Robby's own shoulder, glowing brightly in the black light. Filled to the brim with saline, he hoped it would have a more desired affect than water alone.

Cardboard trees flew by Robby in a blur, but his mind's eye held Sheri in sharp focus. All those stories about this ancient sect, about what they did to their victims – scars so deep, not even the passing of centuries could erode or erase them – turned his insides into tangles of barbed wire. Robby had lost far too many people in his life, people he'd cared about, people he'd *loved*. He was not about to lose Sheri too.

"You smell that?" Preston asked, his nose crinkling.

And Robby did smell it, like they'd just climbed into the stands around Harmony High's swimming pool. Chlorine. And a lot of it.

Robby pinched the axe handle between his knees and his hands rose to the plastic face shield that hung around his neck. "Put your mask on," he warned.

Preston nodded and imitated Robby's movements, quickly strapping his face mask on, then turning the nob on his tank to start the flow of fresh air.

Sheri wouldn't have any protection, however.

Robby knew that there was no antidote for chlorine poisoning. In cases of air exposure, they were to remove and bag the victim's clothing and wash them with soap and water to try and get rid of any residue so that it didn't burn the skin. But if she breathed it, her body would immediately try and reduce the PH by filling her lungs with fluid, and unless they got her to a hospital quick enough to remove it, Robby knew she wouldn't survive.

"Come on," Robby called, trying to be loud enough to be heard through the mask. "We've got to hurry!"

Preston's phone rang, giving both of them a start.

The agent put it to his ear. "What?" He listened a moment, then said, "Yes, it's me! I'm talking through a fuckin' SCUBA mask!" After another moment, his head snapped up. "Where are they?"

"Where are who?" Robby asked.

Preston held up his hand. "Okay. Just...get out of there. There's chlorine gas. Get out to the salt truck." He disconnected the call and put his phone away. "That was Andrews. They were watching on the monitor. He said there's things coming our way."

"What kind of things?"

Something leapt out of the darkness and roared at them. It had long, two-fingered claws like a T-Rex. Its mouth was wide open and filled with fangs.

Preston immediately lifted his gun and shot at it.

The bullet grazed the thing's shoulder. It reached up with its claws to cover the wound, and cried out, "Jesus!"

Even muffled, Robby knew the voice. "Drake? Is that you?"

He reached out and grabbed hold of the thing's head. A rubber mask. Robby pulled it off to find a man glaring at them.

"You fuckin' shot me!"

"You jumped out at a man with a gun," Preston told him, lowering the weapon. "What'd you expect?"

"Sorry," Robby offered. "We thought you were something else."

He reached for Drake's shoulder and the man pulled away.

"Just hold still for a second and let me look at it."

Robby gave the wound a quick examination and saw that it was superficial, no more than a scratch. "You'll live," he said, then pushed Drake back toward the door. "Now get out of here! They're evacuating everyone!"

Drake nodded and stepped away from them, still dazed.

Preston shook his head. "Fuck this haunted house shit," he muttered.

Then Robby saw something crawl across the wall. At first, he thought it was an animatronic, another of Cap's toys. One of those weird props of rubber and vinyl that could be bought at any of the Halloween costume shops which sprung up to fill the vacant stores in the strip malls around this time each year.

There were half a dozen of them now, climbing diagonally from the floor to the ceiling, climbing over and under one another as if racing to see which of them could be first to touch the sky. They looked like centipedes. Plated, flat bodies with countless, segmented legs. And, although Robby could find no eyes of any kind on what appeared to be their heads, he had the feeling that they could see him.

He pointed at them. "Preston, behind you."

"Oh yeah?" The agent rolled his eyes. "Who is it this time? Jeepers Creepers? The *Candyman?*"

"Look out!"

The agent spun around just as one of the things launched itself at him. Its length wrapped around his neck like a noose, and the tip that Robby thought had been its head opened like the petals of some fleshy pink flower – blooming and unfolding to form long, boney mandibles tipped with fangs. The mouth lunged at Preston and, if not for the glass shield of his mask, he would have lost his face.

The creature drew back from his slimed faceplate, and before it could strike again, Preston reached up and wrapped his fingers around its slender body. He held the Glock up to its head, then shot it clean through. Instead of killing the animal, however, the blast only seemed to anger it. The thing tightened its grip around Preston's neck, strangling him.

"A little help, Miller!"

Robby's shocked paralysis broke. He lifted the Super Soaker and fired off a stream, drawing a line of saline across the creature's body. Its flesh smoked as the fluid sank in, eating its way through the writhing body like acid. The thing came apart in Preston's hands, two halves tethered together by gooey strands of melted mozzarella, but it didn't die. Instead, the strands snapped and each end became a separate entity, each with its own pained screech and desire to get away.

The segmented section around Preston's neck loosened its grip and crawled down the length of his body toward the floor. And in his hand, the head whipped around, its mandibles opening and closing as if it were chomping on the air. Preston threw the wriggling thing down and watched in horror as it scurried off into the gloom.

Robby squeezed the Super Soaker's trigger again, firing at the remaining centipede-things on the wall behind him. The creatures seemed to have learned from their brother's failure. They avoided the stream and hurried for the cover of darkness, no doubt following their comrade's pieces toward the exit.

"Come on," Robby urged. He reached for Preston's arm, tried to pull him onward, but the agent recoiled from his grasp.

"Don't we need to go stop 'em?" Preston asked, pointing back after the things with his gun.

"If Hicks has done his job, the salt will take care of that. We need to get Sheri out of here! And we need to do it now, before it's too late to –"

But it was already too late. Robby heard a familiar shriek, one that chilled him to his very marrow.

Sheri recognized that sound...that awful, terrible shriek. It was as if every nightmare held captive in the dark prison of her subconscious mind had suddenly been let loose on her waking reality. There was something horribly comic about the analogy, because Sheri knew that was exactly what had happened. She tilted her head with great hesitation, unable to stop herself, expecting the terror her eyes would meet, yet unprepared for the reunion.

The spider-dog.

It stepped out of the shadows and into the room, its scaly, emaciated body held aloft by those oddly-jointed, spiny-armored legs. The black marbles and eight balls of its eyes were soulless and unreadable, the hungry eyes of a great white shark. And it was not alone.

Sheri watched in stunned fascination as the horror multiplied before her. A second spider-dog followed the first into the room. And then she saw a third crawling across the wall like an Earthly spider from a 50's Sci-fi flick. By the time the fourth creature came into view, she called it what it was: a pack.

When the leader of this pack strutted toward them, Sheri nearly lost her mind. She screamed through her tape, twisted and bucked beneath the weight of her attacker, trying to throw his bulk off of her and scramble away, not even aware of the chains as they bit and bloodied her struggling wrists. The madman who bound her, who held her down, still straddled her, however, and he didn't appear to be frightened or concerned in the least. In fact, he looked positively delighted to see these monsters.

"Beautiful," he muttered, and the overhead spotlights caught a gleam in his eye, as if he might actually shed tears.

The lead spider-dog crawled alongside the altar, then rose up on its hind legs and looked the madman dead in his face. The man's bottom lip quivered and the tears did flow; tears of joy, of adoration. Sheri watched in utter disbelief as he bowed his head, actually bowed down to this...this *abomination*.

"My lord," the weeping man told it, "and my *god*." Then he pointed to Sheri with his blade. "This...this is the sacrifice I've prepared for you. I hope you're well pleased."

It cocked its head to stare down at her, and seen through the metal grid of the muzzle, Sheri felt momentarily safe, a bit like a diver in a shark cage. Her false sense of security evaporated quickly, however, when she remembered that this particular cage only covered her face. The rest of her body was exposed and cut upon; blood in the water.

The spider-dog's mouth flared and a long, slimy tube slithered out like a fleshy straw. Sheri closed her eyes. She felt this weird tongue caress her abdomen, saliva burning into each and every cut as it licked her skin. Her head snapped up, then fell back against the altar as she groaned again in pain.

It's going to kill me! Eat me! It's going to stick that thing into me and turn my insides into goo and there's not a damn thing I can do about it!

The tongue withdrew abruptly.

Sheri opened her eyes again, watching as the spider-dog pulled away and lowered itself back onto the floor. She blinked and turned her head to follow it. The creature rejoined its pack, and together, they bounded off down the hall.

A shadow loomed over her and Sheri looked up once more into the eyes of her captor. "You should feel honored, lass," he said, grinning. "The gods have anointed you."

Sheri didn't feel honored. Not at all. Instead, she felt panic rising in her like the tide.

"Now..." The madman held his bloodied dagger up to her eyes and said, "Where were we?"

Robby remembered the layout of the haunt, knew exactly where they were in the floor plan, and he pushed Preston into a shadowy nook just off the main hall. From this hiding place, a costumed actor would watch and wait, ready to leap out and scare unsuspecting passersby. Now, it was the frightened who were in hiding, hoping that whatever came down this corridor would indeed pass them by and let them be.

It didn't take long for the creatures to make an appearance. They were dark gray in color, but the black lights caused odd glowing bands, diamond shapes, or blotched markings to appear on their skin. Their clawed feet skittered by, and Robby kept count of their numbers.

One...two...three...

His breath caught in his throat.

Four! Jesus, four spider-dogs!

Crouched in their little hideaway, Robby and Earl were only a few feet away from the animals as they passed. The spider-dogs didn't seem to be aware of them, however. Their heads bobbed, up and down, then side to side. Occasionally, they would pause to give a guttural growl or loud snort. Robby held the Super Soaker at the ready, just in case the animals sensed something, in case they turned and attacked.

Then the pack moved on down the hallway, crawling toward the exit on their thorny, chitinous legs. Perhaps they were hunting the centipede-things, or maybe they followed a scent laid down by the first spider-dog over a month ago. No matter the reason for their migration, Robby breathed a sigh of relief that they were gone.

"How long do we need to wait here?" Preston asked impatiently.

"Long enough to be sure they're not coming back."

"You realized, those things came from the direction we're headed, which means they probably –"

"Don't say it," Robby warned him. "Don't even think it. She's alive."

"Fine. But we can't spend forever lookin' for her. We need to blow that gateway before any more of those fuckers decide to go for a stroll."

"All right." Robby stuck his head out into the hall, saw nothing, then motioned for Preston to follow him. They crept out of hiding and continued on to the sacrificial chamber, on to Sheri.

Something crept out of the Fuller house. Officer Hicks steered the salt truck back around to the front of the building, completing yet another circle, and came to a stop. He couldn't believe his eyes. Oh sure, he'd seen the creature lying dead in the woods, the one that attacked Robby Miller and the girl, the thing the media loved to call *La Chupacabra*, but to see it alive and crawling around was something else entirely, and quite frankly, something he hoped he'd never witness.

A second creature emerged from the darkened doorway, and another, and soon they were a quartet. They stood there on the weather-beaten porch, their bodies nearly the same color as the graying wood. Their heads bobbed and weaved as if they were taking in the sights.

So much for another quiet Saturday night.

The passenger's side door opened, nearly giving Hicks a coronary, and Agent Andrews climbed up into the cab. "Why did you stop?" he asked.

Hicks pointed to the creatures on the porch. "You didn't see those things?"

Andrews nodded. "I saw them. That's why we have to keep going. We need to get all this salt on the ground to keep them contained."

"Buckle up," Hicks told him, then shifted gears and stepped on the gas. In his side mirrors, he could see the salt fan out, could see the dark lawn broken by a sparkling swath of emerald crystals, but he didn't understand how it would stop these huge, fierce-looking animals from going anywhere they damn well pleased.

He thought of his wife, Angie, lying at home, safe and warm in their bed, wishing he was there with her, and hoping she could still sleep through the night without getting *that* call.

"We regret to inform you that your husband survived two tours in Hell, but was taken down by some pissed off crabs, jacked-up on steroids. Sorry for your loss."

For a moment, the creatures remained perched on the porch, staring at the big truck as it sprinkled the lawn. But Hicks had not driven more than ten feet before they bounded down the steps toward him.

Oh shit, here we go!

One of the animals leapt up on the side of the truck and the entire vehicle shuddered from the impact. Hicks glanced in his mirrors and saw it hanging there, it's claws actually digging into the metal, its head peeling like a banana to show its teeth.

"Jesus!" Hicks exclaimed in disbelief.

A second spider-thing sprang forward; aiming for what it must have thought was the head of its prey. It latched onto the left front fender and clawed at the hood, the sound of rending metal blending with its piercing shriek. They were like lions trying to bring down an elephant.

Andrews drew his 9mm Glock. The agent climbed out the passenger's side window and shot across the hood. His first bullet went wide and missed its mark, but he aimed his second shot more carefully and caught the creature right in the throat. Dark fluid spurted onto the windshield and Hicks turned on his wipers to clear it away. Andrews fired a third shot into the thing's narrow head, knocking it off the truck; it fell to the ground and rolled away.

One of the animals still clung to the side like a leech.

Hicks reached over, grabbed his shotgun, and said, "Take the wheel."

Andrews nodded and, as Hicks climbed through the window, the agent reached over the seat to steer. Hicks pointed the shotgun barrel at the screeching creature, centering the ghost ring on its weird skull. He fired, feeling the recoil in his shoulder, watching the toothy flower of the thing's mouth get replaced by a sudden bloom of blood and bone.

The two remaining creatures scurried after Number 22 like dogs. Hicks saw one of them drift too far into the truck's wake and crawl onto the piled salt. Its claws started to smoke! The thing danced and shrieked in agony, but as its legs were eaten away, it lost its balance and collapsed onto its side. Whole sections sloughed off its frame, gooey flesh riding steaming rivers of yellow-green pus and India ink, staining the shimmering crystals dark as they continued to melt.

"Holy shit," he said aloud. If he hadn't seen it with his own eyes, he wouldn't have believed it possible.

Hicks blinked, then racked another shell into the shotgun. He raised the barrel, ready to target the sole survivor. They were around the back of the old farmhouse now, and something else caught his eye.

A yellow-green glow.

It filtered through the boarded windows on the first floor, like someone shining a colored spotlight through a fish tank. Bright and shimmering waves of luminosity; it was almost hypnotizing. In fact, Hicks became so captivated by the light that he didn't even notice the final spider-creature closing in.

As they closed in on the sacrificial chamber, Robby felt a sudden wave of nausea. His heart raced and his pulse sounded in his ears. He was panting; his sweaty skin cold as ice.

I'm so fucking scared right now. I don't know what I'm gonna find when I get in there or what I'll do when I find it.

When they were about ten feet from the entrance, Robby flattened himself against the wall and motioned for Agent Preston to do the same.

This is it. Sheri's in there with that bastard cultist. What will I do if she's–

No. He couldn't even think about that right now.

Instead, Robby tried to distance himself, to focus on his training. As an EMT, he'd seen a thousand ways a body could be broken and put back together again. But he'd seen almost as many cases where the damage was too widespread, too catastrophic – cases where all the king's horses and all the king's men were totally useless. And it was these later cases, cases like his friends Danny and Sean all those years ago, like Mancuso tonight, that filled him with dread and threatened to throw him off his game.

Robby turned to Preston, wondering if the agent could tell just how frightened he'd become. If the man noticed anything, however, he never said a word. "Hand me the flash grenade," Robby whispered, trying to present a steady hand.

Preston slipped the duffel bag off his back and unzipped it. "You ever use one before?"

"Never."

"Then best to let me do it, unless you want to wind up blind and deaf by accident."

"Okay," Robby told him, tasting bile and swallowing hard. "Sure. You do it."

Preston rifled through the contents, looking for the grenade; he glanced up for a moment and nodded at the door. "Better make sure he's in there first."

Robby nodded. He moved along the wall, his heart wanting to bolt, but his mind urging caution and restraint. Trying to stay out of sight, he listened for voices, noises, any hint that they were still in the room. He heard one voice, a male voice, speaking in another language.

What did Druids speak? Robby wondered. *Old English? Middle English?*

Whatever it was, it certainly wasn't *his* English.

Robby lingered a moment longer, hoping to hear something from Sheri; a voice, a whimper, a moan...anything that might betray her presence, but he heard nothing to indicate she was –

Alive?

– conscious. He hurried back to Preston. "He's in there all right," Robby told him.

"Okay." Preston pulled the grenade from the duffle and held it up for Robby's inspection. "What we have here is your standard issue M84 stun or flash grenade. When this puppy goes off, there will be a loud *bang*, I mean *really* loud. We're talkin' 170–180 decibels within five feet of the detonation. There'll also be a blinding flash. Now, between the noise and the flash, the bastard should be blind, deaf, and dizzy as shit."

"What about Sheri?"

"Well, yeah, her too. But the effects are temporary, so once this baby goes *boom*, we're gonna need to act fast. Now, when I say – "

Laughter drifted down the hall; it was joyous, triumphant.

"Just throw the damn thing already!" Robby cried, straining to keep his voice down and their position secret.

Preston dropped the duffle bag, but he remained hunched over as he moved down the hall toward the doorway and the sacrificial chamber beyond. He put his finger through the pull ring, yanked out the safety pin, then released the lever as he tossed the grenade inside.

Cayden's finger traced the metal ring at the end of his dagger, traced the five-pointed star inside. His hand was shaking, and his voice trembled as it spoke the ancient words of summoning. Because had never expected to see this in his life. Not really. Yet he *had* seen it.

He had looked into the face of a god, and the god had looked right back at him.

His life flashed before his still-stunned eyes. All the places he had been in his life in pursuit of this moment, all the times he had doubted both his father and himself, all the moments of despair when he'd wanted to give up. But Cayden didn't give up. Not ever. No matter what happened in his life, he had always clung firmly to his faith.

Cayden began to laugh again. He was unaccustomed to triumph, and he found that the taste of victory was indeed sweet.

For thousands of years – ever since the gods had first been forced from this world by ungrateful, disrespecting, and disobedient children – their loyal priests and followers had tried to find a way to bring them back. But try as they might, nobody had ever found the proper door. So therefore, it had not been possible. Oh, they had the proper knowledge of ancient magicks, handed down for generations, and they had the blade, but what good did it do to have the keys to a door you can't bloody find?

How many? Cayden wondered. *How many have longed to stand where I am now – to be the one to open the door for these long-vanquished giants? Hundreds? Thousands?* Millions? *They failed. All of them failed. But not me.*

"Not me," he said aloud.

Now, the prayers had all been spoken. The sacrifice had been prepared, had even been blessed by the tongue of the gods themselves. Cayden only had one task left to perform.

He reached down and dipped the tip of his index finger in Sheri's still warm blood. Then, he touched her forehead and drew a third eye, the all-seeing, all-knowing eye, the eye that saw across the vast expanses of the universe to this place, this single moment in time. She squirmed beneath his touch, still fighting against the inevitable, just as uncooperative as Eve and all of her children, even now in the face of death.

"Goodnight, lass," Cayden told her. "And thank you."

She groaned in reply, her shoulders shaking as she sobbed within his grasp.

He lifted the dagger above his head, ready to bring it down, to thrust it into Sheri's chest and carve out her living, throbbing heart. Then, something moved in the corner of his eye. An object. It bounced, then rolled across the floor – dark, cylindrical.

Cayden didn't realize it was a grenade until it went off.

———

Like an object in the rearview mirror, Hicks didn't realize just how close the creature truly was. It leapt up at the salt truck, leapt up at *him*. Hicks saw movement, a shadow growing larger in the tail of his eye; he lifted the shotgun and fired.

The blast knocked the spider-thing away and it rolled off across the lawn.

Hicks racked another shell into the shotgun and looked around, not wanting to let his guard down again until he knew the coast was clear. He saw no more creatures, however, and so he slid back inside the cab, taking the wheel back from Andrews. "I got it," he said.

Andrews retreated to the passenger's seat, checking the mirror out his own window just to be sure.

"Did you see that light?" Hicks asked him.

"No," the agent told him. "Where was it?"

"It was coming from inside the house. Bright, whatever it was."

Andrews checked the chamber on his Glock, then nodded. "Probably just a flash from the stun grenade."

The flash from the stun grenade wasn't just bright, it was as if a sun had suddenly gone supernova right inside the room. Cayden's arms instinctively formed an "X" across his face in an attempt to shield his eyes, but it was too late. The world was burned away, replaced by white light and white noise, leaving carillon bells to ring through the cathedral of his skull.

My lords? My gods! What's happening? I'm not done! IT'S UNFINISHED!

Cayden screamed. At least, he thought he had. His mouth opened, and he felt the muscles in his throat working to push it out, but he could hear nothing over the deafening song of agony that rang in his ears.

There was another sharp bolt of pain, this time in his cheek and jaw, followed by a sensation of falling – up, down, sideways, he had no way to tell – and then he felt wood slap him hard across the back, knocking the air from his lungs.

Robby held his breath until his lungs ached, waiting for the blast. He did as Preston had instructed; he turned away from the door and cupped his hands over his ears. A moment later, the hallway brightened as if lightning had just struck the room behind them, and Robby heard a muffled roar.

Both faded quickly.

Preston spun around and tapped him on the shoulder as he raced by. "Come on, Miller," the agent said. "Move your ass, let's go!"

Robby followed close behind, and when they rounded the corner and burst into the room, he got a good look at Sheri Foster. She lay completely still atop the altar, atop her own arms, with a leather dog collar wrapped around her neck and her face partially hidden by a muzzle-like mask. A crimson eye had been painted across her forehead, the same drawing that adorned Mancuso's lifeless body, and her blouse had been ripped open – her black satin bra and gory midriff on full display.

Oh, sweet Jesus, no!

The murderer straddled her, the knife he'd used to carve her up still clutched in his hand.

We're too late. Too late to stop him, to save her. Too late.

Numbness stole through Robby's body and the axe slipped from his grasp and fell to the floor by his feet. He gaped at the scene, shaking his head, unable to believe it. His denial quickly turned to rage, however, and his slack, empty fingers curled into a tight fist.

Fueled by wrath and adrenaline, Robby rushed over to the killer and threw a punch into his face. The man was too dazed from the stun grenade to offer any kind of defense. Robby's blow struck him hard across the jaw, sending him tumbling back off the altar and onto the floor.

"*Murderer*," Robby spat as he followed the man down, throwing punches left and right, the Super Soaker that hung from his shoulder swinging and slapping at his back. Robby's fists pummeled the killer until the man's eye swelled, until his lip split and blood spurted from his nose. And Robby probably would have beaten the man to death, if not for the hand that grabbed hold of his arm in mid-swing.

Robby turned his head, his narrow eyes widening. It was Preston.

"That's enough," the agent told him. "They can't give him a lethal injection if he's dead."

Robby looked down at the man's battered face, then at his own bloodied knuckles. He was shaking, panting, his pulse like rolling thunder in his ears. "He killed her."

"No, he didn't." Preston nodded at the altar. "See for yourself."

Robby's eyes shot over to where Sheri lay; he saw her rocking back and forth, saw her knees come up off the table, heard her groan, and his despair turned instantly to joy. *Alive!* Tears flowed up from some deep, untapped well and spilled down his cheeks. *Thank God!*

"Go help her out," Preston told him, aiming his 9mm Glock down at the beaten kidnapper. "I got this fucker."

Robby rose up and hurried over to Sheri's side, taking a moment to survey her wounds. Her abdomen had been covered in a myriad of cuts and lacerations, but these were no random slashes. No. Even through the blood, Robby could make out odd shapes and intricate designs, weird hieroglyphics carved into her soft flesh as if it were soapstone. Some of the pictographs were similar to the ones they'd found in the cellar, while others were completely new and alien to him.

As gory as the gashes had seemed from a distance, none appeared to be life-threatening. Most probably wouldn't even require stitches. The blood was clotting, scabbing over, which was a good sign. And best of all, her beautiful heart was still there inside her chest, where it belonged.

"Not done," the kidnapper cried out from the floor, his voice choked by blood. "Not finished yet!"

The words sent a stream of ice water cascading down Robby's spine.

"Oh no," Preston told the madman, keeping him firmly in his sights. "I'd say you're pretty fuckin' done."

"Sheri?" Robby tried to look into her eyes, but they were still pinched closed. He reached out for the muzzle, attempted to see how it was fastened, but she wouldn't hold still long enough for him to get a good look. "Settle down, sweetie," he told her. "It's going to be OK now."

He managed to remove the leather straps and chains from her head and found that her mouth had been taped shut. Slowly, he peeled the duct tape back, gently freeing her lips. And when she opened her mouth, Robby wondered what her first words to him would be.

Sheri said nothing. Instead, she latched on to Robby's hand with her teeth and bit down hard.

When she heard the explosion, Sheri stopped fighting; she clinched her teeth, slammed her eyelids closed, pinched them together hard, and waited for that white light to scorch her to a cinder. Instead, she felt nothing. No heat, no flames, not even the weight of her attacker pinning her down.

But she knew wasn't dreaming. No. The throbbing, screaming symphony of pain told her that she was still conscious.

Sheri's ears rang. Her head ached. And when her eyes fluttered open, she saw a shape hovering over her, a silhouette. Close. So very close. Its hands were on her face now, lifting the tape.

The bastard wants to hear me scream, she thought. *Well, I'm not going to give him the satisfaction.*

No.

She would give him something else entirely.

Sheri's fight returned and she struggled to ignore the urgent cries from her wrists, from her shoulders and her belly, focusing instead on Robby, on denying this son of a bitch his victory. She opened her newly freed mouth and did what she'd been fantasizing about this whole time, as she laid there, powerless, feeling him cutting and carving, drawing blood. Well, now it was her turn. She bit down on her attacker's hand just as hard as she could, and when she tasted *his* blood, she rejoiced in that small triumph.

Cayden would not be robbed of his triumph. Not now. Not after he'd worked so hard. Not when his life finally had meaning.

The gods...they were counting on him.

That choir of bells in his ears slowly faded to a dull hum. He blinked, trying to focus. Ghosted, spiraling images coalesced. The figure standing over him became twins, then merged into one. A black man with a black gun aimed right at Cayden's forehead.

And, somehow, Cayden had lost the blade.

He lowered his eyes, searched for his dagger, and found it on the floor about a foot away. Cayden returned his gaze to the man with the gun. The gods had helped him move faster than a bullet once before. Perhaps...

Please, my lords, help me!

As soon as he'd finished his prayer, Cayden heard the scream. And he wasn't alone. The man with the gun heard it too; he took his eyes off Cayden and looked away for a moment.

But a moment was all Cayden needed.

The moment Earl Preston heard the scream, he glanced over, surprised by what he found. Sheri held Robby's hand in her teeth, biting down hard enough to draw blood. Earl's eyes widened, then he caught a sudden blur of motion to his right. When Earl glanced back again, he was equally shocked.

The fallen murderer, the one who had been beaten to a bloody pulp and laid wallowing on the floor in front of him, had somehow managed to stagger erect. The man smiled just a little with those split, bloodied lips, and he clutched an equally bloody dagger in his red right hand. The man looked crazed, and his blade appeared to be about eight inches long – a fucking Samurai sword.

How did he – ?

The killer moved then, deceptively fast, faster than Earl would have believed possible, given the man's condition – lunging and swinging his blade like a scythe.

Earl flinched back; he ducked and weaved to avoid being slashed. He lifted his 9mm and fired off a shot. The madman was three feet away, practically right on top of him, and yet, somehow, the bullet missed.

The madman's smile widened and he moved in for another lunge.

Without thinking, Earl lifted his leg and kicked the man in the abdomen just as hard as he could. It wasn't a judo kick, nothing his combat trainer would have been proud of. He simply brought the leg up, more as a shield than anything else, and when the killer ran into it, Earl pushed him back with all of his might.

It apparently was enough. The madman staggered back with a look of surprise, then his eyes narrowed and he made another charge.

Earl leveled his 9mm, fired off a second shot at the advancing figure's chest, and this bullet, too, missed its mark. Or maybe it didn't miss at all. Maybe it just bounced off, as if it were made of rubber instead of lead.

Couldn't have missed. Not from this distance. Not with the asshole dead in my sights. Who is this guy, fuckin' Superman?

Whoever he was, the madman was almost on top of Earl now. His blade slit the air repeatedly, slicing back and forth, back and forth – an advancing lawnmower to Earl's blade of grass.

Earl backed away, thought of firing off another round, then thought again. The 9mm clearly wasn't doing any good against this guy. And Earl knew that, if didn't find something that *would*, and *fast*, he was done.

As he retreated, Earl's heel bumped into an object on the floor. He dared a downward glance and saw that Robby's fire axe lay at his feet. Earl moved fast, ducking to avoiding the madman's killing stroke; he dropped his 9mm and snatched the axe off the wooden floor with both hands. He swung the blade in an upward stroke, as if he were going to throw the axe in some lumberjack contest, and hacked into the meat of the madman's left arm, severing his triceps and chopping right into his humerus. And when Earl pulled the axe free, blood struck the floor with a thick, wet *splat*.

The killer's scream was nearly as loud as the stun grenade had been. He reached over and tried to cover the leaking gulf with his free hand, but it was a poor seal; blood ran through the cracks between his fingers and sprinkled the floor like a busted water main. The madman gaped at it, confusion smoldering in his eyes, then igniting into full-blown alarm.

Earl lifted the axe, made a quick, jerky move toward the wounded killer, and the wide-eyed man stumbled back. "How you like that, motherfucker?" he asked, shaking the handle at him like a switch.

Evidently, the man didn't care for it at all. He took another few clumsy, backward steps, holding his arm close to his side, the dagger still clutched in his hand, though how he managed to hang onto it was a mystery to Earl. Then the killer turned and ran for the doorway on the opposite wall, the one that led deeper into the haunt.

Earl stood by and watched the man bolt, watched him become one with the shadows, then he lowered the axe and turned back to Sheri and Robby. Sheri was sitting up now, her face wet with tears and her bloody hands still chained behind her back, and Robby gently combed her hair with the fingers of his own bloody hand.

"A little help woulda been nice," Earl told them.

As he drove the salt truck around the Fuller place for another completed loop, Officer Hicks cast a glance on the still vacant front door. "They've been in there a while now. You think they need any help?"

Andrews shook his head, seemingly unconcerned. "If I know Agent Preston, he has everything well in hand."

"If you say so."

Their headlamps caught the still melting body of the spider-creature. It lay directly in their path, and the truck rolled right on over it with ease. Hicks heard a pop and a splash beneath the wheels, and when he looked back in his side view mirror, he saw that the remains had been completely flattened; slushy clumps, nothing more.

They swung around to the back of the house, and the yellow-green glow was still there. It seemed brighter than before, however, more intense. Hicks took his hand off the wheel to shield his eyes and said to Andrews, "Tell me you see that!"

"I see it. You're right, whatever that might be, it's definitely not the grenade."

Hicks drove on, trying to figure it out, not liking the ideas that sprang to mind. A dirty bomb, perhaps, building up to detonation? Or maybe the terrorist had some kind of energy weapon? He just didn't know.

He thought of Angie at home, trying to calculate how many miles away their home was, and wondering if it was a minimum safe distance, no matter what happened to him.

"We regret to inform you that your husband died driving a salt truck in circles around a nuclear bomb, but at least your house wasn't vaporized. Please, take some comfort in that."

By the time they pulled past the front porch again, Hicks saw something in the open doorway: a single figure, a man; he stepped from the darkness and onto the porch with a woman draped across his arms. Her hair trailed down from her head and swayed in the wind as her rescuer staggered down the steps and away from the house.

Hicks slammed on the brake.

"What are you doing?" Andrews wanted to know. "Why'd you stop?"

"I don't know who that is," Hicks told him, "but they *do* need our help."

She doesn't know it's me, Robby realized as Sheri bit down, sending waves of pain radiating through his hand and up his arm. *She thinks I'm the son of a bitch who did this to her.*

He cried out, but the sound of a gunshot startled him into silence. Robby flinched and his head jerked around in time to see Preston kick Sheri's attacker hard in the stomach, sending the bastard reeling backward, flailing.

Robby returned his attention to Sheri. He tried to pull his hand free, but her jaw had locked tight like a snapping turtle. "Sheri," he cried. "Sheri, it's me!"

The mask, you idiot! You're wearing a damn face mask! She can't tell who you are!

He reached up and slid the breathing mask up off his face. "It's Robby!"

A spark of recognition finally flared in her dazed eyes. She opened her mouth, released her vice grip on his hand, and began to sob. "Robby?"

"Yeah, it's me." Robby breathed a sigh of relief. With his mask off, he could smell the chlorine, but it still seemed distant, as if there were a pool down the hall. His eyes and nose weren't burning, neither was the skin on his face and forearms. His hand was throbbing, however, each tooth mark drooling blood, but he barely noticed. All that mattered was Sheri. "I'm here," he told her, not knowing if she could even hear him yet. "You're safe."

A second shot rang out, and now it was Robby's ears that were ringing. He instinctively ducked down and draped his body over Sheri's to shield her from further harm. He dared a glance over his shoulder, surprised to see Preston wielding the fire axe. The agent swung it like a baseball bat, buried its blade in the lurching madman's arm, then quickly yanked it free.

Preston cursed at Sheri's kidnapper, threatening another blow, but the man gave no reply. Instead, he covered his wound with his hand and bolted for the nearest exit, retreating down the hall and into the shadows.

Thank God!

"He's gone, Sheri," Robby told her. "He can't hurt you anymore."

He held the back of Sheri's neck and helped lift her head up off the altar. She leaned into him, smelling of sweat and blood, and weeping. "I wanted to fight him," she said. "I wanted to get away, but there was nothing I could do."

"I know." Robby pulled away from her and gently combed her tear-dampened hair with his fingers. "You did just fine. Better than fine."

Preston stepped over, still holding the fire axe. "A little help woulda been nice."

"Sorry," Robby told him, then nodded at the gory axe blade. "Looks like you handled it pretty well without me."

"Yeah, I handled it all right. Still, that dude's nuts, cranked up on PCP or somethin'."

"Or somethin'," Robby agreed. He examined the chains that bound Sheri's bloody wrists, the small lock that held them together, then he glanced up at Preston. "You still have those bolt cutters?"

"I didn't bring 'em in here with me," the agent said. "They're still out in the truck."

"Right." Robby frowned and looked back down at Sheri. She was battered and bleeding, but she was alive, and he wanted to keep her that way. "Preston, I need you to get her out of here."

"What about you?" the agent asked.

"Me? On with the plan as scheduled."

Preston stared at him in disbelief. "You'll get yourself killed!"

"Maybe, but if we don't seal that gateway, a lot more people are gonna die."

"I'm not gonna let you just – "

"*Yes*," Robby yelled, then he lowered his voice again, "you are. You know it has to be done."

The agent looked at him with uncertainty.

"I'll be fine. I know what I'm doing, but I can only do it if I know Sheri's safe."

"Alright," Preston told him. "Fine."

"Right. Good. Okay." With that settled, Robby's full attention returned to Sheri. "This is Agent Preston," he told her. "He's gonna get you out of here, get these damn chains off you, and get you all fixed up."

"No." Sheri shook her head lazily, her voice hoarse and groggy, fresh tears welling up in her eyes. "Not...not going without ..."

"I'll be right behind you." Robby kissed her forehead, then stepped away and nodded at Preston. "Take good care of her."

"You know it." The agent tossed him the axe and said, "You take good care of yourself."

As he watched Preston lift Sheri up off the altar, Robby slowly backed up toward the door, not wanting to take his eyes off her. Finally, he slipped out into the hall and found what they'd left behind: the duffle bag full of pipe bombs and saline solution.

Two great tastes that taste great together.

He snatched the bag up off the floor and slung it over his shoulder, then his hand shot to the leg of his jeans, feeling for the bulge of Sheri's cigarette lighter and finding it still snug in his pocket. He was ready.

Preston passed by with Sheri in his arms, on his way back toward the entrance and safety. "That bastard shouldn't be hard to find," he said to Robby. "Just follow the trail of blood."

"Don't need to," Robby called after them, tightening his grip on the axe handle. "I know where he's going."

The cellar.

As Cayden approached the cellar, he groped his left arm, pressed down hard against the gash, and tried to keep it from leaking like a sieve. It wasn't working. Just when he thought the blood had cooled and congealed beneath his firm grasp, a new eruption would bathe his palm in fresh, hot lava. He felt dizzy, his legs wobbly, as if he might pass out at any moment.

Everything's gone sixes and sevens, he thought. *It's all slipping away.*

Cayden willed himself forward and found that a gaping hole had been punched right through the wooden door, leaving only a splintered frame to hang off its hinges. Light spilled out through the opening, bathing the gory kitchen scene beyond in shimmering waves of yellow-green luminosity. Cayden staggered into that radiance and followed the brightness down.

The stairwell was alive. Steps, walls, even ceiling were covered over in a swarming, wriggling mass of centipede-like creatures. They crawled over and under one another, their individual movements impossible to track. The swarm parted before Cayden's feet like the red sea, allowing him to stumble down the stairs, then closing in again behind him. His blood sprinkled down with each step, baptizing their long, segmented bodies. Some rose up from the floor, or dipped down from the ceiling, and their bulbous faces opened like poppies in bloom, but for the most part, they ignored him.

Cayden was expected.

He was one of them.

A thick, churning fog covered the foot of the stairs. Cayden stumbled off the last step and he reached out for the wall to steady himself. The centipedes scurried away from his hand for a moment, then slowly crept back – licking the blood from his fingers as if it were ambrosia.

The light was even brighter ahead. The gate, the great Old Ones...they were close now. So very close.

He took a deep breath of the chlorine-scented air. The gas burned his nostrils and crept down his throat with razor blade fingers, and when it reached his lungs, it sent him into a fit of wet coughing. Cayden tasted blood; he wiped it from his mouth with the back of his hand.

Blood.

Blood was the key to freeing his fathers from their exile.

Cayden stumbled forward, his feet shuffling across the dirt floor, stirring the fog. There were things moving around down there, hidden in the haze, bulging sacs and hard shells; they slithered and crawled and leapt away from the soles of Cayden's shoes. He could not see them clearly, but he could tell they were as different from the centipedes as they were from each other. And as he hobbled on down the corridor, whatever eyes the menagerie possessed turned up to meet him.

The gods had shown him this place again and again, had beckoned him down this moldy brick hallway on astral feet that felt no fatigue, no weakness, no pain. How Cayden longed for them now.

Another cough brought fresh, warm blood up to his lips, and Cayden wondered for a moment if he would bleed to death before he could complete his task. No. His life belonged to the fathers, and they would give him the strength to see it through. He wrapped his fingers around the black rune stone that hung from his neck and tried to ignore the stabbing pain in his chest and his throat, the dull throb in his arm. Instead, Cayden focused solely on the walking, on putting one shaky foot in front of the other. He had no choice; he had to reach the source of the light, the source of his magicks.

Cayden staggered into the chamber at the end of the hall. The light was everywhere, dancing, flickering, and strobing; it was the most beautiful thing he'd ever seen. He stared in awe as eddies of mist were pulled back toward the light, gaining momentum as they whipped around, like water circling a drain – a spinning, vertical whirlpool, filling the space where a fourth wall should have been. This was the gateway, the tear in the curtain that separated this world from the next, where the gods would make their grand entrance onto this Earthly stage.

A tear ran down Cayden's cheek, and he shouted into the vortex, into the other world, into the very ears of his gods, "I'm...here, my lords!"

He coughed again, blood foaming at the corners of his mouth. "I...I've...done everything you've asked. Everything you...you wanted..."

Cayden let go of the wall and stumbled into the center of the chamber. He stood there, swaying, the light burning his retinas as the chlorine burned his throat and lungs. He fell to his knees in the fog, knowing what must be done, at long last understanding his true purpose.

"Just...Just one task left ..."

Over sixty years ago, Fuller had knelt in that same spot, had uttered those very same words. The farmer had meant for his wife and children to be his final sacrifice, had meant for their blood to open the gate and free the gods, but in the end, he'd failed them. The woman abandoned him in the middle of the night; she fled to Atlanta with her son and daughter, leaving Fuller alone, leaving him with nothing.

In dreams, through visions, the gods had opened a window to these past events and allowed Cayden to peer in, to learn from Fuller's mistakes. He'd seen how Fuller had offered his own blood in place of his family's, but the farmer had hesitated, had been unable to use the dagger on his own flesh. Instead, Fuller flung himself into a thresher, hoping it would be enough.

It wasn't.

No. Despite all the sacrifices Fuller had made, all the innocent blood he'd spilled, his final offering had been inadequate.

But Cayden...Cayden had consumed the heart of a god-killer. Cayden had the power of the gods themselves coursing through his veins this very night. Yes. After all these countless eons, it would be Cayden's blood that would finally grant them their dominion.

He would be the ultimate sacrifice.

Long tentacles emerged from the light. They floated through the air, snaking their way toward Cayden. One of the tendrils touched his cheek, caressed it, rows of suckers on its underside puckering to give him a hundred sloppy kisses. Fresh tears sprang from Cayden's eyes. He reached up, wrapped his hand around the tentacle's pulsing warmth, and said, "My life...My life is yours."

Cayden brought the black rune to his lips; he kissed the all-seeing eye etched in its smooth surface, then let it drop and hang from his neck. Next, he touched his own flesh with the icy finger of the dagger. There was no hesitation, only rejoicing as the blade unzipped his throat. Cayden's blood leapt and danced in the light, bathing the tentacles in his love.

Death is but a doorway. Let my *death be* your *doorway, for now and for all time. Change this world...impose your grand order...make everything* better...

The tendrils became excited. They writhed wildly, whipping at the air as they retreated back into the whirlpool. Cayden's blood-stained lips curled into a wide, beaming grin. As his eyes dimmed, the light brightened. And, when he fell face first into the yellow-green mist, the ground began to tremble.

As Earl Preston carried Sheri down the front steps of the Fuller house, he felt her tremble in his arms. Between her dead weight and the weight of her chains, Earl had worked up a good sweat by the time they reached the lawn, and the night breeze was cool and refreshing against his skin. His back throbbed, but once his feet hit the grass, he somehow managed to break into a run.

Earl's eyes barely registered the huge truck as it rolled to a stop a few yards ahead of him. Instead, he concentrated on the piled salt it left behind –a sparkling line across the darker field of green. Earl felt a bit like a running back trying to score the winning touchdown; he just needed to make it across that line.

"Preston!"

Someone screamed his name, but he didn't stop to see who it was. No. He'd promised Robby that he would get Sheri to safety, and to be safe, they needed to be on the other side of that thick, glittery line.

"Preston!"

It was his partner. Earl chanced a quick glance to his left and saw Andrews running toward him with the police officer who'd been driving the truck. Beyond them, he could see that Captain Davies had done his job well. Most of the cars were gone from the make-shift parking lot, and the emergency vehicles had been moved back to the edge of the woods, their red and blue strobes making rainbows of the surrounding foliage.

Earl spotted an ambulance waiting over there and was grateful for it. Sheri could get these heavy-as-shit chains off, get the medical help she needed. And once Earl knew she was in good hands, he could turn right around and go back to give Robby a hand.

He finally felt the grit of rock salt, and then the ground began to rumble and shake beneath his feet.

Earthquake?

No. While Earl knew a fault line ran through the Midwest, he suspected the cause of this specific tremor was far from natural. And when he spun around to look back at the spook house, he knew that he'd been right.

A yellow-green light poured out through the front door as if chasing him across the lawn. It shone between the slats of boarded windows, and leaked through every crack and imperfection in the wood.

The wormhole, Earl realized. *God...*damn! *It's gonna suck the whole fucking house down!*

Oh, Robby thought as he looked down the cellar stairwell. *This is gonna suck.*

It was like staring into the mouth of Hell itself. Spectral fires blazed from somewhere deep in the catacombs, and the steps, walls, and ceiling were completely covered over by a living, crawling mass of insect creatures. Robby was reminded of a Hieronymus Bosch painting, but the fact that this particular scene was real and right there in front of him made it far more disturbing.

He stood at the top of the stairs for a moment, breathing heavily into his respirator. Imprisoned under glass, his forehead, nose, and cheeks beaded with sweat; his fingers looped tightly around the wooden axe handle, and he tried to come up with a better plan – *Any old plan would do!* – just as long as it didn't involve him going down there alone, a duffle bag slung over his back, loaded down with explosives.

I could just light the fuses, throw the whole bag down there, and run like hell...

No. A concentrated blast in one place might not bring down the whole house, might not close the rift. He needed to space them out, try to blow the supporting walls, and he needed to get them as close to the gateway as possible. Even then, Robby had no idea if it would work.

It'll work, his mind countered. *In 1970, a group of radicals leveled a four-story townhouse in Greenwich Village with nothing but a few pipe bombs. You should more than be able to bring down this rickety ol' farmhouse with what you've got in that pack.*

Yes, but how was he supposed to even get down there? How was he supposed to fight his way through all that with nothing but the axe in his hands and the Super Soaker that hung down from his shoulder?

Too late for second thoughts now, big guy. Just go for it! No hesitation. Kill the fuckers! Do what needs to be done.

Robby took a deep breath, then he shifted the axe into his right hand and lifted the squirt gun with his left. He squeezed the trigger, sent a high-velocity spray streaming down onto the wriggling carpet, bathing the centipede things in his path with warm saline. The creatures shrieked, many dissolving quickly into smoldering rivers of bright yellow pus and puddles of dark goo while others scrambled to move out of his way.

He descended the stairs in a hurry, feeling the extra IV bags slosh and shift in the duffle on his back. The metal pipe bombs clinked together with every jostling, downward step, and each time Robby heard that sound, his heart skipped a beat. Several centipedes dangled down from the ceiling, their faces coming unhinged, dripping mandibles unfurling and lunging at him. Robby gave them each a face full of saline, then ducked and weaved to avoid the thick, slushy rain.

Melted centipede residue slicked the lower steps. Robby lost his footing, then fought hard to regain it. If he went face-first into these creatures now, he knew they would swarm over him, probably within seconds, and when they were done, there would be nothing left but his bones. Perhaps not even that.

His feet entered the thick fog at the base of the stairs, creating splashes of vapor and becoming mired in the hidden muck beneath. Robby looked and saw dark fluids flowing down the steps behind him, cascading over still-melting chunks of centipede like rapids on the river Styx, no doubt mixing with the dirt below. He worked his shoes free, creating ripples in the mist, then started walking.

Light played across the walls and the ancient plumbing that crisscrossed the ceiling, creating luminous shapes and patterns. The centipede-creatures were down here too, and they were not alone. He could see them moving around down there under the cover of this chlorine fog. Occasionally, something would break the surface of this yellow-green sea like the dorsal fin of a shark; long, bony legs...hard, crab-like claws...scaly tails...huge, dark eyeballs riding slender, elegant stalks. Robby sprayed them all and hurried forward through their corridor of screams.

The archway at the end of the hall glowed bright with ethereal flame. And beneath the shrieks of monsters being eaten away, Robby heard a voice. It was weak, unfamiliar, but he knew it was him – the bastard who cut up Sheri.

"My life," the madman cried. "My life is yours."

Robby let go of the Super Soaker, let it hang from his side on its shoulder strap, then he tightened his grip on the axe handle with both hands, ready to use it on the murderer in the next room. When the saline spray stopped, one of the centipedes saw an opportunity; it curled in from the mossy sidewall, lunged at him with its dripping fangs unfurled. Robby saw it in the corner of his face mask. He swung the axe and chopped it cleanly in two. Both halves crawled off in opposite directions, adding their high-pitched screeches to the choir.

He ran into the next room, the chamber where Fuller had performed unknown atrocities, where Sheri's boyfriend Jeff had made his final call and spoken his last words on this Earth. And despite all that, Robby was still shocked by what he saw there.

The far wall was gone. Just...gone. In its place, a vortex of swirling light and mist. Long, squid-like tentacles extended from the whirlpool, surrounding a figure that knelt down on the floor in the center of the room. The madman. He still held the dagger in his hand, and these writhing tendrils embraced and caressed him like their lover.

As Robby watched in horror, the murderer slit his own throat, his blade severing internal and external carotid arteries alike. Blood leapt happily from the man's smiling wound; those frolicking tentacles suddenly retreated from the gory shower, slithering back through the air into the vortex and disappearing from sight. The madman's body leaned forward as if to follow them, then fell face-down, sending ripples coursing through the fog as it sank beneath.

After that, thunder rolled through the earth and the light from the whirlpool flared like lightning. Dust rained down from the rafters as the entire house strummed, a tuning fork responding to the perfect note.

The perfect sacrifice.

Robby had to act quickly. He sprinted into the room and stripped the duffle from his back. The bag landed on the floor with a billowing splash of mist and Robby knelt to unzip it, needing to ready the first of the pipe bombs.

Something stepped out of the rift.

A large, blue, pulpy body held aloft by two slender, oddly jointed legs. It's "feet" looked more like the hands of a concert pianist, with long, delicate fingers instead of toes. At first glance, the creature appeared to have a thick mane of blue-black hair around its misshapen head, but then Robby saw those hairs move independently of one another, saw them reach out and snap at the air, and he realized they were actually hundreds of pincers on long, flexible stalks. A dozen tentacles trailed after it like tails, writhing across the dirt and snaking through the fog.

A bloated, pulsating malignancy hung down from its abdomen – soft pink flesh laced with veins. There were dark shapes moving around within this plump sack; a pregnant womb, filled with a restless litter, or perhaps...perhaps a bloated stomach, squirming with the prey that this horrible thing had swallowed whole – still rebellious meals that now clawed and kicked at the walls of their fleshy tomb as they were slowly digested over time. The creature's lips parted obscenely, forming a vertical smile, revealing crystalline fangs and strings of drool, as if to say that the thing had room inside for more.

Robby stared at the creature, wide-eyed, feeling an odd mix of awe and terror numb his brain. He reached blindly into the duffle, and his fingers found an IV bag. In one quick motion, he brought the solution out and hurled it at the creature before him. The plastic bag burst like a water balloon, drenching it, warm saline gobbling away at its alien flesh.

The thing yowled and toppled over like a stilt walker who'd lost his balance. It landed on its side, kicking at the fog with one leg and reaching up to claw at the stone walls with the other.

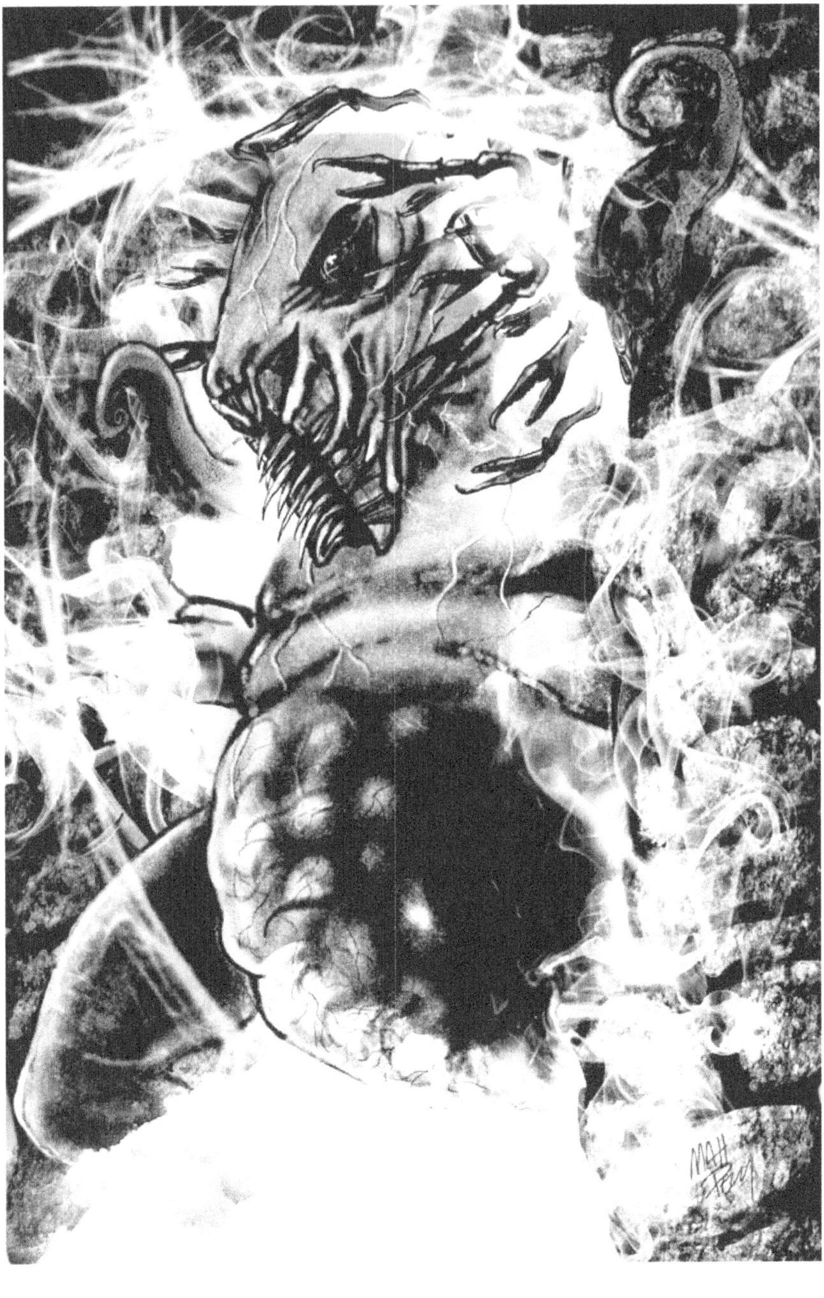

Robby turned away from it and rifled through his duffle bag. He grabbed one of the pipe bombs and brought it out into the light. The fuse was long. It would need to be long to allow him time to escape. The trick would be deciding how long to make the remaining fuses.

He grabbed another bomb, stretched its fuse out, then rubbed the cord repeatedly across the axe blade to cut it down, making it about an inch shorter than the first. When Robby finished cutting, he set the bomb aside and reached into the duffle for another.

The light grew still brighter, painting everything chartreuse, making it hard for Robby to see what he was doing. Wind from the whirling vortex burned the exposed skin of his hands, and he knew that, were it not for the face mask he wore and the bottled oxygen he carried on his back, the chlorine gas would have killed him a dozen times over by now. When he finished cutting all the fuses down to the proper lengths, he stuffed all but one back into the duffle as he rose to his feet.

A creature stood with him, rearing up out of the haze on oddly-jointed legs and snaking tentacles. Its massive, lipless mouth sprung open, flinging spittle in all directions; fangs the size of small tusks jutted at odd angles, each tooth attached to its own flexible stalk of gum, moving independently of one another. The thing's skin reminded Robby of a burn victim – stretched and smooth in some places, grooved and pitted in others, with patches that looked more akin to exposed muscle than flesh. Its eyes – and there were many of them – were albino white, each tiny pupil focused intently on Robby's startled face.

His hand was still in the duffle.

Robby grabbed another bag of saline and chucked it. The plastic hooked on one of the monster's fangs and exploded, draining solution right down its throat. Soft tissues bubbled and smoked, and then the thing's entire head came loose from its body and dropped into the fog like an anchor.

He backed away, leaving the axe on the floor, lost beneath the mist. He got Sheri's lighter from his pocket, thumbed the wheel to spark a flame, and tipped the pipe's fuse. It ignited like a sparkler on the 4th of July, and he gave it a toss.

Robby didn't stick around to see where it landed. Instead, he retreated out into the hall, tossing a second bomb over his shoulder for good measure. The light was now so intense that it bleached everything, flooded every shadowy corner, turning the entire cellar into a negative image of its former self. He ran for the stairs and the door beyond, the Super Soaker banging against his side. Along the way, he lit more fuses and dropped more bombs, one in each archway, another hurled into the side room with the wooden pallets and boxes, still another into the chamber on the opposite side. He saved the few that remained for the base of the stairs.

Things sprang at him from the fog. Robby lifted the Super Soaker's nozzle to hold them off, but the stream grew less potent with each squeeze of the trigger. By the time he got to the steps, he was out altogether.

Centipedes attacked from all sides. They lunged forward, nipping at his boots and trying to find a soft spot above his ankles. He made it difficult for them, lifting and kicking his feet, stepping down on some and shaking others free, all while he tried to pull the remaining two IV bags out of the duffle. When Robby had them, he lit the final fuse, dropped the bomb into the canvas, then let the bag fall.

He mounted the stairs, popped the blue port at the bottom of the IV bags and squeezed, spewing saline solution onto the insect-creatures at his feet and in his path. Thick smoke and fog rose to obscure his view and his ears filled with the screech and chatter of melting, fleeing bugs.

I'm getting out of this fucking house, and nothing's gonna stop me!

Robby made it into the kitchen, but before he could turn and run down the hall, the entire floor exploded into splinters. At first, he thought he'd miscalculated, cut the fuses too short, and the pipe bombs had detonated all at once. Then he stood stunned, watching as long, black cones rose up through the wood, and up, and up...

It took Robby a moment to realize they were claws.

Hicks looked up in time to see a clawed, four-fingered hand rip through the roof of the old farmhouse – two long, middle digits with what looked like a thumb on either side; its palm was as large as the salt truck, maybe larger, and it reached for the moon on a seemingly endless beanstalk of an arm. Tentacles extended from the limb on all sides like wild hairs, whipping and flailing at the stars. And a huge, booming roar filled the darkness.

The crowd around the emergency vehicles gasped and screamed; they shrank back from this monstrosity like extras in a Godzilla film, but Hicks held his ground. He craned his neck, his eyes struggling to take in its dreadful majesty. Other officers actually drew their weapons and fired at the thing. And while Hicks still held the shotgun firmly in his hands, he didn't waste his ammunition. Bullets, he thought, would do no more damage to this behemoth than mosquito bites would to him.

It defied explanation. Hell, it defied *imagination*, for never in his life had Hicks even dreamed that such a thing might exist. It was like the hand of the Devil himself reaching up from the fiery depths of Hell.

Hicks had never been an overly religious man, but as the saying went, there were no atheists in foxholes. He had been known to utter a prayer or two from time to time in the heat of battle; on the streets of Iraq, in the mountains of Afghanistan, and now here, in the woods of Harmony. The prayers weren't for him, however, but for those around him, and especially for Angie. He thought of his beautiful wife, hoping she was still safe beneath the covers and adrift in the blissful ignorance of an equally beautiful dream, far removed from this living nightmare.

"We regret to inform you that your husband was squashed like a little bug by a very, very *big hand. Can you believe it? I mean, what are the odds?"*

Beside him, Andrews' mouth hung open in disbelief and Agent Preston stood transfixed, still holding the woman he'd rescued from the house. She was obviously weak and covered in blood from head to toe, but she was the only one of them who could muster even a single word in the face of this monolithic horror.

"Robby," she muttered.

It was then that the entire world seemed to explode before them, and Hicks lifted a hand to shield his eyes.

Robby ran from the giant, cyclopean hand, his world exploding into splinters around him as the thing burst from the floor and clawed its way up through the ceiling. Light from the rift poured into the room, blindingly brilliant. The gateway was expanding, he realized, opening like the iris on a camera, allowing this monster to finally reach across the universe into his reality.

The hand of a god...

He remembered all that he had read about the Druidic sect that worshipped these things, all the horrid atrocities they had performed in their gods' unholy names. It had seemed so incomprehensible to him then, but now Robby thought he understood. If you believed there were things out there this powerful, this *vast*, things that could crush you to dust beneath their feet whenever they decided to go for a stroll, you would do whatever it took to appease them...even the unspeakable.

How long? Robby wondered. *If the bombs don't go off, if the gate doesn't close, if all these things manage to get through, if people see them,* fear *them, how long until the cults start up again en mass? How long before there are worshippers on every corner performing human sacrifices and the streets run red with the blood of women and children? How long would it take the world to do a swan dive into madness?*

Somehow, he managed to put the brakes on that ghastly train of thought before it went any farther down the tracks. Robby focused solely on the winding layout of the haunt, on getting out, on getting back to Sheri, because it would work, *it would*, and those pipe bombs would –

BOOM...

The entire house shook violently. What little glass remained in the windows shattered to bits. Robby heard joists crack and collapse from behind, then felt heat bake down the hallway after him, licking at the backs of his legs as he ran.

BOOM-BOOM...

A wall of heat now, broiling Robby's entire backside. Plaster, sawdust, and flaming ash rained down into his hair and his path, but thankfully the face mask kept the debris from getting into his eyes. He pumped his legs harder, ran faster than he'd ever run in his life, perhaps even faster than he'd sprinted that long-ago night in the corn, that night when it felt as if there had been demons nipping at his heels.

BOOM-BOOM-BOOM...

This final volley of explosions hit just as Robby entered the first room of the haunt, the fake forest that Captain Davies had been so proud of. Now, its paper trees were being devoured by a very real forest fire as the entire room burst into flames and the floor blew out from beneath Robby's dashing feet.

The force of the blast shot him out the front door like a bullet from a gun. He flew through the air and landed on his chest, landed hard enough to knock the wind from his lungs and to crack the glass of his face mask. Pain radiated from his nose and rang through his sinuses, but he was alive. Slowly, he rolled over, tried to catch his breath, and watched as a fire-blossom bloomed into the night sky above.

Earl Preston watched as the giant monster claw sank back down into the spook house, almost as if it had been yanked hard from below. He saw the yellow-green ghost light turn to red and orange flame in an instant, then witnessed the entire house disintegrate. Brick walls, wooden planks, shingles, Halloween props and decor...all collapsed inward or exploded outward seemingly at random. In mere moments, this structure that had stood decaying for decades gave birth to a fiery phoenix and sent it rocketing skyward with a loud *WHOOSH!*

How long he stood there in the grass, staring into the flames with Sheri cradled in his arms, Earl had no way to know. The image of that monstrous hand was still burned into his mind's eye, and no matter how hard he wished for it, he knew it could never be unseen. He didn't have a clue what unimaginable thing might eventually have come through that wormhole if the house hadn't been leveled, and he hoped never to find out.

Earl suddenly remembered Robby Miller; and no sooner had the thought crossed his mind than he saw a silhouette against the blaze. The backlit figure hobbled across the lawn toward them, and as it drew near, it slid a cracked face mask off its head and smoothed its hair with its hand. "That you, Miller?" Earl asked hopefully. "What kind of shape you in?"

"Much better than the other guy," Robby replied, but when he stepped into the glow of the emergency lights, he looked like death warmed over. He stood there a moment, swaying on his feet, exchanging grateful glances with Earl, with Andrews and Officer Hicks, and then his eyes fell to Sheri.

Sheri didn't remember being put in the back of the ambulance. She heard distant voices, as if from a dream –

"I can't wait to write this report, Agent Andrews."

"I can't wait to read it, Agent Preston."

"Well, it's been fun, but if you gentlemen will excuse me, I'm going to go home, hold my wife, Angie, and give her a great big kiss."

– and when she finally came to, she was free of the chains and there was an oxygen mask strapped to her face. Robby sat next to her gurney, checking her vital signs, evidently pleased by what he saw.

"Hey there," he said with a smile. He looked as if he'd been in a brawl; there were cuts on his lip, his cheek, and the bridge of his nose. In fact, his entire nose appeared swollen, and the black and blue around his eyes matched a huge bruise on his forehead. The skin on his hands had the red, irritated look of someone who'd had an allergic reaction to some sort of medicine or chemical, and one of them still bore a scabby impression of her bite. "Take it easy, don't try to move."

Sheri ignored him; she reached up, wincing at the pain in her shoulder, and pulled the oxygen mask down off her face. "I...I'm sorry I bit you."

"That's okay, sweetie," he told her. "You didn't realize what you were doing, and besides, you'd been through Hell."

Been? They weren't still there?

"The...the Fuller place," she managed. "I saw it blow up?"

"It did. I'll tell you all about it later, but you need to – "

"That man, he said –"

"It's all over, Sheri," Robby assured her. "He can't ever hurt you again."

She nodded, then croaked, "The spider-dogs? The doorway?"

"Dead and gone, in that order," he told her. "Now, try to relax. It's a twenty minute drive to the Stanley U. Med Center, but my man Julian's at the wheel, so we'll be there in ten."

She gazed up at him, still dazed and dumbfounded. "You came for me."

Robby blinked. He smiled down at her, and she could see the affection in his eyes. "Of course I came for you," he said, then he shrugged and tried to act as if it were no big deal. "Hey, you came to my rescue, so I came to yours. Now, we're even."

"I...I didn't realize we were keeping score."

"We're not, 'cause we're even." He reached over, took her hand in his, then added, "We've saved each other."

"Yeah," she agreed. "I think we have."

Sheri Foster smiled and continued holding Robby's hand. In fact, she never wanted to let go of it again. The warming blanket that covered her body labored to combat the chill in her bones, and the motion of the ambulance rocked her gently to sleep. She dozed, content. And in her dreams there was no more pain, no more fear. Not tonight.

epilogue

When Robby picked Sheri up from the Medical Center the next day, he kissed her and held her close. The doctors had prescribed her pain killers, and they didn't want her driving so long as she was taking them. Of course, Robby was more than happy to act as her chauffeur.

The medical personnel at Stanley had been wonderful as usual, stitching and patching her up. She'd dislocated her right shoulder trying to free herself from the chains, and her arm now rested in a bright red sling with white straps. Harmony High colors.

Robby had been there when they questioned her about the attack. He'd held her hand as she went over it in gory detail, occasionally giving it a gentle squeeze to let her know that he was there for her, that he cared deeply, and they'd both shed tears. When the staff started asking Sheri the more personal questions, about whether or not any *penetration* had occurred, Robby wondered if he should excuse himself. But Sheri had wanted him there, and although that madman had done many horrific things to her, Robby was glad to learn that physical rape had not been one of them.

It's the psychological scars that never heal. Isn't that right, big guy? Ornithophobia is an irrational fear of crows. You've got that one in spades, don'tcha buddy? And I don't think they even have a name for an irrational fear of cornfields. My God, man, you're so messed up that they don't even have a name for it!

Hearing every excruciating detail of Sheri's ordeal filled him with a tremendous sense of rage, and as horrible as it sounded, he wished the madman hadn't killed himself and robbed Robby of the opportunity to use that axe on him.

They drove home in the dark. Robby hated driving these roads at night, with the woods to one side and the cornfields on the other, and he would be glad to get Sheri safely home. "You doin' okay?" he asked her, eager to take his mind off their surroundings.

She smiled in the dimness. "About the same as the last time you asked me."

"Sorry. I just worry about you."

"I don't want to worry you."

"No, it's okay." He reached across the seat and took her hand, taking his eyes off the road for a minute to look at her. "It's actually kind of nice to have someone to worry about other than myself."

Sheri's smile widened a bit, then she looked away; suddenly, her eyes widened and she let out a scream. "Look out!"

Robby's attention snapped back to the road. Something ran across their path, caught by the headlights – a dark, sinuous creature with huge, bright red eyes; there and then gone.

Gone into the corn.

He slammed on the brakes and sat there, staring at the still moving stalks where it entered the field and disappeared.

"Tell me that was just a possum," Sheri said with a nervous little laugh.

"I don't know what that was," Robby told her, and then he unfastened his seatbelt. "But I'm gonna find out."

Her left hand shot over and she grabbed him by the wrist. "You think something got out? Something made it past the salt? Maybe flew over?"

"Flew? Why would you think it flew?"

She looked at the road, her lips parted as she searched for words to fill them, then she said, "Okay, this is going to sound weird – "

"Did you forget who you were talking to?"

Sheri gave another nervous giggle at that, then told him, "For a second, I thought whatever it was had wings."

Robby's stomach sank like a stone. He frowned and his eyes shot to the cornfield.

Don't go out there, big guy. That's what they want. They want you to go out there. They want you to come back. You got away once, but you won't be so lucky a second time.

When Robby opened the door, even his truck beeped a warning. "Just...sit tight for a second," he told her, ignoring the alarm. "I'm gonna go have a quick look."

Sheri went completely pale. "That's exactly what Jeff said before he –"

"Yeah, well, I'm not Jeff."

He went to get out and she reached across the seat to grab his arm, her voice becoming shrill, "*No!* You're not going out there! You're not leaving me alone! Come on...Start the truck. Drive away. What does it matter what it is any–?"

"Do you trust me?"

"Do I–?" She blinked. "Of course."

"Then trust me," he told her. "I'm not going to leave you. I'm gonna step over there for a second, have a look around, and I'll be right back. I'll never even leave your sight. I promise."

Sheri stared at him a moment, trembling in the evening chill, then she reluctantly loosened her death grip on his bicep. "Just...be careful."

"I will."

Robby climbed down onto the asphalt and stepped slowly away from his truck. As he moved toward the edge of the field, Robby felt a cold rush of déjà vu. The corn had gone brown, dry and brittle before the harvest, and the wind through the stalks made an expectant sound, like whispering.

Psychological scars never heal.

Robby frowned. No. He made sure of that, didn't he?

And staring out at the neat rows, at the seemingly endless sea of stalks, a sudden wave of revelation washed over him.

He hadn't really stayed in Harmony all these years out of something so noble as a sense of duty. No. He'd been kidding himself on that one. He'd just *settled*, the same way everyone else had settled.

Evil was everywhere. He'd seen enough to know that was a fact.

But the devil you know is better than the devil you don't.

In Harmony, he was still privy to all the town's secrets, both natural and unnatural, and that gave him a feeling of importance, an ongoing purpose. In any other town or city on earth, he'd be just another forty-something man talking about his glory days, but instead of an opposing team, Robby's greatest triumphs and most horrendous defeats came at the clawed hands of monsters and demons. And yet, he still had the feeling that his big game had yet to be played.

Yes, in the pond of this little hick town, Robby was indeed a big fish. Hell, at this point, he probably knew more about the sins and evils of Harmony, Indiana than Father John over at St. Anthony's. But where the Catholic priest was bound by orders and sacraments, Robby was free to act.

And act he would. And soon.

But not tonight.

Robby turned to look back at the truck. The dome light was on, and he could see Sheri plainly, every beautiful line and curve of her face. He took a step away from the shadowy field and headed toward that light.

He climbed back into the cab and closed the door behind him. *Behind him.* In his rearview mirror, his taillights painted stalks the color of fresh blood. Robby glanced away, focused solely on Sheri's face. "I need to tell you something."

"Here?" she asked. "Right now?"

"Yes." He swallowed hard, his mouth now totally dry. "You've had your ordeal, and I've had mine. Mine was a long time ago, and I've never had anyone I could share it with, anyone who would *believe it* until now."

Sheri reached across for his hand, her eyes filled with concern, with *love*. "You can tell me anything."

"I know, and I want to. I want you to know everything." Robby licked his lips, but his tongue had turned to sandpaper. "I've held onto it for twenty-five years, and if I don't get it out now, I'm afraid I never will."

"Okay." She gently squeezed his hand. "I'm listening."

"Sheri," he began, "Have you ever heard of the Wide Game?"

NOTES AND ACKNOWLEDGMENTS

In 2012, I lost a very good friend, and one of the most amazing people I have ever met in my life, Sara J. Larson. Since the early days of my career, Sara had been my biggest fan and my harshest critic. She read the first draft of everything I wrote. I mean *everything*. Every short story. Every novel. And her honest and thorough critiques impacted each work, leaving permanent impressions, like footprints on the moon. While no one would ever attempt or even hope to replace her, a circle of friends and fellow writers did step up to help try and fill the fathomless void she left behind. If not for their considerable time and contributions, you would not be holding this book in your hands right now. So, to Rodney Carlstrom, Nikki Howard, Natalie Phillips, RJ Sullivan, and Kathy Watness, words cannot express the depth of my gratitude and appreciation, but I think the final result is something that Sara would have truly loved, and for that I thank you.

Thanks must also go to: My editor, Amanda DeBord; Tony Acree and the entire staff at Hydra Publications; Matthew Perry for his always amazing cover art and illustrations; Nila Brereton Hagood, for her wonderful narration of the audiobook version – you make my words sound good; Kitsie Duncan, Chris Jay, and everyone at Darkrider Studios; Andrea and Paul Lindeman, Brett Hays at Fear Fair Haunted Attraction (Seymour, Indiana), and the Lawrence Fire and Police Departments for their vital knowledge, advice, and input; all the Indiana Horror Writers; and, of course, my faithful readers everywhere.

ABOUT THE AUTHOR

Michael West is the bestselling author of *Cinema of Shadows*, *The Wide Game*, *Skull Full of Kisses,* and the critically-acclaimed *Legacy of the Gods* series. He lives and works in the Indianapolis area with his two children, Kyle and Ryan, daughter-in-law, Grace, and his two dogs, Gizmo and King Seesar, both rescues.

West's wife, Stephanie, his best friend and partner for 30 years, lost her battle with cancer in 2021. She remains a constant source of inspiration to all who knew her.

When his kids were younger, West turned his garage into a haunted house every Halloween.

Made in the USA
Monee, IL
07 March 2025